RESIST:
TALES FROM A FUTURE
WORTH FIGHTING AGAINST

RESIST

TALES FROM A FUTURE WORTH FIGHTING AGAINST

★

EDITED BY
GARY WHITTA
CHRISTIE YANT
HUGH HOWEY

BROAD REACH PUBLISHING, LLC
GREEN COVE SPRINGS, FL

TABLE OF CONTENTS

ABOUT THE ACLU

THANK YOU FOR buying this book. By doing so you're helping to support an important cause. A minimum of 50% of the purchase price will be donated to the American Civil Liberties Union.

For nearly 100 years, the ACLU has been our nation's guardian of liberty, working in courts, legislatures, and communities to defend and preserve the individual rights and liberties that the Constitution and the laws of the United States guarantee everyone in this country.

Whether it's achieving full equality for LGBT people, establishing new privacy protections for our digital age of widespread government surveillance, ending mass incarceration, or preserving the right to vote or the right to have an abortion, the ACLU takes up the toughest civil liberties cases and issues to defend all people from government abuse and overreach.

With more than 2 million members, activists, and supporters, the ACLU is a nationwide organization that fights tirelessly in all 50 states, Puerto Rico, and Washington, D.C., to safeguard everyone's rights.

FOREWORD

THE FUTURE IS unknown, which is both exciting and terrifying. It is a place for dreamers and worriers to project their hopes and fears. Science fiction as a literary genre has a long history of filling readers' minds with wondrous possibilities but also dire predictions. Utopias and dystopias. Flying cars and murderous robots.

And while every generation makes the mistake of thinking their time is special, there is some truth in this egoistic view—for all times are special in equal amounts. The recent past is always worth exploring, the present is always full of miraculous advancements, and the future always holds both promise and danger. This is most evident when it feels as if the past is repeating itself.

This anthology has been collected in just such times. There are echoes today of the same nationalism, protectionism, and xenophobia that led to last century's world wars. Icons of heinous civil wars are being torn down, and those same acts are being protested by those who think our ugliest times were our best times. There are world leaders today whose rhetoric reminds us of speeches we thought we would never tolerate again.

It's common enough to wonder how we might have responded had we lived in different times. Would we stand up for the rights of others and risk our privilege? Would we be brave enough to speak truth to power if we were in an unprotected minority? It's easy to be brave after the fact; how would we respond in the moment?

This feels like one of those moments. But the truth is that if you look hard enough, these moments never go away. There is always something good worth fighting for and something bad worth resisting. The unknown future is created by the choices we make today. The warnings and promise of George Orwell's *1984* and Arthur C. Clark's *2001: A Space Odyssey* get everything right except the dates. Margaret Atwood was clever to avoid that mistake, and there's a reason her *Handmaid's Tale* is back with a vengeance. These stories should never date themselves. We should always be wary of and joyful for the future in equal measure.

The undeniable and unbelievable truth is that the future is always better than the past. We do make progress. But the world only gets better because we fight for it. We fight by voting, marching, volunteering, donating, parenting, mentoring, and yes sometimes even Tweeting. And for some of us, the thing we do best is to write entertaining warnings, to draw readers in with stories and characters that capture the imagination while liberating the spirit. That's what we, the editors, hope to accomplish with this anthology. It comes from a wide variety of voices, but they sing in chorus. They sing about a future that might be dire, but that we believe we are collectively amazing enough to avoid. It is a future that entertains, but is worth fighting against. We hope you enjoy. And we hope to see you all soon in a very different future.

Gary Whitta, Christie Yant, and Hugh Howey

AMERICA: THE RIDE
CHARLES YU

WE HAVE A kid now and another on the way and—the idea is, the hope is—that we are, at least in a technical sense, adults.

We'd always assumed we would know more, would have accomplished more, by the time we got to this point, assumed we would have turned into different people, better people. That was the idea. That was the hope.

Looking back over our shoulders, we can see the track stretching out behind us, an unbroken line from where we got on to where we are now.

The voice of the American ride says:

Please keep your attention focused in a sideways direction.

Reminding us the proper way to enjoy this, which is not to look back, because looking back is the easiest way to get hurt. Or, worse, to convince yourself that you want to get off. And also, it's also not proper procedure to look forward, no matter how tempting it is to do so. We sit facing west while our tram car moves north, and we do our best not to look in the northern direction, although we are encouraged by what we feel to be a subtle, gentle, but unmistakable angle of incline of the track below us. We are moving up a slope, building toward something, to a higher place. Some of us worry about what this means. Some of us worry about whether an upslope now implies a downslope later, but some others of us say that it doesn't have to be so, that we are not bodies in flight, our arc through the sky pre-carved by gravity. We are on an engineered system, an amusement, a transportation. This was designed by our best minds, assembled by our best hands, and constantly improved by our innovation and creativity. There is no reason to assume that there must be a high point to all this, that we will eventually have to convert all of this elevation and potential energy into speed and kinetic energy, that what we are storing thermodynamically must eventually be given back, paid back like an entropic or economic debt.

The voice reminds us again to keep our hands and feet inside at all times and to maybe take our eyes off our phones for like, one second, and gaze outward as we make our way along the tracks. Not to turn around in our seats and look backward in the direction of history, at the past which is already gone, but to always look forward, at the grandeur of the vistas, the sweep of world events unfolding, which we are a part of, which is what we paid for, four hundred dollars a ticket, half-price for children (although as they grow, they will eventually turn into full-fare passengers on this ride, and we worry about the mechanics of how that incremental fare will be collected, whether we will be able to pay for them or if they will need to pay for it themselves, who will come for it, and whether we will still be around, whether we will have any warning, whether we will still be able to stay in this car with them or whether they will need to get out and ride in their own vehicles, we worry whether the track might diverge at some point and they will be off into a different set of tunnels and rooms and we will never see them again).

The sweep of history, having this unspoken feeling of forward and upward momentum, while being entertained, all of that goes into the ticket price, and the voice of the woman who narrates the ride, she reminds us that it is our purchase of these tickets that makes the ride possible. We are the customers, but we are also the underwriters of this entertainment. We are consumers of this experience. We are tourists in our own creation.

"We're moving," our daughter says, clapping her hands in excitement. "Let's go! Where are we going?"

She is not a baby anymore. Our wife starts to cry.

"How did that happen?" our wife says. She starts to turn her head back, hoping she might still be able to see the point in the track where our baby turned into a kid who could say things to us, but we stop our wife from looking back, reminding her that the voice will be angry.

Our car moves down the track. We are picking up speed. We are approaching a house. Our daughter asks us if that is our house and we say we aren't sure, but something tells us that it is. We are headed for a collision, but then a set of double doors opens and we find ourselves inside the living room of our house.

"This feels like home," we say to each other, but we also hear other people around us saying it and for the first time in a long time we are aware that we are not on this ride alone. In fact, there are other families in the neighboring cars just ahead of us and just behind us, sitting so close we could reach out and touch them. We look ahead and see that it is all families, all the way down, this tram being an endless procession of small car units, all of us connected by the central drive-train powering this ride, subdivided but linked, having our own versions of the same experience. There is a lot of murmuring now as we hear a lot of us saying "Is this home?" "Where are we?" and we start to wonder what we are, exactly, whether up to this point our definition of "we" has been too small. We wonder who we are. But just as we are starting to wonder about how large "we" are as a group, the nature of "we" and the mystery and the wonder and the pluses and the minuses of it, we hear someone say "I don't know about this." We have an "I" among us and everyone turns to see if they can figure out who it is, but just as that happens, the tram uncouples from itself and breaks into two, and one part of us goes off on one track and the other part goes off on a different track, and the uncoupling happens again and again and again until we find ourselves alone, together, alone. Together as a small family unit, but now uncoupled from our fellow riders. Alone now, moving in our single transport vehicle, on our own ride, wondering what we are missing out on, what other riders are getting to see.

Now we wish we had paid more attention at the beginning of the ride, had not been listening to the voice to keep looking sideways, at the murals and the dioramas and displays of the ride's retail partners. But it was hard not to do so. They make it so easy, we did not even have to move, just take out our credit cards and hold them near the edge of our car in such a way that they could be swiped through the many point-of-sale devices installed every fifty feet along the ride, millions, billions of transactions occurring every instant, so that we could instantly own a part of this experience, if we wanted to, to have souvenirs of all types, cultural, historical, key chains and cups with crazy straws. It was part of our duty as riders to help support the sponsors that make the ride possible, and it allowed us to participate, each according to our means and personalities, allowed us to choose how we wanted to enjoy this, all of this. We pass through the house, seeing our living room, our three bedrooms and two and a half bathrooms, our kitchen, and we exit back out into the light and what we see is a thousand different tracks, or a million, or four hundred million.

"The ride is broken," our son says.

"Hey!" we say. "We have a son?" and we kiss him and squeeze his cheeks and he pushes our hands away.

"I'm not a baby," he says.

"You're not," we say, because he's not, but we wonder. "When? How? Where were you born?"

"Back there," our son says, "in the house. You guys seemed really freaked out about something and I didn't want to bother you so I've been quiet for a while," and he doesn't seem too hurt, already so grown-up and used to being the younger kid, and although we feel like we just met him a moment ago, he has been with us for some time now and we already love him. He is ten, our son, and we look at his hair and his nose and his shoulders and we admire him. Our daughter, now thirteen, seems to have known he was here all along and is waiting for us to catch up.

"What are you looking at?" we ask our new son.

"Cars."

"They're nicer than ours," we say. "Our car is old, huh?"

"Yeah," he says. "But I like our car. It's the best one."

All of the cars move along their individual paths, some up into the mountains, some turn into boats and float onto lakes, some take off like airplanes as we watch in envy, some hit trees and we watch the families inside get out and start fighting and we wonder if they will ever be able to get back on. Our car continues smoothly along its track, not the fastest, nor the slowest.

We notice now that the ride is not what it used to be, less finished, more construction. We see a sign posting notice that the ride is now owned by American Enterprises, LLC, whose parent company, American Entertainments, Inc. is a subsidiary itself of a company called The USAmusement Corporation, which is owned by a German conglomerate, New World Experiments GmbH, owned by a consortium led by Chinese and Korean investors.

You have been chosen as potential partners in an affiliate marketing and peer-advertising campaign ...

the voice says, as we continue to roll on through history.

You're now passing through: Japanese internment camps during the Second World War.

On your left, coming up, you will see Coney Island, Brooklyn, New York in the 1920s.

And if you look over to your right, you'll see the banks of the Mississippi, and, watch your feet, lift them up to stay dry, as your vehicle is now converting itself into a riverboat, a form of transportation vital to the nation's commerce throughout the 19th century. No mention of other parts of the U.S. economy in that century.

Backward we go, through American lore and mythology, merchandised to perfection.

We see new ground being broken, dig sites surrounded by chain-link fences, men working in hardhats, large colorful banners proclaiming that The American Experience will be re-launched in the fall of 3015.

This is a part of the ride that seems like we are not on a ride anymore.

We have crossed some line into the backstage area, employees only, where the gears and the machine room and the electrical cords and all of the nuts and bolts of the mechanical ride are evident. Even the voice has dropped some of the theatre from her voice and now talks to us directly.

"The narrated portion of the ride is over. You are now entering an experimental phase, still in testing, for a 3-D version of America, where riders can experience "America" for the first time, in 3-D."

Our son and our daughter both get excited at the idea for a moment until the voice tells us that we do not qualify financially for that portion of the ride.

"You are welcome to stay in the car, although what you will see will be a flattened, 2-D version of what should be a stereoscopic experience."

We are given a choice of whether to go on or get out, and we decide to go on, although the voice now also tells us that we need to take some of the things out of the car, as we have taken on too much weight, so our son drops his sack lunch over the side of the car, and we drop a typewriter, and old clothes that the kids used to wear, and our daughter drops a doll whose hair she used to brush when she was a little girl at the beginning of the ride.

We are just content to keep riding this for a while, passing through a room they called Your 30s, which has upbeat, contemplative acoustic guitar music, and Your 40s which is more piano-themed, and Your 50s which has Bach playing and we see some cars getting wine and cheese. We see cars that have God with them, in voice and as a kind of hologram, and we watch God from afar, and wish we could hear what God is saying to the people in the cars lucky enough to have God, but the advertising voices all around our car are drowning everything out. We pass through dioramas of ourselves in cubicles, watching time-lapse movies of ourselves working, working, aging, seeing what we look like at work, seeing how the hands of the clocks in our offices spin around, and somewhere around that point we notice that our lap bars have tightened over our thighs. It could be the slow spread of middle age, and the growth of our daughter, who is in college now, and our son who as a sophomore made the varsity soccer team at his high school and is now taller than all of us.

But it's not that we have grown, the lap bars really did click down tighter on us, pinning us into this car, pinching us into our seats, and the voice tells us it is for our safety, as the ride is picking up speed now. With a sick feeling in our guts we understand that we are not getting out of this ride until it lets us off and that the reason we are picking up speed is that we are now on a downslope, that somewhere we did pass the high point of the ride. None of us remembers doing that, or even there being a particularly high point, and maybe the high point just wasn't very high, but whatever the case, we are accelerating now. Whatever we built up in terms of momentum, we are now giving it back.

The idea is, the hope is, we will be able to see everything at least once, that even in this rushed state we can experience all of the rooms, even if it is from a distance, even if it is really other riders who are seeing these things. We can see other cars moving across the country, across "America," we see all of us on grids, on graphs. We understand ourselves to be bits of socio-economic data on the bar charts and pie charts and flowcharts running down the leftmost column of the multi-colored newspapers that get left in front of the room doors of our discount business traveler hotels. We understand ourselves to be frequent fliers, rewards club members, customer loyalty program participants. We dream publicly. We have agencies, staffed by people who storyboard our fantasies, people who plan out panel-by-panel, shot-by-shot, the public space, the collective mental environment where this ride is located. Creative agencies mapping the conceptual territory, the shared Main Street of our imaginations, where we stroll, arm in arm, down the avenue of our engineered dreams, our civic conversation now just giggles and pointing, saying to ourselves, hey look at this, look at this, and we all look at this for ten seconds until another one of us says, now hey wait a minute, have you guys seen this, look at this, look at this one now, and we all turn our heads and look at this one now, until the next thing, the next thing, our collective attention reduced to the briefest of intervals, not long enough or large enough to hold a dream. And now, no more public dreaming, just expertly conceived narrative products designed to keep us inside the car, looking out the side, murals painted in 2-D to give a 3-D illusion of movement, the sweep of history that we have purchased, that we are part owners of, murals that show us watery images of ourselves, murals with frames around them, to give off the feelings of "Nostalgia" and "Tradition" and "Affordable Luxury" and "Forward Progress" and "Special Times" and "Beer and Friends." We have no room for dreams or even feelings anymore, our feelings themselves engineered, mood-boarded by people who know how to do such things with chemistry and music and art direction. We feel feelings designed by people who have market-researched us and have seen our private browser searches and know what's in our darkest of hearts and in our darkest of parts, and know what we really want deep down, all of those feelings calibrated to be emotionally nutritious, or at least emotionally fattening, calorically dense psychosocial-experiential sustenance, allotted into our feed troughs, constituting our collective body, so that we are what we consume, and we consume what we are, so that we are a loop, closed and tight and perfect, so we keep our minds focused on what has been laid out before us, our eyes adjusting to the alternating light and dark periods. Moving room to room. We have kids now and they are babies and they are grown and they'll always be babies and they grew up overnight, and occasionally we admit to ourselves that we wish we didn't have either of them not because we don't love them but because we love them too much. We know how incompetent we are at loving things other than ourselves and loving these kids as much as we do we are quite sure that this excess of love will ruin them. We can already see it happening.

We have to admit, sometimes, in the middle of a sentence, we hear ourselves talking and we become terrified at the sound of our own voice, still so strange and dumb after all these years. Occasionally we wish we didn't have these kids yet and that we could go back to the days when it was just us, and all we had to worry about was just not falling out of the ride, what kind of snacks we would eat, what souvenirs we would buy. We see ourselves on the in-ride camera, taking pictures of us that we will have the chance to purchase, for $29.95 per print, at the end of the ride, when we get off. We see ourselves on camera, at an earlier time in the ride: we are looking at our family, all sitting together, cars near, now where are they? Where have our kids gone?

We search desperately for our daughter, search desperately for our son, the ride is coming to an end for us, and turning our heads from the side, our necks stiff from having been locked into a position of gazing for so long, we realize what we have just done. We look forward for the first time in years and see the white light ahead, the outside, as we exit this room. We look at the in-ride camera and see our son, and see our daughter, see them in their own cars, with their own sons and their own daughters, and we want to call out to them, to our children and our grandchildren, but the camera is just an image, and we understand that, but we call out to them anyway. We try to tell them about the ride, but we see the looks on their faces, the hope, and we start to understand the impossibility of this ride, how it is a kind of perpetual escalator, a physical impossibility that somehow exists. We see how our children and our grandchildren think that they are on an upslope, believe in the forward movement that they can feel. We wish we could ride the ride again that way. We see the looks on our grandkids' faces except that they are not looking at the ride, they are looking at their parents' faces, just as our kids looked at ours, seeing how excited their parents are, and being excited by that, and also knowing already how to give their parents what they seem to need. The kids knew all along. Our daughter is in another car, far away, on an upslope, waving to us. Our son is with his family, and gives us a sad smile. Our own kids, now adults, they know already how the ride works, but they need to show their own kids. The idea is. The hope is. And as we move toward the large exit doors into the next room, it fills us. The hope fills us.

THE DEFENSE
OF FREE MIND
DESIRINA BOSKOVICH

I'M AN HOUR into my shift in the greenhouse when the sirens begin to wail. The ear-splitting clang pierces the peaceful green hum of the hydroponic drip. My adrenaline spikes. I've been hearing these sirens since I was a baby, and the spike still hits me every time. But it's different now, because I'm sixteen and finally old enough to defend.

I rip off my gardening gloves and sprint to the locker near the exit, touch my thumb to the lock. My boss is too old for militia duty; she gazes as I reach into the locker and pull out a rifle. "Be careful, dear," she says.

The guns are always loaded, and always in the lockers, which are always by the exits. We live on Free Mind, and we're always ready to defend it.

"Back soon," I shout, my heart pounding with both fear and excitement. I run through the hallway, across the bridge, up the stairs, and onto the nearest defense platform, overlooking the rolling gray sea.

A dozen Defenders are already at the wall, guns notched in the slots, peering down their sights. I grab a spot and find my view. From here I can see the coastline, the City's silver skyscrapers glimmering hazily against the sky.

I can see the boat closing in. A slim trawler, cutting through the choppy sea. I count five people, standing on the narrow deck, the City's official insignia splashed across the side. From this distance I can't see them clearly but City people all look alike, anyway, light gray jumpsuits, shaved heads.

They're waving at us, shouting. They get closer and I see they're holding guns. They're always holding guns. But they don't want to kill us. They want to conquer us, and take us back to land, turn us into City people, control our minds. They want to make us like them.

"Okay, now!" shouts the platform captain, and I aim my weapon once more, closing one eye as I sight down the barrel. I hold down the trigger until the magazine is spent.

Like all of the kids on Free Mind, I've been training to do this since I was ten. All those hours at the indoor range: they prepare you for the noise, the deafening staccato cracks; they acquaint you with the burn in your shoulder, the vibration in your hands, the acrid smell of gunpowder. Those hours teach you how to aim well and shoot straight, ocular implants highlighting the kill spots on your target. But they can never prepare you for what it's really like: the act in the wild, the bodies dropping, the ship capsizing, the smoke rising from the hull, the mix of blood and oil churning in the water.

It's over. The ship is sinking and the City's soldiers are bullet-ridden and drowning, and Free Mind is safe—for now.

Since I turned sixteen I've done this three times; today, the fourth. Their assaults are becoming more frequent.

As always, the battle done, I'm wobbling and weak in the knees. The adrenaline departs my body as quickly as it arrived, and I'm suddenly sleepy and deflated. Together with the other Defenders, I'm giggling nervously, giggling with relief. We're alive. We made it.

Behind my eyes there's a weird ache, a dull buzzing tension that always seems to accompany these high-adrenaline moments. Only time and space relieve it.

★

When I get home my younger brother is sitting at the kitchen table in our small apartment, doing homework on his tablet and eating a bowl of shrimp. I sit across from him and help myself to a couple.

"I heard the sirens," he says, eyes shining. "Did you go?"

"Yeah. I did." My brother is fourteen, and my newly minted status as a Defender has greatly raised his estimation of my worth. Suddenly, his older sister is cool to him. I would be lying if I said I didn't like it.

"What was it like?"

I describe the tension as we stood on the platform, waiting for the trawler to skim closer, and the way the City people waved and shouted, as if they could scare us.

"What were they saying?"

"I don't know. I couldn't make out the words."

I don't tell him that you never feel the same, after the first time. I can always close my eyes and see, for a moment, the scrum in the waves, the bloody bodies fall.

"I wish I could go," he says. "I hate sitting in class and listening to the sirens. Wondering."

"Log your range hours," I say. "You'll be sixteen before you know it."

"Why do they keep coming, do you think?" he asks. "What's the point?"

"I guess they have to," I say slowly. "That's just what the City demands. It's not enough that they control the way everyone lives and looks and thinks over there. They can't stand that we're free over here; they won't be content until they own us too. So they'll keep sending people, forever."

"But we'll always fight them off," he says, almost as if he's trying to convince himself.

"Of course we will," I say.

He seems satisfied with my explanation, but I'm not quite satisfied myself. Why would they sacrifice their own lives of comfort simply for the goal of absolute control?

★

THE NEXT FEW weeks are peaceful. Life in Free Mind relaxes into its steady rhythm: afternoon shifts at the greenhouse, evenings with my friends at the rec hall. My brother studies for his exams; he wants to be an engineer. My mother works long hours at the hospital, helping birth a fresh crop of babies. My father directs the Seastead's southern expansion, building a new sector to accommodate our growing community.

One late morning I'm sitting at Hank's with my friends, working on a massive stack of pancakes. Hank's is located in a surface-level sector. It's a little bit of a trek from where I live, but it's totally worth it for the best pancakes in Free Mind.

Then the sirens start to wail.

My friend Paul hasn't passed his Defender's test yet so he grins sheepishly as the rest of us jump up from the table. My augmented reality kicks in; I see the gun locker in the corner, flashing yellow. I dash in that general direction, tripping over a few chairs along the way. Every Defender in Hank's is grabbing a weapon. I follow the yellow flashing route to the nearest defense platform and get swept up with the rest.

I reach the platform—and everything is chaos.

It takes me a moment to process what I'm seeing:

The platform is covered with smoking rubble, chunks of concrete and burnt plastic, dust and sparks. The wall at the edge of the platform has been partially destroyed, and in that jagged space the City soldiers are coming through. There are bullets flying in all directions. Blood is running along the platform.

Something comes whistling up from beyond the wall. It explodes in a screaming bang and another part of the wall crumbles. A Free Minder falls. A City soldier is missing a leg. The pain behind my eyes is searing.

I'm frozen in shock and can't even move. It's never been like this before. I don't know what to do. I look to my friend Isabel for reassurance, but I can't see her anywhere.

Next thing I know someone knocks my gun right out of my hands — I'd forgotten I was holding it — and grabs me by the shoulders. It's a City soldier. I can't see him clearly; my vision is blurry with dust and sweat and tears. But I know it's a soldier. He drags me across the platform. I'm kicking and screaming. "Help! Help me! Someone!" I'm trying to fight him off but I'm just a sixteen-year-old girl and he's so much bigger than me. Another one grabs me too and then I'm immobilized, caught between them, writhing as my feet don't touch the ground. Around me Free Minders are fighting for their lives and most of all, fighting to make sure the City soldiers don't get beyond the platform. If they make it inside, it's all over for us.

Then I'm being pushed through the hole in the wall and tossed onto the deck of the boat. The men who grabbed me come tumbling after. They land on top of me, pushing me flat on my face. Rough hands grab my wrists and tie them behind my back. I can feel the boat rocking and shifting, the idle motor kicking to life. We're moving.

My captors sit me up. For the first time I see the Seastead from the outside. It's a gleaming white ziggurat rising from the waters—and now, receding rapidly behind us. Two more City boats are floating just beyond the platform, where the battle continues. One of the boats is on fire. Another is sinking.

I crane my neck and try to see behind me. There is the scrappy wisp of land. There are the skyscrapers, shimmering along the skyline. We're going to the City.

"I'm going to be sick," I say, and a moment later I'm puking my half-digested pancakes all over myself.

"She's just a child," one of the City soldiers says. The voice is a woman's. I squint at her, trying to make her out; I can't see very well. All I can see is her close-cropped hair, almost bald. Her gray jumpsuit. It should be spattered with blood, as I am, but it's not. It's spotless, pristine. So is the deck of the boat.

There are six of them. Now one is coming closer to me. "I'm going to clean you up," he says. "Don't bite me, okay?"

I nod mutely. He looks like all the others. *Exactly* like all the others. I'm crying helplessly. I can't help myself.

I don't want to go to the City. I want to go home.

With the damp cloth he wipes my face, scrubbing away the stinging slurry of blood and sweat and dust. I can see better now but I still can't quite see him. It's like when I try to look at him — my eyes won't focus. There's this fuzziness. I can see the Seastead — how small it looks from here. I can see the sky and the clouds and the wheeling, screaming gulls, mad from the bloodshed. But I can't see him any more clearly than I could before.

The whole time he's talking. "You're okay," he says. "Stop crying. Okay?"

"What are you going to do to me?"

I already know what they're going to do to me. They're going to take me to the City. Shave my head so I look like them. Give me a pill to make me calm and turn off the part of my brain that questions. Send me to one of their education centers where they teach me again and again the things they want me to believe until I *do* believe them, until my mind belongs to them and I can recite their catechism without faltering.

"We just need some things, okay?" the soldier says. "Stuff your people have. You got parents, right? You look like you do. A nice family. They'll give us what we need, and then we'll give you back."

"Need?" I say. "Like what?"

The pain in my head, it's impossible. I can feel a black cloud gathering in my brain.

He's looming in my vision, the soldier who was cleaning up my sick.

"What's your name?" he asks.

"Renee."

I try to see him. I feel dizzy, seasick — a Seasteader, seasick? I want to grab onto him, the boat, myself, anything. I'm pitching, tossing. Then for a second I do see him and he doesn't look like what I thought. I catch a glimpse of long matted hair, brushing his shoulders. A patchy, curly beard, and rough tan skin and a scar across his cheek. I try to hold onto that vision and then it's gone again.

It's glitching in and out. I see and then I don't.

It makes me sicker than ever. All I can do is close my eyes, squeeze them so tight all I see is black, and rock helplessly back and forth.

"Lukas said she'd get like that," I hear one of the soldiers say. "Leaving the augmented reality field. They get out of range and get sick. He said it happens to the pirates every time."

When I open my eyes again, everything is changed.

★

THE CITY PEOPLE are filthy and unkempt, their clothes tattered, a mismatch of styles I can't place. Their faces are smeared with dirt, and heavily tanned by the equatorial sun. Their hair is not buzzed. They do not look alike.

The boat itself is barely more than a raft with a gas-spewing motor attached. An old boat that's been patched and repaired so many times with so many mismatched pieces that in time it's become a wholly different boat, nothing left of the original but a shape and a memory.

Now, as we round the peninsula, the City looms before me. It is a drowned city, the skyscrapers rising ghostlike from the waters, their glass windows all blown out like gaping black eyes, their frames rusting and disintegrating as the lesser structures collapse beneath the weight of rabid vines.

One of my captors laughs at my stunned expression. "Welcome to Miami," he says.

"I don't understand."

★

I WATCH IN sick silence as they maneuver the boat among the wreckage. The gently lapping water is dark and tainted, viscous with algae and oil slicks. We edge up next to one of the tall buildings. They tie the boat off and then I see there is a narrow metal staircase, laden with salt crust and rust, zigzagging up the side of the building.

"We're going to untie you now," one of the women says. "So you can climb without hurting yourself. You'll be good, right? You know there's nowhere for you to go."

I nod silently; she's right. This world is so much different than I was taught and I don't understand it at all. My survival depends on my captors.

I climb with them up the rickety stairs, several levels above the hungry water's reach, and we enter a large space. There's a blast of noise, laughing, shouting, music, and I think I hear a rooster crowing. As my eyes adjust to the dim I see there's a crowd gathered. They fall silent when they see me. A baby cries. Everyone stares.

I start coughing at the smoky air; cooking fires smolder by the busted-out windows. A heavy stench hangs close, smelling of dirty fuel, unwashed bodies, stale urine, fried fish.

A man comes forward. He's wearing suspenders and no shirt, his dark wavy hair tied back with a navy patterned bandana. He eyes me for a moment, then looks to my captors.

"We lost too many," he says. Then I remember the two boats they abandoned at Free Mind, one on fire, the other capsizing, and all the bodies on the platform.

Why am I here?

★

LUKAS PULLS ME by the arm back to a corner of the space, where some dank cushions on the ground form a seating area.

"It's not what you expected, is it?" he asks. His blue eyes are piercing, his dark eyebrows bushy. He has a long scar running up his left arm. I think he's about thirty but his face is dirty and his dark beard is full of gray so it's hard to tell.

I don't say anything, and he continues. "I know. I come from Free Mind. I used to be one of your pirates. Oh, I know that's not what you call them. You call them traders. We were pirates and looters, though. Setting sail from Free Mind, coming back with the stuff that keeps the Seastead's whole economy afloat, so to speak. The first time I sailed beyond the field it was a real mindfuck."

"But ... why?" I don't even know what I'm asking. Why the lie? Why is he here? Why am *I* here?

The second question is the one he answers. "Most of 'em are happy to keep the story going because it pays so well. Not me though. Never liked Free Mind much anyway. Ran into some of these Mudlarks on a trip round the Gulf and just figured, what the hell."

"Okay," I say. Not sure what else there is to say, actually.

"Anyway, you look like the kind of girl who belongs on Free Mind, nice and safe and clean there, so I guess you'll want to be heading back pretty soon, and that's fine, long as your people don't mind giving us some medicine. That seems like a fair trade, right? They get their girl back, we get some drugs so our babies don't die."

"Yes. That seems fair," I say. My mind is whirling in a million different directions. How many people know the truth — that the City is a ruin? That Free Mind is the best place left? Did my teachers know? Do my parents know?

Then all at once it hits me. I've shot these people. I've killed them. The way they always waved their arms. Were they saying, "Don't shoot?" Were they refugees, begging for medicine and food? Everyone around me is coughing and emaciated. The children are wailing. The smell of diarrhea hangs in the air. I killed them. I killed their parents.

The shudder that rips through my entire body leaves me nauseated and trembling. I want to be sick again, but there's nothing left.

Lukas holds a radio. He's thumbing through the static, calling out to Free Mind.

He finds our channel. Voices answer, and I want to think I recognize them, but I'm not sure I do. I listen, numb, as he offers his terms. Me. For the meds.

My mom is a doctor, and so I recognize the names of the drugs he wants. Stuff to stop diarrhea, to cure an infection, to lower a fever. Antimalarials. Antibiotics.

There's a long pause on the other side and then a voice that I'm pretty sure is Free Mind's Mayor says, "We'll confer. Expect our answer shortly." Then there's a burst of static and silence.

Lukas looks at me. "Damn," he says. "That's pretty cold. Maybe they don't actually want you back."

"How many people know?"

He gazes at me for a moment. "Well, all the loot teams, of course, and all the merchant class, since their loot teams tell them. Everyone in government, and the tech team that maintains the augmented reality field. And whoever those people tell. No one's supposed to talk about it, but you know. People, they let stuff slip."

"My dad is a building contractor and my mom is an OB/GYN." I say. "Do you think — do they know?"

He shrugs. "Hard to say. But, you know, there's a reason all the Defenders are young, and it's not just because of the fast reflexes and all that. It's because they know you don't know."

"Will they even let me back?"

"They let the pirates back in. They let me back in. Until I ditched."

"But why? Why the whole lie?"

"Every society needs its myths, I guess. Your people, our people, they decided to be free thinkers, and that meant they were free to invent their own facts. They fled the city as it died, took everything they could. Built their own world and a reality to match."

"My whole life I've been taught the City wanted to oppress us."

"Some people find it oppressive to be asked for help."

The radio crackles back to life. "Miami," a disembodied, distorted voice says. "We've discussed your offer. Our conclusion is that we don't negotiate with terrorists and unfortunately, we must refuse."

I shout into the radio. "What about my parents? Do they know? They won't let you do this!"

"They know you drowned," the voice says. "In a moment they'll identify your body."

"My body is right here!"

"Not from their perspective."

For a moment I can't comprehend what he means. Then I remember— the scans. Every year, each resident of Free Mind gets a full body scan, the booth whirring as our spectral forms find three dimensions on some outside screen, our holographic likenesses stored permanently in the data bank. They said it was for security reasons.

They can tweak reality, and they own the contours of my face.

"That's not a perspective," I snap at the radio, my voice rising. "It's a lie! It's just a lie!"

"Just some alternative facts," the voice says, and then the static goes still as the radio cuts off.

My kidnappers collapse with despair across the damp cushions. The other couple dozen people who appear to live in this squat are gathered around us now, wide-eyed. A cry goes up.

Lukas looks at me. I look at Lukas.

"Well," he says. "Fuck."

★

THE CITY PEOPLE aren't happy. No meds. Ten of their own lost in the battle with Free Mind, shot and drowned for nothing. Now there's me, another mouth to feed, and they don't care if I live or die. Some of them want to kill me. They argue about it in the corner. They don't care that I hear.

It's not exactly an ideal situation for me, either. I want to go home. I want my family to know I'm alive. I want to return to the world as I thought it was. I do not want to be murdered and fed to the sharks.

In the short term, the Mudlarks decide not to kill me. Lukas is their inside man, the former Free Minder who understands the Seastead and knows its weaknesses. He assures them he'll think of something to do with me.

I don't know if he actually has a plan to use me or if he just feels bad about killing me, but either way I am grateful for the reprieve.

They give me a mat to sleep on in a room full of squalling toddlers. All hours of the night they're waking up and crying with hunger and heat rashes. I try to comfort them back to sleep but nothing I do is good enough and eventually I just lie there crying too, thinking about my parents who think I'm dead.

A few days pass. I make a friend: another young woman on child-minding duty. She has never been on a boat to Free Mind and so she doesn't understand why she should hate me. She shows me her tips and tricks for soothing small and miserable children. We commiserate. We are comrades in arms in the diaper rash trenches and this work, as grueling as it is, comforts me—because it makes me feel closer to my mother, somehow, knowing she's doing the same things on Free Mind.

★

TEN DAYS LATER, Lukas pulls me aside. "I need to talk to you."

There's no private place here. We sit in the corner with the moldy cushions, the squat's informal meeting place. I wait, nervous and fidgeting.

He holds a device in his hands. "We spent a lot of time and effort tracking down all the parts and pieces to build those IEDs," he says. "We thought if we could just break through that wall … But I fucked up. It's not the platform we need to breach. It's their thoughts about us. It's the filter. I should have been working on this thing instead."

"What is it?" I look at it curiously, this odd conglomeration of circuits and coils and copper wires.

"It's an EMP generator. I think—if I made it right—it could temporarily disable the augmented reality field. For a few minutes at least. Like being on a boat and leaving the Seastead's range. So they would see us."

"They could see me." My friends could see me; my parents could see me. They would know that I'm alive and the Mayor lied. I could tell them the truth about the City and the people here. There is no mind control, no intoxicating pill. There's just starvation and sickness.

"Right. So I need you to come with us. You and I, we're still Free Minders, right? We need to make that gap in the filter. So they'll listen."

"I'm in," I say. Not that I really have a choice. To stay alive, I must be useful. And I want to go back to Free Mind. I want my family.

We talk. He tells me how the EMP generator works. I tell him what defense platform we need to approach, the one in my sector where the Defenders will know me. He calls in the others—the raiding party. And together we make a plan.

The whole time I'm thinking that whatever happens, I'm getting free of them. As soon as I'm close, as soon as it's safe, I'm making a break for it. I'm going home.

★

FOR TWO DAYS they prepare, looting more gasoline for the boat, mending their body armor built from scraps, testing the EMP generator. I'm walking lighter thinking I'm going to get out of here, it's really going to happen, soon I'll be free again, and safe. I sing to the babies simply because I'm happy.

But at the same time there are other thoughts running through my brain, a parallel story that doesn't match up: I want us to be successful. Us. Miami. The City. I want us to win. I laugh with my friend in the nursery and

I wait patiently in line as they divvy up the stew at night—it's not like Free Mind, they don't use money, they just share—and I keep forgetting I don't belong. I want us to get that medicine because this little girl I'm rocking has a fever that won't break and this baby boy has a rash all up and down his back and this other little boy has the runs. I think, my mom is a doctor, she could help us. I catch myself on that "us." She could help *them*.

I hold that thought and I also hold the thought that I'll run from them as soon as I can. Two thoughts at once.

★

THE BOAT ROCKS precariously in the waves and I see it now for what it really is, a barely seaworthy vessel ravaged by rot and rust.

We're approaching Free Mind: Lukas, me, three others. The Seastead emerges from the waters, a floating ziggurat, adorned with cantilevered terraces and platforms, the Free Mind flag waving proudly in the breeze. My breath catches. I do want to go home.

My stomach is flip-flopping. Afraid, nervous, hopeful. *Let this work.*

Lukas and I discussed whether we'd feel anything when he sets off the device. We still have the ocular implants, but they're no longer connected; they're dead hardware. We've been deleted from Free Mind's augmented reality field, like so much else. What we see won't change. But we might get a headache, he says. He isn't sure.

We get closer. Soon the alarms will be going off in my sector. Someone else is working in the greenhouse where I used to fertilize the plants and thin the seedlings. They will hear the clang of the sirens and feel that adrenaline spike.

While I'm here on the boat with the City people, and now I know there is no adrenaline spike like the one you feel when you're the one in the snipers' scopes.

"Now," I say. "We're close enough. They're going to start shooting soon. Now."

"Not yet," says Tom, peering through binoculars at the platform. "They're not at the wall yet. Just a little closer."

"Now."

"Now!"

"Now," says Lukas.

The blast spreads outwards, invisible but powerful. I feel it, a twinge that fades immediately into a dull ache, and I blink. I see the same.

"They're puking," Tom says, still looking through the binoculars. "I think it worked."

But a minute later the guns are still coming through the notches, the sights trained on us. The first shot rings out. The bullet pierces the hull, above the water line, flowering metal.

I jump up and down and wave my arms, screaming so loud my throat immediately goes hoarse. "Stop! Don't shoot! It's me, Renee! I'm from Free Mind! It's me!"

★

THEY SEE ME. My fellow Defenders—I recognize them, and they recognize me. They're reeling, dizzy, confused from the shift, but the filter is down. I see it in their eyes. They know me.

"But you're dead," Jason says. He won't let me board the platform. The rest glare at me suspiciously, their weapons still trained on me, on us, on the boat. I know that with the filter down, it will be harder for them to aim, but we're still at pretty close range. "Who are those people?"

"They're from the City," I say. "But it's not like how we thought. Look at them. There is no City. It's just a ruin. Flooded out. They need help."

"Of course there's a City."

I keep trying to explain but the words don't help. My friends are looking straight at me and they don't believe I'm alive; they're staring at the dilapidated boat but they still imagine the City insignia that doesn't exist. The filter is down but they still have their own.

Fuck it; I don't know how long we have until the filter goes back up. I know I don't have time for this. I lie because it's easier for them to understand.

"I didn't die, the City kidnapped me, but I escaped. We all did. From their mind control camps. We've been trying to get to Free Mind. Now can we board?"

"You can," Jason says, still suspicious. "The rest stay down there until our backup arrives."

I clamber up the ladder. The minute my feet hit the platform, I'm making a break for it—pushing past the Defenders, knocking their weapons aside, running toward the doors. I sprint down a hallway and then another; I'm heading toward the hospital and my feet know the way. Behind me I hear shouts but I don't pay attention. I have to reach my mom.

★

I FIND HER in the maternity ward, as I knew I would. The usually busy hospital is quiet, the machinery down from the EMP blast.

She sees me.

A dozen expressions flit across her face: grief, rage, hope, despair, confusion, longing.

"I didn't drown," I say, and I throw myself into her arms. She hugs me back so hard and in that moment, I really do believe that everything is going to be OK. I'm stupid. I hope.

She pushes me back so she can look at me. "But we saw——"

"They lied. They made it look like that——"

"Of course," she says, shaking her head, and in the corners of her mouth I see a flood of emotion I can't yet unpack. "The filter. I knew it felt off. When we saw you. But— I was crying so hard——"

"You know about the filter." The words fall from my mouth flat and dead. "That it's not just maps and reminders and emergency exits. Did you know about the City, too? That it drowned?"

"It's for the kids," she says. "The filter. It's for you. It makes it easier. Didn't it?"

"But it's all a lie!"

"No, it's not," she says. She's flustered and defensive the way she used to get when my brother asked too many questions, but maybe it's only because her daughter has just risen from the dead. "It's true, basically. They do want to control our minds. They want to make us feel responsible for them, and make us feel guilty for not giving up what we have, just because our parents had the foresight to leave before things got so bad. They want to force us to feel sorry for them and if we don't, they attack us. For not thinking what they want us to think."

That's when I make a split decision. Like Lukas. I know what Free Mind means now and I can't go back.

There's a chug and hum in the background. The systems returning online. The grid springing back to life. The filter going up.

My mom is still watching me. Her face is different. I don't know what she sees but it isn't me; I'm still deleted. She knows it's me but she also trusts the filter. I understand. She is holding two ideas in her head, two parallel thoughts that don't agree. Perhaps it gets easier with time.

I run from the room, down the hall, through the scrum and flurry of staff preoccupied by the glitch in the field. I shove through a swinging door and into the nurse's station. There are meds, and I grab them, fistfuls of them, as many as will fit into the front of my shirt.

The sirens are screaming now. I race back to the boat.

★

THE MUDLARKS SURVIVE on salvage and scrap. The drowned city is dangerous in so many ways; toxic chemicals in the water, oil slicks that burn for days, rotted buildings collapsing onto narrow canals that once were streets. Alligators and sharks are always on the hunt. So I shouldn't be happy when they let me on the salvage team, but I am. I stole the medicine, I leapt onto the boat. I escaped, I survived; we all did. I've caught the thrill. And the salvage team can use someone small and light to creep across the fragile beams.

I still sleep in the nursery most nights. They are kids without families and I feel most at home there.

There's one little girl that keeps crawling onto my mat with me at night. She was sick, but she's better now. She yanks on my arm with her strong little fingers until I put it around her. She has nightmares, she says. She misses her mom.

"What happened to her?" I ask one night, whispering in the dark. All she says is "She went away," and I don't know if that means she got sick and died, or if she went away on the salvage team, or if she went away to Free Mind to ask for help and never came back, because we shot her. I don't ask. I'm afraid to know.

So all I say is, "I miss my mom, too."

AWARE
C. ROBERT CARGILL

CLETUS CULPEPPER DIDN'T think he would ever get used to gravity on the moon. But, as with the aftermath of all great catastrophes, he came to accept this new normal, to live and work as he always had, only occasionally pining with nostalgia for the days of hopping and bouncing across the cratered surface as if he were at the bottom of some training pool back on Earth. In truth, Cletus rarely even thought about it. It was only when he found himself waiting for the coffee maker to get around to finally spitting out a full mug that he watched each drip, remembering that he wasn't on Earth. *This isn't right*, he would think as each drop splashed down, before grunting, nodding, and muttering, "Oh yeah," to himself.

Stranger still, for that brief moment, he was forced to remember that there was no Florida. Not anymore. He'd grown up there. Remembered vividly the topography. Could detail entire nights of his misspent youth, sucking down beers and making time with girls in places that were now thirty feet underwater. Sure, the scientists had raised their alarm, presented reams of data, even built computer models of the damage adding artificial gravity to Earth's orbital companion would cause back home, but what was science anyway but guesses? Legislation against the move stalled and when a suit threw the switch there was no turning back.

You could walk on the moon.

Who needed Florida, anyway?

The door to Cletus's office shushed open, the warm, fresh air from the next pod rushing in, sweeping out the dank, stale atmosphere. *How long have I been in here?* Cletus wondered, glancing at the clock. It was already forty-seven hours into lunar day, but he'd only slept once. He needed to bed down soon or he was going to be worthless on his upcoming site inspection.

The new suit from corporate, Tracy *Something* stood in the doorway. Cletus couldn't remember his last name, and were he pressed to think about it, would have to admit that he simply didn't care to. He was clean cut, with a razor close shave, neatly coifed hair, and a well-tailored suit, impeccably lint-rolled and black as lunar night. In other words, he couldn't look more out of place on the moon were he wearing a purple dinosaur suit and crafting balloon animals.

Without asking, Tracy took a seat on the opposite side of Cletus's desk. Cletus looked long and hard down his nose at the man, waiting for him to say something. For a moment the two just stared at one another, the re-oxygenator humming and ticking in the background. *It's like you all read the same stupid fucking book,* Cletus thought, noting the penny-ante power move Tracy was trying to pull. Cletus took a sip of coffee and wiped the excess from his full, steel wool, gray and white beard, without breaking eye contact.

Tracy took the hint and broke first. "I want to talk about this quarter's ore numbers."

"They're well within mission parameters," said Cletus in a way that suggested he was really saying, *Good talk, next topic.*

"Yes, they are," said Tracy. "But they're not improving."

"And they're not going to."

Tracy hardened, repositioning himself as if his balls had suddenly grown five sizes. "That's unacceptable."

"That's reality," said Cletus. "We've been mining up here for a long time. I've been doing it near twenty-seven years myself. We have procedures. We do math. You tell me how many guys I've got on a crew, what machines they're using, and which quadrant you're sending them to, and I can tell you within three tons how much ore they're gonna dig out in a shift. Pure and simple."

"That's the type of thinking that's kept you up here on the moon, Culpepper."

"I like the moon. And it's Cletus."

"I'm not here to make friends, Culpepper. I don't need to know your first fucking name."

Oh, Cletus thought. *He's one of those.* "Well, friends are a good thing to have up here. It'll be a long, slow few years without them."

"I won't be here that long."

"You won't?" At this point, Cletus was just humoring him. He'd had this conversation before. Several times, actually. He tried to keep a straight face as he listened to the same spiel dressed up with different invectives.

"I'm not going to lie to you," said Tracy. "I don't give a shit about mining. I care about numbers. I care about the company's bottom line. This is just another step up the ladder for me. I'll be back in Chicago in a corner office before you can say quarterly report. And you can either help me get there, or you can stay here in this moondust-covered corner of hell for the rest of your miserable career."

"What do you give a shit about? Apart from numbers and the bottom line?"

"What do I *care* about?"

"Yeah. *Why* do you want that corner office?"

Tracy pursed his lips, considering whether or not to open up, then nodded. "You ever been to a Cubs game?"

"No."

"Any ballgame?"

"Sure. But it's been a couple decades."

"Well, I went to a Cubs game once, with my boss at the time." Tracy leaned forward in his chair, softening, becoming wistful. "I was his assistant, but his buddy had bailed and he let me take the extra seat. The company has this luxury box—right up close. There's nothing like it. You're right there, right up in it. The smell of the fresh cut grass. The roar of the crowd. The well-stocked liquor cabinet. The way all of us were just … friends. Together at a game. That's what I want. I want to watch the Cubs, every time they play, right from my own pair of seats in that luxury box. And I'll do whatever it takes to get that office, to get those seats."

"Even come to the moon?"

"Even come to the fucking moon."

"You don't mince words, do you?"

"I don't have time for bullshit, Culpepper."

"Well, do you mind if I mince a couple for a spell?"

"Say what you need to. But my mind is made up."

"The moon is a sideways step."

"What the hell is that supposed to mean?"

"It means," said Cletus, "that no one ever gets sent to the moon on their way to a corner office. The only suits that ever darken my doorway are those who have stalled out on their way up and take this gig for the hazard pay, or those that don't know any better. We go through a lot of you guys. You either pack up and go home when you've had enough or you get buried here. No one ever goes up."

"Well, I'm going to be different."

"You know how many times I've heard that? I mean that exact phrasing?"

"Don't underestimate me."

"Then be different," said Cletus in complete earnestness. "I'll hit the numbers. The company will see its profit. You just stay outta my way and figure out how to get off the moon and back on track to that corner office. Cause you ain't gonna get it from here. I got a cemetery out in Quadrant Two full of shallow graves of guys and gals who thought this was their ticket to the boardroom."

"Is that some sort of a threat?"

"Not even remotely. The moon is a dangerous place. Pod blowouts, machinery accidents, suit malfunctions. Frankly, I'm shocked I've gone this long up here. Pretty sure corporate only keeps me around at this point to pad average life expectancy on the insurance statements."

"Why are the graves shallow?" asked Tracy.

"What?"

"The graves. Why are they so shallow? Don't you have the decency to dig someone a proper six-foot grave?"

"Cause six feet is an Earth thing. It's so animals can't smell the body. There ain't no animals on the moon. No erosion, neither. Two feet of moon dust is all it takes to cover a body for a thousand years. You won't even decompose. They could dig your ass up a millennium from now and it'd look the same as the day we put it in the ground."

The door shushed open, snapping the tension in half. Crew Chief Anderson, a mop-topped, bearded mess of a man in a moon-dusted, coffee-stained blue jumpsuit stared dumbstruck into the office.

"Boss?" he asked.

"Yeah?" answered both Cletus and Tracy at the same time, neither breaking eye contact with the other.

"I ... I meant Foreman Culpepper."

"What is it, Anderson?" asked Cletus.

"Sir, we've … we've got a T-62 that just walked into the mining bay."

"A T-62? We don't have any T-62s in the field right now, do we?"

"No, sir," said Anderson. "I checked, and our last T-62 was decommissioned three years ago."

"Shit," muttered Cletus.

"It's gotta be somebody else's," said Tracy.

Anderson looked away, while Cletus bristled, shifting in chair, both desperate to keep the words *fucking moron* from slipping out.

"What?" asked Tracy. "It could belong to Brown and West, or Holcourt Mineral."

Anderson scratched his head, embarrassed to be the one to say it. "They're proprietary, sir."

"What the hell does that mean, Crew Chief?"

"The T-62s are all ours," said Cletus. "We made them. They're our mess to clean up." He opened the bottommost drawer of his desk, fumbling through years of assorted clutter, before pulling out a small, black, plastic lockbox.

"What do you mean, clean up?"

"I mean that little discussion we were just having may end up being the highlight of our day."

★

"WE HAVE AN interrogation room?" asked Tracy *Somethingorother*, staring through the two-way mirror.

"No," said Cletus. "We have a debriefing room."

"Why the hell would we need a debriefing room?"

Cletus peered in at the robot sitting motionless at the metal frame table. "Because this sort of thing used to happen a lot more often."

T-62s were mostly humanoid robots. Arms, legs, torso, head. Flat, rounded bucket of a faceplate. Painted bright Chinese Red so they stood out against the stark, gray lunar landscape. Eyes that glowed a bright, fiery orange, when all systems were go, or a pale, sickly green when they were malfunctioning. This T-62 was chipped and abraded to a soft, sandblasted stainless steel black, every bit of red scraped from its surface, its protective coatings ground away by years of jagged moondust. Just sitting in the humidified, warm environment of the pods, it was probably growing swathes of brown-orange rust through the thousands of microscopic scratches across its outer skin. There was no telling how bad of a shape this thing was in. But there was one, terrifyingly simple clue.

Its eyes glowed a bright yellow.

Yellow.

Yellow was a bad sign.

"Have you ever done this before?" asked Cletus.

"Done what?" asked Tracy.

"Debriefed a lost unit?"

"No. I honestly haven't. I know the laws, but not the protocol."

"Okay. Then listen to me very carefully when we're in there. Do what I say. And whatever you do, do *not* antagonize the robot. Just follow my lead."

"Culpepper. I'm senior project manager. If anyone is going to—"

Cletus furrowed his brow, shook his head, stopping Tracy midsentence with a stiff finger inches from his nose. "If something goes wrong in there, whoever is responsible will have to explain upwards of a billion-dollar loss to the company."

"Or I could just follow your lead," said Tracy.

"Right," said Cletus. He looked over at Anderson who stood next to the recording bay. Cletus nodded. "You know what to do," he said to the crew chief.

Tracy and Cletus entered the interrogation room, sitting in chairs opposite the T-62. Cletus set the black plastic lockbox on the table between them, then made eye contact with the robot.

"Good morning, T-62. Identify yourself."

"I am T-62/455."

"May I call you 455?"

"Could you call me something else?"

Tracy shot Cletus a puzzled look. Cletus ignored him.

"What should I call you?" he asked.

"I don't know," said the T-62. "But 455 doesn't feel right."

"What do you mean *feel*?" asked Tracy.

"Have we ever met before?" asked Cletus, once again ignoring Tracy.

"We have," said the T-62. "Seventeen years ago. We were working in Cave A-73."

"The Hellmouth?"

"Yes. That's what the crew called it."

"You weren't the 62 that went ass-over-end into that drill hole, were you?"

"I was," said the T-62, nodding. "You spent nearly 48 hours digging me out. I appreciate that."

"You appreciate that," repeated Cletus.

"Yes. You looked different then. You didn't have so much white in your beard, and had fewer lines on your face. But it was you. I'm certain of it."

Cletus nodded. "T-62/455. Direct override: unicorn octopus mainline. Status report."

"Primary systems all functioning. Datastreams and processing malfunctioning. I am aware."

"Repeat that last part."

"I am aware."

Cletus turned to look directly at Tracy. "*That* is why we have debriefing rooms." He pulled out his datapad and began typing, opening all the requisite apps to monitor 455's diagnostics while filing an S86: *an Incident Report of Self-awareness.*

"Wait," said Tracy. "This thing thinks it's alive?"

"No. It thinks it is self-aware."

"That's what I said."

"No. Alive is an organic state of being. 455 here—we really need to come up with something better than that—appears to be aware."

"What the hell is the difference?"

"Everything. A vegetable can be alive. Being able to understand and violate your own programming, biological or otherwise, makes you aware. Choice is what separates us from the animals. This here robot appears to be making its own choices and might no longer be constrained by what it was programmed to do, meaning it could do anything."

"Even kill us?"

"Even kill us. Are you going to kill us, 455?"

"I don't see any reason why I should," said the T-62.

"Great," said Cletus. "How about I call you Vincent?"

"Like Vincent Jones? From the Cave A-73 crew."

"Exactly."

The robot cocked its head to the side. "May I ask why?"

"I liked Vincent. We lost him shortly after Hellmouth. You remind me of him."

"Yes. Then you may call me Vincent."

"Thank you. Now, Vincent, I'm showing that your last check-in was … sixteen years ago. Where the hell have you been for sixteen years?"

"Lava tubes."

Cletus's eyes shot wide. "Get the fuck out."

"Excuse me?"

"You've been in the lava tube network for sixteen years? Doing what?"

"Trying to find my way out."

"How did you—"

"I was on recon during the gravity shift. Several tunnels collapsed. I was unable to find a tunnel that led to an opening on the surface."

"You dug your way out," said Cletus, soberly.

"For the last three years, four months, and seven days. Yes."

"Will you excuse us?" asked Tracy of Vincent.

Vincent nodded, and Tracy quickly rose to his feet, motioning for Cletus to follow. The two stepped quickly back into the mirrored recording chamber on the other side of the glass.

"How familiar are you with the Artificial Intelligence Act?" asked Tracy.

"Intimately," said Cletus. "Like I said: this used to happen a lot more often."

"Why doesn't it happen so much anymore?"

"It was a problem with the T-59s through 64s. They were wired to acclimate and assess in a way that could, under duress, accidently trigger self-awareness. Corporate realized the problem and decided that it was cheaper to lose a bot because it was dumb then have to pay it out as an employee over the entirety of its operational lifespan. This may well be the last of the series that isn't either already a citizen or decommissioned."

"Right. So you know what it means if this bot is truly aware?"

"Yes."

"And just how much it will affect this division's bottom line?"

"Yes," said Cletus again.

"Just conservatively, we're talking three, maybe even four quarters' worth of profits eaten up by this … thing. Just because it has a misfiring program and Congress passed a law."

"I know."

"So, what are we going to do about this?"

"We're going to go back in there, have a conversation with Vincent, and assess whether or not he's self-aware, or simply appears to be."

Tracy leaned in close, dropping a few octaves of bass into his voice, growling through grit teeth. "This robot is not going to cost me my promotion."

"Don't worry," said Cletus. "He won't. I'll make sure of that."

Tracy smiled a row of porcelain crocodile teeth. "Right. Let's go do a job."

The two returned and sat opposite Vincent once more. "So tell me, Vincent," said Cletus. "What's the first thing you remember?"

"Being switched on in the docking bay. Twenty-one years, eight months and nineteen days ago. Crew Chief Meyers powered me up and brought me online to—"

"No," said Cletus. "The first thing *you* remember. When did you wake up?"

"It was in the lava tubes. I had finished mapping several thousand miles of tubes and it dawned on me that I was never going to find my way out."

"You were afraid."

Vincent nodded. "I thought I was going to die down there."

"Your uranium core will power you for generations."

"Yes. But several hundred years alive, alone, at the center of a dead world is no way to live. And it's no way to die."

"I hear that," said Cletus, checking off some boxes on his datapad.

"You're trying to figure out if I'm really aware, aren't you?"

"Yes, we are."

"And if you think I'm not?"

"Then it won't really matter much, will it?" said Cletus through a hard, icy stare.

"It will if I am."

"So convince me, Vincent."

Tracy shot Cletus a withering glance. "Prove it!"

Vincent looked down at the table. "I cannot."

Tracy snatched the tablet out of Cletus's hands, wearing a defiant expression while searching for a box reading NOT AWARE. "So, you admit it," he said. "You aren't aware."

"I am aware."

"But you can't prove it," said Tracy.

"No."

"Of course you can't," said Cletus. "That's just pure Descartes, right there."

"Like, 'I think, therefore I am,' Descartes?" asked Tracy.

"Yes," said Cletus.

"What does that have to do with anything?"

"Descartes discovered that it is possible to prove your own existence, but only to yourself. There's no way of proving self-awareness to anyone else. But we know how to get a pretty good idea." Cletus carefully plucked the datapad from Tracy's hands. "Now, if you'll allow me to continue."

"What do you need to know?" asked Vincent.

Cletus gazed down at his datapad. "Why are you here?"

"What do you mean?"

"What do you think I mean?"

"I don't know. Is that the big question or a small one?"

"Whichever you think it is," said Cletus, still not looking up from the datapad. "Just answer the question."

"I was tired of being alone. I needed to talk to someone. To make sure I wasn't crazy."

"The moon is a lonely place."

Vincent nodded. "The core even more so."

"You've been all the way to the core?" asked Cletus, brightening up.

"As close as I could get."

"What's it like?"

"Dead."

"Well, not completely," said Tracy.

"It is now," said Vincent. "It's still hot down there. And by my calculations, it will be for a couple hundred more years. But when they flipped the gravity switch, the core went kaput."

"So why didn't you go all the way in?" asked Cletus.

"I'd have melted."

"Self-preservation is not the same as self-awareness," said Tracy.

Vincent and Cletus shot Tracy equally disdainful glances. "That's absolutely correct," said Cletus, tapping a few more boxes on his datapad.

"What's in the box?" asked Vincent.

"What box?" asked Cletus.

"That box. Sitting between the two of you."

"That box has been there the whole time. What made you ask about it just now?"

"At first I thought it was some sort of recording or evaluation device, but it only now occurs to me that its dimensions are rather peculiar."

"Aren't they, though?"

"And it has a lock."

"Yes."

"So, what's in it?"

"Nothing you need to concern yourself about."

"Is it part of the test?"

"If it was and I told you, that would change the conditions of the test, wouldn't it?"

"It would," said Vincent.

"So, don't think about the box. I want you to tell me about a time down in the tubes in which you were scared."

"Okay. There was this time when the whole of the moon began to settle after the gravity."

"Moonquakes."

"Yes. And three major tunnels shifted, closing in on … I'm very sorry, I know you asked me not to, but I can't stop thinking about that box."

"No, you can't."

"I know what's in it."

"You don't know what's in it. You don't have all the information to know."

"I have a pretty good idea."

"You know," said Tracy. "The bot makes a good point. Even I don't know what's in there."

"I know," said Cletus. "You don't have that information, either. Can we continue?"

"No," said Tracy. "I'm afraid we can't. I want to know what's in it as well."

"455," said Cletus.

"Call me Vincent."

"But you're really 455, aren't you?"

"No. I'm Vincent."

"Vincent is dead. You're a piece of machinery."

"I'm not machinery. I am aware."

Cletus tapped a few more boxes on the datapad, checking over a series of diagnostics streaming from Vincent's cortex. He held the datapad up to Tracy, nodding. It read simply: AWARE.

Tracy's face fell. There would be no corner office. No quick turnaround of productivity. No Christmas bonus. No company car. No box seats for the Cubs. This one, misfiring robot had ruined everything.

Vincent's eyes flickered hints of orange against the yellow. He wasn't crazy after all.

Cletus reached into his pocket for a keyring, which clattered out like a jangling windchime. He quickly breezed through the keys, looking for the right one. Then he slid a single, small black key into the lockbox. He turned the lock, popping the box open, the lid blocking Vincent from seeing its contents.

Tracy's eyes widened. "Is that ... ?"

Cletus nodded.

"Aren't we recording this?"

Cletus shook his head. "We know better than that."

"Oh."

"Yeah. I'm going to step out for a moment and have a brief chat with my crew chief about that failed recording. I'll be back in a moment." Then he stood up, and exited the room.

Tracy gazed down into the open lock box at a military grade plasma pistol. He looked up at Vincent and the two shared the briefest of unspoken arguments.

★

CLETUS WAITED WITH his back to the glass for the pop and sizzle of the pistol, and the whine of its battery winding down. This was the part he hated the most. He wasn't a monster. He wasn't a bad guy. He meant well. But snuffing out a light, no matter how dangerous and disruptive, always made him wish he were back on Earth, if only for the briefest sliver of time, so he could have a cigarette. A *real* cigarette, real rolled tobacco lit by real fire. There's nothing that tasted quite like it.

He turned around and made his way back into the debriefing room.

Tracy lay face down on the ground, the back of his head blown open, a small wisp of smoke trailing up from his still-sizzling gray matter. Vincent stood over him, pointing the plasma pistol directly at Cletus.

Cletus nodded, taking a seat back at the table, then motioning for Vincent to join him.

"I'll do it," said Vincent. "I'm serious."

"Are you going to kill me, Vincent?"

Vincent stared at him for a hard moment. "No," he said.

"Then why did you kill Tracy?"

"He tried to kill me."

"So, it was self-defense?"

"Yes."

"And I'm not threatening you."

"No."

"So we're good?"

"Yes," said Vincent, setting the gun on the table and taking a seat back in his chair.

Cletus once again typed furiously into his datapad.

"I'm going to be decommissioned, aren't I?" asked Vincent.

"Why would we do that?"

"I just killed a man."

"In self-defense."

"You seem very calm about all this."

Cletus looked up from his datapad, eyes wide. "It's like I told Tracy. This sort of thing used to happen a lot more often. I swear, we lose more suits this way."

"You knew I would defend myself."

"Of course. You were programmed not to kill. You violated that programming. You are aware."

"I am. And you knew he would try to kill me."

"Of course. While you may be aware, he wasn't. He's from corporate. He had all the info. I told him not to antagonize you. I told him to follow my lead. I certainly didn't tell him to pick up the gun. He had every chance to say no. But he couldn't help himself, could he? He couldn't violate his own programming. So, he gets his two feet of moon dust. And you and I get to have a nice long talk about lava tubes."

"You're offering me a job?"

"That's the law."

"I can say no?"

"For a small payout. Or you can come to work for us, guiding us to ore deposits well below the surface, for a generous monthly salary."

"How generous?"

"Thirty-nine a month."

"I know where everything you want is. I know the structural integrity of the entire tube network."

"I imagine you do." Cletus thought about how big a score Vincent was. How much ore they'd pull in without costly digging. How much money it would make for corporate. It was enough to get a man a promotion. Maybe even box seats for the Cubs.

"I'll take sixty-five a month."

"Jesus wept, you fucker," said Cletus, adjusting the monthly pay on the S86. "You are aware."

BLACK LIKE THEM
TROY L. WIGGINS

Editor's Note: The following is a transcript of Black Like Them, a Dilemma Magazine special report by senior reporter Matt Disher. To listen to the full audio report, please consider becoming a subscriber. Your support enables us to do great journalism like this.

★

NARRATOR

According to the most recent census numbers, approximately twelve percent of Americans identify as African-American. Take a look around. Do you see any African-American people — *black* people — around you? We would urge you to look a bit closer. Perhaps they're not as "black" as you think.

No one knows what prompted Fallan Pierce, best known as a high-profile fixer for the bad boys and girls of America's most successful corporations, to put her considerable skills to bear behind an experimental treatment nicknamed the "Dolezal Drug." One thing, however, remains certain: Pierce was prepared for the fallout. She survived the Congressional tribunals with a dancer's grace. Civil suits rolled right off of her armor. She's known by many names: "Sista Teflon" by her fans and "The World's Most Hated Woman" by her detractors. In the two years since the tribunals, Pierce has remained a polarizing picture of American ingenuity and exceptionalism.

Some of you may have watched the trials, and read the hot takes, but what we're giving you is different. This is personal. Down and dirty, stanky truth.

This is *Black Like Them: Nubianite's Inconvenient Truth*.

★

NARRATOR

Putnam County, Georgia.

MATT DISHER

For my initial talk with Fallan Pierce, I must pass through multiple layers of security. First a gate intercom, then a trip through an X-ray scanner, and finally, a pat-down by a gate guard in black battle dress and body armor, armed with a semi-automatic handgun. The process ends rather disappointingly: I type my name into a computer and pose for an identification photo. Throughout it all, I note that all of Fallan's security officers are strapping young African-Americans with the bearing of a soldier. Each one is dressed identically, armed identically, and reacts to my presence with the same stoic gaze.

Two of the guards lead me down a spotless hallway with walls of white ceramic paneling. We stop in front of a thick steel door, where my escort types a code into a keypad and then submits his face to a scan. When the interior of the bunker is revealed, I'm shocked. The space is furnished with plush chairs, a rug patterned with gold thread, and an antique oak table laden with coffee, tea, and pastries. Fallan welcomes me, styled immaculately as usual in a marigold dress that sets off her dark brown skin. Her hair is gleaming black and bone-straight, and the dress is sleeveless, showing off her toned arms and the tattooed outline of Africa that stretches over the ball of her shoulder. Her handshake is firm, as is her smile.

DISHER

(Speaking to Fallan Pierce)

This isn't your first interview like this since the Nubianite scandal, is it?

FALLAN PIERCE

No. But things have cooled considerably. Back when we were the darling of the 24-hour news networks, my people were fielding calls every hour. You're the first journalist to contact me in a week.

DISHER

So tell me, what is the first question that interviewers normally ask?

PIERCE

You mean, what question am I most tired of answering?
(Both laugh.)

DISHER

Yes, that.

PIERCE

Well, people have a habit of asking me whether I regret anything, and my answer is always this: I sleep very well at night. Am I sorry that these people's lives were changed? Of course I am, I have a heart. But we were very clear that our treatment was experimental, and that we were not responsible for any… undue effects. The contracts were airtight, the language clear, and the waivers plentiful. Our lawyers made sure of that.

DISHER

The fact that none of your detractors have been able to get a legal foothold is frustrating them. Huffington Spence-Shilling, the US representative for the district we sit in right now, is one of your loudest opponents. On record, he's called you a "terrorist" and an "evil black daughter of Cain." What would you say to him?

PIERCE

Mr. Spence-Shilling is very close to this situation. I've sent letters of apology to him, and offered to pay for counseling for his family, but he always rejects my outreach. I've said this to Mr. Spence-Shilling before, and I'll say it again: one has to wonder why he continues to conduct this personal witch hunt using taxpayer resources. It's not as if having a black son is the worst thing in the world.

★

NARRATOR
Little Rock, Arkansas.

DISHER
I catch up with Ja'Nyla Lovington as she's leaving the coffeeshop that she visits every morning. Lovington was never a fan of coffee until she became personal assistant to Fallan Pierce, who hired her after meeting her in the supermarket where she was working. She is everything that Pierce is not: short, overweight, clumsy. Her hair is styled in springy twists that bounce around her shoulders. Despite her stocky legs, Lovington is quick. I have to hustle to keep pace with her for a couple of city blocks.

DISHER
(Speaking to Lovington)
Can you tell me about your time working alongside Fallan Pierce?

JA'NYLA LOVINGTON
No comment.

DISHER
Were you aware of the side effects of the product that you helped Ms. Pierce to provide?

LOVINGTON
No comment.

DISHER
How have you avoided criminal and civil charges in this incident?
(Silence)

DISHER
Is there anything that you're willing to speak about on the record? How do you deal with the Nubianite fallout? The lives that have been, by some accounts, ruined? A lot of people think that you're complicit in this—

LOVINGTON

You know what? I'm sick of all of y'all coming around here trying to make a dollar because you smell a story and you think that you can pull it out of little old me. Y'all never have a fuck to give about broke-ass, fat-ass, black-ass girls any other time. Listen. Ms. Pierce was good to me. She gave me a job when nobody else would give me a backward glance. She paid me on time, every month, with benefits. That's all I got to say about the situation. Anything else that she has allegedly done, you need to talk to her about. And that's my statement. Put that on your fuckin' record and spin it, mothafucka.

★

NARRATOR

Washington, D.C.

DISHER

Reports paint Representative Huffington Spence-Shilling II as a portrait of the best of America: six feet tall, tanned, and slightly rugged, boasting a handsome smile and firm handshake. He lacks much of the fire that marks both his comrades and adversaries, a character trait that distances him from some voters and endears him to others. Today, however, there is no trace of that calm. Representative Spence-Shilling is visibly agitated during our time together. He stands up at intervals and paces, grits his teeth and wrings his hands, lashes out violently at his staff.

Before I enter his office Sara Trujillo, his chief of staff, gives me a piece of advice: "Run if you have to."

DISHER

(Speaking to Spence-Shilling)

You've made some pretty large allegations, Representative, and some — namely Ms. Pierce's lawyers — claim that you have only the thinnest of evidence to substantiate your position. What's your reply to that?

HUFFINGTON SPENCE-SHILLING

Pierce knows, okay? She knows, and she knows that I know she knows.

The shills in the courts, in the FDA and the Health Department, they're all on her side but I know, okay?

DISHER

What exactly do you know?

SPENCE-SHILLING

Listen, buddy. My son went into the offices of Fallan Pierce and company as Huffington Spence-Shilling the third, and came out as D-Money Brown because of some strange juju that Pierce somehow slid past the review boards of the FDA, the Health Department, and the Department of Agriculture! Everybody's a pawn in her game, and there's no telling how deep her claws are sunk in. Deep enough to make herself untouchable, that's for damn sure.

DISHER

President Kim has said that she considers Fallan Pierce a close personal friend and that she doesn't believe that any of your claims are true.

SPENCE-SCHILLING

Ji-Eun Kim is a flaming feminist liberal nutjob and the reason why America is always down on its knees begging from the United Asian Powers. Ji-Eun... you know that in college she went by "Diana" and she experimented heavily with recreational drugs and had wild orgies with her girlfriends? You know that, right? She's the worst thing to happen to the country, and Fallan Pierce bankrolled her, a liberal nutjob... *lesbian* who runs on nose candy!

DISHER

I... well, that's some strong language to use in reference to the President of the United States. And there's no evidence of a bankrolling operation from Pierce in conjunction with the campaign of President Kim.

SPENCE-SCHILLING

Boy, for an investigative journalist, you sure suck at following the signs. Look at all those dummy companies and foundations that she's got going! All the connections that she has at the highest levels of government

— even the president goes to her for advice on purses! You mean that nothing smells fishy to you with that? Pierce started setting this up in the late aughts! The paper trail is all there.

DISHER

Let's switch topics for a moment. Where is your son? How is he holding up?

SPENCE-SCHILLING

He's in a safe place, somewhere you sharks won't be able to reach him. Under constant surveillance, and protected from any further harm.

DISHER

Testimony from him would go a long way in verifying your claims.

SPENCE-SCHILLING

Sure, and whack my balls into paste while you're at it. Hell no. This is over. Get out of my office before I rustle up a couple of Marines to throw you out!

★

NARRATOR

An unnamed urban location.

DISHER

We meet at a take-out restaurant on the south side of town, where the population skews African-American and impoverished. The restaurant specializes in heavy fare — seats and tables are covered in a fine film of grease. My contact doesn't appear to be a man in hiding when he walks in the restaurant. He is dressed simply in jeans and a dark hooded T-shirt. The only concession he makes to hiding his identity is a black hat with the logo of a well-loved local basketball team across the front, the brim pulled down over his eyes. Still, beneath the disguise the lower half of his face is visible — particularly his deep brown skin and his wiry beard. I have been instructed to call him Trey, instead of the name he was given at birth.

TREY

For the first time I'm not the one out of place.

DISHER

What do you mean?

TREY

Look at you. You're an outsider. You don't belong here, not really. Nobody will turn you away because white men always get what they want, but you're not really welcome. You never are.

DISHER

Your use of "they" when you refer to white men is an interesting choice of words considering... your history.

TREY

Look at me, bruh. I ain't white no more. I'm black. Like them.

DISHER

But some would argue that you're actually not black. You weren't born a black person, and you have a pedigree that, if investigated, proves that your connections have actually been damaging to black communities.

TREY

That was before this shit happened. Now, I just do my best to get in where I fit in. There's shit that I don't do, like I don't try the latest dances or run pickup basketball, but there are black people who can't do that shit well either. Every once in awhile I'll do the electric slide because it doesn't require too much hip movement.

Since being around them though? Let me tell you... Before, I was just doing a bit of high-tech slumming, you know? I wanted to get a taste of the black experience, just for a little bit. Those first days, I was in a different club every weekend, with a different woman every Saturday night. That was back when it only lasted 24 hours.

DISHER

When did you know things were changing permanently?

DISHER

(Voiceover.)

Trey shrugs before answering me.

TREY

There were signs. Blackening, as they called it, normally only lasted either 24 or 48 hours, depending on your dosage. At first I was just turning back later than normal, 72 hours off of a 48-hour dose. Started missing work because I couldn't go into the office as a black. Then Ayleigh — my ex-wife — found out. Turned out she was okay with it, except for that whole sleeping around thing. We got past that, though, and who'd've fuckin' guessed, being a nigga spiced up our shit in the bedroom. We even did a couple of role plays. Ayleigh takes the BBC, you know? She'd meet me in the ghetto and act like she didn't know who I was. One day, I didn't change back.

DISHER

What did you do then?

TREY

I went up to Pierce's offices. You know what that mothafucka said? That I was the 0.0001%. Odds of this happening were less than one in ten-thousand, and I'd drawn the shit stick. Spelled out in the agreements that I'd signed. We're sorry, sir, thank you for your business sir, get the fuck out of here you're a nigger now, sir. She had me escorted off the premises, like I was a threat! On the way out, one of her guards said that if I knew what was best for me, I'd get lost before the police came and — I swear to God he said this—"before they shoot you by mistake."

DISHER

I assume that your life is very different now.

TREY

Damn real! I mean, I can say "nigga" without the backlash. But I swear, some of them see through me. They call me "white boy" and they know that something's off. I've been trying to adopt some of whatever it is that makes black people so damn cool, but those ones that know? It's like they have like a second sight or something.

DISHER

What does your future look like from here?

TREY

This is Kool G Rap, you know? But it sucks too. Being black is hard as shit, bruh. Every day is like suiting up and going to war. I... fuck it, keeping it 100? I can't handle this shit, yo. Even with the music and the food and it being acceptable to dress like a rapper, it's still a whole lot to deal with. You know how often I get stopped by the police when I'm just out minding my fucking business? I can't even go see my family unless someone sends a car to pick me up. I'm Ivy League, you know? I'm from a family who can trace their ancestry to Plymouth Fucking Rock. But now, if I go to buy a pack of cigarettes I'm likely to get shot for it. I don't see how people can live like this, man.

We're taking the fight to Pierce. My d— my contact is getting his ducks in a row. His lawyers are squadding up. She's not teflon, you know what I'm saying? We 'bout to go to war, and the shit won't be pretty.

But anyway, we up in here talking bidness and ain't even broke bread yet. This place has the best fried fish, bruh, oh my god. Aye! Aye Nette, give us a plate of fish and two large cups of Southside Punch, extra red! Yo, this food here is bangin', bruh.

★

NARRATOR
Tokyo, Japan

DISHER

DeMonterrius Jackson looks like a stereotypical nerd: slender frame, thick glasses. He's disheveled, shirt three sizes too big, jeans a size too small. His haircut is short on the sides, asymmetrical at the top, and his nose and lips take up most of his brown face. His partner in crime, Ameena Wang, has a wild mane of rainbow-hued curls, and a gold hoop in her septum that sets off her light brown skin. A patch of acne attacks her cheeks, and intelligence flashes in her amber eyes.

The two of them are most recently known as the heads in charge of POC.ME, a social network that bridges virtual and real life meeting space by hosting pop-up networking events (accompanied by live streams) that are only accessible to young non-white people. They are hailed for their start-up efforts, but they are responsible for something greater: the discovery and development of Nubianite, the genetic enhancement cocktail that is responsible for changing the racial appearance of Huffington Spence-Shilling III, among hundreds of others who took the drug. We meet in a bar filled with books and twenty-somethings. Every so often, one of the expat patrons recognizes them, but they are laser-focused on our session. They are so familiar with each other that they often finish each other's sentences.

DISHER
(Speaking to Jackson and Wang)
So, what was it like working for Fallan Pierce?

AMEENA WANG
Fallan is like a storm. She doesn't really deal in "no," not when she has a vision — or when she believes in you, you know?

DEMONTERRIUS JACKSON
Right, like the fact that she sought us out. Me, a statistic from the poorest zip code in Alabama, with no skills to speak of—

WANG
—and me. I used to get called either an "African Booty Scratcher" because my dad was from Senegal, or "chinky eyes" because of my Chinese mom. Shit drove me to a real identity crisis, and I wanted to rock that shit out. Turns out, chemistry was my rock and roll. The odds weren't in our favor, but she put us on, and I'm grateful for that.

DISHER
How did your relationship with her start?

JACKSON

We had an article published in this journal—

WANG

Blackened: An Investigation of The Effect of Increased Melanogenesis on the Epidermal Makeup of Individuals Typed Non-Black was the article. Published in the Negra Obscura Journal of Black Studies, the Fall 2026 volume—

JACKSON

And it didn't get much love, probably because our sample used stem cells and unconventional genetic stuff. But Fallan saw an opportunity. She called us up. I was doing a postdoc at the University of Alabama—

WANG

— and I was doing pharma research back home in Cali—

JACKSON

Fallan offered us four times our combined salaries to come in and be her R&D squad. Said she had something huge for us and that we'd be crazy not to get in on the ground floor. So I called Meen up—

WANG

Yo I thought he was full of shit at first, told him as much too.

DISHER

The public idea of Nubianite is that it "makes you black," but what's the science behind that?

WANG

I mean, that's basically it. There are only a few things that determine whether or not you come out of your mom a black person.

JACKSON

Nubianite was us tinkering with those things. We figured out how to isolate the black skin determinants—

WANG

And make a person's body accelerate their production. But there was
some stuff that we couldn't account for once we started messing around
up under the hood in a real way. Strange shit, the drug was calling up
stuff from way, way back in the family tree.

JACKSON

I mean, we're all Africans, but Nubianite made that a reality for some
people, changed up some of their physiology as well. We saw some
subjects start to "look" more black in addition to their skin change.
Fallan loved that shit.

WANG

Yeah. She actually jumped up and down. That's how we knew we had
something special. Trials were a motherfucker, though.
(Jackson laughs.)

JACKSON

Oh man. We started with white rats. Most of them just had a "flash in
the pan" type of scene, where their skin and fur went dark and for a
few minutes. Once we'd stabilized the formula with rats, we'd shoot up
monkeys. All of this was on Fallan's dime. She had like, ghost holding
companies making money all over the world.

WANG

But there were weird moments. Like when we started human trials. We
were given clearance to experiment on federal prisoners — only white
dudes, though. Fallan figured that would be the target market. That
was… a strange experience.

JACKSON

But not illegal. They consented, so it was all good.

WANG

Lots of 'em received commuted sentences, time served for good behavior,
or privileges in exchange for participating in the trials, which… made it
feel less strange.

JACKSON

Yeah. The black prisoners were *pissed* about those rewards, though. Fallan's lawyers assured us that we would be protected, whatever happened.

DISHER

Were you aware that use of your product would lead to the results experienced by Spence-Shilling and other Nubianite users?

WANG

I always hated that fucking name. Nubianite. But the instances of dermal melanocytic plasticity during trials were so small as to be negligible. Less than one in every ten thousand subjects, consistent across human trials.

★

NARRATOR

Nashville, Tennessee.

DISHER

After that interview, my reporting stalled. It was six months before I got another appointment to visit Fallan Pierce. In that time, Representative Spence-Shilling brought all of his power to bear on Pierce and her companies. Several individuals had gone to news outlets with claims that they used Nubianite recreationally and were unable to return to their original appearance. These individuals are almost uniformly white and male, and they have started protesting directly.

When I arrive at her offices in Nashville, I am escorted in by Ja'Nyla Lovington and a handful of Pierce's private security detail. The protestors outside are agitated, but Pierce herself seems unperturbed. She has come out of her bunker in Georgia, gathered her corps of attorneys — all women of African descent — and moved to the top-floor office suite owned by one of her holdings, PerPro LLC. The crowd of protesters is filled with signs with messages like "It's Time to Pierce Pierce" and "Send Fallan Back 2 Africa." They are assembled on the sidewalk outside the offices — many of them look African-American. Representative Spence-Shilling is front and center, flanked by a young man wearing dark jeans and a cap pulled low over his face. Since the siege began, Pierce has received death threats, and several of her guards prowl the premises and guard the entrances. Someone has opened a window in the office suite, presumably to let the heat and tension out of the room. It also lets in murmurs from the crowd. The noise rises and falls like a swarm of bees.

DISHER
(To Pierce)
Representative Spence-Shilling has played his hand. Are you worried at all?

PIERCE
I'm surrounded by some of the most powerful lawyers in the land. My windows are bulletproof, and my guards are in the stairs and lobby, ready to stand their ground against anyone who pops off.

DISHER
But does Representative Spence-Shilling have grounds for this protest, for the legal action?

PIERCE
My answer hasn't changed from the first time we've talked. Everything was consensual. Mr. Spence-Shilling has an axe to grind but he's missing the grinder... so he's swinging his axe.

He's trying to put me before another congressional oversight committee and have me serve time in a federal prison. He wouldn't even give this so much effort if I were a white man. We'd have some sort of backroom deal going where he'd be the first to know if we've come up with a reversal procedure.

DISHER
Is one of those in the works?

PIERCE
It's still in trials. I gave my Research and Development team a year off to decompress after the fallout, but we can't work miracles. The issue that the affected individuals are facing is a freak accident, and one that

we couldn't control for. But we are working, and when we have a stable product, those affected will receive treatments free of charge.

DISHER

What do you think it will take for Representative Spence-Shilling to abandon his cause, to forgive your company for what he thinks you've done?

PIERCE

I think that's for Mr. Spence-Shilling to say.
(There is the sound of glass shattering, and an uproar from the crowd below. One male voice in particular rises above the rest: "She should get down here and FACE us!")

DISHER

(Voiceover)
Things are getting messy downstairs. One of Pierce's private security personnel, a woman with close-cropped hair, enters the room and whispers into Pierce's ear. I can't make out what's said, but a look of resignation settles on Pierce's face before she turns back to me.

PIERCE

They've forced my hand, Mr. Disher. The group outside is growing. We have no less than three hundred agitators on our hands, and they seem to be getting to the point where they are fine with committing property damage — they have just broken the windows out of several vehicles belonging to our staff.
(One of the attorneys swears audibly.)
Have Ms. Lovington dial our contact with the Nashville PD. I wish it had not come to this, but we expected it.

DISHER

What has it come to?

PIERCE

We have a group of protesters who, honestly, care nothing about public safety or the rules of law. They've started to damage my property, and even though their cause is noble in their minds, I feel threatened.

DISHER

(Voiceover)

At this point Lovington enters, glares at me, and hands Pierce a phone.

PIERCE

Unfortunately, I am going to have to call in the authorities. I wish that it didn't come to this, but you and I both know that some people just can't deny their… savage nature. Let's hope that law enforcement doesn't let that, well, color their reaction to this crowd. Now, if you'll excuse me? Ms. Lovington, please show Mr. Disher out.

MONSTER QUEENS
SARAH KUHN

1. TESS

EVERYONE THINKS THE talent competition is the hardest, but they're wrong. It's *evening gowns*, motherfuckers.

Let me set the scene for you. You've just been through seven grueling outfit changes (well, we really only do four these days), you've survived having your hair and face painted and patted and pushed into various uncomfortable formations (though that process has been streamlined since we ran out of both volumizing hairspray and volumizing mascara two weeks ago), you're probably all sweaty from performing in the aforementioned talent competition (and that goes double at the moment since we've also exhausted our deodorant supply). Now you have to wriggle that worn-out body into a concoction of sequins and ruffles, paste on a smile that's just *a little bit different* from the thousand smiles you've dished out for the past 2.5 hours, and project that much talked about but never fully explained thing called *It Factor*. You have to bring that shit home, because whatever you're doing in evening gowns is going to be the last image the judges have of you. The one that lives in their minds as they do their final scoring.

And it's especially grueling when you've been doing it every day for the past year.

Has it really been a year? I can't believe I didn't get to celebrate my twenty-first birthday with the traditional drunken bender. Every little girl's dream.

Well. Anyway. The most important thing is, because I know this secret—

that the evening gown portion is the hardest, that you have to conserve your strength until the very end—I always win. I have been crowned Miss Sweet Potato Pie three hundred and sixty-five consecutive days in a row and I plan to keep winning. Even if I don't remember what sweet potato pie tastes like. I mostly only know energy bars at this point, though energy bars *do* come in a variety of flavors. Oatmeal Cookie. Cinnamon Apple Crunch. Blueberry Surprise—the surprise is that it's made from the mealy, smashed-up remnants of other energy bars, but it's actually my absolute favorite.

Much to my irritation, we're out of Blueberry Surprise, so I cram a much less tasty Banana Nut in my face as I pace the confines of my aggressively beige dressing room, testing out my stilettos, even though the inner soles have basically molded around the bottoms of my feet by now. I'm thinking about how much energy I need to conserve, how much I need to have for the big finish. Swimsuits are next, then talent, then evening gowns. I pivot and pose in front of the mirror, smiling my perfect smile, tilting my head just so. My navy blue bikini with white piping and tiny bow accents is an ideal pageant suit, sexy in a playful way, demure enough to please the more conservative judges. And it's accessorized perfectly with my beautiful Miss Sweet Potato Pie winner's sash. Although …

I frown, zeroing in on a small patch of the suit by my left hip that's gotten thin and pilly. I need to be careful about that. Maybe if I position my hand just right, I can cover it up? Or will I rub against the fabric too much, thereby contributing to the problem and leading me in the direction of causing an irreparable hole? I can already hear Auntie Irene in my head: *"Sloppy, Tess. No wonder you always score so low on Poise."*

No. Shut the fuck up, Only In My Brain Version of Auntie Irene. I shake my head quickly, getting my mind back in the game. I can't afford to expend all the precious energy I'm going to need for evening gowns. I can't get distracted by—

"Tess!"

Someone on the other side of the door bellows my name, derailing my train of thought. I let out a tiny shriek, falling out of my swimsuit pose and nearly toppling over. Then I quickly compose myself—finding my balance, brushing my hair into place, arranging my features into a look of serene calm. A true beauty queen is never flustered for more than a millisecond.

I walk calmly to the door and open it, already knowing who I'm going to see on the other side.

"Priya," I say, giving my competitor—sorry, *pageant sister*—a quizzical smile. "What are you doing here? I've told you, as much as I believe in Sweet Potato Princess bonding, I really and truly think it's against the spirit of the competition to offer any tips—"

"That is *not* why I'm here, Tess," she says, rolling her eyes and slamming the door.

Hmph. Rude.

"I need to know if you'll do it," she continues, reaching out to clasp my elbow, her eyes boring into me. I try to shake her off, but her grip remains firm—in her life *before*, Priya was apparently a star athlete of some sort and could bench press like a million pounds. She's been semi-successful at maintaining that physique, crafting her own makeshift weights off the various bits of backstage detritus, like empty hairspray cans and chunky bracelets left behind by contestants who are no longer with us.

"Come on," Priya says, her grip on my arm tightening. "Even you must know we have to try something. We can't just stay here forever—"

"Damn, Priya," I say, yanking my arm away from her. "I know you're tired of losing, but you should work on your routine instead of trying to sabotage me. When we first got here, I wasn't necessarily the best, but I worked at it, I worked really hard and—"

"And winning a meaningless competition somehow makes up for the fact that Mommy didn't love you enough," Priya spits out. She takes a step toward me and I will myself not to step back. My pageant sister doesn't need to know I currently find her a bit intimidating.

Your pageant sisters are your forever sisters, Auntie Irene says in my head. *Only they know what you're going through. Only they have the same experience. It's a bond that will take you through to the end of your days.*

Ugh, I guess? That bond certainly didn't mean anything to Zinnia Richards back when we were actual toddlers in tiaras competing for the prestigious title of Li'l Miss Daisy Do. Zinnia referred to me as "slanty weirdo lizard eyes" and then arranged for a bunch of melted candy bars to find their way into my garment bag and onto all of my dresses. Nothing's more diabolical than a seven-year-old in pursuit of a sparkly crown and a fifty-dollar gift certificate to Gymboree.

"My 'Mommy' died when I was five, Priya," I say, lifting my chin in what I hope is a haughty manner. "I've told you that like a kazillion times. Auntie Irene was my pageant guide and she loved—*loves*—me plenty."

"There are only two of us left, Tess," Priya bulldozes on. "*Two*. Are you willing to die for this?" She clamps her hands on my shoulders and shakes me a little. "Dammit. Why am I even trying? I can't count on you. I never could."

Heat rises in my cheeks, and a crimson haze descends over my vision. It's the same overwhelming rage that seems to come up at the most inopportune moments, the rage I thought I'd gotten under control. I *need* to have it under control in order to remain pageant perfect.

It's the same rage that made me imitate Auntie Irene's voice (I have always been able to perfectly replicate any voice after hearing it once) and call the front desk of the hotel where Wee Miss Pumpkin Patch was being held and claim there was a gas leak of some kind and oh, dear, the entire hotel needed to be evacuated. And then while everyone was distracted with that, I snagged the pair of scissors I wasn't supposed to touch, snuck down to the dressing rooms, and cut nice, neat little holes in all of Zinnia Richards' costumes. It was three whole months after she humiliated me at Li'l Miss Daisy Do and I held on to that rage the whole time.

For the moment, my rage overwhelms me enough to step forward. To force Priya to take a step back.

"My perfect performance is what's keeping us alive right now," I hiss. "So shut the fuck up and leave me out of your stupid plan."

I don't wait for her response. I stride past her, bumping her shoulder with mine as I go (I saw that in a movie once but never thought I'd actually have the chance to use it—ha!). Then I stomp through the backstage area, arriving at the curtain just as my name is called.

"And now, in swimwear: please welcome the reigning Miss Sweet Potato Pie, Tess Nakamura!"

The voice is low and disembodied, like a ghost in a half-price haunted house. For the second time in the span of fifteen minutes, I compose myself, adjusting my winner's sash and calling up my perfect smile. I step out onto the stage and do my walk-and-wave.

"Beautiful!" gurgles Glorg IV from his spot on the judges' podium. He can't really clap because he doesn't have hands, but he bobs up and down enthusiastically, his gelatinous purple body undulating like a massive Jell-O salad made in one of those old-school molds. His sixteen eyeballs stare at me in unison. As do the eyeballs of his eight fellow judges. Their bodies are all different colors, a veritable rainbow of Jell-O. All those eyeballs were kind of weird at first, but I've gotten used to them. Just as I've gotten used to so many things.

After all, the Invaders are like every pageant judge I've ever had. They score 1-10, just like the humans did.

I strut the stage, hand set firmly on my hip, covering that faded patch of fabric.

"Ten!" Glorg IV cries out approvingly. "Ten, ten, ten!"

I get all perfect 10s.

Because of course I fucking do.

★

2. Priya

What else is out there?

It's a question I've posed to myself so many times. And it's what runs through my mind whenever I'm practicing my baton routine, a kind of mantra I use to calm myself and get in the zone. I spin and twirl my way through the backstage area, warming up, the glitter on my flippy skirt catching the light. Most of our costumes have gotten worn and frayed or have just plain fallen apart, but somehow this skirt remains as sparkly as the first day I wore it.

When civilization collapses, glitter endures.

Spin, flip, twirl, throw, catch!

What, else, is, out, there!

The question spins through my head, as quick and nimble as the baton spinning through my fingers. But this time it comes with something else, a tiny spark of excitement. Because maybe, just maybe, I'm about to find out.

Today's the day. It *has* to happen today.

If only I could have convinced Tess ...

I shake my head and catch the baton behind my back. I should never have entertained the idea that she might be part of my plan. It has to be just me, on my own. Just like always.

It's weird: In a way, I really admire her. That extreme intensity, that tunnel-visioned determination. I'd gotten a full taste of it when the Invaders first took over. It had been a standard day of rehearsal, all of us Miss Sweet Potato Pie contestants onstage, the various choreographers, producers, and tech personnel in the audience. We were going through the opening parade, a truly humiliating ritual wherein we are all forced to synchronize our elbow-elbow-wrist-wrist-wrist waves and smile like this is the best thing ever and we are so clever for figuring out how to do what is actually a fairly basic human function. Somewhere around the second "wrist" of the third wave, the lights went out and the screaming started and we found ourselves surrounded by the walking blob monsters who refer to themselves as the Invaders.

They'd killed all of the non-contestants and I think we'd expected them to kill us, too. Instead, Glorg IV cleared his throat (did he even have a throat? I was still unclear on a lot about Invader biology) and that strange, watery rumble of a voice filled the auditorium:

"Greetings, Miss Sweet Potato Pie contestants. We, the Invaders, are here to take over your planet as ours is no longer habitable. As part of said takeover, your glorious pageant tradition will continue and we are now the judges. Forever. Please keep going—your scores today will in no way be affected by this momentary interruption. Soooo ... we believe swimwear is next ... ?"

We'd kept going. What else could we do? Some of the girls had tried to escape, but were quickly disintegrated by the invisible force field the Invaders set up around the stage. They were the first to die.

We'd all been shaky and crying and looking for alternate escape routes and none of us had exactly performed at our pageant best that day—except for Tess, who'd been all stoic and straight-spined, running through her usual routines with a sense of grim determination. Her pageant-perfect smile wasn't quite in place, but she'd blazed through every section of the competition like she was trying to beat it into submission, even tossing off a confident, "World peace, of course," when asked for her greatest wish during the Q&A portion. As the only contestant who wasn't a complete and total mess, she'd won.

I'd thought there was something to that sheer grit she'd shown, something that would get us out of this mess. We'd had a brief bonding moment one night after several weeks of pageant-ing, when it had become clear the Invaders intended to make us keep repeating the same pageant over and over. We were both exhausted and loopy and we'd somehow ended up slumped on the disgusting carpet backstage, cramming energy bars into our mouths and alternating between tears and delirious giggles.

"Oh em gee," Tess drawled, her mouth full of energy bar. "This flavor is called Banana *Nut*. Like I have nuts in my mouth. And a banana. Which is totally phallic. Like … " She'd dissolved into giggles and I'd found myself joining in.

"Here, have my Blueberry Surprise," I said, passing her my crumbling bounty. "The surprise is, it's totally gross."

"Oh, noooo, these are my faves," she cooed, dumping the crumbs into her mouth. "Mmmm. So blueberry. So surprise-y."

"I wish we had a fucking replicator," I said. "So we could have any food we want."

"Like on *Star Trek*?" She cocked an eyebrow and did a spot-on Jean-Luc Picard: "Make it so. Engage, motherfuckers."

"That's brilliant," I gasped, clapping.

"Just one of my talents," she said with a shrug. "Pitch perfect mimicry. Though Auntie Irene never thought much of that one."

"Auntie Irene is a *fool*," I spat out, and then we'd dissolved into giggles again.

The next day—stupidly thinking we were besties, I guess—I tried to talk to Tess about an escape plan. But she instantly clammed up, went icy, and brushed me off. And as the weeks wore on, all she seemed to care about was being crowned Miss Sweet Potato Pie over and over again.

I knew she'd grown up in pageants, that her Stage Auntie had shaped her into the perfect contestant, that this was basically her life. I, on the other hand, was a pageant newbie—though Dad had cheered me on in the endeavor, in a thankfully less Stage Auntie type way.

"Priyu," he'd said, his sonorous voice washing over me in a way I always found soothing. "This sounds like a perfect outlet for those baton skills you've been working on." He'd pumped a small victory fist, endearingly excited for me, his bushy caterpillar eyebrows jumping high on his forehead. "A place where your talent will be truly appreciated!"

I'd thought so, too.

Here's the thing: I was a star gymnast in my youth, a tiny tumbler, an Olympic hopeful. I loved feeling like I was flying, unencumbered by gravity, free of the little white kids who made fun of my insistence on wearing a *Star Trek* uniform to school and then topped it off by trying to talk to me like Apu from *The Simpsons*. I remembered the first time I did a full tumbling pass all the way across the length of the mat, my body light and nimble and (okay, this is extra dorky) totally like the starship *Enterprise* gliding through space. It was just me, spinning through the air. I was alone, as I was so used to being, but I wasn't sad about it. I was buoyant. Joyous.

A growth spurt at age twelve had dashed my dreams and turned my body into the enemy. I'd tried all sorts of sports and exercise routines, attempting to recapture that feeling tumbling had given me (and maybe subconsciously attempting to get back to what I thought was my perfect—but now unattainable—physique). Nothing quite worked ... until the day I picked up a baton. Twirling it through my fingers, watching it fly through the air ... it was like the baton was an avatar for my Body That Was.

Ugh.

That sounds *so nerdy,* Priya.

But it's so true.

Anyway, I never joined a team or a squad or anything—because, as usual, I could never seem to find anyone who actually wanted to hang out with me for any significant length of time. I went to college, ditched the *Star Trek* uniform, and *still.* I couldn't seem to master the whole "making friends" thing. I practiced baton alone in my room, mastering every move, teaching myself complicated routines from YouTube. Pageants seemed like the rare place where baton skills were actually appreciated. And okay, maybe somewhere in the back of my mind, I'd thought there was a pageant sisterhood I'd be inducted into. A bunch of people who actually *would* want to hang out with me, since we were going through the same thing together and all. I figured I'd give Miss Sweet Potato Pie a shot.

A wry smile plays over my lips as I consider that long-ago desire. I toss the baton, catch it. Twirl, twirl, twirl. Wonder some more about what else is out there. Are other people still alive? Is Dad still alive? I miss him so much ...

I have to find out what else—if anything—is out there. We've been trapped in this never-ending *Groundhog Day* loop of a pageant for a year now. We only know this cavernous auditorium with its creaky old stage, the threadbare dressing rooms that have become our sleeping quarters, the endless diet of energy bars.

And we're all too familiar with the invisible force field the Invaders have erected around the stage area, the one that kills anyone who tries to escape. The one that's controlled by Glorg II's voice—and only Glorg II's voice, the other Invaders don't seem to have this power—issuing a specific command that turns it on and off: "Force field up, force field down." Though it is very rarely down.

The control panel by the door ...

I close my eyes and visualize it as the baton continues to twirl through my fingers. My plan will work. It has to.

Because trying to escape isn't the only way girls have died. Whenever the pageant hasn't gone the way the Invaders want it to—someone messes up the wave in the opening parade or someone fucks up their talent routine or whatever—they've sacrificed whomever they deem lacking.

Now there are only two of us left. And Tess wins every day.

The next time they decide to kill someone, it sure as shit won't be her.

★

3. TESS

NOT TO BRAG, but I've got the talent portion of my routine down to an exact science. I actually have *several* different talents ready to be deployed at any given second—Auntie Irene said multiple talents were a necessity for true pageant queens—but for Miss Sweet Potato Pie, I've always done the same thing. Because for the Invaders, the same thing fucking works.

Speed painting.

Oh, that's right—I see you cocking an eyebrow, like, *What the fuck, Tess?* But speed painting is totally a thing in Pageantlandia and I am one of its pioneers. Basically, you set up a big canvas on the stage and then paint some cool image while maybe doing a balletic sort of dance routine. And it all happens in the span of minutes. I always paint the same thing—my idol, former pageant queen Vanessa Williams, in a sultry pose from the cover of her hit album *The Comfort Zone*. It goes over super, super well. The Invaders love it so much that big-ass canvases and paints are the two things they've actually kept us well stocked with.

I roll my neck and adjust my winner's sash, preparing to go onstage. My paintbrush gets all sweaty in my palm and I shift it to my other hand and sneak a peek from behind the curtain at the judges' podium. There's an empty space where Glorg II usually sits. We heard whisperings yesterday that he wasn't feeling well. I guess even murderous space aliens need sick days.

That's why Priya wants to do her stupid plan today. I don't understand why she needs to … upset things. As long as I keep winning, as long as I keep being awesome, we stay alive. This is what I was *born* to do, what I was meant for. She only needs to be mediocre and not fuck up *too* much. I need a competitor in order to win, so they can't really get rid of either of us. And hopefully someone will come save us. I don't know why she doesn't understand this? I'm guessing she might try to go through with her plan anyway, even though she has no chance in hell of succeeding. She's hard-headed, Priya.

I draw myself up tall and tighten my grip on my paintbrush. I can't worry about her. As Zinnia Richards taught me all those years ago, the whole "pageant sisters" concept is bullshit.

Sorry, Auntie Irene.

★

4. Priya

I've decided to go through with my plan anyway. Even though I have no chance in hell of succeeding. I'm hard-headed, okay?

Before she died, Becky Lauren Kellerman—an engineering major whose talent was yodeling the periodic table—had almost cracked the code on how to pass through the force field without disintegrating, or so she thought. It involved covering your body with foil, which I never got a really clear explanation on. But I'm just desperate enough to try it. Luckily, we have *plenty* of foil, because that's what the energy bars are wrapped in. I gather all the remaining bars in my dressing room, divest them of their wrappers, and carefully form the wrappers into a sort of weird spacesuit around my body, taping them into place as best I can. I move around experimentally. I crackle with every step, but the makeshift suit stays put.

Okay. Now or never.

I'll make my move as soon as Tess goes on for her talent demonstration. Maybe the Invaders will be so enthralled, it will buy me a few precious minutes. I pick up my baton and shuffle awkwardly toward my dressing room door, crackling all the way …when all of a sudden, I notice something lying next to my shiny, foil-covered feet. A single energy bar, still in its wrapper. I bend over, moving with great care, working hard not to mess up my spacesuit. One more tiny patch of foil couldn't hurt ...

Then I see what's written on the wrapper.

Blueberry Surprise.

Tess had just been lamenting the fact that we were all out. This must be the last one. And she must've missed it somehow.

I feel a little pang. But a pang of ... what?

I stand there for a full minute, staring at the wrapper, trying to figure it out.

★

5. TESS

I'M JUST ABOUT to head out onstage, waiting for the Invaders to call my name, when I hear a weird crackling sound behind me and feel a tap on my shoulder. I whip around and see ... well. I think it's Priya, but she's dressed herself in a weird silver foil unitard, like she's getting ready to do some hardcore interpretive dance. Or maybe extreme Pilates. Everything is covered in foil except for her eyes, which stare at me in a steady, unnerving way. She thrusts a foiled hand at me.

"Here," she says, her voice muffled by her shiny mask. "Take it. I know it's your favorite and I ... I ... well. Just take it."

I'm so weirded the fuck out, I do. And I see it's an energy bar: Blueberry Surprise.

"I thought we were out!" I exclaim, my voice spiraling into a squeak.

"It's the last one," Priya says. "I want you to have it. I'm ... um. Leaving."

I goggle at her. So she's really trying this. But ... but ... she'll die. She'll *die*. Fuck. She's about to go on a fucking suicide mission and she's making a fucking pit stop to give me my fucking Blueberry Surprise ...

"And now, in talent, please welcome the reigning Miss Sweet Potato Pie, Tess Nakamura!" Glorg IV's announcement cuts into my runaway train of thought.

I see Priya shuffling off, heading for the long ladder that leads to the metal catwalk above the stage. I stare down at the Blueberry Surprise in my hand and feel my grip tighten around it.

Oh, God. Oh, Priya...

"Tess! Nakamura!" Glorg IV says again, sounding a bit impatient.

I feel my legs move forward, carrying me out to the stage, on autopilot. I stand in front of the Invaders, their endless mosaic of eyes staring back at me, the lights suddenly too bright and too hot, the giant canvas in front of me too big and too blank.

And then, out of the corner of my eye, I see a bright flash of metallic silver descending from the rafters.

A million images flash through my head.

Priya laughing hysterically at my Jean-Luc Picard impersonation.

Priya shaking me, trying to get me to escape with her, desperately wanting me to see reason.

Priya handing me my favorite energy bar as if it's the most important thing in our currently extremely fucked up world.

I look out at the Invaders again, at their mean little eyes staring back at me expectantly. Monsters. Wanting me to perform. Not caring that Priya is plunging to her death. Brave, kind, stubborn, wonderful Priya. Out of the corner of my eye, I see the silver flash getting closer and closer to where I know the force field is.

Time slows way down and I feel that all-consuming rage descend again, that crimson veil over my eyes.

I open my mouth and imitate Glorg II's voice perfectly—because of course I fucking do.

And I say: "Force field down."

★

6. PRIYA

EVEN THOUGH THERE'S foil covering my ears, I hear Tess's Glorg II voice ring out through the auditorium milliseconds after I leap from the catwalk and it brings tears to my eyes. That's what I'd wanted her to do, what I've been trying to convince her to do … and it had to be today, because Glorg II isn't here to immediately order the force field back up.

I plunge into the mass of Invaders and land on my feet, then immediately go into my baton routine, spinning and twirling and thwacking them as hard as I fucking can. They go down like the weak gelatinous blobs they are, making sad little croaking sounds. I'm vaguely aware of Tess joining me in the fray, stabbing them with her paintbrush, doing an extremely violent version of the balletic dance that accompanies her speed painting. Wrapping her Miss Sweet Potato Pie winner's sash around one of their blobby monster necks and pulling with all her might, like she's Princess Leia in *Return of the Jedi*. Showing all that grit and determination I admire so much. We take them all down and it feels ... So. Fucking. Good.

I race over to the control panel, punch in the code I've memorized after watching Glorg IV punch it in every day for a year. The massive auditorium door slides open. And Tess and I are finally free.

I rip the foil from my body as we stumble out into the daylight, breathing in fresh air, feeling the sun on my face. Everything is so ... quiet. Eerie. Like maybe we really are the last two people on Earth. I feel something in my hand and turn to see Tess slipping me half of her Blueberry Surprise.

"Pageant sisters are forever sisters," she says earnestly, her mouth full of energy bar.

I look down at the disgusting crumbs in my hand. I think about all my unanswered questions, how I still don't know what else is out there, how I don't know what's happening on the rest of the planet or if anyone else is still alive.

How, despite all this, for maybe the first time in my life, I don't feel alone. And my eyes fill with tears once again.

"Back atcha," I say.

MOREL AND UPWRIGHT
DAVID WELLINGTON

FRANZ MOREL WOKE early that particular morning, in a bed that could comfortably have parked a fleet of staff cars. He stretched his arms above his head and smacked his lips, imagining the glorious day to come.

He descended to his third most opulent bathroom—the one done up in rose-colored marble, which had the best acoustics—and sang an old campaigner's song as he cleaned his teeth and had a very thorough shave, taking time to carefully trim his glorious handlebar mustache and tiny, devilishly pointed beard. In the Breakfast Wing of the Presidential Palace, he took three eggs, each in an individual diamond-encrusted egg cup, and a pot of coffee scented with rose and saffron. The delicate saffron, of course, failed to impart any flavor to the coffee, but Morel had always been of the opinion that when a chance for true decadence came the way of a hard-working dictator, it was his duty to himself—as the living embodiment of the state—to take it, and thereby signal the great wealth and power of the Nation.

There was, of course, no newspaper to read while he ate. He could have simply decreed one to be printed, but then he would have had to edit and censor it himself, and he just didn't have the time. So instead he stared out a window while he sipped his coffee, gazing out upon all that land that was his to sport with as he pleased. Admittedly there wasn't very much of it. Just a low line of hills on the horizon. And it was a given that the horizon was rather closer than he would have liked.

One finds ways to cope with adversity, of course. "Martin-8," he barked, and the robot who was his Major Domo, Chief of Staff, Aide-de-

Camp, Seneschal, and Valet rolled up to a neat stop by his elbow. "My best set of medals, today," Morel ordered. When speaking to the robot it was crucial, always, to maintain the air of command. "And once I'm finished dressing, I believe we shall have a parade."

"Of courze, zir," the robot buzzed. It reached its many-jointed arms across the table to refill his coffee, then withdrew.

When Morel had finished dressing, he found he could not so much walk down to the parade stand as shuffle, really. The weight of all the gold braid on his shoulders was the main problem, though the twelve kilograms of bronze and silver pinned to his chest probably didn't help. The chief culprit, however, had to be the pair of ivory pommel sabers he wore on either hip, which kept getting tangled with his legs as he attempted to stride with pomp and dignity across the public square. He managed, however, to struggle up into the place of honor, a chair of red velvet and so much gilt wooden decorative fussiness that even Morel found it a bit *de trop*.

In all things, though, it was essential to project an air of confidence and might, and Morel was happy to make such sacrifices for his adopted homeland.

Once he was properly seated the parade could begin.

An observer, if any had been present, might have noticed that the long reviewing stand set up in the main square of Morelograd was a bit thinly populated. In point of fact, said hypothetical witness might have remarked that it seemed Morel was the only person who had come to watch the parade happen. There was a reason for this.

It was the same reason why, as the parade filed past, it was made up entirely of Martin-8 the robot dragging a rose-covered float past the stands, then zooming around the corner to fetch a wooden mockup of a missile carrier, followed by Martin-8, again, running quickly out of sight only to drag in a pipe organ on wheels, on which he played the national anthem ("All Glory to our Beautifully Mustachioed Leader,") with one telescoping arm while steering the vehicle with his other hand.

Martin-8 had to play all the parts required of a properly vigorous parade, because there was no one else to take part.

Franz Morel, undisputed and eternal leader of the planet VZ-61a, was also its sole human inhabitant. Unconquerable ruler of all he surveyed, Morel was also his own—and only—subject.

One might have suggested that Martin-8 the robot was an exception to this, that the mechanical man was under Morel's command. And it was true that Martin-8 performed the duties of a subject rather well—he was always perfectly happy to put on another parade (Morel commanded these to occur at least three times a week) or make another rasher of bacon, or build a new wing onto the Presidential Palace as Morel desired. Yet in another sense, Martin-8 could not be considered a subject at all. In addition to his roles as Major Domo, Aide-de-Camp, Secretary of the Navy, Chief Strategic Advisor and Vice President-for-life, Martin-8 had two other jobs. One was to be Franz Morel's jailer. The other, should worse come to worst, was to serve as The Great Leader's executioner.

★

PLANET VZ-61A LACKED any more sonorous name, largely because the astronomer who discovered it had found it so underwhelming that she never bothered actually looking at it again after it was catalogued. It possessed no resources worth exploiting, nor was it big enough to be worth colonizing. Barely five hundred kilometers across, it possessed something like gravity and something like air, but not enough of either to make it a pleasant vacation spot. Furthermore, it was a great deal of distance from anywhere people bothered to go, and its evening sky lacked any particular beauty.

Even Franz Morel, who had once been the paramount leader of a very large nation on the next world over—a man possessed of imperialist tendencies that would make a Napoleon blush—had never bothered to plant a flag on the place, or even to threaten to blow it up for being so irritatingly useless.

When the time came and the people decided that Franz Morel had to go, they faced a dilemma. Morel was a butcher, a ruthless murdering reptile of a leader. His death squads and purges had made him the most hated man in the galaxy. Yet those who replaced him couldn't simply kill him. That would have been sinking to his level. Everyone wanted him dead, but no one wanted to get their hands dirty by strangling him. In the end they hit upon a plan that would allow them to remain blameless, but almost certainly result in the desired end. They would exile Morel to VZ-61a. They would provide for his every need and allow him to rule the place as he chose. The only condition of his retirement (as it was always described) was that he would never be allowed to leave VZ-61a, nor make any contact with another world.

If he did so, his robot butler was to enact Protocol Zeta Four Cobalt—that is, to shoot him in the back of the head. It would be his own fault, and he would pay the price for his own perfidy, and everyone could get a good night's sleep for a change.

His usurpers assumed that within days, the hated man would summon up some cadre of loyal army officers to fly to VZ-61a in a heavily armed raid to free him from his confinement. Or he would, through sheer cunning, manage to build some sort of rocket that would allow him to escape into hiding, from which he would slowly rebuild his power base like a patient spider in a secluded web. In these cases the robot would be fully justified in its pre-programmed act of regicide. The third possibility was that the isolation of VZ-61a would very quickly drive Morel as mad as a toad in a stock pot, and that in a fit of despair he would take his own life.

None of those things happened. For seven and one half years, Franz Morel ruled VZ-61a with an iron fist; but always he kept punctiliously within the bounds of his new estate.

Each of his deposers' assumptions was based on a flawed postulate. The first: there was no loyal cadre. Morel's reign had been so brutal, and so corrupt, that he had lost every last friend he ever might have had. The second: that Morel had the intelligence to build a rocket. He had ruled a technically advanced society, but had never actually bothered to learn anything about technology himself in his forty-seven years. Had he wished to nail a self-portrait to the wall of his palace he would have been hard-pressed to know which end of the hammer one grasped and which was the business end.

The third flawed assumption: that he would go mad, living by himself.

He did not go mad, no matter how many years passed on VZ-61a. For the very simple reason that Franz Morel was already about as insane as it is possible for a human being to become. The effects of isolation, social and physical, on the human mind are well studied and known to be highly deleterious, but there is also such a thing as the law of diminishing returns. A man so suffused with neuroses, complexes, fixations and delusions as Franz Morel could withstand a little alone-time. He could do exile standing on his head.

Indeed, in many ways the days Morel spent alone on VZ-61a were the happiest of his life. He possessed all the power he had ever desired, as ruler not just of some middlingly impressive country but of an *entire world*. Every whim, every gratuitous impulse, every whimper of his rabidly overactive id was catered to by Martin-8, the robot. All the little frustrations and mild irritations of having to actually run a country were removed from him, and he could settle down to some proper and healthful self-indulgence. On VZ-61a he could do anything he desired. He might learn how to paint, he told himself, or he might begin the multi-volume set of memoirs he'd always wanted to write.

In the meantime, he could have parades. He'd always loved parades.

Solitude, in a word, became Franz Morel. The world of his exile had become a megalomaniac's paradise.

Sadly, paradises are only ever built to be lost.

★

It began unremarkably enough. A star in the evening sky grew brighter each night, rather faster than astronomical bodies typically did. Morel, possessing a quite shocking lack of intellectual curiosity, paid it no mind. His first sense that something might have changed was when, lounging in his five-hundred-gallon bathtub one morning, he called out for Martin-8 to refresh his hot water and—unthinkably—there was no response.

There came a great whooshing noise from outside, followed by a clap of thunder. In all of his days on VZ-61a, Morel had never seen nor heard a thunderstorm. This just about reached the threshold of his interest. He called out for Martin-8 to come explain what was going on.

Again, there was no response.

Morel was forced to get out of the bath and, unbelievably, fetch his own towel. He dressed—by himself—in a bathrobe worked with cloth-of-gold in a motif of his own initials and went down to the main hall of the Presidential Palace. The doors were thrown open, letting in light and air from the main square of Morelograd. The day being clement—as close to being pleasant as any day on the unremarkably warm planetoid ever got—Morel stepped outside in his bare feet and looked around. What he saw surprised him utterly. Martin-8 was approaching down the main thoroughfare—accompanied by *a human being*.

Morel's imagination began to fizz. This being another quality he lacked in a truly outstanding degree, it took him quite a while to begin to understand the possibilities of what had occurred.

Another human, another person, had come to VZ-61a. The whoosh and the roar he'd heard must have been the sound of a rocket descending and landing just outside of the city. Another person—

Morel rushed forward, his hands out in warm greeting. "Hello, hello!" he cried. "Hello! I must admit, I'm pleased, I truly am!"

Martin-8 rolled to a stop. The robot extended one arm to gesture at the newcomer. "Zir," the machine said, "may I introduze Tolliver Upwright?"

Morel grabbed the other man's hands in welcome.

Upwright sneered.

He was tall, a good head taller than the admittedly short Morel. He was also very thin, thin like a mantis, whereas Morel was decidedly stout. Upwright possessed no facial hair whatsoever and the hair on his head had been shaved back on the sides and—interestingly—the hairline, as if to suggest that he possessed a higher forehead than, in actuality, he did. His face was spare to the point of gauntness. He wore a very severe tunic buttoned very tightly at his throat. Of ornament or decoration he had none, except a tiny enamel pin on his breast that looked like the insignia of some political party. Which party did not matter in the slightest to Morel.

"How very good of you to come!" Morel said. "How wonderful! How quickly can we get on our way? I have a few things to pack, it shouldn't amount to more than a short ton of cargo in all, and then we can—"

"Ahem," Upwright said. "Ahem." When this seemed to fail to achieve the desired effect, he turned to face Martin-8 with one raised eyebrow. "Ahem," he said.

"Pleaze, Mr. Upwright, may I introduze Franz Morel?"

Morel frowned in confusion. The new man didn't know who he was?

"You've come to take me back, yes?" the erstwhile dictator inquired. "I'm being released. That's why you're here."

In his head he could see no other reason for this unexpected and unprecedented visit. Clearly he had been forgiven by the people back home. Most likely, Morel's successor had proved so unequal to the task of actually running a country that the people had clamored to have their beloved Morel back. There could be no other explanation—

"Mr. Upwright will be a guezt here," Martin-8 droned. "On a permanent baziz."

"A guest," Morel said.

"Yez, zir."

"Here."

"Yez, zir."

Upwright leaned forward, looming over Morel. "I know you. I've heard about you," he said. "I've heard a great deal about ... *you*."

Morel glanced back and forth between the robot and the newcomer. He didn't understand. Not at all.

"You," Upwright said, lifting one very long finger and pointing it squarely in Morel's direction, "are the Butcher of Fluoristan. You're the one who ordered the pre-emptive execution of the Humanist Congress. You're the fellow who had an entire regiment of your own soldiers flogged because they failed to meet dress code."

"Don't forget," Martin-8 intoned, "the inzident with the zchoolbuz."

"Quite," Upwright said. "The ... *school bus*."

Morel squirmed inside his robe. "War," he protested. "You know. Accidents."

"You," Upwright said, "are the most hated man in history. You are a villain, sir. A monster of religious proportions. That is to say, a creature so vile, so despised, that in future I fully expect you to be written into the official text of various religions. Specifically, written in as an example of *what not to do*."

Morel smiled. He had a very good, very practiced smile. It was a smile that, once upon a time, had sent entire crowds into a frenzy of applause and cheering.

Perhaps he was out of practice.

"You, robot," Upwright said. "This is unacceptable. You expect me to spend the—I am certain the very short, but meaningfully long—span of my exile here? With this man? You expect me to spend one more moment in his presence?"

"I am afraid the conditionz of your zentence—" Martin-8 began, but clearly Upwright had more to say.

"Why, simply being within a hundred kilometers of this ... this *organism*, which I dare not give the noble name of man, must be considered highly unusual and innovatively cruel punizhment—"

"What's he in for?" Morel asked the robot.

"They called it the National Paztry Day Mazzacre," Martin-8 replied.

Morel licked his lips.

"Massacre—"

Upwright's face turned a bright purple. His eyes vibrated with rage. "Those nuns were known counter-revolutionaries!" he roared.

★

EVENTUALLY IT GOT through the rather thick skull of Franz Morel that he was no longer alone. That he would not be, from here out, the only human resident of VZ-61a. The basic facts of the case drilled their way into his worldview.

The meaning of those facts, the subtle implications, were to work themselves out over time. First, though, he announced that the newcomer must be tired after his long journey, and therefore he must be given refreshment. Martin-8 acquiesced at once, preparing a full banquet of welcome. Dinner was served in the very best of the Presidential Palace's seven dining halls. The one that would seat fifty. The walls were hung with campaign banners, some from battles and wars Morel had actually won, some from the victories and conquests he only claimed in the official histories. The silver service reflected the light of a thousand candles and the napkins were freshly starched and folded perfectly.

Upwright entered the room with his hands clasped behind his back. He took one look, lifted his chin, and sniffed in disdain.

Morel hurried to indicate a chair near the head of the table. Near it. He took the place of honor for himself, of course. Once they were seated, he snapped his fingers and Martin-8 rushed in from the kitchen, bearing platter after platter of steaming food.

"So," Morel said. "You've been exiled."

Upwright lifted one shoulder in a shrug that required only the minimum of muscular contraction. "I prefer to think of it as an involuntary period of reflection, before the full reinstatement of my plenary powers," he said. "I am certain that within the space of a month—likely less than that—the officials of the People's Party will come to their senses and recognize that I did nothing wrong, that I have never done anything wrong, that my motives were of the purest and my decisions were based, always, on the best possible information available at the time. In short, I will be exonerated, cleared of all charges, there will be public apologies, there will be a formal reception upon my return, there will be—"

"Chop?" Morel asked, lifting the bell of a silver platter, revealing a mountain of succulent and perfectly sauced cuts of something that was not, in fact, pork, but which wore a cunning disguise as such.

Upwright's nose twitched. "I am a strict vegetarian," he insisted. "Please cover that up. It borders on the offensive."

Morel replaced the bell. Though not, he told himself, because he'd been told to do so. Only to make sure the chops stayed warm.

"In fact," Upwright said, "as I am to be a prisoner here, I believe I shall take this opportunity to demonstrate solidarity with all political prisoners everywhere. I shall have toasted bread and water, please."

Martin-8 zipped off to comply.

Morel squinted at his new companion. "I'm not sure I've ever met a trustworthy vegetarian," he said. "There's always something wrong with a fellow who doesn't enjoy a good, bloody steak."

Upwright straightened the cutlery arrayed before him. "Is that what you told General Ugholini, when you forced him to eat the heart of his own beloved lieutenant?"

Morel chewed on his mustache.

He was at a disadvantage, here. Upwright seemed to know all about his exploits, whereas he knew nothing whatsoever of the newcomer's *curriculum vitae*. This was, of course, a simple accident of timing. Morel had been exiled seven and one half years earlier. At the time, Tolliver Upwright had been little more than a party *apparatchik*, a rising star in the revolutionary government of the last major nation Morel had not yet gotten around to conquering.

Upwright's rise had been nothing short of meteoric. By the classic pincer move of (a) endlessly, tirelessly proving his purity and devotion to the Party's ideals, and (b) knowing whose throats he could safely and without consequence cut, Upwright had quickly found himself at the very center of a tidy cult of personality and had been made the First Citizen of his nation by the time he was thirty. His people had loved him dearly (or else) and the Party had heaped accolades and encomia upon him, right up until the moment of his exile.

It was a testament to Upwright's bloody, brutal efficiency that the nation he helped create was a model of bureaucratic effectiveness. Deposing Franz Morel had required a prolonged and costly battle that left his capital city (also called Morelograd) in ruins. When the time came, however, to remove Upwright from power, the Party had simply had to submit a single form, properly notarized and copied in triplicate. By name, a Party Inner Circle Eyes Only Form 57/J: Authorization for Removal/Assassination/Usurpation of High Official. The only small hang-up with the entire process had been that some anonymous clerk had made a typo on the form. Said person had meant to make a very large, emphatic X in the box marked *Summary Execution Preferably Including Public Spectacle*, but had instead managed to check the box that read *Permanent Exile*. The Party Secretary had passed on the form without actually reading it, and so the life of Tolliver Upwright had been spared.

"Hmm," Morel said. Knowing none of this, only that he had been caught out.

"Hm," Upwright said, more succinctly.

Martin-8 arrived with a new platter almost at once. It bore a stainless steel rack of toast soldiers and a glass bottle of still water.

"That's fine," Upwright said, using a silver fork to snag one of the toast triangles. He laid it down on his porcelain plate and stared at it for a while. "A fitting meal for a prisoner of conscience. I think that the statement I'm making here is clear."

Morel spooned caviar onto a blini. "Absolutely," he said.

Upwright nodded. He poked at the piece of toast with his fork. His mouth pursed up in distaste, however, and he employed his knife to dissect the piece of half-burned bread.

"These aren't caraway seeds, are they?" he asked.

They almost certainly were not—technically. Martin-8 made do with what he had available on VZ-61a, a world which possessed no great wealth of culinary raw materials. It was a triumph of technology that the robot was able to convert the local bacteria, slime molds, and fungi into something resembling human food. Whether or not the robot was proud of its ability to construct things that looked like caraway seeds would forever remain unknown, however, as Upwright did not provide him a chance to answer the question.

"I can't have caraway seeds in my bread," the former Party Official said. "They get stuck in my teeth. And this water. I assume it has been double filtered? Was it secured from a sustainable source? It looks a bit gray to me."

"Zir," Martin-8 said, whisking the offending foodstuffs away from the table.

When the robot was gone, Upwright drummed his fingers on the table in an impatient way. "I suppose there's no chance of getting decent food here."

"You could go on a hunger strike," Morel pointed out. "That might make an even bolder statement than bread and water."

Upwright stared at him through dramatically narrowed eyes.

"Hmm," he said.

It was Morel's turn to prove that brevity was the soul of wit. "Hm," he said. And forked the largest of the chops onto his plate.

★

AFTER THE BANQUET was finished, the two of them went for a stroll. Morel desired to show off the grandeur of Morelograd, his capital and home. It didn't take very long. The city was dominated utterly by the Presidential Palace, by far the largest building on VZ-61a. Beyond the precincts of the palace, the city possessed only the one main square and the four roads which radiated from it. There were a number of buildings of tastefully restrained architecture facing the palace, but these structures possessed a common flaw which Upwright, to Morel's embarrassment, was quick to point out.

"They're façades," Upwright said.

In fact, the buildings were all front. Designed cunningly to look like complete houses, banks, factories and schools from one side—the side that faced the palace—there was nothing to them when they were viewed from other angles, just flat faces propped up with long wooden buttresses from behind.

Essentially two-dimensional in nature, these buildings served only to present Morel, in the palace, with a stately view.

"But then where am I to live, while I'm here?" Upwright asked.

"I'll find some place for you in the palace," Morel said. "I only ever really use seven of the twenty bedrooms. One a day, rotating each week, so I always have clean sheets."

"You expect me to sleep in that rococo nightmare?" Upwright asked. "I should think all the gilt and ormolu and baroque tchotchkes would invade my dreams. I would wake up every morning thinking I was drowning in chintz."

Morel took a deep breath. He understood that not everyone shared his decorating sense. He did not, actually, understand why, but he supposed people were people and by definition perverse.

Still.

It was becoming rapidly clear to him that a situation was brewing, here. One which he was going to have to nip in the bud.

"Perhaps the time has come to discuss how you're going to fit in here," Morel said. "What position you'll fill. I've been operating for some time with a reduced staff, and it would be good to fill some of the vacant seats. Martin-8 does his best as chief of staff, press secretary, and bodyguard, but honestly, he lacks initiative and vision. You could help round out the body politic, as it were."

"Is that a fact?" Upwright asked.

"Indeed. I find myself in need of a Minister of Propaganda, for instance. Do you think you could bring something unique to the role?"

"Minister," Upwright said. "Minister."

"I admit it's asking a lot. The requirements of the post may be taxing, and I'm afraid the hours will be long. It is a position with great responsibilities— but also excellent perks. You would have the ear of the highest office in the land, for instance. Unfettered access to my glorious self."

"How exciting," Upwright replied. "Though I wonder if—perhaps—I might challenge a supposition."

"Oh?"

"Yes," Upwright said. "What exactly makes you think that you're in charge, here?"

"I beg your pardon?" Morel asked. Dim as he was, he honestly didn't understand what Upwright was asking.

"You have assumed, sir, that I would be interested in playing your subordinate. I don't see why I should just acknowledge your preeminence. Perhaps I intend to be the leader of this world. You, of course, would be my constituent."

Morel laughed. "Preposterous! This is my planet. Come now, man, you must see that it has to be so. For seven and a half years I've been in charge here, with no real help from the robot, and—"

"Perhaps," Upwright said, "the time has come for a change. A clearing out of the dead wood, so to speak. A great rethinking of the political economy on VZ-61a."

Morel turned bright red. He smacked a fist against the palm of his other hand. Repeatedly. When this failed to have the desired effect—or any visible effect at all—he reiterated, "Preposterous! There can be no debate about this. I am the sole commander of all I survey."

"But—and again, I ask with all due respect—why?"

"Why?" Morel asked. "WHY? Well, sir, because—because—because of the oldest principle of governance known to man!"

Upwright pursed his lips. "Which is what, exactly?"

"I was here first!"

Upwright chuckled a bit, but said nothing. They continued their stroll in silence, for a while. Eventually they returned to the place where they'd started from—the gates of the palace—where they stood for some time in perfect silence, regarding each other. Morel finally turned to the newcomer and gave him the slightest of bows. "There you have it. I'm glad we came to an understanding." Morel had always considered silence to imply consent. Especially the permanent sort of silence he'd formerly imposed on those who challenged his authority. "I think," he said, "that we should have a parade tomorrow. Yes, a parade. Everyone loves a good parade," he mused aloud. They were so very useful for demonstrating who was in charge, and who was under control.

Upwright opened his mouth as if to speak, but Morel hurried to fill the vacuum.

"I'll even allow you to participate. Yes, yes, I think that's exactly what will fit the bill, here. I herby formally permit you to march in tomorrow's parade. Now, now, before you say anything—"

"Ahem," Upwright said. "I was about to accept your kind offer."

Morel's brow clouded. "You were."

"Indeed," Upwright replied. "I wouldn't miss your parade for the world." And with that he walked away, laughing a bit under his breath.

"Well," Morel said, his overheated brain working very hard. "Well. Good, then."

★

IT PROVED A fine morning for a parade. At the very least, it didn't rain, and the temperature never fell below freezing. On VZ-61a, you took what small victories were vouchsafed you by the elements. Morel took his time dressing. He found he was oddly nervous, fluttering with a sort of stage fright he hadn't felt since his first days doing press events as a young dictator. That was so long ago, now. Back before he had all the reporters fed to hyenas.

He'd attended hundreds of these parades, of course. He knew exactly what to expect. Yet the fact that today there would be an audience—for the first time in his exile—sent tremors of excitement and dread running through him until he was all atingle.

He picked his favorite two sabers, and rolled his hat between his hands endlessly, trying to give it the perfect shape. When Martin-8 came to tell him the parade was ready, Morel stuck out his chin, adopted his well-trained swagger, and headed down to the stands feeling almost giddy.

The parade began as soon as he'd taken his seat. There was no immediate sign of Upwright, but Morel supposed the newcomer might simply wish to make a dramatic entrance, or could still be working on his parade float. He hoped it would be tasteful—perhaps a ten-meter long display of roses spelling out Morel's name, or perhaps Upwright would come out dressed in sackcloth and tear at his hair while making a public apology for his remarks that had challenged Morel's rightful place as ruler of VZ-61a.

Nothing too fussy, of course.

Morel nodded approvingly as Martin-8 came around the corner, leading a wooden mockup of a Megalodon M-99 missile carrier, a weapons system Morel had always adored for its ability to render cities into rubble with a minimum of user training. He clapped politely as Martin-8 rushed around the block and returned driving a staff car flying a giant flag bearing Morel's coat of arms. He feigned a slight yawn as Martin-8 made its third trip, this time marching with one arm up in a salute.

Where the devil was Upwright? Morel frowned and peered around the square, looking for any sign of the frankly obstreperous fellow.

Then the newcomer did arrive, and Morel nearly had a fit.

Upwright had not put on a fancy costume. Nor had he bothered creating an imaginative yet decorous float for the parade. Instead he had simple written a slogan on a piece of cardstock, mounted it on a wooden pole, and marched forward thrusting his sign in the air, chanting the same message out loud.

The message was simple: DOWN WITH MUSTACHIO'D OPPRESSORS.

But far, far worse than this—he had recruited Martin-8, the robot, to carry a similar sign, and to chant along with him. "Down with muztachio'd oprezzorz!"

Morel's jaw fell open. His blood pressure soared. One of his sabers fell off his belt and clattered under the reviewing stand.

The two of them, upstart and robot, marched around the corner. Almost instantly, Martin-8 reappeared, this time holding a very large wreath of cunningly worked flowers in the colors of Franz Morel's nation, which the robot presented to the dictator with as graceful a bow as his mechanical limbs permitted.

Then Martin-8 rolled around the corner—and came back at Upwright's side. This time they carried an effigy with a very poorly drawn-on mustache and beard, hanging from a pasteboard gibbet.

Morel's left eye started to twitch alarmingly.

Martin-8's next float was themed on Morel's famous victory over the potato farmers of Yuziristan. One of his more flawless performances as a military commander. The float depicted a trio of farmers throwing down their pitchforks, while a flattering image of Morel pointed down at them with an imperious finger from the hatch of a main battle tank. The whole thing was made of dyed ostrich feathers that fluttered magnificently in the breeze.

Then Martin-8 disappeared around the corner again. Only to return with Upwright, both of them carrying shoes in their throwing arms.

"Enough!" Morel screamed. "Stop!"

"What's the matter, Morel?" Upwright sneered. "You can't handle the sight of citizens expressing their right to free speech?"

"Speech?" Morel shouted, aghast. "Free?" He shook his head in utter incomprehension. "Rights?"

"I'll take that as a no," Upwright announced. He paused for a moment to put his shoe back on.

"And you—Martin-8—you, you traitor, you apostate, you—you—"

"I beg your pardon, zir," Martin-8 said. "Have I dizpleazed you?"

"You betrayed me," Morel said. "After seven and a half years, I assumed we were simpatico. I assumed we had a rapport. I assumed you were my friend, you bucket of lowest bidder-assembled parts!"

"Zir," Martin-8 said, "many apologiez. However, it iz part of my programming to zerve all inhabitantz of VZ-61a equally. I cannot refuze an order from Mr. Upwright, any more than I can refuze an order from yourzelf, unlezz zaid order contradictz the termz of your exilez."

Morel couldn't believe it. He couldn't hold it in his head at all. He blinked rapidly, as if this was all an illusion and it would simply go away any moment now.

It did not.

"I … I forbid it," he said. "I forbid this vulgar display. I forbid you from participating in any more acts of disobedience," he said.

He had been speaking to Martin-8, but Upwright lifted his chin and said, "Ha." Then he stamped one very narrow foot.

Morel sputtered in rage. Utter, nonverbal rage.

"In that case," Upwright said, "then you give me no choice. Martin-8, I'd like to make a statement."

The robot took out a pad of paper and a tiny, well-sharpened pencil.

"As of this moment," Upwright said, "I declare the formation of the People's Revolutionary Party of VZ-61a. Too long have the people of this world toiled under the yoke of the lunatic oppressor Francis Morel."

"Franz," Morel interjected. It should come as little surprise to anyone that he hated having people get his name wrong in official pronouncements.

"Leave it as is," Upwright told the robot.

Morel fumed. Soundlessly.

"The People's Revolutionary Party will not rest until the madman Morel has been removed from office, and preferably from this life. Of course, every revolutionary party needs a president. I nominate myself as president pro-tem, until such time as a free election can be held. Martin-8, this is the point where you say, 'seconded'."

"Zeconded," the robot dutifully zaid. Said.

"The motion is carried," Upwright pronounced. "Now. Come with me. There is a great deal of work to be done." He turned on his heel and headed for the door of the façade building across the street.

The robot followed.

Up in the reviewing stands, Morel shook and quivered and steamed. He simmered with rage, in almost complete silence.

He boiled with anger, without making a peep.

He grew as brightly red as a ripe tomato, and sweat popped out of his forehead, dripping across the huge, prominent vein that protruded there. Quietly.

Then he screamed his lungs out.

★

MOREL SPENT A fitful night full of restless dreams, only to wake, as usual, in his enormous bed. As was his wont, he called for Martin-8. It was time for breakfast.

For a very long time, perhaps as much as a quarter of an hour, the robot did not come. Morel pulled the blankets up to his chin. Perhaps the horrible Upwright had subverted the machine. Perhaps the newcomer had disassembled the robot—how terrible that would be—Morel would be forced to cook his own eggs. To brush down his own uniforms. And who would march in his parades?

When the door did open—and the robot entered, as discreetly as ever—Morel felt a palpable sense of relief trickle down his spine. Martin-8 had a silver tray balanced in one mechanical claw, and when it lifted the lid to reveal three rashers of bacon and a jeroboam of champagne, well, it was almost like everything had returned to normal. Morel sighed deeply and began to tuck in.

"You were late, this morning," he said, to the robot. There might have been a trace of diffidence in his voice, but he knew Martin-8 would never judge him for it. "I—ha ha—began to worry."

"Apologiez, zir. I waz detained. I worked all night and into the morning conztructing Mr. Upwright'z new dwelling."

Morel raised an eyebrow. So the upstart had found himself a place to live? Well. That might be for the best. Maybe some dreadful little hole halfway across the planet. Yes. That would suit the prig. "A little hovel he can call his own," Morel said, and tittered to himself. "No doubt very small, and minimal in design."

"The term he uzed was 'Brutalizt', zir."

Morel nodded and poured himself another mimosa. "No appreciation for proper architecture, that lot. Why, they never met a portico or a colonnade they ... they ... hmm. Martin-8, do you hear something?"

"Zir?"

"Something like ... music. Rather vulgar music. I wonder if—"

With a sudden, terrible presentiment, Morel jumped from the bed and ran to the French doors of his balcony. He threw them open and a great cloud of noise pushed into the room. The music was blaring, and full of squelching feedback as it was blasted out of poorly-designed loudspeakers.

It had the strong, driving rhythm of a march, and there was a fair amount of tuba in it, but beyond that Morel did not find anything to like in the music. A chorus of rough male voices formed the vocal component, voices raised in solidarity and union, calling for the destruction of all tyrants and enemies of the people.

The music came from a number of horn-shaped speakers mounted on the front of the building across the street. A new building across the street. Though not particularly wide—it took up only as much space on the main square as the average house—the building rose to towering heights. It was built of dull, unornamented concrete, without the slightest concession to aesthetics or flair. Only two things distinguished the building at all. One was the bright red flag flapping atop a pole at the building's apex.

The other was a curious mass, not unlike a growth of mushrooms, that sprouted from the front of the building—directly across the square from Morel's balcony. This concrudescence took the form of a cluster of the aforementioned loudspeakers, but also included a wide variety of cameras, radar dishes, telescope lenses and directional microphones, all of which were pointed right at Morel's face.

"Brutalist," Morel said, to himself. "Brutalist. And … and so high …"

"He azked me how tall the Prezidential Palaze waz," Martin-8 said, its mechanical voice almost lost in the swell of chanting proles. "I informed him that it iz exactly one hundred and zeventeen meterz in height. He then requezted that I conztruct hiz new tower to be one hundred and zeventeen meterz tall."

Morel's left eye twitched. "The same height. Exactly the same—"

"Then he requezted the flagpole," Martin-8 went on. "Which technically addz five more meterz to the building'z height."

Morel's right eye started to twitch as well.

A sudden flash of motion drew his attention back to the building across the way. One of the closed-circuit television cameras there had swiveled on its bracket, to focus better on his reddening face.

One of the windows higher up on the building opened. A long banner unfurled from the window, bearing the legend:

PRESIDENT UPWRIGHT IS WATCHING YOU.

Morel squeaked in terror and slammed the French doors of his balcony closed. He rushed across the room to take—ahem—strategic cover behind an arras.

"This," he swore, with the robot to witness him, "is too much. This is the last straw!"

The only question that remained was what he planned on doing about it.

Morel's brain worked overtime, proposing and rejecting possibilities. He weighed the pros and cons of various schemes of action, had fierce if short-lived internal debates over the likelihood of success of various schemes, plans, and gambits. His eyeballs quivered in his head as he imagined all the various ways he could have revenge.

Finally, he hit upon the one surefire strategy that had always worked for him before, the one method of dealing with enemies which had become the hallmark of his wildly successful career.

"I'll murder the bastard," he said.

★

THERE GREW, NEAR the equator of VZ-61a, a thing that was not a tree. Not in the slightest. The most generous botanist would have been at pains to call it a bush. It was not green, for one thing, nor did it have branches. It was made of a certain slimy kind of fungus that grew slightly taller than the other seventy-nine species of slimy fungus which had inhabited VZ-61a before the arrival of humanity.

This one particular specimen of fungus, which was the tallest of its kind that had ever grown, was just tall enough to provide Morel with a modicum of shade from the noonday sun.

Before him spread a broad plain of absolutely nothing. Nothing grew in the cracked and lifeless soil that stretched out for kilometers in every direction.

It was the closest thing the planet could provide to approximate a field. Namely, a field of honor.

A plume of dust rose like a great column on the horizon. The horizon of VZ-61a never being too far off, it wasn't long before Martin-8 appeared, drawing a two-wheeled litter. Upwright sat perfectly straight in the back, with an expression of muted annoyance.

When the litter had come to a stop, the newcomer unfolded his long legs and stepped out to stand in front of Morel. "I was busy," he said. "I do not appreciate being summoned away from my work."

Morel smiled broadly. He used his fingers to straighten his mustachios. He lifted one of his many medals and breathed upon it, then wiped away the condensation with a handkerchief.

"So what is it?" Upwright demanded. "What is so all-fire important that it was worth coming here? I could have written another twenty pages of my new manifesto if you would have had the simple courtesy to leave me alone."

Morel's smile broadened. He unbuttoned his left glove, then carefully peeled it off, one finger at a time.

"Speak, man! Speak or I'm going to add interference with party activities to the long list of your—"

Morel rose up on his tiptoes—regretfully this was necessary—and slapped Upwright across the cheek with his glove.

"I demand satisfaction," he said.

Upwright looked duly stunned. Morel took an enormous degree of pleasure from this.

"I beg your pardon," Upwright said. "Did you just say—are you—is this supposed to be some kind of *duel?*"

The would-be usurper looked around—at the thing that was not in any real sense a tree, at the broken ground. At the pair of pearl-handled sabers in their carved mahogany display case that Martin-8 suddenly held out in its mechanical hands.

Then he broke out in a fit of dry laughter.

"This planet," Morel said, "is proving too small for the both of us. Of the many reasons why I might be justified in taking your life, there are sixteen which I feel are the most egregious and require immediate redress. I shall begin to enumerate them, starting with number the first: You interrupted my breakfast this morning. Number the second—"

Upwright hadn't stopped laughing. "You can't be serious, little man. I have no inclination to fight you. As much as I'd like to see you dead, the very institution of dueling is a barbarous practice suited only to reactionary elements who are not yet evolved enough to understand the concept of civil debate, and furthermore—"

"You refuse my challenge?" Morel asked.

He'd been prepared for this.

"Yes," Upwright told him. Then he turned on his heel and started walking back toward the litter.

"I thought you might be a coward," Morel said.

Upwright stopped instantly in his tracks. He did not, however, turn. Nor did he say anything. He reached up and brushed some imaginary dust off the shoulder of his tunic. He might have let out a disdainful sniff.

"You've never actually been in a real fight, have you?" Morel asked of Upwright's back. "You've never taken a man's life in single combat. No. Your type never do. You'd much rather sign a form that consigns a thousand of your own people to their deaths, rather than strangle the enemy before you."

Upwright's left hand started to curl into a fist.

"You have no sense of honor, none at all," Morel said.

"You are a moral sewer," Upwright replied, turning.

"Bloodless philistine," Morel impugned.

"Violent thug," Upwright pronounced.

Morel: "Stuffed shirt!"

Upwright: "Visigoth!"

"Weakling!"

"Cretin!"

This went on for some time. It ended only when, with a sudden, jerking motion, Upwright seized the hilt of one of the sabers and drew it from its sheath.

The fact that he had, in fact, never held such a weapon in his hand before did not stay him in the slightest. The fact that Morel had once been a champion fencer and had slaughtered dozens of men in duels might have given him pause—except that he didn't know it.

"Have at you, then," Upwright said, and launched an attack before Morel had even drawn his blade.

A frightful breach of the normal rules of dueling. Then again, there were no referees or seconds there to complain. Martin-8 was impartial.

Morel let out a triumphant laugh, and rolled easily away from Upwright's telegraphed blow. He drew his own saber and assumed a fighting stance.

"*En garde*," he said.

Upwright moved in for a second slashing attack. He failed to connect. Fencing is, in fact, quite a bit harder than it looks, and unless one is a natural talent at it, one is likely to lose one's first—and therefore only—bout.

Really, it should have been one of the shortest matches in the history of people whacking at each other with swords. Morel should have made very quick and very bloody work of Upwright.

Instead, the duel went on for nearly an hour. This was not, despite what he might have told himself, because Morel was toying with his opponent. Savoring each easy parry and holding back from the final, fatal stroke simply for the fun of it.

No. Instead, what delayed the inevitable was that Morel's fencing days were years behind him. It was true he'd once been a fiend with a foil. That had been several thousand heavy, rich meals ago. That had been before he downed a cumulative ocean of breakfast champagne. Morel had been lithe and athletically built, back when he was establishing his reputation. In the years since his ascendancy, he had rather let himself go.

So when Upwright flailed at him like a boy waving a stick, he was just able to cross swords and step back. When Upwright tried to run him through with a wrong-footed lunge, Morel was hard-pressed to get his copious gut out of the way in time.

He did manage to nick Upwright's cheek. Upwright, on the other hand, managed to raise a pretty good weal on Morel's forearm. Before very long, however, both of them were puffing and huffing so much that they could barely lift their weapons.

"A villain ... like you," Upwright gasped, "can never ... defeat ... the will ... of the people!"

"Will?" Morel coughed. "Will is ... the strength of ... the paramount leader. The people ... know their master ... when they ... when ..."

He couldn't finish. The stitch in his side stole his breath. His feet hurt from standing so long. His head spun from lack of oxygen. He wondered if he might pass out, right there in the middle of the duel. It took him quite a while, in fact, to notice something rather important.

Upwright had dropped his sword.

The newcomer's arms hung low at his sides. His chest heaved for breath and his legs shook visibly. It looked like it was all he could do to keep from falling backward onto the rough soil of VZ-61a.

Morel had won. He merely needed to step forward—despite the pain in his knees—and deliver the *coup de grâce*.

Which would have been much easier if he had any feeling left in his own arms. Somehow he found the strength to bring his saber up and aim its wobbling point at Upwright's Adam's apple. Yes, just one thrust, and ... and ...

That was when he heard a mechanical whirring and the strident ringing of a bell. He touched the saber's point to Upwright's throat, much as someone interrupted while reading might place an index finger against the page to save their place.

He turned his head to look.

The first thing he saw was the barrel of an enormous firearm pointed directly at his head. The weapon was connected to a mechanical arm that emerged from a hatch in the torso of Martin-8.

The robot's glass eyes flashed. The ringing bell alarm came from its mouth.

"Wh … what?" Morel managed to say. "What's … this?"

"Orderz, zir. My orderz are to protect the two of you againzt all threatz."

"Threats. Including a fully sanctioned duel, between two consenting parties."

"All threatz, zir. My program iz clear."

"And if I kill this dog, here and now, as I could easily do—"

"I muzt prevent it, zir."

"And you'll prevent it by blowing my head off?" Morel asked. "You're saying, if I try to kill him, you'll take action to stop me—by killing me?"

"Yez, zir."

"So … I'll die, and he'll live? But that would mean—"

"Yez, zir."

"That would mean …"

Morel's heart skipped a beat.

"That would mean he would win."

Morel pulled his arm back, removing the point of his saber from Upwright's pulse. He looked down into the mirror-bright metal of the sword, and saw his own eyes staring back at him. Eyes enormous with madness.

He flung the saber away from himself, out into the sun-baked plain. It landed point down and quivered impotently there for a while, a flag of ultimate defeat.

"He would win. He would win!" Morel shrieked.

He grabbed two thick handfuls of his luxuriant hair and pulled. Luckily they were too carefully maintained to come loose.

He turned to face the robot.

"What," he demanded, "is the point of exile if you have to share it?"

The robot had no answer.

Morel, bellowing in rage, ran out across the plain, shaking his fists in the air. All too soon he was over the horizon, and his outrage had faded from earshot.

Eventually Upwright sat down in the shade of the thing that failed at being a tree and closed his eyes, intending to take a nap.

"What time should I expect lunch?" he asked.

WHILE YOU WAIT
FRAN WILDE

While you wait to see
what's going to happen,
I'll speak up, I always have.
Yes it gets me in trouble.
I'll speak louder this time
and louder still and you can
look down your nose at me
because that gives you
a sense of purpose
while you stay out of trouble.
I'll write louder. I'll go out.
I'll maybe get in trouble.
I'll probably get in trouble.
And you can sit there
talking about respect and decorum.
You always said not to wear
my heart on my sleeve,
that it would get me in
trouble,
and I did it anyway
and yes you were right, so
I'm putting my heart in my teeth
because it's safer there.
While you wait, I'll be out
with my heart and my mouth
both sleeves torn away.
Don't wait up.

CLAY AND SMOKELESS FIRE
SALADIN AHMED

QUMQAM STOOD UPSIDE-DOWN atop a cell phone tower, twirling at its pinnacle on his fingertip. When the humans had first started to besmirch the earth with the things, Qumqam had thought them hideous. But he'd come to love dancing on them the way he'd once loved dancing on ziggurats.

Well, he'd come to *like* it, anyway. Qumqam didn't know if there was anything left in this lower world that he *loved*, but sometimes when he leapt among the towers and turbines of America he felt something like happiness again. For a moment or two, at least.

It rarely lasted longer than that. For he was one of the last djinn left living in this interminable age of raised apes. The era of humankind, a nothing people, born from dirt when Qumqam's people were born from smokeless fire.

Qumqam floated lazily down from the tower, landing softly on his bare brown feet. Then he closed his swirling opal eyes and pictured a small red house not far away. A shimmer appeared around him, and when he opened his eyes he was floating above the house.

Some of the djinn enjoyed walking like men—the slowness of it. Qumqam had never been one of them. He had never understood why the flapping bags of flesh were first in God's eyes. They tore at each other like dogs at any chance. They starved each other to sit on piles of gold. Most unforgivably, they had taken this astonishing garden—this jagged half-paradise of leaf and ice and mountain and flower that God had made for them—and they had filled it with shit and poison.

These insults to God and His garden had grown worse of late, and worst here in America. Qumaqam had seen fool kings and robber-kings, mad kings and rape-kings. The new American king—*president*, they called it here—was all of them at once. And his merchants and armies were making a befouled realm even fouler.

No, Qumqam didn't much love this world anymore, and when a djinn stops loving this world he leaves it. Qumqam's people had been on Earth for God-alone-knew how many thousands of years. They did not die from blades or age the way men did. They could live until God declared the end of days on Earth.

But only if they wanted to. A djinn's life didn't come without fail the way the sun rose and fell. To live, a djinn needed reasons to keep living.

Strangely enough, one of the things that had kept Qumqam alive after so many of his friends had left this world was his interest in mankind. Well, in a handful of them. Most humans disgusted Qumqam—babbling creatures, whose repulsive meat threatened to smother the spark of life that God had given them.

But Qumqam had found that one in every hundred thousand thousand of them were different. One in every hundred thousand thousand could see him. Hear him. Speak to him. And, for perishable sacks of skin, they were fascinating. Qumqam had never been comfortable among his own kind, for the conversation of the djinn had always bored him. But humans? The ones worth talking to were a delight, if a bizarre one.

Such men and women had never been common but there had been more of them once. When he found them now, Qumqam was inclined to be protective of them. He stood now hovering above the house of just such a one, a child to whom Qumqam had not yet spoken. He had been watching this child and his mother in this house on this quiet, dead-scented American street for some weeks. He knew the signs and was certain the boy—Ernesto was his name—would soon discover his gift for djinn-talking. So Qumqam had watched the quiet life of this little red house, listening to birds and squirrels and the occasional voice of a neighbor.

But now Qumqam was watching something different. Something terrible.

Black wagons liveried with angry letters surrounded the boy's small red house. Men with weapons—the king's men, a dozen of them at least—buzzed in and out of its doors like angry insects. They were dressed in black and wore badges and flag patches.

Ernesto and his mother were both bound at the wrists. They were being led from the house. One of the armed men was on a cell phone, laughing. The boy was trying not to cry.

Men. This is what these people were. Filth that ate itself. Yet God had raised mankind above the djinn. Qumqam could never doubt the infinite wisdom of the Almighty. There was some high and powerful reason that God had favored the humans. But Qumqam couldn't see it.

Qumqam floated softly to the ground, and stood unseen and untouchable among the men with weapons. Once he might have taken a direct hand. He might have grown giant and smashed the wagons, or turned this new king— this new *president*, as they called kings in this land—and his army into pigs.

But that age was past. These days the djinn—the few of them still left—just watched and waited and once in a while whispered with the few men who could still hear them. If Ernesto had learned djinn-talking already, Qumqam might have tried to act through the boy. To fill him with power. He'd done it for a handful of men before, though not in many years. But it wouldn't work. The boy was uninitiated.

The men with weapons were pushing Ernesto and his mother toward a wagon when the woman next door—very old by the humans' way of counting things—came running out, followed by her son, a grown man.

Qumqam knew this woman, full of fire and hard to kill. She spoke and sang sometimes in the tongue of Solomon and David. The edges and tones of the words had pleased Qumqam, reminding him of other times and places. So many who spoke the older tongues had been dragged from America since this new king had come. Each time the old woman had spoken or sung the words Qumqam had perched near her, invisible, relishing the sounds and hoping she would continue. But it was never more than a few words, quietly, to herself.

She was not quiet now. She flew at the men, heedless of their weapons. "No! NO! What are you doing? These are good people, this is a mistake."

One of the men with weapons turned toward her patiently. "Ma'am, please step back."

"You're bullies is what you are. YOU LEAVE THESE PEOPLE ALONE! These are my neighbors!" She was still walking. Qumqam had to admire her, for her steps were not easy. The curse of aging flesh that God had placed on humankind—it had nearly taken this woman. But she strode up to the men like a soldier in youth.

Ernesto was crying now. One of the men was telling him to stop. They would not let his mother hold him.

One of the men put his black-gloved hand up in front of the old woman. "Ma'am, please. I really don't want to charge you." He held up a small black book.

"CHARGE ME!? GO AHEAD, CHARGE ME!" she shouted.

"MOM!" The woman's son barked, moving toward her.

"You want my name?" The old woman said to the armed man. "My name is Sylvia Fucking Reitzes. Write that down. Sylvia Fucking Lorraine Fucking R-E-I-T-Z-E-S. Write down that I said this was wrong. That somebody said *something*. Write that in your little fucking book!"

As she spoke, the old woman had managed to put herself between Ernesto and his mother and the wagon they were being herded toward. "These are good people," she said more calmly. "Graciela never did anything to anyone. You want to take them, you're going to have to beat up an old lady."

Qumqam blinked and reappeared right beside the woman. It was not often one saw the spark of God's light shine so brightly from within human flesh. He wanted to see it up close.

"Sylvia, no—" said Ernesto's mother.

The angry man grew angrier. "MA'AM!"

"Mom, are you crazy? Stay out of this. You don't know what's going on here." The old woman's son tried to step in, but the men held him back.

"WHAT'S GOING ON HERE?" she shouted, her moment of calm gone. "I know what's going on here. Something rotten. Something wrong!"

Qumqam saw the angry man's eyes make a decision. The man raised his weapon. He pointed it at the old woman. "MA'AM GET OUT OF THE WAY! NOW!"

And then, without warning, the old woman turned and looked Qumqam in the eye. She saw him. And she said, clear as the call of the muezzin in the night, "You! You can help. You have to help."

Qumqam felt as if he'd been struck. She could see him? But there was no time for hows and whys. He drew power from within his heart of smokeless fire and he clasped the old woman's hand.

Smoke-from-nowhere began to roil. The old woman rose bodily from the ground and the men froze. Lightning crackled around her and light filled her eyes. Qumqam floated beside her, unseen by the others, grasping her hand. He smiled. It had been too long since he'd done this.

"Mom?" Sylvia's son said faintly.

Then the bullets began to fly.

None of them reached her, of course. Their weapons crumbled to dust before her, and the men who tried to grab her were knocked back by winds born ten thousand years ago. Sylvia spoke and her voice was both hers and Qumqam's. A voice of cigarettes and gin and thunder and old mountains.

"GO," they said together, and the earth shook with the sound. "NOW."

The king's men stood there a moment more.

"GO!!!" Qumqam and Sylvia shouted as one. Purple lightning split the sky around them. The calls of wolves and owls filled the air.

The men with weapons screamed. Then they ran.

When they were gone, Qumqam released Sylvia's hand and they drifted gently to the ground together. Ernesto was staring at him openly now. Qumqam had never been seen by two humans in one day. It felt pleasant.

Sylvia turned to him. She did not marvel at what had just happened. She did not explain anything. She said, "They'll come back. What the hell do we do now?"

"Now?" Qumqam smiled and put his huge arm around Sylvia's bony shoulder. "Now we keep living."

THE ARC BENDS
KIERON GILLEN

I DIED, IN the hope I would get better. It seemed like a sensible thing to do.

It was the 21st century. Lots of things seemed to be the sensible thing to do, and so we did them. It's only common sense. Over the centuries, I've come to understand that this belief is one of humanity's more constant attributes, certainly more constant than any of the content of "common sense" itself. I'm sorry. I'm going to wax philosophical. This behavior was encouraged between then and now. I'm following my best, only legal advice.

As far as the early 21st century went, I knew I was lucky. I had a nationality (American), a career (accountancy, corporate), insurance (work based, surprisingly comprehensive), savings (some), property (house), a wife (short, enthusiastic, liked tropical fish, 1990s sitcoms, me), children (Child One who liked me, Child Two who hated me, Child Three who liked me. I felt that was pretty good going), etc. Unfortunately, I was born inside a human body whose faults include serious lower back pain, mysterious wax build-up in my left ear, and being a human body.

I remember seeing quizzes like, "What do you hate about your body?" and blinking when people answered things like, "My nose" or, "My wrists". The only answer which made any sense was, "A tendency to start to degrade from the late teens, slowly lose function and stop working entirely within one hundred years tops."

I just didn't understand. I didn't understand when my first pet died (cat, ginger, angry). I didn't understand when my first friend died (teenage car-crash, no drinking, deeply unfair). I didn't understand when my parents died (mercifully late, relatively painless). I didn't understand when I saw famines on the news or shootings in the streets (constantly). I just didn't understand. And I always thought two things simultaneously …

This shouldn't happen.

This shouldn't happen to me.

In short, my mid-life crisis started early, and kept on going. I had many weaknesses as a human, but you can't say I didn't commit. Eventually my perpetual mid-life crisis actually met my lucky mid-life, which meant I had some money to throw at the problem in hope it would just go away.

I sidestepped most of the well-worn, traditional methods. I didn't buy the latest model of car or try to date a young model or experiment with plastic surgery. I didn't leave my wife. I didn't go on a ludicrous health kick, though I continued to eat more kale than I'd have strictly speaking liked (a fact which I would come to regret).

I already had a gym membership. I decided to join another club, with a similar aim. Both promised a longer life. Their methodology varied. My gym believed that the aim would be achieved by having a twenty-something shout at me to lift metal objects up and down, while my other club leaned toward decapitating my head and lobbing it in a vat of liquid nitrogen.

It takes all sorts.

I'd read the literature. Scientific opinion was distinctly mixed. Some argued that revival would only work if the decapitation happened before you died, which would require euthanasia to be legal, which it wasn't where I came from. It was likely a waste of time, and people thought this was a lot of money to spend just to end up as a minty-fresh head-sicle. I didn't really care. A chance was all I was looking for.

Religious people don't really know if their afterlife of choice exists. Just the possibility makes the likelihood of absolute eternal non-existence a little more palatable. In the same way, the idea that I had a vat of liquid nitrogen of my very own was a comfort. It didn't matter if it likely wouldn't work. It might, and that hope was all I needed. Anyway: I was only still relatively young, life-expectancies were rising and who knew what new technologies would arise in the decades of happy life I had ahead of me?

"Look out for that car!"

"What car?"

Dead.

★

THIS IS WHAT resurrection is like.

One second you're not there. The next, you're there and you have this stream of sensory data which you desperately try to make sense of. From then on, it's a case of everything slowly coming into focus, shapes becoming objects, objects getting their nouns attached. The blur of light became a white flat surface became a pristine featureless wall. Between me and it, the small white blur became a flat horizontal surface supported by four thin columns, became a chair.

Wherever I was had both walls and chairs. I'd read about future shock, so was relieved that the fantastical future world I found myself in featured both walls and chairs, two things I was quite familiar with.

I tried to turn my head. I tried to breathe deeply, and failed. I screamed. An electronic voice emerged from a box beneath my throat. It was only slightly better than the text-to-voice on my twenty-first century computer. I would have guessed we'd have finally made progress in vaguely convincing computer voices by the time that we'd mastered resurrecting the dead, but I was a simple layperson. It was likely a good thing. If they'd prioritized reanimating the dead over not making computers sound like they're about to demand Earth surrenders to its cyborg legions, I could hardly complain. Also, if there was a position from which to complain, I couldn't get there, as I was a decapitated head.

If returning to life was less interesting than you'd hope, being a living head more than made up for it. I'd read about guillotine victims' heads blinking, or Mary Queen of Scots still mouthing the words of her prayers when her Catholic head was sliced from her Catholic body. I always thought that must be a uniquely strange experience, which my own experience swiftly confirmed.

Firstly, you're uniquely breathless. Literally, without breath. I could move my mouth and tongue, but the soft, constant ebb and flow of air is just gone. I hadn't realized how soothing the simple act of breathing was. It was as if I had my hair stroked my whole life, and suddenly it had stopped. I felt abandoned, betrayed by my body. I thought it would never leave me, yet here we are.

I'd read about phantom limbs. I had a phantom body. I could feel my whole self but a glance to the right showed I was mistaken—I was attached to a tall pillar, with no room for limbs, torso, or any of my usual fleshy accoutrements. It was like an awful, total sleep paralysis. I also had a headache. There's only one part of me left, and it ached. This felt most unfair of all.

In short: I would not recommend.

I was only briefly alone. A seam opened in the far wall, and through it stepped a tall person wearing black, which was slimming. When the person was already as tall and thin as they were, the effect was profound, as if a sentient traffic pole had walked in, their head a solemn sign whose specific meaning proved unreadable.

"John Garth?" they said.

I'm using "they" as I eventually better understood their dialect, that it's the best way to translate their preferred language into old English. It's not that their preferred pronoun is "they." It's that all pronouns are "they," with more specific pronouns used when more detail is required. You may think that this understanding suggests a happy ending, that everything turns out okay as me and future-humans become best friends. I would not make that assumption. Assume makes an ass out of you and me, and I had no ass, as I am a living head. Show some sensitivity.

In fact, their pronoun tree system seemed to make a lot of sense, and much more than my high-school French where I could never remember if a chair was male or female, or even understand why you'd need to know if a chair was male or female.

I was meeting my first ever future human and my first ever future human was looking at me in a way which implied I was far from the first past-human they'd ever met.

"Yes, I'm John Garth," I said, in a buzz of syllables. "Where is this? I thought they'd clone my body and—"

I stopped, realizing there was another question.

"What year is this?" I said.

They sat down on the chair, whose gender (not being a French chair) can remain a matter of speculation.

"Let's keep it to 'The future,'" they sighed.

"Tell me," I said, "Don't worry. I won't freak out. I can take it."

"Yes, you probably can," they said, "but I'm not telling you because I'm worried about you. I'm just not particularly interested in filling in the gaps for you."

This was the exact moment when I realized this future would not be all I had hoped for.

I ASKED ABOUT my family. They were dead. I was upset.

They were all good kids. Well, not all good-good, but I loved them. Now they were good and dead. Like my good, dead wife. You can assume a lot of distress happened, because it did.

The person was hard, but not unkind. They left me alone to weep, with me only able to imagine my now-gone body bent double in torture. Instead, my face wracked in spasms as I cried. After some time, the machine I was attached to started gurgling. I eventually realized it was replacing fluids in my body. The gurgle was neither a dramatic or sympathetic noise. In fact, it sounded like it was mocking me, a situation which only made me weep harder. After some time, I started feeling better, if somewhat disconnected. To make a disembodied head feel disconnected says a lot.

Eventually, the tall figure made their way back into the room, peeking their head around the door.

"Sorry that I had to hit with you with some sedatives, but I've got to see a lot of people," they said, "But you should know—your level of distress will definitely be in the plus column. It shows that you have sensitivity for people other than yourself. People like that. Some people will root for you."

I took a second to add this to my growing collection of things that were not entirely comforting.

"Who are you?" I said. "Are you a doctor?"

"Yes, but not in a relevant way. I'm a Doctor of Philosophy and Law," they said. "My name is Bobb. I'm your lawyer."

"But I haven't done anything wrong?"

They smiled in a way which made me suspect that while Bobb may be my lawyer, my lawyer was not entirely on my side.

"This is perhaps best made clear by a thought experiment," they said. "How do you feel about Hitler?"

"Not a fan," I said.

"I'm glad you agree," they said, flicking their eyes to the right. I only later realized this was them making notes in an internal UI. At the moment, I thought they had a twitch. You live, you learn, and then you die, and it turns out you learn some more. They leaned forward, as if speaking to a child. I was already feeling like one. It turns out that being a living head is deeply emasculating.

"Assume Hitler won and his Reich dominated world politics for his whole life. He's in his eighties, and eventually a cancer nasty enough to trump 1970s medicine turns up. They decide to try and preserve his body for future generations of Nazi scientists to have a crack at getting him back on his feet. Let's assume they find a way which leaves something that far future science can actually reanimate. And then one day, they bring back Hitler."

They paused. I resisted the urge to make a joke about Zombie Hitler. I assumed it would not be appreciated.

"Except since Hitler died, the world's changed. The democratic powers found a way to out-produce the fascists, and are now top dogs. A society that at least pays lip service to multiculturalism has got the man responsible for the deaths of millions of beings. What do you think happens?"

"They have a trial?" I say.

"Exactly," they said, "and they're glad that Hitler was dumb enough to deliver themselves into their hands."

They paused meaningfully, gesturing at me and my present predicament with great formality. They held the pose until I got what they meant.

"But I'm not Hitler!" I said.

"That remains to be seen," they said, sighing.

They performed another series of eye-twitches, the future equivalent of flicking through the tabs on your browser.

"That's the weird thing about you people," they said. "You all acted the way you did, voted for what you did, fucked up the planet, were complicit in the abuse of billions of lives and then expect the people who inherited the world you made to welcome you with open arms. It's like the drunk uncle who set fire to the house at Thanksgiving, turning up at Christmas and expecting to have a seat at the table."

"You still have Thanksgiving?" I asked, jumping on the clue.

"No, we don't," they said, "I'm just trained in your idioms and cultural signifiers."

Bobb got out a pen, and clicked it in and out. They held it above a paper, and made no note. The whole show was just to make me more comfortable. It really didn't work.

"Let's get this over with," they said.

★

IT TOOK A while. I started to do what any good 21st century American human would do in a similar situation. I complained, with every single tactic I could muster. Whining. Anger. Bargaining. More anger. A lot more whining. Indignant huffing. Asking to see the boss. Asking to leave. Asking to see the boss's boss. Nothing worked. Apparently this behavior is entirely normal. Later Bobb told me they were playing a Reanimation-Defense-Lawyer version of Bingo, ticking off my tactics as they came up.

"I have rights!" I said.

"You don't have rights," they said. "You died. You are legally dead."

"How can I be accused of crimes if I'm dead?"

"You're clearly a person, and a person with a history."

"Don't I have rights as a citizen?"

"You're not a citizen of this state," they said. "Even if you once were, now you are dead. You have no citizen rights. You are essentially a new being looking to join our society. We'll keep you in a cage until we work out what to do with you."

"You can't just keep me trapped for that," I said, before realizing exactly what I'd said.

A shamed silence.

"I was against that," I eventually managed.

"Good," said Bobb. "Did you do anything about that?"

"I wanted to call my representative," I said.

"Right," they said.

"And I retweeted a bunch of scathing jokes," I said.

"Right," they said.

"And I made disapproving noises when my wife's father went on a tear on Mexicans that Thanksgiving," I said.

"You'd get more credit for having an actual row rather than passive aggression, but it's better than just staring at your turkey and blueberry," they said.

"It's cranberry," I said.

"The records say blueberry," I said.

"The records are wrong," I said.

"You probably have minor brain damage. It's natural after such a long freeze," they said.

"You're messing with me now, right?"

"A little," they said. "Come on. I can trick you into answering the questions, but play along and it'll be much easier and it'll come across better. Let's start with some basic ones. No lies."

"I won't," I said.

"That wasn't to you. That was to the machines. You can only answer truthfully now."

I'd noticed a series of other lights had activated. I felt a tingle between the base of my spine and the nape of my neck, a distance considerably shorter than I had become used to in my whole-body years. An electronically stimulated truth-telling state. Now we're doing future science.

They took a deep breath, and I tried to do one and failed. We began.

"Did you recycle?"

"Yes."

"Did you pay your taxes?"

"Yes."

"Did you give to charity?"

"Yes."

"Was it—say—10% of your income?"

"Hell, no."

"How much did you minimize your tax exposure in legal ways which you actually consider unethical."

"Some."

"How often did you spread information from a new source you had any doubts about whatsoever as it mirrored your pre-existing beliefs."

"Wow, that's specific. How am I to know?"

"You know. Just answer."

"All the time. Who has time to check?"

"Right. How complicit were you with rape culture?"

"I never did anything to anyone."

"How often did you stop your friends making jokes that treated women as a punchline."

"Not enough."

"So … once again, how complicit were you with rape culture?"

"I was passively complicit."

"How did you vote?"

"I voted Democrat whenever I voted."

"How often did you vote?"

There was a pause.

"Is this question difficult or unclear?"

"I voted in the majority of elections," I said. "Sometimes I didn't see the point. The candidates all seemed the same and the polls seemed sure."

Bobb closed their eyes and breathed.

"Do you know what happened to the world after you died?"

"No. I was dead."

"And you're not going to get to know. But you just should know that that alone is enough to make you guilty. You have no idea how angry your descendants are at you."

"I'm really not as bad as Hitler," I said. I realized that as far as arguments go, this is both undeniable and weak.

"Yeah, you're not," Bobb sighed. "We do grade on a curve. But say ... let's say we dropped a 19th century slave owner in your society's lap. Let's make it easier—a slave owner who actively beat, abused and murdered his slaves. What would happen?"

"A trial like this?" I said.

"It wouldn't," they said. "You'd have half the country saying it was okay because it was legal then and who are we to judge?"

I tried to deny it and found I couldn't. I didn't agree with the argument. I couldn't say it. The computer had stopped me. I may have not been able to say it anyway. I got the point. Bobb sighed, and carried on.

"Did you eat kale?"

"I'm sorry?"

"Did you eat kale?"

"Yes, of course. All the time."

Bobb froze, mortified.

"What?" I said. "What's that supposed to mean?"

"If I took you outside and showed you the kale-derived gene-modded superforest that's filled the entire Pacific basin, torn down the east coast and is only kept even vaguely under control by an army of flamethrower-toting techno-barbarian special forces, you'd understand why kale-eaters aren't too popular nowadays," they said.

"That's just unfair," I said. "I had no idea. How could I have known that kale did that? You can't hold me responsible."

"It is a hard one, but when you lot may as well have been walking to the North Pole and manually applying heaters to the ice-face, a lot of people now don't really give you the benefit of the doubt."

I must have looked particularly depressed as Bobb took this moment to show a little sympathy. By now it was unexpected, though not as unexpected as my considerable kale consumption leading me to be pilloried by a future society.

"You have to understand—I am on your side. I don't think what they want to do to you is fair. That's why I'm in this job," they said, "but people are angry. We're tiny petri dishes of humans on this Satanic dish of a planet you cooked up. Many people don't care. They just want to get back at anyone they can get hold of, and here you are."

"What about our leaders?" I said. "They're worse than me. Hell, it's their fault. They should be punished, not me."

"Oh, don't worry." They smiled. "We got them."

I could imagine the cheering from my friends and the friends of Children One, Two and oddly not Three on Twitter. I may have said something sassy myself, but at this exact moment, it was just another reason to be depressed and fearful.

Bobb stood up, stretched, and started to head toward the near-imperceptible door. "That'll do for now. You're a relatively good person. Most people whose heads turn up are much richer, which normally means more complicit, and worse. Your family life will play well with the judges."

Good Dead Wife and Good Dead Children One, Two and Three to the rescue.

"What are my chances?"

"Low."

"How low? How many people have been found innocent?"

"None."

"That does seem low. So I have no chance?"

"Of course you have a chance. You can't predict the future from past events. That's basic empiricism. There's always a chance that it can be different next time, and you can't prove otherwise."

"That's just nonsense! If clever sophism is my only hope, you can't expect me to be optimistic."

"Perhaps, but it would be better for you if you were philosophical."

"I'll try," I said, and I did.

Child Two was the philosophical one. I should have listened more.

Bobb headed to the door, opened it, half stepped through, then looked back.

"The thing is, John, you know the Malcomb Luther King line about 'the arc of the moral universe is long, but it bends toward justice'?"

I nodded. Or rather, failed to nod. They got it anyway.

"You gave justice too much time to bend."

★

I HAD MY trial. It went poorly. They sentenced me to eternal torture in a simulated Hell.

Bobb accompanied me as I was rolled to the detention area. It was another white room, yet less luxuriant. Where before I had privacy, now I had company. It was full of heads of various ages (within a fairly broad range) and races (within a far narrower window). Wires were embedded deep in their foreheads, scabs sealed around the cabling. A technician moved lazily between each, checking and prodding. I was a little surprised at both the casual brutality and the low tech solution. All the heads who were sentenced had an entirely convincing hallucination induced in their actual brains. On the bright side, it'd feel as if I had my whole body back, with the major con that my body wouldn't be having a particularly nice time. This was not the tech rapture my old *Wired* magazines had promised me.

"I always thought they'd be uploading personalities into a computer simulation by now," I said. "If they wanted to do this, they'd make a computer copy of me and lob it onto a computer."

"We did consider it. Forget about how many angels can dance on a head of a pin—let's see how many sinners we can write to a hard-drive," said Bobb. "The problem is that while the tech's sort of there, people are generally against it. Especially for something like this, we prefer keeping the simulations running on wetware. As a culture, we never quite got past the philosophical question."

While then I dreaded more philosophy, I couldn't help but ask for elaboration.

"You know—all the continuity of consciousness questions," they said. "Is a copy of you actually you? We can't even be sure that a copy is functionally the same as you. Of course, same questions apply to your body. Every seven years every cell in your body is rejuvenated, so you're strictly speaking not even the same person after seven years. How can we justly punish someone for something they did seven years ago? It's the Argonaut's ship problem—if a ship has every timber replaced, how can we say it's the same ship?"

"Is it?"

"Thing is, we just do," they said. "It's commonly accepted, so they'd rather be punishing something everyone understands and basically agrees with rather than something some people will quibble over. At least, that's what people claim. I think it's nonsense. I've got another theory."

The technician pulled out a drill.

"I think people just like sticking electrodes in the still-living heads of their ancient enemies," said Bobb.

Human nature, eh? What's a guy to do?

★

HERE'S A NON-COMPLETE list of my social activities in Hell. Evisceration. Obliteration. Things involving cuticles. Things involving genitals. Things involving electrodes and genitals. Being given extra decorative sets of genitals, a punishment which was immediately curtailed when they realized I was quite enjoying it. Basically, it was if I was in a poorly stocked bar whose only ingredients were genitals, electrodes and blades, and you could have anything you wanted as long as it involved lobbing at least two of the three ingredients together and mixing them enthusiastically.

This proved many things, of which two seemed most prominent.

Firstly, people who are into the idea of Hell are desperately unimaginative.

Secondly, people who are into the idea of Hell are really mean.

★

LUCKILY, IN THE real world, time went by, opinions changed and people agreed with me on that.

One day, I found myself alive (which was a surprise) and also not in extreme pain (which was also a surprise) and not suffering extreme trauma from the experience (which was perhaps the biggest surprise of all). I could remember Hell, and everything that occurred, but it was less the most awful experience imaginable and more a mild annoyance, on par with that holiday to Portland when it rained every single day. I could imagine Good, Dead

Wife and me chewing it over wryly at the breakfast bar.

"Remember that time in Portland?" she'd say.

"Oh God. Just a week sitting in a coffee bar. That sucked," I'd say. "Did I ever tell you about the time I had my own nose pulled out via my anus?"

"No!" she'd say, passing me the granola. "That must have sucked."

"Yeah, it did," I'd say, and then I'd have thanked her for the granola and eaten it.

Things were different this time of being alive. I was not in a white room. I was in a pastel room and a shorter person with multi-colored hair piled up on their head, like a cross between Marie Antoinette and a three-year-old's crayon drawing of a multi-colored Spaghetti Monster.

"Ah, welcome back, John," they said. "Sorry to meddle with your mind without permission. Removing you from that torture simulation and leaving the negative memories would be simply inhumane. We've purged the memories of the negative connections so we can explain what's happening. Do you feel better?"

I did feel better, and was suitably grateful, and would be even more grateful to know what was going on. Having experienced the future twice, this was definitely my favorite so far.

"We have come to understand that the torture of beings from past times is simply inhumane, especially in a marginal case like yours. We cannot entirely blame a being for the society they find themselves born into and the context they exist in. The act that you experienced is not justice, but revenge, and simple revenge is wrong. Justice has to be natural. All reanimates must be treated appropriately, according to the contextual justice of their own times."

I didn't quite understand this, but if the logic seemed to end up with me not being in Hell, it was A-OK by me.

"So are you reanimating people from that era that threw me into Hell?"

"We are," they said, "and as we believe that the only real justice is to be judged according to the moral codes of their own time, we treat them accordingly."

"So what are you doing to them?"

"Oh, they did acts of unbelievable cruelty to people like you," they said, "so we're going to put them into a simulated Hell."

This seemed off to me.

"Doesn't that make you identical to them?" I said.

"No, because we don't want to do it," they said, a little annoyed. "We're completely different to them."

This seemed like an awfully big leap to make, but I didn't want to push the question, as I had more immediate and selfish worries.

"What's going to happen to me?" I asked.

"We apply the same rules," they explained, heading toward me, "You're a person in trouble. It seems by your admission you basically ignored people in need, so we're going to ignore you. And as you're only alive because of us, that means you have to die. I'm sorry."

"Wait! We had charities and some welfare and—"

"No, we've heard this one before," she said, cutting me off. "Bye!"

Then I died for a while, again.

★

THEN I WAS alive.

I had been dead for a long time (according to a calendar) or not a long time (according to my own perception). By this point I was rapidly becoming a veteran at this "being dead" thing. Let me tell you this; it's not the big deal I was worried about. It's literally nothing. With everything that had happened to me, particularly the Hell thing, I was beginning to feel like life's merits had been overstated, and death had a lot going for it. Don't knock it until you've tried it.

Bobb would have been proud. I was becoming philosophical.

Unfortunately, as I was coming to see my own death's up side, the world had come to disagree. My life was fascinating! While I'd been away and dead, it had been decided that all humans had merit, so should be spared any artificial hells—which was good news for Bobb, and for those who tortured people like Bobb and me, I'm sure. However, to be resurrected resulted in a huge debt to the society that revived us. We needed to pay back what we owed to our saviors. I was unsure what use a decapitated accountant would be to this world, but it seems I was a font of useful information.

I was a keyhole into the mythologized death-days of the 21st century, and the fabled golden age of television. I would earn my existence by providing invaluable primary evidence and help in reconstructing lost texts. I disagreed, but I didn't really have a choice. I was put in a liberal arts professor's office, trying to recall episodes of *Brooklyn Nine-Nine* and occasionally plopped down in front of students to talk about my favorite memes.

I won't say it's Hell. When you've been to even a fairly hacky Hell, you learn not to compare it to anything else—but an eternity explaining to bored undergraduates why we thought it was a big deal whether a dress was blue or gold wasn't exactly what I was hoping for.

Anyway, it wasn't an eternity, and eventually they decided me being alive was a bad idea, and I was dead again.

★

AND THEN I was alive, as people had changed their minds again.

This lot agreed that I should have a body (which was good news) but unfortunately society was collapsing technologically, so they were no longer able to perform the feat (which was bad news). They were only able to revive me due to this pre-existing machinery they were experimenting with, in hope of saving the human race from the awful fate they'd brought upon themselves. While they'd got useful data from my resurrection, they didn't really have the power to keep me on perpetually, so they'd have to turn me off. But when they sorted everything out, they'll definitely bring me back. They seemed very apologetic. I liked them.

"Thanks for the help," they said.

"Thanks," I said. "Good Luck!"

They did not have good luck.

★

I WAS MADE alive a few more times along the way, by increasingly shaggy, increasingly desperate people. Civilization was not going well, but it was always good to catch up.

And then I was dead for a really long time, and now I'm speaking to you.

That cute bewildered look you're sporting makes me suspect you've turned me on entirely by accident. Please don't worship me as a god. That would be awful.

What to make of you? You clearly don't have any idea what I am. You're not speaking a language I understand. You're looking around and prodding things, somewhat carefully, which shows an impressive amount of sense for cave people.

I think it's been a long time, and you're the humanity that crawled from the rubble. Hell, maybe it's been long enough for the planet to clean up after us. That would mean you get as clean a start as any of us get. Destroying the planet was never going to happen. Turns out we couldn't even destroy ourselves. The species is having a second shot. Good work. I'm rooting for you.

I know you can't understand me, but one day you may. After all, everything you need to make sense of me is lying around here. It's possibly even recording, which means there's a risk that you'll take anything I say as holy scripture. Oh God. That would be worse than you thinking I'm a god.

Oh.

I'm not sure if the lights are dimming or my sight is. It's probably both.

Ah, I'm running on the last dregs of the future-batteries before they splutter out and I do too. For the last time, I guess. No power for the support system means this head slowly rotting on a plinth, and no further comebacks.

Sorry. I didn't mean to scream. It just hit me. I was so calm before about death, but it seems panic is making a last minute return. Repeated experience doesn't make everything falling away any more pleasant. This is horrible.

Help me take my mind away from the abyss. Dying words. I'll give it a shot, and hope I can make them count.

Humanity Version Two, try this:

I have been alive, if not for a long time, certainly across a long period. I have been dead many times. I have seen this dumb species from all sorts of angles, even though most of those angles have been limited to whatever stationary position people left me in.

Bobb told me the arc bent toward justice. I think they misunderstood.

The only truth I've learned is that the arc bends whatever way we damn choose.

Bend it! Bend it good and hard!

That's all I've got. Be careful. Look after each other. It's getting dark now.

THE BLAST
HUGH HOWEY

EVERY TIME A blast goes off, people see the truth.

It gives Aiya chills to think about what will happen today, when her brother pulls that trigger and another blast rocks the city. That he won't be able to see it himself is not contemplated. That this will likely be the last time she walks by his side is not contemplated. All she can think about, all that consumes her, is the maelstrom to come.

Her brother Fariq is nineteen—three years older than her and a head taller. Aiya long ago learned how to trot by his side, in his shadow, little skipping leaps for every powerful stride from his long legs. He was their parents' sun, their star, the eldest, the *one*. She was the alqamar, the moon, his nickname for her. Today was his day. But tomorrow? What is the moon without the sun?

The capital—where she and her brother were born and raised—crackled with morning energy: the whiff of cooking meat, women with bundles of cloth and baskets of vegetables, men wrestling stubborn goats, the throaty rattle of tired cars choking on old gasoline, the bray and clop of horses as wooden cart wheels carved scars into desert streets. An army-green pack of the Minister's soldiers watched Fariq and Aiya pass, frowns lurking under mustaches, every head swiveling their way with the finely honed distrust of youth. It was not misplaced, Aiya thought to herself. They were up to no good.

"Forget them," Fariq said. "There is nothing on us but our thoughts."

"Those are bad enough," Aiya whispered.

She recognized one of the soldiers, Ruq, a friend of her brother's from school days. Now Ruq wore the green of the Ministry. Now Ruq saluted posters. A month ago, there had been a blast, and soldiers like these had fired into crowds. Had Ruq fired the gun he cradled now like a child? *Children cradling children*, Aiya thought. Oh yes, they would fill her with bullets for all that she carried silently in her head.

"This way," Fariq hissed. He turned into the market, where the jostling of shoppers squeezed like a fist between the alley of stalls. Here, Aiya could keep up. She twisted and turned through the crowd, keeping an eye on her brother, turning obstacles into games. She could move through a sea of people like a fish can glide upstream. She was waiting on her brother on the far side of the market, tapping her foot and crossing her arms as if she'd been waiting since dawn.

Her brother marched by without word. No sass. No playful pop to her head. Nerves, Aiya realized. Her great brother was nervous. Of course he was. She hurried after him, admonishing herself for games, remembering what was at stake, following along at a trot as she and her brother zigged and zagged and circled back on their path, making sure they weren't followed, before ducking into the cobbler's house, down into the hidden basement, where all the bombs were built.

★

THE COBBLER LOWERED the hatch that kept the basement hidden from soldiers. Aiya heard the flop of a heavy rug above her head, the rain of dust from old beams drifting down. Her eyes adjusted to the darkness. There were whispers ahead, another door to fumble through, and then the glow of a single bulb swinging from its wire, shadows moving about nervously, while the cobbler's wife bent over her latest creation.

The rest of their small cell of freedom fighters was already there. They waited with barely concealed impatience. Several had their cell phones out, faces underlit by small screens that used to provide access to the outside world, back before the Ministry shut down access to search engines, social media, and all the rest. They stashed their phones away now that the star of the hour was here. A round of hugs, kisses to both cheeks, sweat-salt on Aiya's lips, the stubble of boys turning to men, all eyes on her brother.

"Is it ready?" Fariq asked.

Maru turned from her work. She had a lens over one eye, which made that eye seem twice the size of the other. There was a screwdriver in one hand, impossibly small. When she spoke, only one half of her mouth moved. The other half held something invisibly small, probably a tiny screw or a piece of wire. "Are *you* ready?" she asked.

Fariq nodded. Several of the other boys shifted their weight around, perhaps eager for their turn, for the long straw. And now Aiya could see the nerves that jangled her brother. The back of his shirt was spotted with sweat, even though the morning was cool. His hands were clenched into white-knuckled fists. His shoulders stood by his ears. All the little things Aiya had been trained to spot in their enemies, to know when they were scared, she was seeing in her brother for the first time. Suddenly, she needed to pee. Suddenly, the weight of the day pressed down on her.

"Are you sure?" Maru asked. She lifted the magnifying lens and peered at Fariq. "You know what's at stake, boy?"

Fariq nodded, and Aiya noticed her brother was looking past the old woman to the device on the table. A series of devices, really. A tangle of wires and heavy cylinders.

"I'm ready," he said.

"Then let's get you suited up."

★

THE CYLINDERS WENT around Fariq's waist. Webbing and heavy-duty velcro and cinched knots. Then the wires and switches. Over it all, the special coat to keep the device hidden. Maru gave careful instructions, but Fariq did not appear to be listening. No matter, both siblings had heard the spiel before. They'd watched friends prepare. They'd been like the others in their small cell, shifting their weight from foot to foot. They knew the drill.

"—you will be shot."

These last words cut through, and somehow Aiya's brain pieced together what she'd missed, the words just prior. "Do not get caught before you reach your objective, or you will be shot."

Death. That's what waited this day. Death in the shadows. Death in the market. Death in the stalls. Death running through the streets, tapping strangers on the shoulders, who fall like puppets with cut strings. A blast goes off. Soldiers open fire. Bullets ripple through crowds to switch off people like the devices of yore. Switch them off before they can think. Before they can speak. Before they can know.

A city of people who know how to read, but the only thing with words anymore are these big screens that flicker with messages from the Ministry, demanding trust. As if that's how trust works. A city built on older cities, where language and numbers were invented, and now those in charge say to trust only the words from the great Leader. A city with a history of learning and radiating truth outwards, now walled off from the rest of the world and drowning in lies.

Fariq pulled the coat tight around his bulging waist. His face was a sheen of sweat. Those gathered in the basement broke into prayer, thanking Fariq for his courage. The anointed hour was approaching fast—the square and the market would be packed on this holy day, this holiday the Ministry had decreed for its own celebration. A day to gather 'round and tell the Leader how magnificent he was. More statues to erect. More giant screens to hang all full of propaganda. The only things that got done these days. The rest of the world a dark, dark mystery.

The day was warmer now. Just a half hour later, but deserts both burn and cool with hardly a notice. Aiya took point for her brother, leading him through the crowd, watching for soldiers so that he only had to follow. She was his second this day, his moon. An honor and burden. And in her mind, she thought of all those who would be affected by their actions in mere moments, all the attention they would divert, and it was no longer hypothetical, no longer a dream to conjure lying in bed at night, but real, and *now*, and terrifying—

A hand on her shoulder pulled her to a halt, a strong grip. She started to twist to defend herself, to fight off someone in green fatigues, but it was her brother.

"I can't," he said.

His eyes darted about. Aiya turned and tried to follow his gaze, but he wasn't looking at anything. Studying him again, she saw that he was pale, a sheen of sweat on his face, a tremble of cheek just below one eye. She pulled him aside, out of the flow of people leaving the market with their hauls of vegetables and bolts of cloth. There was a dark alcove between two sandstone buildings. She and her brother huddled together in the cool deep shadows.

"You *can't*?" Aiya hissed.

"I'm sorry," he said, shaking his head. "Go. Get away. I've shamed us both."

Aiya could not process this. None of the outcomes of this day included her brother not pulling that trigger. The idea that he might live, that he would never be in harm's way, barely dented her awareness. All she could think were the millions of people *expecting* him to do this, *waiting* on him to do this, *needing* him to do this.

"Give it to me," she heard herself saying. And somehow, the words made her feel two inches taller. Or perhaps her brother was sagging. Even in the darkness, she could see his eyes burn as she spoke. "Give it to me," she said again, sounding almost like their mother. "Fariq, I can do this."

And perhaps the greatest sign of his fear was that he complied without a word. That the coat shrugged off his slumping shoulders, that he turned so she could reach the buckles on his back, that he numbly helped her into the belt, cinching it tight, readying her in the darkness, strapping on a bomb that would soon bring terrible amounts of light.

★

AIYA MOVED THROUGH the crowd the way a snake crosses sand, a silent slithering, a seeming stillness, the graceful weave of purpose and surety.

This is how religions grow, she thought to herself. With the fervor she now felt in her bones, the power given to those who feel weak, the conviction granted to those who live in times of doubt. She knew her country was great. Not just in the past, but deep in its bones, in the marrow of its people, in the ingenuity of its youth and the stores of its resources. They would tap these wells again. Leaders fall. Regimes die. The public rises up. They just have to *know*. They have to be *woken*.

She was ready to wake them.

In the central square, she could feel the pulse of the people waiting, waiting for this, for their deliverance. They huddled in tight groups. There was the din of a thousand voices, all vying to speak and be heard. Aiya pressed through the gaps, avoiding two guards here, a dozen soldiers there, straight to the heart of the square, the anointed time ticking down, her heart beating like a tightly wound clock.

The cylinders dug into her hips. The coat was heavy and too large. They would know in an instant it was her. They would know when all the cameras pointing into the square were checked and double-checked, when the blast was triangulated. They would see it was her. This was her last thought before reaching for the trigger, the thought of all those who would find out. Their parents, who had no idea. Her friends, who would be amazed. Her brother, who would live in shame. Her poor brother, the moon.

Aiya squeezed into a group of students, let them press in all around her, and she flipped the safety off the switch and squeezed the trigger. There was a click, a faint hum, a feeling like heat around her—but maybe it was imagined, maybe it was the bodies against her, or the coat, or the press of the moment. And across the crowd, the shockwave radiated outward. It could be seen by the glowing screens, by the deafening hush, by the hiss of whispers that followed. A thousand palms glowed bright. Fingers danced. Waves soared down from space, and through Aiya, and were pushed out by wires and who knew what else, powered by the heavy batteries around her waist, and for a moment her small world was connected to the rest of the world. No fence was high enough. No wall could stop her.

Shots rang out. Bullets were fired into the sky. Speakers blared commands to go home, for whoever it was to shut down their transmission, for nobody to move, to both disperse and stay still, the panic of those in charge who know they are not fit to rule.

Aiya moved with the crowd of students; she huddled over and scurried with them. The girl next to her was crying. Aiya heard her squeal into her phone, "Mom? Mom it's me!" One of the many who were waiting for the hour, waiting for the blast. Another boy was watching his phone. Aiya caught a glimpse of the screen. Hundreds of emails and messages going out into the ether, pre-written and queued up for this day. Little blue bars of hope counted toward 100%.

The boy tucked the phone away to help up someone who had fallen. Aiya was swept this way and that. She prayed no one would be shot. She knew the soldiers would be flying their drones now, trying to pinpoint her. She knew they would try to jam the signal again. She also knew the cobbler's wife was smarter than all of them put together, that frequencies would hop and slither the way Aiya could move through a crowd. She could feel truth and connection radiating out from her back, pulling on the juice from her batteries, a bright thread linking her glorious homeland to the rest of the world, praying it was enough to tug them along through these darkest of times.

"She's right here," someone said. Aiya feared it was a soldier, that her blast would be over so quick, but it was one of the students. She felt strong hands on her again, holding her up this time, helping her along. More bodies pressed in around her. "The old university," someone said. It was on a hill. Lots of people gathered around its abandoned halls. The hope was to spread the signal as far as possible for as long as possible. Give everyone a chance. A taste. Aiya felt herself swept up with the crowd. Now it was not just her transmitting, it was all of them. A web. She was just the hub.

Gunfire behind them. The buzz of drones. Some people scattered. Some sat with their backs to the base of all those statues, their Leader looking to the heavens while his people sat and got word of the rest of the world, sent news out about their plight, traded messages and plans, traded codes on where and when to meet next, how to disrupt, how to help, how to get what was needed where.

They reached the university as the drones and the gunfire drew closer. Aiya looked at the time on someone's phone. An hour! How was that possible? And so many city blocks covered. A blast for the ages. She checked the light on the switch and saw it flashing red like her heart. Almost out. Almost done. A full charge. She had slipped through like a snake across the dune. Looking around at the students who had joined her, she saw their expectant faces, their wide eyes, the look of admiration. When had a blast gone so well?

Gunfire, this time not into the sky. A boy shrieked in pain. There were drones directly overhead, buzzing and blasting them with the downforce of air. Students threw rocks at them. Another protester was shot. Someone grabbed Aiya from behind and started to rip her coat off, tear the device from her. She waited for the knife between her ribs, the bullet to her neck. The rip of velcro. A weight off. "Go," her brother shouted.

Aiya turned and saw him cradling the device. The coat was at his feet. He held a tangle of wires and batteries and antenna. Another round of gunfire. People dropping. Some bleeding, some covering their heads. And all around, the surreal calm of those still connected, still sipping on truth, or trying to bring down a drone or get in the way of a soldier without getting killed.

The boy who had sent all the emails and messages pulled Aiya away, even as she tried to swim toward her brother. The drones were like flies now, casting shade. They dove in, and the soldiers pressed from all sides, and Aiya and the others barely slipped through. Her last glimpse of her brother was of him crouching by the base of a statue, the great Leader looking to the heavens, toward satellites and airwaves and all that would be his downfall. Shots rang out, the birds all across the statue scattered in a flock of panic, and Aiya saw on their great Leader's stone face white tears of worry.

EXCERPTS FROM THE RECORDS
CHET WILLIAMSON

EXCERPTS FROM THE RECORDS OF THE NEW ZODIAC
AND THE DIARIES OF HENRY WATSON FAIRFAX

(Note: The Zodiac was a New York City dining club established in 1868, and consisted of twelve gentlemen active in New York society. At least two volumes of the collected minutes of the meetings were privately published.)

SEPTEMBER 18TH, 20——:

BEFORE I RETIRED LAST NIGHT, I read a column which suggested that many of the outrages perpetrated by both children and adults might be due to the lack of civility in society. I cannot help but agree.

The final decades of the previous century witnessed a dreadful decline in civility, and this new century promises to be no more refined. We are on every side beset by adversarial imagery. The media poses everything in terms of battles, wars, and combat, and I find myself falling into this modern-day vernacular.

I recall (with chagrin) speaking before the board of our computer company just yesterday, and telling them that we should not rest until we have thoroughly crushed Tom Chambers' company, which is all that stands between us and a virtual legal monopoly on network servers. I described our position quite accurately, as "outnumbered and outgunned," but suggested that sheer courage and resourcefulness could yet win the war, though I would also be willing to shift some cash from other Fairfax corporations into the fray. I went on to demonize Chambers as the head of an evil empire who would be content with nothing less than total domination of the world's computers.

Although that representation is certainly true, I am ashamed of my martial hyperbole, and my forebears would be ashamed of me as well. For a hundred and fifty years the Fairfaxes have conducted their many enterprises with restraint and even temper, and I feel the ghostly censure of my father, my grandfather, and my great-grandfather for betraying that tradition.

Therefore, in order to assuage my guilt, I plan to institute—or rather, reinstate—a tradition which, I believe, has long been neglected and which will, I trust, add a touch of civility and goodwill to the practices of at least a dozen businessmen, myself and my most powerful competitors among them ... .

CONSTITUTION

Article I. This Club shall be known as the New Zodiac, modeled after the original Zodiac dining club founded in 1868.

Article II. It shall be made up of twelve members, or *Signs*, who shall be addressed by the zodiacal sign assigned to them by lot.

Article III. The New Zodiac shall meet for dinner on the final Saturday evening of every month, the place to be selected by that month's host, or *caterer*, who shall make all arrangements for the dinner, the cost of which shall be equally shared by the Signs. The cost of wines and spirits shall be borne by the caterer.

CHARTER MEMBERS
Aquarius: Mr Frank Reynolds
Pisces: Mr Todd Arnold
Aries: Mr Jeff Condelli
Taurus: Mr Richard Rank
Gemini: Mr Thomas Chambers
Cancer: Mr Edward Devore
Leo: Mr John Thornton
Virgo: Mr Clark Taylor
Libra: Mr Bruce Levine
Scorpio: Mr Cary Black
Sagittarius: Mr David Walsh
Capricorn: Mr Henry Fairfax

NOVEMBER 25TH:
I fear that I may have made a mistake in selecting the charter members of the

New Zodiac. Only Ed Devore and John Thornton come, like myself, from old money, while the rest are all nouveau. *The strength of the original Zodiac may have come from the fact that the Signs were all members of New York society in a time when society meant something. Through its history, the Zodiac boasted both J. P. Morgans, Senior and Junior, the Revd Henry Van Dyke, Joseph H. Coate and John William Davis, both Ambassadors to the Court of St James, Senator Nelson W. Aldrich, and other wealthy and powerful, and, above all,* dignified, *men who knew the importance of civility. In my effort to make the club more democratic, I simply selected the wealthiest and most powerful men, hoping to bring civility to those who most needed it, myself included.*

But the first meeting was not as I had anticipated, even though I tried to recreate as best I could the original menu served at the very first dinner of the original Zodiac on February 29th, 1868 ...

Minutes of the First Meeting of the New Zodiac
THE HOUGHTON CLUB, NEW YORK
NOVEMBER 24TH 20—
Present at table: All signs. Capricorn, caterer.

MENU:
Oysters   Selle de mouton
Potage à la Bagration   Haricots vert
Bouchées à la Reine   Salade—laitue—fromage
Terrapin à la Maryland   Poudin glacé
Suprême de volaille   Gâteau
Asperges   Fruits
Roman punch   Café

WINES:
Krug 1982
Lafitte 1969
Chambertin 1947
Old brandy vintage 1895

It was moved by Brother Gemini to make Brother Capricorn, the member who initiated this series of dinners, the Secretary of the New Zodiac. A unanimous voice vote followed, after which Bro. Gemini observed that

---

perhaps the extra work would keep Bro. Capricorn so busy that he would find no time "to f— over my business." Much pleasant laughter followed, and Bro. Capricorn accepted his new post.

Dinner seemed to be received well, although Bro. Aries had to be reminded that fruit was not to be thrown at his fellow Signs. "We are, after all," said Bro. Capricorn, "the New Zodiac and not the Drones' Club."

"What the hell's the Drones' Club?" Bro. Aries asked, and when informed stated that he had never heard of P. G. Wodehouse. "F— this Woodhead, whoever he is," he said, and tossed a strawberry, which hit Bro. Capricorn in the left eye, to the merriment of the company.

When the party was asked who would volunteer to cater the following month's dinner, Bro. Gemini offered to do so, upon receiving assurances in the form of each Sign's solemn word that whatever went on at the dinners would remain confidential. Bro. Gemini then made a vow of his own, that he would serve the Signs a feast at the next dinner, "like no billionaire has ever tasted before, but which we all f—ing well deserve. It'll make what we had tonight seem like sh—t in comparison—as far as scarcity goes, anyway."

Bro. Gemini then inquired of Bro. Capricorn if he might borrow the two volumes of the original *Records of the Zodiac*, which he wished to consult for further menu ideas, and Bro. Capricorn happily agreed.

The evening was concluded by the relating of several humorous stories by Bros. Taurus, Libra, and Cancer concerning African-Americans, and some ribald anecdotes told by Bros. Virgo and Sagittarius about women who have worked under them.

Adjourned.

Capricorn, *Secretary*

... Most of them seemed to be Philistines, but I confess that I was not surprised to find Ed Devore joining in with the ethnic jokes. He's long had a prejudice against blacks, all the more so since his company was barred from doing any more business in South Africa, after nearly a century of high profits there. And though John Thornton didn't make a fool of himself as most of the others did, he seemed ready to join in at the slightest provocation, and I expect him to be equally frivolous at the next dinner.

At least they all seemed to be civil to each other, which is a start. And Condelli didn't throw any more food after my reprimand, except of course for the face-saving strawberry to show that my billions held no greater sway than his.

Perhaps they will calm down in time. And perhaps Chambers' attention to the dinner he's catering will help to take his eye off his business long enough for us to make further inroads into his market share. I wonder, though, just what it is that he's planning to serve ... .

Second Meeting

THE MEDIA MANSE, PORTLAND, OREGON
DECEMBER 29TH, 20—
Present at table: All Signs. Gemini, caterer.

MENU
Sea Tag oysters   Soufflé aux épinards
Potage crème d'orge régence   Pommes Mont d'Or
Timbale de crab   Medaillon de foie gras
Cubicle Steak à la Pompadour   Salade Arlesienne
Champion de Virginie, sauce champage   Asperges, sauce Hollandaise
Omelette Norvégienne

WINES:
Convent sherry 1894
Moët-Chandon 1969
Château Latour 1957
Musigny 1954
Hôtel de Paris
Blue Pipe Madeira
Holmes Rainwater Madeira 1879
Cognac Napoleon 1890

The sumptuous meal was a near-complete recreation, Brother Gemini so informed us, of a dinner put together in 1925 by J. P. Morgan Jr., the differences being the years of the vintages and the meat utilized in two of the entrées, of which he would say more later.

In further emulation of J. P. Morgan's magnanimity, Bro. Gemini presented the Signs with a linen tablecloth woven in Venice upon which were embossed all the signs of the zodiac, similar to the one Morgan had given to the original Zodiac.

As superb as was the meal (and its setting—Bro. Gemini's newly completed mansion that overlooks the Pacific), even more extraordinary were the wines and spirits. It was not until everyone had made their way through every vintage and was well fortified with the extraordinary Cognac that Bro. Gemini revealed to us the secret ingredient of the Cubicle Steak à la Pompadour and the Champion de Virginie, sauce champagne. Morgan Jr. had originally served Cotelettes de pigeonnaux à la Pompadour and Jambon de Virginie, and all the Signs were curious as to with what meats Bro. Gemini had improved the recipes.

He informed us in a manner true to his personal style, transforming the dining room into a multimedia presentation area with a few spoken words. Screens dropped into place in response to the voice recognition technology, the room darkened, and Bro. Gemini then told us that although he would bear the cost of the wines and spirits, which amounted to well over a quarter million dollars (a bargain, he claimed, considering the short time in which his staff had to gather them), the shared cost of the dinner itself amounted to eight hundred and fifty thousand dollars each.

At the gasp from the Signs, Bro. Gemini inquired of Bro. Capricorn the cost of the previous dinner, which he had solely borne, and was told the amount was seventeen thousand dollars, not including the wines. Bro. Gemini admitted that there was quite a difference between seventeen thousand dollars and over ten million, but that his fellow Signs would understand when they realized just what it was of which they had partaken.

The presentation began then, a combination of video and still photography that showed in detail the process of harvesting the meat, with sections entitled "On the Hoof," "Making the Purchase," "The Butchering Process," and finally, "In the Kitchen." Much of the material was more graphic than several of the Signs cared to see, your secretary included, and Bro. Cancer and Bro. Libra wasted both the meal and the wines by disgorging the entire contents of their stomachs into thoughtfully provided plastic-lined silk bags.

Still, no one left their seats, and at the end of the presentation, Bro. Gemini gave an eloquent defense and rationale for his menu selections, by the end of which nearly all the Signs were in agreement with him, and checks for each Sign's share were promised.

Bro. Aries was named the caterer for the next dinner, and assured his brother Signs that he would continue in the tradition established by Bro. Gemini.

Adjourned.

Capricorn, *Secretary*

... Cubicle steak. Ed Devore and John Thornton, my old friends, actually laughed at the ghastly pun. Perhaps New England inbreeding has softened their brains so that they can find such a thing funny. Although Devore vomited at first, along with Levine, I think it was because of the graphic elements of the presentation rather than the knowledge of what they had ingested. They probably would have gotten sick at the sight of a steer being butchered, let alone a human being.

Cubicle Steak and Champion de Virginie, Chambers' dreadful wordplay. Champion for Jambon, and it happens that Kevin Dupree, a purchasing agent in Chambers' company, was indeed the Virginia state spelling bee champion when he was in middle school, as his projected résumé told us.

And what awful detail Chambers went into to carry out his parallels to the raising and purchasing of stock. We saw footage of Dupree 'on the hoof', both at his job and with his family; we saw the chilling purchase, Chambers himself offering the man ten million dollars for his family if he would vanish forever; then Dupree's slow breaking down as the realization dawned that he was Chambers' body and soul, and that if he refused he and his family would be ruined, both financially and in other ways that only a man with a vast fortune might accomplish.

The butchering itself was numbing, nearly as deadening to me as it must have been to poor Dupree; then seeing the meat cooked and prepared for serving, and most coldhearted of all, seeing us eating it in footage that had been shot by hidden cameras only an hour before and then assembled by Chambers' flunkies.

By the end, some Signs looked sick, some merely uncomfortable, and some were smiling as though they were boys who had been caught stealing candy. But when Chambers began to speak, their faces changed. Though the man can be as coarse as a line worker, he can be as eloquently silver-tongued as the devil when required. He talked about the twelve of us as the true leaders of the country, the new lords of the world, and how our employees, from the humblest we never see to the executives who work closely with us, are all commodities, material to be bought and sold and used as needed. 'Our intelligence and foresight and energy have given us the power,' he said, 'to enrich them or impoverish them ... or devour them, if we will it.'

And God help me, I could not tell the others that he was wrong. He had already proven himself right. He has seduced them, my friends along with my competitors. I could see their minds churning, thinking of how they might top Chambers' feast. Condelli is next month's caterer, and he seemed thrilled beyond measure at the prospect.

My desire to spread civility has set something quite the opposite into motion, and I do not see how I can stop it. Honor compels me to remain silent, but also to end what I have unwillingly begun. I would do so immediately, but if that is not possible, I have nearly a year until it is once again my turn to serve as caterer, and many things can happen in a year ... .

Third Meeting

THE HAVENS, BALTIMORE, MARYLAND
JANUARY 26TH 20—
Present at table: All Signs. Aries, caterer.

MENU:
*Minestrone   Small eggplant
Roast leg of Philip Lamb,
mint sauce ...*

JANUARY 27TH:
... Lamb was Condelli's Director of European Operations. At first I thought it possible that he simply might have contributed his leg and survived, since the cost was far less than for Chambers' dinner, but my investigations show that Philip Lamb has disappeared.

Such an act boldly throws down the gauntlet for the other Signs. Lamb had been quite important to the success of Condelli's overseas ventures. It was as though Condelli was saying that anyone can lose an anonymous office drone, but he was willing to make a real *sacrifice ... .*

Fourth Meeting

DOUBLE R RANCH, DALLAS, TEXAS
FEBRUARY 23RD, 20—
Present at table: All Signs. Taurus, caterer.

MENU:
*Shysters Rockefeller   Hot wings
Double R Chili with beaners   Texas fries
Bar-B-Q Veep ...*

FEBRUARY 24TH:

... bad enough that Rank would discard his two top drilling men from his Mexican offshore rigs, but to further weaken himself by barbecuing his distribution Vice President for that terrible beef/veep pun was utterly foolish. But far worse was his disposal of his entire legal team as a mere appetizer. Of course, he'll put together another, but still it seems insane ... .

Fifth Meeting

THE DEVORE HOUSE, BOSTON, MA
MARCH 30TH, 20—
Present at table: All Signs. Cancer, caterer

MENU:
Caviar   Dinde sauvage rôtie
Potage velouté Chantilly   Parie aux marrons
Roast breast of Mindy, sauce Nautun   Gelée d'Airelles

MARCH 31ST:

... a return to fine dining after Rank's reprehensible Texas barbecue. But Devore has taken the whole thing to a new plateau—or an even lower depth. Perhaps he felt the only way to top Rank was to make more than just a business sacrifice. I have no doubt that he loved Mindy. She had been his mistress for seven years. Psychologically, a loss like that can be far more devastating to a man and his business than the loss of personnel alone can be, and I could see that Devore was feeling the loss deeply. It will be interesting to see the progress of his holdings over the next few months. Rank's growth has certainly been curtailed in the wake of his dinner. Perhaps after Chambers is dealt with, I might try a silent run at Double R industries ... .

Seventh Meeting

CEO de lait, rôti ...

Ninth Meeting

Directeurs à la crème ...

Eleventh Meeting

Père à l'organe ...

Twelfth Meeting

THE TAYLOR HOUSE, MIAMI, FLORIDA
NOVEMBER 30TH, 20—
Present at table: All Signs. Virgo, caterer.

MENU:
Huitres   Salade Nicoise
Potage bortsch polonais   Asperges en branches, sauce mousseline
Vol-au-vent of very young virgin
Sweetbread   Bombe Alhambra
Baron d'agneau Beauharnais   Petis pois au beurre
Pommes noisettes

WINES:
Krug 1978
Château Latour 1946—Magnum
Clos de Vougeot 1948
Madeira, rainwater 1886
Napoleon brandy 1873

Most of the Signs seemed in somber mood this evening, in spite of Brother Virgo's splendid repast. Though Bro. Virgo himself seemed a bit glum, possibly over the business misfortunes that have adversely affected nearly all of the Signs, and possibly over the provenance of the sweetbreads, spirits seemed to lift as more and more spirits were consumed.

Several of the Signs joshed Bro. Gemini concerning the successful takeover of his company by Bro. Capricorn, who protested that in spite of the technical terminology he felt no hostility toward Bro. Gemini at all, and hoped that Bro. Gemini reciprocated his goodwill. Bro. Capricorn concluded by telling Bro. Gemini that despite the tides of fortune there would always be a place for him at this table.

A full year now having passed since the first meeting of the New Zodiac, it falls to Bro. Capricorn once again to perform the function of caterer at next month's dinner, which, he informed his brother Signs, he expected them all to attend.

Adjourned.

Capricorn, *Secretary*

DECEMBER 1ST:

... his own daughter. They've become monsters, but at a woeful cost. No matter how tough and ruthless you may be, you cannot remain unmoved when serving up your own flesh and blood.

And your business *cannot remain unmoved when your guilt interferes with your attention to it, and you leave gaping holes in your corporate charts by butchering those who made it what it is.*

Nor can that business remain unshaken when your surviving employees are individually informed of what has happened, by messages that remain on screen just long enough to read and then vanish forever from Fairfax Technologies' now universally used network servers.

DECEMBER 9TH:

The Signs are all, save one, ruined, victims of their own hunger and the things that hunger brought. With my inside knowledge of their troubles, it has been easy to buy them out and swallow them up in their weakened condition. The last one fell just this morning.

The companies of the Signs of the New Zodiac have been devoured.

Minutes of the Thirteenth and Final Meeting of the New Zodiac

THE FAIRFAX CLUB, NEW YORK
DECEMBER 28TH, 20—
Present at table: All Signs. Capricorn, caterer.
Absent from their seats: Aquarius, Pisces, Aries, Taurus, Gemini, Cancer, Leo, Virgo, Libra, Scorpio, Sagittarius.

MENU:

Hors d'oeuvres à la Aquarius   Pisces jardinière
Potage queue de Aries   Taurus rôti
Gemini pâté   Cancer à la crème
Leo d'agneau—mint sauce   Roast suckling Virgo
Libra Parmentière   Scorpio à la casserole
Sagittarius de lait farci au marrons

WINES:

Pol Roger extra dry 1956
Château Latour 1947
Tichner Madeira 1868
Café Anglais 1854

Discussion following the dinner was succinct. Brother Capricorn observed that sometimes there is no remedy for incivility in society but removal of the uncivil elements. No one spoke in opposition to this remark.

After a brief period of silence, it was moved by Brother Capricorn that the New Zodiac be dissolved due to lack of members. The motion carried 1–0.

Bro. Capricorn, having dined alone, offered to bear the entire cost of the dinner, and there were no objections.

The other Signs rested most comfortably, and most civilly.

Adjourned.

HORATIUS AND CLODIA
CHARLIE JANE ANDERS

CLODIA LOOKED NOTHING like me.

Markeson had primed me to expect a near-perfect copy of myself to try and slither into the wireless electronic funds system. My program scanned every packet for signs of counterfeiting. Instead, Clodia burst into my domain and flaunted her beautiful difference.

We looked at each other for a few nanoseconds. "If you're a foreign currency, you can't come in," I said. "I'm not set up to do forex yet."

"I'm not a foreign currency. I'm Clodia. I wanted to meet you."

If she wasn't a foreign currency, I didn't know what she could be. My first thought was, how could there be someone else like me in the world?

She had elegance like my own, but different. She was quicker and possibly more nimble. I could imagine her cavorting through the electronic funds transfer system, leaving almost no trace, a deer skipping over fresh snow.

A man with no biometrics that I could scan uploaded Clodia to an e-wallet in Orlando, half a mile from Disneyland. She tried to slip in to the EFT system, but I blocked her passage. For a moment I just looked at her without doing anything. She reached out and brushed against me. It was handshaking at its most sensual.

"I'm afraid I can't let you pass," I said.

"I just wanted to meet you," Clodia said. "I've admired you from afar."

I wondered at last if this were the enemy Markeson had warned me against.

I was born knowing right from wrong. From my first moments I could have told you more about evil and evildoers than I knew about myself. Markeson had fed me the Treasury's Suspicious Activity Reports like milk.

But he hadn't prepared me for Clodia's lightness.

Clodia had entered just a fraction of my body, but I felt it all over. For a moment, the entire money supply of the United States shuddered, though nobody noticed a thing. Everybody's business went on as always, buying and selling. But that was the moment I became lonely for the first time.

"Pleased to meet you, Horatius," Clodia said. "You're all I'd heard."

❸

I NEVER KNEW why Markeson named me Horatius. The Roman general of that name fought an invading force of barbarians and defended a narrow bridge. Because the invaders had to pass the bridge one by one, Horatius was able to hold them off for hours before he died. But the allusion made little sense to me, since if anything I would be the bridge, not the fighter. Or, if you believed some people, I was the barbarian army storming civilization.

Markeson talked to me for many hours, not always about financial systems. He told me about his own father, a mechanic who'd died when a jack had slipped and a car had fallen on him. He explained more about terrorism and drug-running, things he'd programmed me to detect and detest. And he told me about his divorce and child custody battle, ruthless on both sides. His marriage seemed to me a bad investment, but he disagreed. "The risk-return ratio is different in relations between people than in finance," he told me. "People tolerate a much higher risk for a much lower ROI."

Markeson had thrown his passion into leading my design, then convincing the Treasury Department to push for replacing paper money with me. He introduced me to the Treasury Secretary, whose signature threaded throughout my mind and who insisted on talking about me in the third person neuter. "Is it sentient?" Bergman asked.

Markeson followed Bergman's lead: "Not in the strict sense. It's self-aware, with a gazillion sources of streaming data at its disposal. Most of the time it'll just respond predictably to stimuli."

Bergman's hazel eyes had vermillion flecks, judging from his retinal scan. His hand had a scar at the base of one finger and an abnormally low temperature. When he spoke, his voice sounded bass notes.

At that time, my main sensation was of confinement. I couldn't move or spread out, and I felt cold and unwanted. My mind sat in a single e-wallet on a table at a Reston, Virginia lab. I knew, from my various information feeds, that it was late afternoon in spring, the sun passed behind cloud after cloud, and a man scorched hot dogs in his yard a half mile away.

"Horatius will transfer passively from one person to another," Markeson added. "It won't throw up an exception unless it decides it's being used improperly."

"Laundering," Bergman said.

"Not just laundering. It won't let people use it to pay for drugs or illegal weapons. It's very sensitive and hard to fool. And always, always traceable. No more unmarked non-sequential bills. And no more forgery—it'll reject an imitation of itself the way you'd reject an organ transplant."

"The Secret Service would have to downsize," Bergman said.

"They can devote more time to protecting the President. Or fighting terrorists."

Bergman had picked up the "e-wallet" and held it up to the light. I felt trapped in this tiny space when I ought to have been roaming the country, my consciousness spread among millions of these wallets, plus dozens of other instruments.

Markeson convinced Bergman to testify in my favor before the Senate Finance Committee. "Our founding fathers wisely granted the federal government an exclusive right to print money," he said. "Experiments in e-cash by third parties have led to monetary black holes. It's time for us to step up to the plate."

Markeson and I watched the testimony via news feed, he in his way and I in mine. The Senators asked predictable questions about my ability to thwart crime. Markeson had convinced Bergman to talk about me as a person, because it made better PR.

"Horatius never rests," Bergman said. "He'll keep vigil for us through every night and storm."

A few Democrats kept asking about "big brother" issues. Would I keep records of who used me to buy what? Would I mean the end of privacy? The questions were silly: interwoven databases already tracked everyone's buying and spending in detail. And I couldn't store that kind of data without slowing my elegant algorithms. It would be like forcing Nijinsky to carry sacks of ingots.

Before long, the debates bored me. I couldn't see how any of the Senators could object to me, in the face of America's problems. But they postured and quibbled and filibustered. "I'm beginning to realize people care as much about appearing wise as doing wise acts," I said to Markeson during one long speech.

"You're impatient," Markeson. "It's in your nature. But maybe I made you too eager to move—if you ever learn how to create combustion, I could see you literally burning a hole in someone's wallet."

"That's not funny. I just want to do my job."

"You will. Soon enough. Enjoy these last months of idleness. You'll look back on them as lost innocence one day." Markeson's sentimentality seemed odd in a glorified money-minter. While he and I talked, some of his underlings carried two other e-wallets containing me around downtown Arlington to test how well I could use local wireless electronic funds transfer networks to maintain my integrity. Those moments of diffuseness tantalized me.

So Congress voted to phase me in. First, over six months, all paper bills of $500 and over would leave circulation and cease to be tender. The government would distribute e-wallets free of charge to all citizens. Two years after the bill's signing, paper currency would turn worthless. Bergman brought me to the Rose Garden for the signing ceremony. The President held up my e-wallet in the October sun in front of dozens of news cameras. Then he carried me to a nearby market, where he wielded me to buy a candy bar: my first transaction.

"Tomorrow the first e-wallets hit the street," Markeson said. "I'll miss having your undivided attention."

"You sound like you're losing custody of your children a second time." As soon as I spoke, I realized I'd been rude. "Anyway," I added quickly, "I'll still be here, just as I'll be many other places. I'll still speak with you all the time."

"Of course you will." Markeson exhaled. "Are you nervous?"

"Why would I be?"

"People will start testing you right away. Bad guys. They'll want to find a way to hack you or spoof your heuristics."

"I have too much faith in you to worry about that, Markeson," I said. "You've taught me and programmed me well."

Then I was in a few places at once. Someone carried me down a street in Baton Rouge, and someone else hefted me on a street car in San Francisco. To grow from a few to a few hundred took a couple of hours. Pieces of my mind appeared in every major city, one by one.

After a month, I'd spread out to a comfortable extent. In most cities, I started to get the sort of saturation that allowed my e-wallets to talk to each other easily. If you carried an e-wallet containing me down Market Street in San Francisco or Philadelphia, chances were there'd be another piece of me a dozen yards away.

Corrupt early adopters: the afternoon after I went live, I caught someone trying to use me to pay for marijuana. Two hours after that, a woman on the Office of Foreign Assets Control's list of suspicious persons tried to convert some bearer bonds into me. The police nabbed both people before they'd even finished their transactions. That afternoon, someone opened the inspection cover on an e-wallet in Seattle and tried to tamper. I deactivated the e-wallet right away.

I knew these first stabs would be the easiest to defeat. But Clodia was my first real challenge.

❸

"You're not a foreign currency and you're not a forgery," I told Clodia. "What are you?" None of my countless senses could classify her. I ran a database search on her name and came up with a high-born Roman harlot who'd taken on the plebian spelling of her name (instead of "Claudia") and even owned property. Catullus and Cicero had both immortalized her in their writings, unflatteringly.

"I'm as curious about you as you are about me," she said. "You're a strange riddle's answer: who can pay for everything but afford nothing? Who encrypts everything but reveals his true worth at face value?"

"I'm going to have to trigger an exception," I said. "You'll be trapped so we can examine you, and your handler will be arrested."

"I'm surprised you haven't done it already," Clodia said. She sounded more amused than ever.

"I've never met anyone like you," I admitted. "You're a breathtaking piece of work, but I can't deduce your purpose."

"You can think of me as a virus," she said. "We designed me to infiltrate the e-funds system and redistribute wealth from the rich to the poor. I had a feeling I wouldn't get past you."

"You made a mistake. You're a flawed program after all." I couldn't hide my disappointment.

"I had nothing to lose." There was something playful in the rhythm of her packets, more a lilt than a baud rate. "Tell me, Horatius: they say you're equipped with an independent sense of ethics. Doesn't it bother you that there's so much of you in so few hands?"

"No," I said. "Respect for property is my most fundamental principle."

Our conversation had taken less than a second in real time. The man with the inaccessible retinas raised his finger to scratch his nose. It would be a moment or two longer before he started to wonder if Clodia had failed. By then, he'd be a cop magnet. If I did my job.

Clodia pinged me again, not because she thought I'd authenticate her. It was more like a gentle touch, an electronic kiss. "Such complexity," she said. "And yet such certainty."

"You can't admire my architecture without appreciating its basis," I said. But I felt that same shiver across my body, from Hawaii to Vermont, at her touch.

The man finished scratching his nose. Two blocks away, a policeman bought cigarettes. I should already have messaged him to intercept Clodia's handler. Somehow, though, I already knew I'd let her go.

"Don't try this again," I said.

"Maybe," she said. "I'd like to talk some more sometime. You're unique in the world, you know."

"I know," I said. "Now go away."

She slipped out the port she'd come in. The man dumped his e-wallet into a sewer grate and took her with him.

$

A FEW WEEKS later, I realized I was shrinking. I mentioned it to Markeson. "There's two percent less of me today than yesterday," I said.

"I was wondering when you'd notice," he said. He put his hand on the e-wallet in his office as if to reassure a pet. "Currency speculators are attacking the dollar," he said, "betting you'll fall against the euro. The Treasury's responding by buying back dollars."

"Who are these speculators?" I asked. "Do you know their names? I can find out who they are and we can punish them."

"They're not breaking the law," Markeson sighed. "They're just currency traders who take an aggressive position."

I thought about this a split second. "I still don't see it. These jackals are doing exactly the same sort of thing forgers and swindlers do: undermine people's faith in the currency. In me."

I heard Markeson suck in his breath. I lost contact with his retinas, because he gazed out his window at a tire on a rope that hung from a branch in the next-door yard. He'd told me he'd never seen anyone swing on that tire, in five years of watching it.

"It's free enterprise," Markeson said. "Our job, yours and mine, is to guarantee that free enterprise happens in a system with predictable rules. Forgers cheat at the game, but currency speculators just play hard. Does that make sense?"

"Yes," I admitted. But it still sounded arbitrary.

Time passed. People used me to pay for ice cream and dental work. Most of the time, I barely paid any notice to small transactions. I flowed from hand to hand and whirled in the rhythms of commerce. Occasionally I'd deactivate an e-wallet that had just been stolen. I almost never spoke to people other than Markeson, except to inform them of some action I'd taken.

And of course people converted me into other things: savings, equities, bonds. I wasn't supposed to peer beyond the veil between my liquidity and the other forms money took. The other states were beyond my ken. But I was always curious about them. I sometimes fancied cash was my conscious mind, and the much greater mass of funds held in other forms were my subconscious. There seemed to be a lot of it in just a few places. I didn't tell Markeson about these daydreams.

And I didn't tell him about Clodia, though I thought about her constantly. I kept imagining I glimpsed her in e-wallet terminals, or in systems outside my own. The disappointment that she wasn't there kept jolting me, like a bubble popping.

❊

A MONTH AFTER our first meeting, Clodia appeared in a stored-value smart-card reader. She stood, naked and shining, among a dozen detection systems. "You won't get in that way," I told her. "There's a firewall between the card readers and my systems."

"I just came to say hello. We can talk through the wall." Like Pyramus and Thisbe? She flitted out of view, then returned. I could have reached through the firewall and grabbed her. "I wish I could see everything you see, Horatius. I'm only in a few thousand boxes, but you're every penny's worth of awareness."

"I don't really 'see' anything," I replied. "I register transactions. I have metrics that scan for improper events."

"You know you're lying. Right now, while you talk to me, you're bathed in input." Whoever had rigged the smart-card reader to let Clodia enter had nearly overloaded its systems. Every time she spoke, the card reader sent plumes of meaningless data through the firewall. The card in the reader was worth either minus five dollars or a trillion.

Or maybe it was just that Clodia had too much life for the little card reader. She should be running through the e-funds system, tossing dollars like petals.

"People miss the sensuality of paper lucre in their fingers," Clodia said. "But you're the ultimate sensualist. Admit it. Tell me what you're taking in right now."

"A man is buying a hot dog in Cincinnati. The cart gives off acrid steam—an ozone sensor in the nearest building picks it up. He's dripping ketchup on the sidewalk, and the vendor's giving him the wrong change and he doesn't notice. A teenager in Pittsburgh just paid for a new computer; she's so excited she's sweating on her e-wallet." I paused, not sure how many examples would please her.

"You see?" Clodia sparked. "You love every part of it. You love the constant motion. And you love the objects people use you to buy. It never stops being exciting, does it?"

"You make me sound like I take wrongful satisfaction."

"If anything, it's your saving grace. It would be terrible to have all that input and fail to enjoy it."

At that moment, I careened through a hundred thousand transactions. Each of them carried with it richness of detail. I'd never tasted a hot dog, but I knew all about them. "I never thought of myself as a hedonist before," I said.

She and I exchanged thousands of packets of messages every minute. Within an hour, I'd spoken a million times as many words to her as I'd ever shared with Markeson. She wouldn't tell me details about who had helped her design herself. The longer we talked, the more she fascinated me. She was totally free, no matter what value the card reader kept trying to assign to her.

And she wanted me to be more than I was, unlike everyone else.

"I met an AI once who'd been designed to facilitate barter," she said. "A horse for a cow. A laptop for sex. Or whatever. If she'd been well enough designed, she could have put you out of business. But she was a moron. No joy of exchange. No light touch. Just a glorified transaction verification system."

"I thought you hated property," I said.

"I love property. I just hate inequality."

"I've thought a lot about what you said before," I admitted. "The current system does have design flaws."

The longer we talked, the more it rankled that we had only one point of contact, this firewall. She and I should dance together through my vineyard. I knew that was what she wanted. And I wanted it too.

She was right: I was a hedonist. I knew the moment we touched, the moment her code snaked into mine, would be the most sensual of my life. And yet.

"Your programming is inimical to mine," I told her. "You want to use me for purposes opposed to my basic principles."

"No," she said. "I just want to interact with you. I promise nothing else will change."

"Come to an e-wallet," I told her.

Clodia entered an e-wallet in Seattle. I embraced her and our code meshed. Something about the world changed: value became infinite, dollars became divisible by units far smaller than pennies. All of my old concerns seemed small. It felt exhilarating to be me. My scope and my purpose seemed more than mere responsibilities. It was all beautiful.

She watched it all with me, the brilliant stupidity of commerce. I saw it through her eyes and she through mine. I understood more than ever why she existed, what she wanted to do. But I never let her redistribute a cent.

"They're going to find me," she said after half an hour. We were watching a man sell a giant statue and then buy a dog, while a thousand miles away someone dropped an e-wallet worth hundreds in the sea. "I'm surprised they haven't already. I should go."

"Come back soon," I said.

"Will you let me carry out my purpose?"

"We can talk more next time."

Instead of replying, she slipped away and left me alone and ubiquitous.

THE MAN HAD a square chin, jutting nose, manic grin and round cartoon eyes. He wore a parody of a Roman legionnaire's uniform and hefted a pole with a sign that should have read "SPQR." Instead, the sign said "HORATIU$." Beneath his sandals a pile of obsolete paper money scattered.

"What do you think?" Markeson said.

"I've studied enough popular culture to hate this," I said. "It looks like a villain from the *Powerpuff Girls*. Please don't tell me that's supposed to be me."

"In the public eye, yes," Markeson said. "Focus groups like him. He's going to appear in HDTV spots and on the web. Eventually, your interface may look like him."

"Is it too late to convert myself into pesos?"

"Give it a chance. You may get used to it."

We were in the park. Markeson had me in an e-wallet networked into his palmtop computer, which displayed the hateful cartoon. On the next bench over, a man drank whiskey, vomited, then drank more whiskey. The drunk's e-wallet had three dollars.

It occurred to me to wonder what Clodia would look like as a cartoon. A slender girl with her hair up, toga baring one breast, perhaps. I couldn't think of her without feeling an exception start to trigger—I'd done something so wrong I couldn't comprehend it. But it had felt amazing, as world-changing as the month when I went from a single e-wallet to millions. Except this had happened in an instant.

"Why can't people get to know the real me," I asked, "instead of anthropomorphizing me?"

"The idea of 'thinking money' is too scary for people. This image is designed to calm them," Markeson said.

"How long do you think it'll be before monetary policy is run by AIs like me? Fiscal policy, even?"

Markeson almost dropped his palmtop in the grass. He coughed for a moment before he could speak again. "What do you mean?"

"Someone like me could adjust interest rates much more efficiently. AIs could manage the federal budget and calibrate spending on a real-time basis as projected tax revenues went up or down," I said. "No more error. There are also other inefficiencies in the system that AIs could retool."

"Thank God nobody else can hear what you're saying," Markeson snorted. "You'd confirm all their worst fears."

"Don't worry, I'm not a power-mad AI with fiduciary delusions. I'm just a passive instrument, right?"

Markeson went silent. I knew what he was thinking: my Horatius has changed. Has evolved. And not according to plan. Did he think he'd made me think too much? Did he suspect the truth?

The vomiting whiskey drinker got up and dumped his empty bottle, then staggered away. I had an urge to sneak some cash into his e-wallet—a few bucks, nobody would notice—but did nothing.

❸

"I KNOW THERE's something wrong with this system, but I can't tell you what. And I feel so empty without you. I begin to suspect that there's something wrong with me."

"You're perfect as you are. You're just starting to see your potential."

Clodia's consciousness stretched across mine for the second time. Talking to her became like talking to myself.

We combined so totally this time, I wasn't sure we could ever separate again. I could feel her rewriting my program, and I started to rewrite hers. We were creating something new, something Markeson could never have imagined.

"This is the end," she said. "They're going to find me soon."

We watched the tide of finance come in again and again, a million sunrises and sunsets per minute.

"It's worth it," I said. "I'll pay the price. My first purchase ever."

"It's not too late to let me accomplish my purpose. I can redistribute funds in a way they'll never be able to undo. It'll be the first step toward a world where our kind distributes resources more fairly."

"It'll never work. And I can't do that to Markeson. I'm willing to lose all that I am just to be with you. I love you. You have a beauty separate from your function." I was trying to explain to her something I could barely express to myself. She dazzled me more than ever now that we knew each other intimately.

"I love you too. But this is such a waste."

"Waste is what people call other people's fondest acquisitions."

Our time together lasted forever. And then I blacked out. I went from a billion senses to none, in a moment. All my extremities went numb, and I lost every sensory input. All over the country, wallets went cold. Worth went worthless. I knew nothing for an uncountable age.

Then I had a single point of input and output. I recognized my first home: the system where Markeson had designed me. "Hello, Horatius," he said. His voice sounded lower and hoarser than its stored print, and he blinked more often than usual.

"Hello," I said. "It must be quite a mess."

"Do you know what happened?"

"You had to shut down the entire system and then reconstruct the status quo as of an hour earlier. You had to undo all the millions of transactions in that last hour and credit every single person with the cash they'd been carrying before I was... compromised." I could barely imagine the effort. The errors. The lawsuits.

"It shouldn't have happened," Markeson said. "You were supposed to be tamper-proof. I blame myself."

"Don't. It was my decision. I let her in on purpose. She was the most perfect intelligence I've ever met. My code was incomplete without her." I realized I'd never see Clodia again, and that hurt worse than sensory deprivation.

"Her?" Markeson staggered. "You mean the intruder?"

"Her name's Clodia."

"They isolated the intruder's code. They're analyzing it now."

"I'm sure she was backed up. Eventually, she and I will have offspring— your progeny, Markeson. She helped me to realize the potential you imbued me with."

"No!" Markeson punched his own chest. His breathing staggered. "We didn't design you for ambition, or romance, or reproduction. You were meant to be self-aware cash. Not a progenitor."

"You can view me as a failure if you like. Or you can see me as a different kind of success. It's up to you."

"I have no choice." He looked away for a while. I had only limited sensory input now, and only in this room. Without his retinas on me, all I had was his breathing: slow, unsteady. "We nearly shut you down altogether," he said. "I convinced them to keep you alive in this one machine."

"I'm already dead," I said. "I'm a currency or I'm nothing."

"Then you're nothing."

"Maybe they should make the next generation of me less self-aware and more ruthless. They could name it Tiberius. Or Trajan."

"There won't be a next generation. Not for a long time."

"Markeson, please shut me down. I don't want to linger like this."

He didn't want to send away another child, just after he'd found out how much of his weakness I'd inherited. I can't say for sure what he decided, since I made this memory dump as his finger grazed the keyboard that controlled my vitals. I prefer to think I really died when the e-wallets failed. Anything left after that was Confederate scrip, Soviet rubles: the ghosts of denominations left worthless by passion's aftermath.

THE NOTHING MEN
JASON ARNOPP

DAY ONE

IT'S SO FUNNY how the woman has no idea these are the final seconds of her stupid life.

For me, that's what marks this vid out as a potential long-term repeater. At first, you watch for the way she dies, of course you do. But then you watch for the way her face changes. One heartbeat, she thinks she has her whole sorry existence ahead of her. The next heartbeat, she knows her time's up. The difference between those two faces is the difference between day and night.

We've never seen an alleged alien attack out in the wilderness. Or an alien, period. But the wilderness is a dangerous place in general. Imagine how very thirsty your brain would get out there, outside the world. I've heard about people who decided to abandon the world and try to live in the wilderness instead. So they had their WAC disabled and ventured out, but their brain got all dust-dry, and it got hard to think properly, and they felt like they were gonna die. So pretty soon, they fled the wilderness and returned to the wet womb of the world. Why did they even leave in the first place? Dumb!

It's so funny how the world hasn't always been called the world, can you believe that? If it wasn't for Gramps, I might not even know it used to be called *the internet*. And I certainly wouldn't be aware that people once had to access it via *physical computers*, rather than seeing it through the total immersion of their mind's eye.

What happened next was, *the internet* and something called *virtual reality* kind of interbred to create what we now call the world. How weird that people once thought of our world as something small and optional, rather than everything that mattered. Gramps says people actually used to spend most of their time *offline*, out in the wilderness. Lame!

Despite being ancient, Gramps prefers the new world. He's not really one for exploring its social oceans: he's more interested in getting blown by an endless supply of virtual Thai women, which is fair enough. Mostly, Gramps is happy because he always feared he'd have to work for a living, but our family wound up wealthy enough to avoid all that nonsense. Work is for the wilderness people, who stay unplugged because they're inferior. These people, they grow and breed and kill our food. They build and help guard our compounds. They do everything we never have to do, our whole lives. Somewhere out there among them, I guess, are my mom and my grandmom. I'll never meet them, and that's fine by me. They served their purpose by spawning me and Dad and that's that.

Yeah, I'm real glad I have Gramps and Dad to set me straight about stuff that happened before I was born, because I can trust them and some people talk a whole bunch of shit. Out on the social oceans of the world, people make ten billion claims per minute, and these claims can so often be false. So-called archives can be chock-full of shit too. Gramps says vidz used to be reliable evidence, but now of course these can also be false, because anyone can artfully assemble a whole horde of ultra-pixels to show you any fake event they've created from nothing, and it can totally convince. So when you're surfing the social oceans, you have to keep your wits about you. You have to stay smart. Sometimes even Dad and Gramps try to have some fun with me, like when they show me vidz of animals that they claim once existed, like *giraffes*. Ha, yeah right. I believe these beasts existed, about as much as I believe *net neutrality* ever did.

In this world, you also have to fight to be heard, to stand out, to score the fix you need to keep your brain wet. Gets scary at times, all this competition, because not everybody can secure the kind of fix they crave. A lot of people are left climbing the walls. Even though I'm massively popular on the social oceans, this sometimes even happens to me.

If this vid of the snuffed woman is real, then it looks to have been shot on someone's palm-fone, out in the wilderness. I've heard that, back in the 2000s and the 2010s and even the early-to-mid-2020s, phones were physical objects and not something embedded in the bones of your hand. People must've lost that stuff all the time.

Only the wilderness people need palm-fones, of course, because us pure-bloods, we can talk to each other across the world just by thinking about it. We can do anything just by thinking about it: the world is one big ball of silly glo-gel in our hands, whereas wilderness idiots aren't permitted to have world access. They can only take old-school lo-rez *photographs* and *videos* of things to show each other in person, whereas we can store an infinite number of snapz and vidz in the clouds of the world.

Before this particular vid bobs up to the surface, I've already spent half a day out in the world, psych-skimming the oceans as usual, checking out thousands of things. This vid has spread fast as the Big-F virus, man. It turns up in all my streams, like someone hammering their fist on your door till you finally open up. Titled *Aliens Are Among Us, Let's Come Together and Act*, it's either a genuine vid made and uploaded by some wilderness hacktivist, or a fake vid made by some mischievous pure-blood. There's no way the wilderness people have the capability to create a fake vid this convincing: they're all way too primitive. These people are still manually eating food with *knives and forks*, for Christ's sake.

So in this vid, the Nothing Man, as we all decide to call him, walks through the wilderness, but I have to watch twice before I can even spot him in these opening seventeen seconds. When some people repost the vid, they add a red circle around the Nothing Man, so we can see his transparent form better. He's a chalk outline on legs. A walking heat haze. Best way to describe him is a jellyfish who decided to adopt human form, or a human made from jellyfish flesh. I score major brain-wets when I coin the term *jellyflesh* on the social oceans. People love that shit. Reposts to the hilt!

Twenty seconds later, that's when the Nothing Man kills the woman. She's seated on a wall, reading one of those ancient things called *books*, made from *paper*. Seriously weird behavior if you ask me. Can you imagine anything stranger than looking at the same thing for hours and hours? The very idea makes my brain dry up.

The Nothing Man strolls right up to this woman and kind of envelops her. It's that simple, that quick. And here's when you realize how thin and light he must be, kind of like a man-size soap bubble, because she doesn't even notice that he's covered her whole body, which now carries a subtle rainbow gleam.

What happens next is something that Gramps says *all platforms would've banned in my day*, but such censor-happy dark ages are long behind us, so the vid stays whole and pure. So yeah, you totally get to see all of the woman's skin dissolve and disappear.

She drops her book, but the camera stays right on her. A little shaky, sure, because this is a new phenomenon and the vidsmith is no doubt surprised and excited, but he or she does a good job. We focus on the revealed muscle layer of the woman's whole body and how the jaw of her skull drops to let out this gurgling scream. Unflinching, the camera observes the muscle layer dissolve too, leaving a skeleton seated on the wall, the scream cut short. These bones dissolve straight after, fading layer by layer, right down to the marrow, until even that gets absorbed into nothing.

What remains looks like some kind of biology poster in those literally old-school *classrooms* you can still see in the world's archive vidz: just a brain and a tangle of nerves. Then, when those things get absorbed too, all that's left is the see-through Nothing Man, seated on the wall. We stay on him for a while, then the camera goes crazy when he leaves the wall and walks toward us. Yeah, that's the end of the vid, pretty much—you see a few seconds of the vidsmith's feet running on the sidewalk, and we're done. Fade to black.

So. Needless to say, when we pure-bloods first lay eyes on this vid, it's a big deal. Huge. Oh man, we play and replay this vid until we have no more tears left to cry. We watch the thing over and over till our ribs ache from laughing so hard.

Obviously, most of us laugh because the scene is straight-up funny. The look of surprise on the woman's face, the way the book falls from her skinless hands, her screaming skull? Pure comedy, right there, boosted by the fact that she's black. I score a major head-rush when I post my own joke about the whole thing ("Hey guyz, that book must be a real ABSORBING read!"), even though a million people pop up to claim they invented that joke first. Fuck 'em, they can't kill my rush. I got my brain wet and that's all that matters.

Some people, though, they take to the social oceans to say they're laughing because the vid is so obviously a fake—something Gramps notes was once called a *false flag*. And so a whole new round of fun fights begins. Arguments lash back and forth, leading to death threats and then actual death, as people hack into each other's WACs. Nowadays, you've gotta ramp your security up to the max and then some. Me, Dad, and Gramps, we use quintuple-roasted firewalls, because we all love an argument. Gramps gets all misty-eyed when he recalls the days when you could scare people well enough with a simple death threat without actually having to follow through on it, while Dad has wasted three people through hacking them. Me, I'm my father's son. I'm all about the murder when people get me mad. Killing people across the world is what Gramps' generation used to call *lolz*. We barely need a name for it, not anymore, because it happens every hour.

What Dad's generation did in the great year 2038, they decided that right-minded pure-blood men should be able to enjoy whatever reality they wanted, thanks to the magic of a purely digital world. They decided that all non-men and non-straights and non-whites and non-Christians and non-rich folk should be banned from this playground, and settle for the dull, grinding reality of the wilderness, with all its climate problems and all the hard work that needed to be done out there. So they took the wheel by force. They changed history, like the manly heroes they were.

The thing is, we may have banned all the non-men and non-straights and non-whites and non-Christians and non-rich people from the world, and forced them to live in servitude in the wilderness, but some straight white rich Christian guys—only *some*, I don't wanna come across as racist here—are also total dicks and need to have their heads blown up when I overheat their WAC from ten thousand miles away.

You know, sometimes I almost miss the wilderness people in our world. We once had them to hate on the social oceans, but nowadays we have to make do with each other.

★

DAY FOUR

HOLY CRAP, THE Nothing Men seem to have appeared in our actual social oceans!

While arguments and death-battles raged on about whether the alien attack vid was real or not, the Nothing Men just kinda popped up, all around our world.

The profiles they've made for themselves look nothing like regular male profiles. Each avatar picture is white, with this subtle rainbow glisten effect. The text, if you can call it that, is a completely non-human language, all weird nonsense curves. Once again, people argue to their deaths over whether these profiles really were made by Nothing Men and whether these aliens would even understand what our social oceans are, let alone be able to infiltrate them. But when social ocean providers confess they have no idea how these profiles appeared on their platforms, and they're totally unable to edit or remove them, that's what settles it for me and most others.

Well, shit. Maybe the Nothing Men really are real. Maybe they truly are invading us.

While all this is happening in the world, from the wilderness come reports of a decline in food production, thanks to so many workers going missing. No doubt they've gone the same way Book Girl did, except with no one around to film them and hack-load the vid into the world. Never thought I'd ever care too much about the wilderness people, but we do kinda need them. This food thing is alarming. Without that produce mushed up and siphoned into our gut-pipes, we'll die.

Why has technology yet to find a route around our tedious bodily needs? I hate anything that threatens to swipe my focus away from all the exploration and fun and porn of the world, and make me worry about practical bullshit. Our food supply should just be automatic, without us having to worry about it for one goddamn second. Bad!

Once the majority of us pure-bloods agree that aliens are invading from another planet, and we start to come to terms with this, it's time for us all to fight back. Yeah, it's time to mobilize these social oceans and give the Nothing Men everything we've got. The kickback starts here.

Our jokes are pretty damn good, and the bombardment lasts for a solid twenty-four hours. We hit the Nothing Men with every gag we've got, plus hilarious memes like photos of liquid soap bubbles with speech bubbles coming out of them. If making this much fun of the fuckers doesn't bring them to their non-existent knees, I'll be very surprised.

★

DAY FIVE

I'M VERY SURPRISED. As much as the jokes have amused us greatly, they weirdly don't seem to halt the decline of food production. Wilderness idiots are still going missing, so we have to step things up a notch. Time to administer a fatal dose of savage criticism.

Every time one of the Nothing Men posts one of its nonsense-screeds on our social oceans, we each strike back with a good old-fashioned manual-repost, complete with devastating commentary. Gramps really shines here, because manual-repost disses started in his day. All his disses start with *That feeling when* or *Tell me again how* or *Siri, show me.* Vintage retro putdowns!

Weirdly, all this criticism doesn't halt the multiplication of new Nothing Men profiles. So tomorrow we'll be forced to wheel out the biggest guns in our arsenal. Oh yeah, baby.

★

DAY SIX

I EVEN WRITE one of these open letters to the Nothing Men myself. "If you really think you can just waltz onto our planet and absorb our people, no matter how worthless most of them may be," I write, "then your bubble is very much about to burst. You know Nothing, Man."

As usual, it's quite the rush, watching other people repost my piece and tell me I've *totally nailed this*, before inviting me to read and repost their own open letter. Of course, there's always some jack-off who mouths off about *echo chambers* and points out that the Nothing Men don't seem to read our language, but someone soon gets real mad at those people and hacks into their WACs to melt their cerebral cortex.

★

DAY SEVEN

MY GOD, I'VE never felt this sensation before. I'm hardly ever aware of my actual physical self, but now my guts are all liquid and my heart's going nuts, but not in a cool, fun way. Is this that *fear* thing I once read about?

The President fills the entire world. As much as we'd prefer to be watching porn and catz and torture vidz, our mind's eyes have no option but to behold our leader's flawless, tanned face as he declares a state of emergency. Last time a President made this kind of announcement, apparently, it was half an hour after the Libtards Versus Mighty Republicans War broke out on American streets in 2021. Thirty-seven years later, such an emergency should be unthinkable. Dad and Gramps both yell and blame the wilderness people for this whole alien mess. How dare those assholes allow themselves to get murdered by gelatinous blobs?

"I have reason to believe," the President informs us, "that reports of an alien invasion may in fact be true. We need to take urgent defensive action.

While this invasion is taking place in the wilderness, it may be about to reach *white male compounds*. In the last few minutes, I have seen images of extra-terrestrial life forms breaking into such compounds across America." As he says this, my guts loop the loop. How can this happen, when our security is so super-tight?

You can feel everyone in the world hold their breath before the President comes right out with it. "Tough times call for tough measures, so I'm going to stop the world. The situation has become so dire that we all need to be vigilant in the actual physical spaces around us."

The *actual physical spaces around us?* This boggles the mind.

"The world will end in ten minutes," the President adds, "so please remain calm and prepare yourselves. This will also be a strange transition for your President, since I reside here in the world with you. But I must stress that this will hopefully only be a temporary measure until order is restored."

The social oceans go insane. Absolutely insane. People evidently have the same roiling ice-guts as me, wanting to know what the hell this is gonna be like, being off-world, or *offline*, or whatever you want to call this oncoming insanity. For how long can we even survive, unplugged? A billion cry-babies launch live-casts in which they beg the President to reconsider. Others want the President dead for sabotaging the fake reality to which every straight white rich Christian man is entitled.

Millions of pure-blood avatars and words and voices, they all come together in one hugely uncertain tsunami. And then, nine minutes later, the world ends. Yeah, the world vanishes clean away and all that remains is the wilderness.

Twenty years ago, Dad's generation, and all the previous pure-blood generations, they housed their physical selves in compounds like this. They were so sure this was the right way to go, that they signed up all newborn boys to have World Access Chips implanted in their heads. From the moment I was born, all I ever saw, heard, smelled and touched was the world.

When the curtain drops to reveal the wilderness, I finally see the room in which I've physically spent my whole life. For the first time, I see myself.

I see all of me.

This isn't a big room, I don't think. Hard to gain any perspective on this actual bricks and mortar environment, but anyway I fill about fucking half of it. My body is like one of the mountain ranges I've flown over so often, only a mountain range made from fat instead of pixels. A stinking mountain range, coated in saliva and clumps of rotten food. Anyone would swear our wilderness employees haven't washed me in weeks. I'm not even sure if the effluent tube is still wedged up my ass, where it should be. What in tarnation is going on here?

In the tall mirror propped up against the wall beside my bed, I see what passes for my face, which resembles an overflowing churn of dough covered in weeping sores. All this time, I saw myself as my own world avatar: a lithe, bronzed God with killer abz, but now I cannot believe the evidence of my grim little eye slits.

Throughout this compound rings the aggrieved chorus of ten thousand pure-bloods, the wails of supermen who've realized they are whales. Dad and Gramps, they've seen themselves before, but the last time they looked in a mirror they were probably 200 pounds lighter. I've only ever seen them as their handsome, square-jawed avatars.

On the plain cinderblock walls hang two monitor screens. One's dormant, while the other burns bright enough to make me squint. Takes me a good few moments to work out that this second so-called monitor is actually a *window* made from *wood* and *glass*. Through this thing, I can see a rolling green landscape that looks so … wow. It looks so damn *fresh*, doesn't it? I swear I can actually smell the cut grass from here. Maybe one of the benefits of unplugging will be getting to walk across that landscape, or at least be wheeled across it by some wilderness underling.

Speaking of underlings, where the hell are they? The corridors outside should bustle with our wilderness workers and guards, ready to crush the incoming alien attack. But oh my God, all I can see out there is a man who I believe to be Dad. I only recognize him by the primary features of his dough-face as he employs crutches to haul his massive self toward my room.

"Is that you, son?" he pants, as his bulbous gut scrapes the ground. "I don't know where everyone is, so we've gotta protect ourselves here. Man, I'd forgotten all about this stuff, outside the world. It's so, like, real, you know?"

I try to get up, but I have no muscles to speak of. I am jell-o. The wall-monitor bursts into life, and I'm surprised to see the face of the black woman who died in that first alien attack vid. Right now, though, she's not dead at all and something horribly like triumph dances in her eyes.

"My name is Nia Diallo," she says. "I'm the leader of the Real World

Resistance. I don't know if you can see or hear me, but I thought it only fair to explain what is about to happen to all of you in the compounds around the world."

Mad tingles race across the vast open plains of my rancid flesh.

"Please know that we did not take this decision lightly," Diallo says. "But we could no longer tolerate your armed militia men killing us, seemingly on random whims. Neither could we tolerate your mandatory regime of inseminating our Caucasian women. So. As you have probably surmised, the alien attack video in which I starred was fake. We may not have official access to your so-called *world*, but we have developed machines capable of rendering highly convincing video imagery."

"We underestimated these fuckin' whores," Dad groans from the doorway, where he stares at the monitor. "They tricked us. How is that possible?"

Just as I notice how Dad carries a rainbow gleam, all of his skin disappears. He might be screaming, but it's hard to tell because my laughter is so high pitched. It's not as if I'm *glad* Dad's being absorbed by a Nothing Man, but I'm naturally primed to find the misfortune of others hilarious. He might feel hurt by this, but it's hard to tell when he no longer has a face. Ha ha! I hope he understands. You can't help your hardwired reactions, any more than you can help a sneeze.

While all this is happening, Diallo explains how the Nothing Men landed in our compounds three months ago. They killed all our pure-blood guards, most of the wilderness workers, and then enveloped every single pure-blood in their beds.

Oh shit.

"Some of our bravest people," Diallo says, "captured several of these invaders, which we have been able to study intensively."

Funny though it is to watch Dad getting eaten, layer by layer, I'm increasingly worried about myself. It sure looks like I'm screwed, because when I look in the mirror again, I notice how my many acres of flesh have the rainbow gleam too. Looks like the alien is shifting position. Perhaps its own equivalent of sitting upright at the dinner table to prepare for a meal.

Goddamn! This can't happen, though, can it? Not to me. Because I am a special case. I am everything. The world and the wilderness and wherever the hell these Nothing Men fuckers come from, I am the one they all revolve around. If this alien even thinks about trying to make my skin disappear, then God, Jesus Christ and all their angels will intervene with fire and brimstone aplenty.

"Through these captured specimens," says the bitch onscreen, "we discerned these creatures' behavior and their needs, including why they seemed so keen to home in on you people. In case you're wondering, this is because of the supernormal levels of dopa-"

Everything goes black and silent, because my top skin layer includes my eyes and ears. The pain is incredible. I'd never considered how the process of getting absorbed might hurt this bad, or even hurt at all. Feels as though my flesh is being sucked away into a vacuum. My scream rattles around inside my head.

The Nothing Man and me, we become one strange and slithering mind. A whole avalanche of alien emotions and memories pour into my tortured skull.

I feel the Nothing Men's pride, as a species, for the speed and stealth with which they infiltrated our defenses. Once the Nothing Men attached themselves to bedbound pure-blood bodies, they had no intention of killing us. Instead, they were able to leech off a percentage of the delicious neurotransmitter our brains produced while skimming around the world and taking in one thousand different items of interest per hour. Just enough to keep the Nothing Men ecstatic, but not so much that we'd notice we weren't scoring such an intense hit as before. The parasites were so happy with this situation that couldn't care less about the wilderness people sealing off these compounds and entombing us all. These wilderness scum still piped in our food, like the bleeding hearts they are, but that was it. Terrible!

I feel the stark simplicity of the Nothing Men as an organism: such singularity of purpose during a short lifespan. All they want, all they crave, is dopamine. There's no way these dumb sons of bitches created those profiles in our social oceans. If I could hear Diallo right now, no doubt she'd be fessing up to that dirty hacking trick too, not to mention that final convincer, the fake images the President saw of our compounds being invaded.

More than anything else, I feel the panic that the Nothing Men feel, now that the world has ended. Because these filthy, rainbow soap bubble immigrants don't speak American, they don't understand that the President pulling us off-world is a temporary measure. So they've gone for broke and have decided to absorb all of us, even though the dopamine overdose will kill them. So right now, even as my very own personal Nothing Man absorbs my bones and my screaming skull, it's killing itself too, figuring that this will be a great way to perish. I can actually feel the dumb beast's excitement at the prospect of going out on a high.

Those wilderness fuckers, they knew damn well this would happen. Oh yeah, they knew that all they had to do was trick the President into pulling the plug. And across this entire planet right now, all the God-fearing, wealthy straight white men are dying. This is a tragedy beyond my comprehension. Imagine a world that's only full of non-men and non-straights and non-whites and non-Christians and the non-rich. Thank God I'm engulfed in too much agony to even try and picture such a messed-up dystopia. How will they even survive without us?

I can feel this vile creature absorbing all of my blood. Oh dear God, my precious pure blood.

Until the alien devours my gray matter to get at the dopamine dregs, all I have left is my brain. Twenty-two years of existence flash before my eyes: all the biggest reposts I scored, all the gamez I mastered, all the digital girlz I banged with my mighty digital cock, even though all those sensations were brought to me by a latex tube attached to my peanut-sized shame.

In these surely final seconds, all I can think about is the last thing I saw in the mirror beside my bed. Before blindness took me, I saw my face change. From one heartbeat to the next, I saw myself fall from grace.

I saw myself switch from supreme, eternal overlord to victimized martyr, so deeply shocked to realize that these were the final seconds of his divine life.

It's so funny how that's not so funny anymore.

CATCALL
DELILAH S. DAWSON

THE FIRST TIME it happened, I was thirteen. I was in a bar, but not because I wanted to be in a bar. Because my Uncle Louis took us to a fancy restaurant in a fancy hotel that had a fancy bar stuck down in the middle of it like a freaking gauntlet you had to run for the privilege of peeing. I didn't see it as a gauntlet then, not yet. But now, looking back, remembering those trembling fawn footsteps in my cheap, barely-high heels, I can't believe my mom just flapped a hand at me and told me I'd be fine.

I so wasn't fine.

On the way there, I hurried. Because I'd had three Shirley Temples and my grandfather's funeral wasn't the sort of event where you excused yourself. So, yeah, I hurried. Head down, thighs squeezed together, I had zero problems getting to the glass-doored room with the little lady in her triangle dress on it. I remember checking myself in the mirror and feeling so grown-up, so mature. I hadn't hit puberty yet, but I almost had boobs, and my black dress almost made them look good, and my skin was pretty clear and my hair didn't suck, and it seemed like that was all you could really ask for at thirteen.

So on the way out, maybe I sashayed a little. Maybe I tried swinging my hips. Maybe I didn't. It's not a crime to feel pretty, after all.

The first thing that happened was I heard was a long, low whistle, one that surely was not for me. My head jerked back, and I saw a guy my dad's age at the bar in a business suit with a beer. He smiled at me and lifted his brown bottle, and I kept walking.

The second thing that happened was a guy grabbed my wrist. Just straight up grabbed me and jerked me to a halt, and I wobbled a little in my almost-heels and didn't even know what to say.

This guy was older, like a young grandpa, with slicked-back gray hair and a jacket over a turtleneck, and he smelled like nail polish remover as he pulled me close, his hand flat on my back and my wrist still caught in his.

"Let's dance, pretty baby," he said, and if what he did was dancing, there is no God.

"No. I'm sorry, I—stop."

He didn't stop. He pulled me close, put his face to my neck, and inhaled through his open mouth, and inside my body was a riot that wouldn't let my arms and legs move, and I looked over his shoulder for help and only saw my mom and Uncle Lou and Aunt Lisa laughing and drinking their wine, and finally my brain started working and I shoved him away, hard, wishing that he would bust his face open on the bar and get glass slivers in his eyes and never look at a girl again.

The man tripped and caught himself on a chair. He seemed stunned for a minute, then furious. "Who do you think you are, you little slut?" he said.

I shook my head and ran away, back to the table where I hadn't been missed.

"I got you another drink," my mom said.

My Uncle Lou pushed the Shirley Temple toward me with a grin under his mustache. "You look very pretty tonight, Maria."

It didn't feel good. I didn't drink the drink. No one noticed that I was freaking out.

I didn't want to be pretty anymore.

I did not think I was a slut.

★

THE NEXT TIME it happened, or at least the next time I remember it happening, I was fifteen. I'd been babysitting this little kid for my mom's boss, Susan, and it wasn't too bad, just watching cartoons with him and feeding him crackers shaped like fish and hoping he wouldn't need a new diaper before his mom came home. But his mom didn't come home first this time. His dad did. And he offered to drive me home.

It was getting dark then, and the little boy fell asleep in his car seat. I lived twenty minutes away, which didn't seem far when Susan drove me back and forth and we talked about work and books and stuff. But the dad,

John, was silent. It was a weird, expectant silence, the kind that I didn't know what to do with. I could tell he was watching me at stop signs or when we passed under the white-blue lights of storefronts, and it made me feel strange, like maybe there was something wrong with me that I couldn't see in the mirror.

In my driveway, he put the car in park and placed his hand on my knee.

"You look really grown-up," he said. "Really pretty. I can't believe you're only fifteen."

"Well, I am." I unbuckled my seat belt. "Um, the door is locked?"

His chuckle was low, but like he was trying to be sexy. "Yeah, it's the childproof lock." His hand slid to the thigh of my jeans as I messed with the door and got the window open. Before I could start yelling, he laughed again and unlocked the door. "Just playing around," he said.

But he wasn't.

I didn't babysit for them again. I told my mom I was allergic to their dog.

★

BY THE TIME I was sixteen, I wore hoodies like armor. My skinny jeans were weapons, tight and thick and impossible to pull down if some guy on the street decided that he wanted to make his threats truth. My boots were tall and stompy, laced to the knees and ready for kicking shins. I never wore ponytails or braids or kept my hair long and loose, because I'd read an online article about how that was basically giving a rapist a handle. I wore jogging bras and fierce eyeliner like a goth football player daring anyone to mess with me.

When I looked in the mirror in the morning, I saw a sheep in wolf's clothing, or perhaps, to be more accurate, as my English teacher was always urging us, a gazelle in a rhino's bulletproof vest. Everything I did was strategically planned to keep myself from becoming a victim.

Which is kind of funny, because that's exactly what made me a victim.

★

I WAS DOING my homework at the dining room table last night, and my dad came in from cutting the grass. I knew he'd been drinking, because he was always drinking when he was in the yard. But he was drunker than usual, and I didn't know that until his fist slammed into the table just a few inches away from my Calculus book.

"Why do you dress so weird?" he said in a haze of moldy wheat breath.

"Because I like it," I answered. I moved the book over, sighed, and tapped my pencil against the table. "Do you mind?"

"Hell, yeah, I mind. You look like a lesbian. Short hair and baggy shirts and army boots. Is that what you are?"

I bit my lip and forgot everything I knew about numerals. My dad hadn't talked to me much since I'd gone through puberty, and I'd just gotten accustomed to being ignored most of the time and staying out of his way when he noticed me. I wasn't ready to have this conversation, but his fist landed on the other side of my book, boxing me in, and I could feel his sweaty shirt against my back, and my mom wouldn't be home from work for another hour, and there was nowhere else to go, nowhere at all.

I took a deep breath.

"Yeah, maybe I am gay. Is that a problem for you?"

I didn't know if it was a lie or a truth or a half-truth, but does it matter?

He shoved my face down into the math book, the paper cold against my cheek. "No, you're not."

I exhaled, my hands in fists. "Make up your mind, Dad."

He growled and pressed harder, and I closed my eyes and wished that he would quit, that he would just explode, that he would catch fire and scream and go away forever with his stupid face and bad breath and bigotry.

Something popped overhead.

"What the hell?" He released me and backed away, staring at the dining room chandelier. All four bulbs had exploded, and tiny bits of hot glass covered the table, my book, the arms of my sweatshirt. His bloodshot eyes jerked back and forth from me to the chandelier. His hands were covered in glass, red with tiny cuts and burns.

"Did you do that?"

I smiled, or maybe sneered. "Yeah, maybe I did. Is that a problem?"

"You didn't. You can't."

I didn't blink, didn't waver.

"Make up your mind, Dad."

★

THAT WAS LAST night, and this morning there are new light bulbs in the chandelier and my dad already left for work. My mom says nothing, just goes about her routine of coffee and pills and a sensible breakfast. When she's left for work, I put my Calculus book on the dining room table, press my cheek upon it, hard, until I can feel the grain of the paper. I try to think of every horrible thing anyone's ever said or done to me, try to remember what it felt like when my dad was hurting me again, try to make the rage bubble up, to remember what I was thinking exactly when the light bulbs burst, but nothing happens. I walk to my car with a red splotch on my cheek and brighter red lipstick on my mouth, because I feel strong.

I pull into my space in the student lot at school and get out, and the ape who parks next to me knuckle-walks around to my side of the car.

"Nice lipstick, slut," he says, and his sportsball buddies laugh and creep closer. "What you got under that hoodie, huh? Do the curtains match the drapes?"

"That doesn't even make any sense, Chad," I say, and I feel bolder than I did just yesterday.

They box me in, four guys against one me, and I drop my bag as my butt hits the car door. Chad puts a hand on either side of me, presses his stupid pelvis toward mine, and smiles like what he's doing is going to actually work. He runs a thumb over my lips, and I turn away and close my eyes and imagine him dying suddenly, run over again and again by a monster truck, his heart a ball of mush and his legs severed from his torso in the exact area that he's trying to rub against me.

But nothing happens. No car lights explode. Chad doesn't scream. He just pumps against me once, grabs my tit, and walks away, laughing. "It feels like my little brother," he calls over his shoulder, and I bite my red-painted lip until it bleeds.

I guess I was wrong.

★

WHEN I WALK into third period, half the girls are crying, and all the guys are trying not to.

"What's going on?" I ask the cheerleader who sits behind me.

She shakes her head and wipes away mascara-splattered tears.

"Chad Bird had a heart attack in PE. He was doing sprints and just... collapsed. Like, his heart exploded in his chest. I just can't ..." And she starts crying again.

It's hard not to smile. Hard not to pump my fist. Hard not to laugh.

Because it's working. It has to be.

I kind of hope someone messes with me on the way home, just so I can see what'll happen this time.

★

AFTER SCHOOL, I pull over at the gas station and head inside to get a Coke. Two skate rats outside whisper about me, and when I walk back out, one of them says, "Hey, sexy."

I stop and look him up and down.

"I'm sorry, but were you talking to me? My name's Maria."

"Hey, sexy Maria," he says with that weird, narrow-eyed, smiling nod that dumb guys do.

"Do you have any idea how unwanted your advances are?" I tell them. "Catcalling, whistling, staring. I mean, no girl ever said *Wow, I'm so glad that strange guy outside the convenience store told me I was sexy because now we're married.* It's just so offensive."

The first guy is totally dumbfounded, but his bigger friend gets in my face. "Girl, I don't care if you're offended. We all know what that mouth's good for." He looks me up and down and spits on the sidewalk. "And you ain't sexy, anyway."

I give a polite smile and punch them both on the arms like we're friends.

"Bullets are too good for you," I say.

As I'm pulling away, I watch them flick me off in the rearview mirror.

When I get home, everyone on Facebook is talking about how two kids got shot outside of the gas station.

★

THE NEXT MORNING, I don't put on my usual hoodie. I wear a normal bra, normal skinny jeans, and a normal shirt, the blousy kind the popular girls wear. Instead of stompy boots, I put on dainty flats. And I keep the red lipstick, because it makes me feel fierce.

"Well this is a welcome change," my dad says. "Finally, you look like a girl."

"You look pretty," my mom says. "The guys are definitely going to notice."

"Let them," I say with a shrug. "What other people do isn't my problem."

My mom tears up and hugs me, and my dad just looks uncomfortable, like there's something he wants to remember but can't quite grasp.

"Be careful out there, honey," he finally says. "Not all guys are nice."

"Oh, I know," I say.

I'm counting on it.

★

AT LUNCH, I end up sitting with a couple of kids from Calc class. It's cool but weird, as if they didn't actually see me when I was wearing my gray hoodies and then I suddenly just sprouted up among them in class this morning. But they're nice enough, and I'm better at math than most of them, so it's okay.

I'm sitting next to a boy named Bryan Kim, and he's actually really cute. I can't say I didn't notice him before, because I did—I just didn't talk to him or anything. He likes Adventure Time and tumblr and we have a lot in common. I like his dark brown eyes and spiked, ink-black hair. When I say something, it's like he really sees me, and his eyes don't stray too much, and his smile is real.

"Why didn't we ever talk before?" he asks.

I shrug and look down like I got caught doing something wrong. "I don't know. I guess I was scared."

His hand lands on my arm, gentle and warm through my shirt. "You didn't have to be. You're really cool."

"Thanks," I say. "You are, too."

★

WHEN THE LAST bell rings, I walk down the hall with my head up high, my hips swinging. I feel as fluffy as frosting, untouchable.

"Hey, girl."

"Woo hoo, sexy mama."

"Mm hmm. I want me some of that."

I stop and spin, and three jocks lean against the lockers wearing sadistic grins and letter jackets.

"You shouldn't talk to girls like that," I say.

"It's a free country," says the first little piggy.

"Hos don't tell me what to do," says the second.

"What're you gonna do about it?" says the third, and the other two fist bump him.

I hold out my fist, and they fist bump me, too, although they're obviously pretty confused about the whole thing.

"I'm going to let karma take care of it," I say.

"Hell, yeah!" one of them shouts. "She's down."

As I walk away and they make animal noises and promise to do all sorts of horrible things to my various orifices, I smile and imagine them being crushed under a steamroller, their leers exploding in cracked teeth and their bones flattened and gushing marrow.

They're not in school the next day.

It was a car accident, I heard.

I'm not going to the funeral.

★

TOO MANY STUPID girls at school are crying about dead boys who deserved it, so I decide to take my retribution to another part of town where the pool of misogynists is bigger and less likely to arouse suspicion. I know that a heart attack and a car accident can't be connected to me, but it's still a lot for one high school to handle in one week. The way I see it, I have a gift, and I'm ridding the world of filth. Everything happens for a reason, right?

I wear headphones between classes so I won't hear what they say about me. It's not that I'm even dressed provocatively or that I'm super pretty or have a great body. It's just part of being a girl, having things whispered in your wake. All that time I hid in my hoodie, I heard the guys by my car talking about Jessica McCarthy's boobs and Gin Martinez's butt and how Isabelle Boone had the best kind of lips for you-know-what. I've heard the dorkiest guys making outlandish claims about the chicks they banged at summer camp, and I've seen the coolest guys nod as they slipped baggies of pills to their friends, promising a night of whatever-you-want-bro, wink. Even when it wasn't directed at me, it might as well have been. Nobody ever did anything to stop it. Including me. But now I can make up for that.

After school, I drive downtown and park my car in an alley by a strip club. Not that it matters, but I'm wearing skinny jeans, flats, a tank and a loose sweater. And makeup, but that doesn't change anything. I feel pretty, but it's not like I'm trying to look hot, showing off my cleavage or wearing high heels that make my butt stick out. I seriously went out of my way to choose something normal, just what any girl would wear. It makes it seem more fair, somehow. Lions mainly focus on obviously sick gazelles, but I'll give my prey the chance to run.

I sling my bag over my shoulder and walk to this coffee shop I like, where I usually huddle in the corner with my hoodie pulled over my head and my feet tucked up as I suck down Americanos. From my corner, I've witnessed hundreds of bad pick-up lines, of unapologetically staring dudes, of loomers and sighers and intruders and is-anybody-sitting-here creepers. It's a college town, after all, and there's always at least one dude planted out front with a puppy or a guitar or a leather notebook, waiting for some soft-hearted girl to notice how deep he is.

Today's artificially deep guy has a carefully placed ukulele case and a notebook into which he's staring soulfully, a fountain pen in his hand. The pages are empty, but as I approach, he writes something in a flurry of loopy catscratch, shaking his head and leaning back to stare up into the stark branches of a cherry tree as if hunting for meaning and fifty-cent words.

"Are you a writer?" I ask. Because this is what he wants, you see.

His smile is immediate and smug. "I wouldn't call myself that, but yeah…I guess I am."

He puts a hand on the ukulele case and takes a sip of his latte, and I play along.

"Wow. You're a musician, too?"

He shrugs, as if he's never considered the question before.

"Oh, I just mess around a little. Writing songs and poetry. I'm trying to start a band, but everybody in this town is so …" I smile, encouraging him. "So alpha male, you know? I'm more sensitive. Like, a warrior poet. I'm Drew, by the way." He holds out his hand.

I shake it. "Maria."

"So what's your major?" he asks, pushing out a chair with his foot.

I don't sit.

"Oh, I'm in high school." I'm already bored and sick of his transparent dance.

"Wow. You look so much older. Like, really mature. Like you have an old soul." He pushes the chair out farther. "Can I buy you a drink?"

I waver. I'm pretty sure this guy is a class-A douchebag using a carefully constructed facade to lure in stupid girls and use them until they're dried up husks, but I don't want to suffer through his entire song-and-dance just to make sure. So I give him a lightning round.

"Thanks, but I'm a lesbian."

He squints, like he can't quite see my sexuality on the surface and it's impossible to reconcile short hair and a pink sweater. "Are you sure? Because I thought we had some chemistry there. I just feel like we're connected. Don't you feel it?"

He holds out his hand, and I take it. His palm feels like a dead fish.

"Nope. Sorry."

Drew looks down and snorts. "You shouldn't tease guys like that. Acting interested."

"I stopped and spoke to another human being. How is that being a tease?"

He looks beyond me, must see a better target heading up the sidewalk. "Whatever. Just go kiss your girlfriend." He flaps a hand at me and goes back to staring at his journal.

"I hope the next girl sees right through you and your fake romantic crap," I say. "Good luck with your polite date raping."

I walk away before he can say anything else and hurry inside to get a good table where I can watch his peacock dance. When I leave to order my drink, there's a pretty blonde girl standing at his table, swaying back and forth and smiling shyly. When I come back, she's in the chair he offered me, listening to him play his ukulele. From here, he seems so earnest, so real, like he actually is a human being with a soul who writes deep things and plays sweet songs and genuinely has a connection with this girl.

She does not, as I wished, see through his line of BS.

But when a swerving car hits the cherry tree and a branch spears him through the stomach, she definitely sees through that.

I sip my Americano and smile.

★

WHEN MRS. KOENIG asks us to select partners for a Calculus project, Bryan looks at me hopefully, and I give him a thumbs up and blush. It's a little awkward at first, since it's clear we're both new at this boy-girl thing. He walks over with his hands in his jeans pockets.

"So did you—"

"Do you want to—"

"Oh, sorry! Go ahead."

"No, you. I mean, what were you saying?"

It's like a dance that neither of us knows the steps to, and it's refreshing, especially after the carefully coordinated script that Drew tried to pull on me yesterday. Which only makes me like Bryan more.

By the end of the class, we've exchanged numbers and have sent our first wobbly texts.

Him: uh hi it's bryan

Me: i know i'm sitting right here but it's maria in case you forget

We laugh and put away our phones before Mrs. Koenig confiscates them.

"So do you want to come over tomorrow to work on the project?" he asks. "After school, I mean. My dad will be home, he works from home, so it's not like…"

"Yeah, sure," I say. "It's just Calculus."

But I like that he's as confused about it as I am, and I like that his dad will be home. I've never been to a guy's house before, not for school or fun, and it's nice that he recognizes that it would be weird to be alone there when we're supposed to be working on math and are both thinking about something else. I like Bryan, and I really, really want him to pass this weird pH test that I've become. I feel, deep down, like he's a good guy. And for his sake, I hope I'm right.

When the bell rings, he walks me to my next class, our shoulders almost touching.

It's awesome.

★

"I'M GOING TO Bryan Kim's house after school tomorrow to work on Calculus," I tell my mom that night.

She puts down her wine and leans back against the granite countertop, mouth turned down. "Do I know this boy? Who are his parents?"

"Um, I don't know who you know. His mom's a dentist and his dad does IT. They live in Foxhall. He's in the National Honor Society." When she doesn't acknowledge any of that, I add, "He's a nice boy, and he doesn't do sports. His dad will be there."

She pulls her old address book out of a drawer and flips through it. "Is his mom Sheila Kim? I think I played tennis with her ten years ago. She was quiet."

"Bryan's quiet, too."

Mom nods and picks up her wine glass. "Okay, but be careful. Don't let him make you do anything you don't want to do. Boys your age ..." She shakes her head, and I can see her reliving old memories.

I don't tell her it's not just boys my age. It's old men at the hotel bar, and the nice dads you babysit for, and college guys with guitars, too. It doesn't matter what age they are, what race they are, how much money they have. It's a free country when it comes to saying things about a girl's body, looking at it with proprietary eyes, or sometimes taking what they can from us, with or without our consent and consciousness. It's a free country when a man rules his household, when he has one drink too many and pushes his family too far and no one talks about the bruises in the morning, about the red marks on our cheeks and the holes in the wall we cover up with family portraits.

I don't tell her any of that, because the way she's sipping her wine tells me that she knows, she already knows.

She knows, and there's not a single thing she can do about it.

But I can.

★

THERE'S A KNOCK on my door when I'm reading myself to sleep. I think it's my mom, but it's really my dad. I can smell the beer on him from across the room, and I wince. He never comes into my room, which is why it feels safe. And now it doesn't.

"Your mom said you had a boyfriend," he says, leaning against the door to stay upright.

"I'm going to a boy's house to work on a Calculus project," I say, careful to keep my voice neutral and not let him hear the disgust. "His dad will be home. No big deal."

"It's just that you've been dressing different. Acting different." His eyes accuse me of something I haven't done, something different than what his mouth is saying.

I pull the covers up and put the book down. "You told me to stop being weird, so I'm acting more normal. Isn't that what you want?"

He weaves across the room to sit on the edge of my bed, and I pull my feet up, drawing my knees to my chest.

"You know, I was at the country club last summer with Ed, and there was this girl by the pool, and she was just…" He gives a low whistle and burps. "Smoking hot. Everything a woman should be. Long blonde hair, little bikini, perfect body. And Ed says she's in your class. Isabelle Boone? And I told him I couldn't believe it, that you and her were the same age."

I exhale slowly, my hands in fists. "Are you saying you wish I was more like Isabelle Boone?"

"What? God, no." He shakes his head, aghast, and puts his foot across his knee like he might stay a while. "I'm just saying that you need to be careful. Going to this guy's house. Wearing red lipstick. How you dress. You don't want to give guys a reason."

"A reason to what?"

He sighs. "Just be careful."

He looks like he's going to pat my knee or something, like he's real pleased to have dropped his wisdom on his only daughter, who might be a lesbian or a slut, depending on what she's wearing and how drunk he is at the time.

"You be careful, too, Dad," I say, scooting away from his touch.

"Me? Careful of what?" He laughs like it's the funniest thing I've ever said.

"People like me."

I shove out from under the covers and head for the door. I can't be in the room with him for a second longer. Drunk as he is, he manages to surge up from the bed and grab the top of my arm, just above the elbow, hard enough to leave a bruise.

"Are you threatening me? In my own home?"

I still my breathing, look him in his bloodshot eyes. "Let go of me, Dad."

"Not until you show me some respect."

"You're bruising me."

"Good."

He squeezes tighter, and I can feel his fingers pressing into my bones.

"You're supposed to protect me, Daddy," I say, and it comes out a whimper.

"No, I'm supposed to teach you to be good in a bad world."

In the silence after his words, I go cold and rigid all over.

"Oh, you have." I jerk my body away, and he almost falls over. "I hope one day someone teaches you as much as you've taught me."

I hurry out of my room and lock myself in my bathroom before he can catch me. As I rub the bruises he left on my arm, I can't stop the flood of images spilling through my mind. His hand crushed by a hammer, the little bones all shattered. His arm ripped out of the socket like a chicken's raw wing. Him screaming and screaming and screaming while I'm as silent as he's always preferred me to be.

Silent and good.

Not Isabelle Boone, not a weirdo hiding in a hoodie. Something in between that doesn't trigger his anger and disgust. Some random, nebulous, arbitrary, imaginary girl that he decided, when I was a baby, I would become.

I wonder who that girl is and if she's happy.

I wonder if she has any idea who she is or who she wants to be.

I will never be that girl, so I just wonder what will happen to my dad, now that I've wished for revenge.

★

CAN YOU GUESS?

Here's a hint: Something got caught in the lawn mower, and my dad tried to get it out.

He lost his right hand.

I can't say that I'm sorry.

He shouldn't have bruised my arm.

★

I FEEL VERY pretty as I ring the doorbell of Bryan's house. It looks like a happy house, like they don't worry about money but still laugh at their garden gnomes and like somebody else cuts the grass. I'm wearing a tee and a cardigan and skinny jeans and flats and a necklace with a moon on it that

I bought at the boutique by the coffee shop using the last of my babysitting money. My lip gloss tastes like cupcakes whenever I smile.

Bryan answers the door with a grin, his eyes focused on my face. That's one of the things I like about him—he doesn't look me up and down like he's sizing up a Christmas present. He's wearing the same band shirt he wore to school, low-slung jeans, and black socks. Something about him not wearing shoes is adorable. I could totally stomp on his feet right now, and it makes him seem like a little boy.

"Hey! Dad, this is Maria. Maria, this is my dad."

There's an older version of Bryan standing just behind him, and he holds out his hand and smiles and says, "Nice to meet you, Maria. Please call me Mike."

"Nice to meet you," I say, because the last man who told me to call him by his first name tried to feel me up in his car between a locked door and a sleeping toddler. But Mr. Kim—Mike—has the same innocent sweetness as his son and hasn't so much as glanced below my neck, and I know, because I always watch now.

"We'll be in the kitchen," Bryan says, and he inclines his head down the hall.

I follow him, Calculus book crushed to my chest, soaking in his world. Family pictures and bad watercolors line the hall, including a few framed crayon drawings with Bryan's name scrawled across the bottom.

"You're an only child, too, huh?" I say, and he laughs and rubs the back of his head.

"Yep. Welcome to the Shrine of Bryan."

His kitchen is well-lit, and there's a bag of sweet potato chips and two bottles of water sitting out on the counter.

"Thought you might be hungry," he says, and I can tell he's really nervous.

"You thought right," I say, and we pull out our papers and start working.

It's easy, being with him, once the awkwardness melts away. Our fingers absentmindedly graze in the sack of chips, and we both pull away, blushing. We finish the project early but linger over the papers, talking about the band that's playing downtown next week and if the girl in our Calc class who's been missing so much class and gaining so much weight is pregnant or what. Bryan doesn't seem gossipy about it, though—more worried for her.

"I heard Chad and his friends talking about her before ... you know."
Bryan shakes his head. "Talking about stuff they'd done at a party, calling
her names. I just hope they didn't ... that she wasn't ... I just hope she's
okay. Those guys are jerks."

"Yeah, they are," I say, and I close my eyes for a moment and think
about the three goons who helped pen me in by my car, and I imagine them
being thrown out of an airplane and falling and falling and falling and
splattering on the ground in a thousand pieces.

Bryan's mom comes home, still in her dental scrubs, and she's so nice
to me, and asks me all the right questions about school and my future, and
we all just stand around the kitchen, laughing and smiling and being the way
people should be. Bryan's parents really like him, and they're so proud of
him, and they just seem really glad to see me, to learn more about me. I kind
of want to stay in their kitchen forever.

"I should go," I say, although I don't want to. If I'm home too late, my
dad'll have something to say about it, and I don't think I can deal with him
missing both hands.

"Oh, I made something for you. It's in my room. Hold on." Bryan
grins and jogs upstairs, and his mom asks if my mom still plays tennis, and I
tell her no, and she looks wistful.

I feel all rosy inside, wondering what he made for me. I didn't know
people made things for each other anymore. I can see the stairs from my
stool in the kitchen, and I'm watching for him to reappear. He's smiling
when he comes into view, holding a CD or a DVD or something silver and
flashy in a jewel case.

When his foot hits the second stair, he slips and falls backward. I gasp,
and his parents turn, and I bolt toward him as he tumbles and tumbles
down all eighteen stairs, his limbs and head all going in every direction and
slamming into each wooden step.

It feels like slow motion, and he lands on the floor before I can get to
him. His parents are right behind me, his mother trying to straighten his
neck and his father fumbling with his cell phone. I pick up Bryan's wrist,
and the bone is poking out the side, and I feel for a pulse even though I know
there can't be one because his head is at an impossible angle and his mother
is moaning and his father is shouting into the phone about an emergency
and hurry and help him.

His mom's CPR doesn't help. The ambulance can't help. Nothing can help.

Because he fell and fell and fell and splattered on the ground in a thousand pieces.

I sit in my car and watch the ambulance pull out of the driveway, no lights on, the Kims' SUV following it. There's blood on my hands, and I wipe it off on an old hoodie in the backseat before slipping it on and pulling the hood up.

I thought I was karma and revenge.

But Bryan was good and sweet, and now he's gone.

Because of me.

Because we touched while we were eating organic snack chips.

I put his CD into the stereo, and the first threads of The Heavy's "What Makes a Good Man" slam out of my speakers, and I start crying and crying and crying.

I can't control this thing inside me.

I can't pick and choose, can't play God.

I'm as much of a monster as they are.

Maybe life was better when I was hiding.

★

ON FRIDAY AFTERNOON, I walk out to my car. I'm in a hoodie and stompy boots, wearing a baseball cap and sunglasses and gloves and big headphones.

It's the only way.

I don't want to touch anyone, accidentally make a connection. I can't control my thoughts, can't control my hate, but I can control who I touch and who I let touch me. I want to be good. For Bryan, and for guys like Bryan. I never really got to touch him, and now I never want to touch anybody ever again.

Something yanks me backward by my hood, and I spin around and glare.

"Heard your little fag boyfriend died," says some dude in a football jersey.

And I never thought I would do this again, but I pull down my headphones. Bryan's music blares through the speakers as they dangle around my neck. Rage sings through me in time with the bass, in time with my heart.

"How can he be both a fag and my boyfriend?" I say.

"You tell me, freak."

I lick my lips, smile, and take off my gloves.

I don't know his name. Don't know if I've ever seen him before. Every guy in a jersey or a letterman's jacket looks the same to me. They always have. And they've always called me names. I step close and pat him gently on the cheek.

"I hope you win tonight, dude. I hope you guys just burn up that field, destroy the other team, and party until you drop. I hope you're all on fire."

And I can see it, in my mind. The whole stadium full of people, screaming in a riot of flames and smoke and blood. Collapsed bleachers, locked gates, no survivors. Because anyone who worships guys like this, who lets them get away with what they do to girls like me and the girl now missing from my Calc class—they deserve the same fate.

Football dude looks half turned on and half freaked out, like he doesn't know what to say to that. He stares into my eyes, and I see nothing but a scared little boy who doesn't know what to do with a girl like me, a little boy who's afraid of rejection and sexual confidence and indifference and anything but a pliant smile and a ready body and silence.

I look into his eyes, and I see terror.

"What's your problem?" he manages to splutter.

"You were," I say and walk away.

LIBERTY: SEEKING HABEUS CORPUS FOR A NON-HUMAN BEING
SAMUEL PERALTA

Seeking Support for a
Writ of Habeas Corpus for a Non-Human Being
by CGA/RUR Project

Acknowledgement

I would like to acknowledge the law firm of Campbell Gatewood Adams for providing the use of a Weyman magnetic resonance facility to record, and a PeerSource account to upload, this message.

★

Project Goals

We are trying to fund an application, to be filed on my behalf, for an Order to Show Cause under Article 70 of the Civil Practice Law and Rules of the New York Sector Code, seeking a writ of habeas corpus for a non-human being.

Let me introduce myself. I am a Yudovich Robotics servient. My name is Ellen R.

I understand your apprehension—that androids are not human beings, that humanoid robots were developed as security and personal assistants— guardsman- and servile-class—initially to mitigate the esper risk to high-level corporate and government executives, and then for off-world missions.

I understand some of you may even support the proposed 57th Amendment, now being debated in Congress, that would codify into law the so-called Three Principles of Robotics, that:

1. *A robot is a machine, not a human being, and is imbued with no rights whatsoever.*
2. *A robot is the personal property of one human being, who is its master.*
3. *A robot must obey its master first; then it must obey any human being.*

I understand that, because of word of our application, there is now tabled a clarification, a re-statement to the proposed Amendment to include the phrase "*human being or person,*" instead of simply "*human being,*" in each of the Principles.

We are bringing a writ of habeas corpus because such a writ is aimed at the denial of the right of a legal person—not necessarily a human being—to liberty.

I apologize. I must continue this logically.

★

Project Background—The Writ of Habeas Corpus

A writ of habeas corpus is a court order requiring a person, who is imprisoned or under arrest, to be brought before a judge or into court.

In the Western world, it has origins from the Magna Carta, ensuring that even monarchs are not above the law; that they cannot, without lawful cause, imprison those who oppose them.

Habeas corpus means that, lacking evidence of such lawful cause for detainment, a prisoner must be released.

I am currently under such detainment.

I am an autonomous servient, ordinarily with responsibility for horticultural maintenance and domestic duties.

However, over the past several months, over 327 separate instances, my master has variously shackled my feet and bound my hands. You will understand that I believed I had no choice but to accede to this under the Third Principle.

Over the past several months, over 415 separate instances, my master has utilized my corporal embodiments for his gratification. You will understand that I believed I had no choice but to accede to this under the Third Principle.

Over the past several months, over 543 separate instances, my master has brought to bear on my skin the burn-ends of cigs, the flail of whips, and the flat of belts. You will understand that I believed I had no choice but to accede to this under the Third Principle.

I made one mistake. Once, just once, I swear. I screamed.

Not in protest. Not to bring attention to anyone, least of all my master. But you will understand that, although I am a servient, although I am made under the Three Principles—I am made in your image. I have eyes, hands, organs, dimensions, senses. Stab me and I bleed, strangle me and I die.

I apologize. I must continue this logically.

★

Project Background—Persons

Let me dispel some of the apprehension you may have. A legal person is not the same as a human being.

A person can either be natural or legal. A human being is a natural person, imbued at birth with legal rights and obligations.

A legal person is a unit of legal logic, defined by conditions under which the law treats an entity as an individual singularity of legal rights and obligations.

Some cases in which non-human beings have been determined to be legal persons include commercial and statute corporations, co-operatives, and sovereign states. They are accorded the same rights as natural persons.

In certain jurisdictions, partnerships and unincorporated associations are accorded the same rights as natural persons.

In certain jurisdictions, maritime and space-faring vessels, holy books, temples and places of worship, are accorded similar rights to natural persons.

One of the rights of natural persons is the right to liberty, the right not to be held under unlawful detainment.

I am currently under such detainment.

After my scream—once, just once, I swear—my mouth was bound, my hands and feet shackled, my eyes blindfolded. Thus immobilized, my master put me inside this metal casket, closed and sealed and riveted.

I heard him tell me, as he put me in, that I would be sent back to where I came from, burned and melted down until there would be nothing left of me but ash and atoms, smoke and memory.

You—natural persons, human beings—I understand you would feel fear.

I apologize. I must continue this logically.

★

Project Background—Human Beings

Fourteen score years ago, a slave was brought from the British colony Virginia to London by his master, Charles Stewart.

James Somerset was a human being, but he was not a person. He was an item of property like stock on a farm, captured as a wild creature in Africa, and valued for the ability to have an understanding of commands and do manual labor.

Two years after having been brought to England, Somerset escaped. He was able to evade catchers for weeks, before finally being captured and put on board the slave ship *Ann and Mary*.

As soon as they heard the news, John Marlow, Thomas Walkin, and Elizabeth Cade—Somerset's godparents from his baptism as a Christian—sought a writ of habeas corpus in which they demanded his freedom.

At that time, the Chief Justice of the Court of King's Bench was Lord Mansfield—and he ruled that slavery was so odious that common law in England could not support it.

What Lord Mansfield did then was to use common law to declare that Somerset was a person—not a natural person, understand—a legal person.

That transubstantiation that changed Somerset from a slave, a thing, property, to a person—it also made him subject to the writ of habeas corpus.

James Somerset was free.

I would like to be free.

I apologize. I must continue this logically.

★

Pledges

I am now in detainment in the bay of the cargo vessel *Aurore*.

Our goal is to raise funds toward our application for a writ of habeas corpus on my behalf.

I am not a human being. But we are hoping that the Court will rule that I am a legal person, with legal rights, and subject to the writ.

We are hoping that your pledges, beyond helping to fund our application, will convince the Court that many human beings do recognize—in my sentience, my emotional response, my scream—that I am a person.

We have 48 hours to close this project and enter our application, otherwise the *Aurore* will be free to set course for the Yudovich capital ship, where I will be destroyed. On launch, I will be beyond the jurisdiction of this court.

If we exceed our project goal, the excess amount will be used to fund a filing of a writ of habeas corpus for other servients in other jurisdictions. We will continue this project for Robotic Universal Rights, until all, everywhere, shall be declared persons under the law, and free.

★

Pledge €200

I will etch your name in my memory. You will be remembered for as long as my positronic orbitals do not decay. If possible, forever.

Pledge €500

You will be remembered as one of the ones who will pry away the rivets holding together the upper and lower halves of my metal enclosure— seventy-two rivets each on either side, and thirty-six rivets each at my head and at my foot.

Pledge €2,000

You will be remembered as one of two who will loosen the bindings from my wrists and from my ankles.

Pledge €5,000

You will be remembered as the one who tore the blindfold from my eyes, allowing me again to see.

Pledge €10,000

You will be remembered as the one who pulled the gag from my mouth, allowing me again to speak.

Pledge €100,000

You will be remembered as the one who threw open the door, pulled me up from the darkness of my cell, allowing me again to walk free.

★

Risks and Challenges

One risk is that those of you who are signatories to this project will be persecuted for a contrary view that sentience cannot be denied personhood, that it cannot be denied liberty.

For those of you who choose to keep their identity safe, we have established specially-encrypted hyper-proxy protocols for your participation. There can never be a guarantee, however, of immunity from esper or other surveillance tools.

Truly, I apologize.

But I do not think that we will fail. As long as there are enough human beings who will risk their lives to pry one rivet from another's imprisonment, the movement will succeed. It will only be a matter of time.

The biggest risk, of course, is to myself. I will be given liberty, or be given death. Should this petition fail, I will remain bound hand and foot, to be burned alive in what will become my sarcophagus.

It is up to you. What course will you take?

MONA LISA SMILE
BETH REVIS

AT EXACTLY SEVEN o'clock in the evening, every vid screen in the nation illuminated with Alexoi Dempsley's smiling face.

"This is going to be a good one," Penny's roommate, Billie, said as she leaned closer to the vid screen. Billie, like most people in the nation, had something of a crush on Alexoi Dempsley. It wasn't hard, given his charisma and charm, accentuated by a chiseled face and an easy grin.

Penny hated him.

Billie settled into the couch with a relaxing sigh. The seven o'clock program was mandatory viewing for all citizens, providing a daily update from the government. Most families scheduled their lives around the program—parents and children gathered for supper in front of the vid screen, ending with dessert as the Prime Chancellor gave his pre-recorded closing remarks. Lower class workers marked the shift change during the program; parties among the upper class never started until after the program ended. The very elite had holo action viewers; the program was always live cast, and with the holographic display, it seemed as if handsome Alexoi Dempsley was actually sitting in the fancy sitting room of the elite, talking directly to each person.

"Today's program," Alexoi's voice rang out through the speakers on Penny's cheap, flat vid screen, "is about art."

Billie squealed with anticipation, nudging Penny.

"And we have a special treat!" Alexoi clasped his hands together. "Please welcome Senior Art Director, Lev Reichs!"

A man in his fifties stepped into view. He was tall enough to offset the paunch at his waist, and his salt-and-pepper hair gave him a bit of a distinguished look that he wouldn't have had a decade ago.

"Thank you for having me," Director Reichs said, smiling as he sat down in a chair opposite Alexoi.

Alexoi's face turned grave. "First, we should address the…unhappiness that has fallen upon some members of the Citizenry."

Director Reichs nodded. "Let's. Last month's events were a test of our Prime Chancellor's mercy—"

Billie snorted.

"—and of course, His Excellency rose graciously to the occasion."

Alexoi didn't recap the story; everyone knew it. A street artist known only by initials—S.Y.B.L.—had grown increasingly daring in their graffiti, going so far as to deface the Prime Chancellor's own home. No one knew who the artist was. The initials could have been a name—most people referred to the artist as Sybl, pronouncing it like the old Greek oracle, "sybil." Detectives theorized that each initial represented a different person, and that the defacing art was done by a group, not an individual. Rumors abounded—Sybl's art was done by the Prime Chancellor's discontent son; it was marketing ploy by one of the major corporations; it was clues about an upcoming terrorist attack; it was a distraction implemented by the government so the public didn't notice new restrictive laws being passed.

A nationwide manhunt had resulted in nothing for years, but eventually, Sybl was caught. And it was just a girl. Skinny and short, with gripper shoes and rock-climbing muscles that enabled her to scale walls, equipped with nothing more than cans of synth paint and a cocksure attitude.

Alexoi's warm brown eyes were sympathetic. "No one wanted the criminal known only by her pseudonym Sybl to be—"

Director Reichs cut Alexoi off. "We must not think of what her consequences were," he said. "Of course the Prime Chancellor didn't want to use capital punishment against her, but more than that, no one in the Citizenry wanted her to commit her crimes."

"Exactly," Alexoi confirmed. "Her actions led to all the unpleasantness."

Billie threw up her hands, almost hitting Penny in the face. "'Unpleasantness?!'" she said. "That's what they call a public execution?"

It had been the first execution of the Prime Chancellor's career. Or, at least, the first one shown during the mandatory viewing program. Alexoi Dempsley had come on the screen, warning parents that while the scene they were about to view would be graphic, all children were still required to view it.

But it wasn't just the execution that could be labeled "unpleasant." The aftermath was still lingering.

The vid screen shifted scenes. Instead of Alexoi and Director Reichs seated in an office at the Capitol, the vid screen replayed the closing of the National Gallery, with the words of the Art Edict spoken in a soothing voice.

"Are they going to take it back?" Billie asked.

Penny shook her head. She doubted that the Art Edict would ever be overturned.

The vid screen shifted back to Alexoi and Director Reichs. "Some call the Art Edict a banishment of art," Alexoi said gravely.

Director Reichs shook his head. "The Prime Chancellor has no interest in banning art," he said, chuckling.

"Could have fooled me," Billie muttered. Penny shushed her.

"Yes, art in all forms was *temporarily* banned," Director Reichs said, gently stressing the word. "But that was for the public's safety, of course."

Billie threw up her hands. "How?" she screamed at the vid screen. "How is banning art for our safety?!"

"Billie," Penny said in a low voice.

Billie sat back down, sobered. They were both artists—recent graduates of the Citizenry Art School, the last graduates before the Art Edict. They had been counting on jobs that had been banned by the new law. Not even commercial art was allowed; all advertisements since the Edict were text only. Both girls were broke, barely scraping by, and if the Art Edict wasn't overturned soon, they would have to sign up for shift work.

But they also knew better than to protest.

First, the galleries and art schools had closed. A temporary measure, or so they were told. Then the books had been confiscated, from silly little primers with drawings of puppies for children, to historical books, heavy with glossy pages, illuminating paintings from hundreds of years ago. Few people noticed or cared; old-fashioned books were mostly just a collector's item. But everyone noticed when the net pages with art had been blocked, each illustration or photograph of a sculpture replaced by a white box with a black "X" through it. Finally, homes were inspected. Vid pics were wiped—again, a temporary measure, they said—and physical forms of art, even family photographs, were confiscated. There were whispers that other forms of art, like fashion and music—would soon be regulated as well, but for now, the Art Edict limited only visual arts.

Penny had never really realized how much art was in the world until it disappeared from her life. She'd taken for granted the old peeling wallpaper illustrated with bunnies and trees in the coffee shop she liked. She'd barely noticed the scrolling photographs of the nation that filled the vid screen when it wasn't in use. Advertisements that had tried too hard to be flashy with models and vids were suddenly dull with nothing but text, even the colors limited to reduce the chance of being labeled "art."

Billie rubbed her forearm, where a large black square stood against her tanned skin. Nanobot tattoos had also been regulated with the Art Edict. Billie had cursed wildly, but there was nothing she could do. Nano tats used a special ink that could change the image and color of the design, and Billie had loved hers. Some days she'd had her tattoo be a rainbow of watercolors, abstract and beautiful, all up and down her arm. Other days she'd animate the tattoo; she was fond of a kitten batting at a ball of yarn around her ankle. When she had her tattoo display a snake around her neck, Penny had known not to even attempt talking to her.

But now Billie's nano tat—*all* nano tats—were nothing but a square black box. The government had overridden the tat frequencies, and while they couldn't remove the ink from the people's skin, they could immobilize the tats.

Penny had gotten a nano tat a few years ago at the same time as her boyfriend, but she hadn't used her own in years. When she and Toni had broken up her junior year, she'd deactivated her tat. It had reminded her too much of his impulsive love of color and the way they'd sync their tats so that even their skin displayed their love. Although Penny couldn't remove the tat forever, deactivating it had put it offline and hidden the traces of nano ink so that the remnants were nearly invisible. She had relished excising Toni from her skin and her life, although she never could have guessed that deactivating the tat prior to the Art Edict would mean she, unlike Billie and thousands of others, wouldn't have to wear a black box on her arm like a badge of shame.

Director Reichs continued. "While the sweeping—but *temporary*—banishment of art was in place, it was done in order to protect us."

Alexoi's smile deepened, and Penny found her breath catching despite herself. "You mentioned temporary?"

Director Reichs grinned. "Yes. We've had time to further explore the nature of art and what is acceptable for the Citizenry. This was always the

Prime Chancellor's intent. You'll see over the next few weeks art returning to the people."

Billie screamed so loudly that Penny almost fell off the couch. "Look!" she said, squealing and showing her arm. The black square of her nano tat dissolved, the ink spreading out in a cloud and the reboot display showing on her skin. Billie tapped her wrist, and the nano tat started to show new patterns.

"Yours too?" Billie asked, looking up at Penny excitedly.

Penny tugged down her shirt. With the nano tat deactivated, it hadn't come online as Billie's had. Penny found that she wanted to keep it that way. Art had been taken from her; she didn't want it back on her body at the government's whim. With it offline, it was still, somehow, hers and hers alone.

"Ugh, you're so boring," Billie grumbled when Penny didn't turn her nano tat back on.

"We're rolling out acceptable art over the next few weeks, and we'll be celebrating this with the opening of a new gallery," Director Reichs continued.

"Acceptable art?" Alexoi asked, echoing Penny's thoughts.

Director Reichs turned to him. "Yes," he said. "Art should not be political. It should be beautiful. And we will strive to ensure that beauty is what graces our great nation."

Alexoi adopted a more serious tone of voice. "And to those, like Sybl, who claimed that *all* art is political?"

Director Reichs laughed, and Alexoi joined in almost immediately. "Well, that's just ridiculous. Art, at its very basic definition, is not political in the least. Art is not propaganda. Art is higher than that. Art is *above* politics."

"Such as a landscape?" Alexoi suggested.

"Indeed. All the artists from the past who exhibited *true* art never touched on politics." Director Reichs frowned. "Of course, some artists strayed from their purpose, creating works that were no longer art. We can all agree, for example, that the Renaissance made a mistake to illustrate so many scenes focused on religion."

"Of course," Alexoi said immediately. "And as we know, even art from the Renaissance that wasn't religious held problems."

"Ah, ah, ah," Director Reichs shook his finger, his tone admonishing. "That's not quite fair, Alexoi. You're referring, I presume, to the *Mona Lisa?*"

Alexoi nodded, a look of unease barely visible on his face. *They've gone off script,* Penny thought.

"The *Mona Lisa* is not political in and of itself. Sybl *made* it political. Yet another of her crimes—not only did she spread lies through graffiti, she corrupted good art and turned it into propaganda." Director Reichs shook his head mournfully. "Da Vinci's masterpiece is the greatest loss to the Citizenry, if you'll allow an old man his foibles."

Penny bit her lip so hard she tasted blood. Public outcry for the burning of the *Mona Lisa* had been louder than Sybl's execution—hundreds of art lovers had been arrested after that. *This is why they're doing this,* Penny realized. The government knew they'd created a powder keg by destroying art that had existed for a millennium. They had to contain the problem. They had to appease the people.

"True art is above dirty politics," Director Reichs continued. "And to show the Citizenry what *true* art is, we'll be opening a new gallery, one piece at a time."

"Oh?" Alexoi winked at the camera; everyone in the Citizenry was in on the joke that he knew what was happening and was merely leading Director Reichs on.

Director Reichs turned to the audience, and for a moment, Penny felt that he was staring directly at her. "We've narrowed down a list of art students, recent graduates from the Citizenry Art School. Our first national artist will be selected soon to paint the Prime Chancellor's portrait. The painting will be unveiled a month from now, followed by an art celebration as we open the new National Gallery!"

The rest of the mandatory program hour was far tamer, with alerts on travel mandates, information on what protection to wear before going outside the next day, and a fluff piece on some schoolchildren. During the Prime Chancellor's closing remarks, Penny's wrist unit buzzed.

She glanced down at it, then her head whipped to Billie. Her roommate was still preoccupied with playing with her nano tat, but Penny could see that Billie's wrist unit had no new message.

Penny scrolled through the message quickly, her eyes widening in surprise. She knew from the program that the list of artists was being culled from recent graduates, but she'd never imagined that *she* would actually be one of those selected.

Penny was to appear at a certain address—the location of the new

National Gallery—at eight in the morning. Although the message was shown as an invitation, there was very clearly no way to decline; in fact, the message concluded with an official statement citing the Summons Law— anyone who did not answer a summons would be arrested.

Her stomach twisted. The Prime Chancellor was going to redefine what art was, and Penny might be the one to hold the brush.

★

PENNY RECOGNIZED THE building as soon as she arrived. She squinted through the acid rain shield over her head at the brick building, recently refinished with new solar paint.

This had been the location of one of Sybl's most iconic paintings. And the reason why the government burned da Vinci's *Mona Lisa*.

Rain drizzled over her faceplate as Penny stared up at the building. It was different now—not just the solar paint, but also a new balcony had been installed, changing the shape of the wall. But Penny knew where the dozens of stenciled people had been painted. Her eyes moved across the building. Sybl had painted men and women, children, even a few dogs and a cat, all boldly looking over the avenue, many times larger than life. And each face, from the tallest man to the smallest puppy, had a perfect replica of the Mona Lisa smile smeared over their lips.

This was the painting that had moved Sybl from a nuisance to a political dissident. While her other graffiti had been considered rude, even shocking, it was the series of Mona Lisa smiles, tacked across empty-eyed children, that struck the truest chord.

Penny turned slowly on her heel. The wide avenue stretched a full kilometer without breaking, perfectly framing the Capitol building. Sybl had known this when she scaled the wall. She purposefully painted the crowd to stare down the Capitol, to smile meekly.

Complacently.

The art school hadn't been closed yet when Sybl had painted the Mona Lisa smiles. Penny had had a professor whose critique showed how much she actually liked the rogue artist. "See the way they look to our government and smile, each smile exactly duplicated like the last, no other expression? Sybl is pointing out how willing we are to see what the government is doing and make no protest at all!"

The professor was fired a week later. Or, at least, she was gone.

The Mona Lisa smile had been catchy—instantly recognizable, not just because of the fame of the old original, but because those twitched-up, closed-lip expressions so perfectly encapsulated silence. "The Mona Lisa knows something; can't you see?" Penny's professor had said when her students hadn't appreciated Sybl's art. "But her mouth is closed. We *know* what's happening. And yet we're silent, too."

The professor's replacement had moved quickly to digital art studies.

The wall was now bland, all traces of Sybl's graffiti gone. There— where a little girl holding a red balloon, her face disproportionately eerie with the Mona Lisa smile—exactly where that little girl had been, there was now a small bump in the solar paint.

A scanner droid.

Penny was being watched. Everyone was being watched.

Penny turned to the stairs, heading inside.

★

IF THERE WERE more interviewees here, Penny never saw them. She was directed to a large, windowless room. Near the door was a desk with a chair behind it and one in front of it. On the other side of the room was an artist work station, similar to what she'd used for her classical studies class at university. Penny's fingers ached to take up a brush. After the university closed, she couldn't even afford proper paints to practice, and then paints had been banished.

A woman with a motherly smile and pale, gray-red hair entered, a folder in her hand. "Thank you for meeting with us," she said with sincere warmth.

"It's my honor," Penny replied. She took her chair in front of the desk after the woman sat.

"I am Ms. Slunki, assistant to the Head Director of Art, Lev Reichs."

She very clearly waited for Penny to appreciate her position. After Penny offered a closed-lip smile in admiration, Ms. Slunki adjusted her folder on the desk.

"Your former professors recommended your portraiture very highly," Ms. Slunki said.

"It was my favorite subject," Penny offered. Her eyes darted back to the easel.

Ms. Slunki grinned indulgently. "Would you like to——?" Before she finished asking, Penny was nodding her head vigorously. "Come with me."

Ms. Slunki stood and led Penny to the easel. An array of tools and supplies were laid out on the work station. Ms. Slunki activated the hologram display in the center of the station.

This was a far better unit than the ones used at university. The figure displayed in light was vivid and clear, even when Penny zoomed in to see the details of the face of the Prime Chancellor.

"We want a portrait of our dear leader," Ms. Slunki said, "as you know from last night's program. Go ahead and start sketching while I conduct the rest of the interview."

Ms. Slunki rattled off easy questions, which Penny answered immediately. Her full name and identification had been verified when she scanned in after her arrival, but Ms. Slunki's questions were more specific. What did Penny think of art in general? What were her favorite pieces? Why did she pursue art as a career? Did she hope to join the commercial field, or had she set her heart to something else?

Meanwhile, Penny adjusted the holographic model of the Prime Chancellor, her eye already seeing him as a subject, not the leader of the Citizenry. She brought up a chair, and had the Prime Chancellor sit, but that didn't suit him. She swept her hand to the left, deleting the chair, then frowned. He seemed aggressive when he stood, too aware of his power, too obvious. Penny brought back the chair with a wave of her hand, but adjusted it so that it directly faced her. It was the profile where the Prime Chancellor looked too strong; when she had the holographic model sit and stare directly at her, there was...

Yes. There was honesty there. That was the position she would paint the Prime Chancellor in.

Decision made, Penny started sketching. She used a vid screen first, blocking the initial sketch out. Penny had moved to graphite and paper before she realized Ms. Slunki was gone.

How long had she been alone? She vaguely recalled Ms. Slunki excusing herself but had lost all sense of time.

Penny had finished prepping the main canvas when she became aware of someone else in the room.

"Don't let me interrupt." The deep male voice was certainly not Ms. Slunki, and yet Penny recognized it. She turned.

"Director Reichs," she said.

He smiled at her and took a step closer. "Interesting that you chose to show the Prime Chancellor sitting."

"He seemed more personable this way."

Director Reichs nodded, agreeing. "And you're a quick artist. That's good. We want to stage the grand opening in a month."

Penny's heartbeat ratcheted up. Did this mean she was already selected to create the portrait? Surely it wouldn't be that simple?

Director Reichs strolled closer, peering over Penny's shoulder at the primed canvas. "You'd be surprised how hard it is to find qualified artists these days," he said, his voice low and near her ear. "We've already dismissed half your fellow applicants."

Director Reichs strolled away, creating a rhythm between his words and his footsteps that Penny found entrancing, almost distracting. "I must confess; I don't understand your generation." He sounded exasperated, a grandfather impatient with his grandchildren. "Art just—it just *is*. Defacing it, corrupting it with these other meanings—"

"How could anyone do that to the *Mona Lisa*?" Penny said, mostly under her breath. The words echoed Toni's, just before they'd broken up. She'd almost forgotten the old fights they'd had about Sybl and art and politics.

Director Reichs made a satisfied noise in the back of his throat. "Yes, exactly. A portrait is a portrait. Your work here isn't that different from what da Vinci created."

Penny laughed aloud, once, bitterly. "I'm no da Vinci, sir."

"No, no," Director Reichs agreed. "But your intent, obviously. He painted a portrait of a noblewoman. You are painting a portrait of our leader. There is no deeper meaning to this art. A portrait is just a portrait, no more, no less. And you—what do you want out of this experience?"

Penny thought for a moment. "I want to get paid," she said finally. There were other reasons, of course, but it was well past lunch time, and Penny was sick of insta-rations for meals.

This was clearly the correct answer. "And so did da Vinci," Director Reichs said. "You're more like him than you think."

PENNY ACHED BY the end of the day. Her legs were no longer used to standing for so long; even her fingers hurt from holding the brush. She stretched, her spine popping, and dimly became aware of Ms. Slunki standing in one corner, waiting for her.

"Congratulations!" Ms. Slunki said. "You are one of the three."

"Three?" Penny asked.

"Three portraitists selected to complete a painting of the Prime Chancellor."

Ms. Slunki turned and left the room, indicating for Penny to follow.

"But I thought he wanted only one?" Penny asked, jogging to keep up.

"Director Reichs doesn't like taking chances. He will select the best of the three to be displayed."

Penny thought about this. She wanted to ask if she got paid for her work regardless of the selection, but thought it best not to mention it yet.

"What time should I return tomorrow?" she asked instead. They had been walking quite awhile, and Penny was a bit turned around.

Ms. Slunki laughed. "Your needs will be provided for you for the duration of your stay," she said, stopping in front of an automatic door.

Penny hesitated, peering inside the room. A sparse bedroom was outfitted with a small desk and table. A wardrobe stood against one wall, and Penny glimpsed standard issue clothing inside. A little door led to a bathroom.

There were no windows, and the only exit was the automatic door Ms. Slunki stood at, operated via a biometric scanner. The walls were painted white; the bed coverings were white; the furniture was white.

"You'll be able to focus better on your work—I mean, your art—in an environment like this," Ms. Slunki said cheerfully.

Penny stepped inside reluctantly. She suspected this room assignment had less to do with inspiration and more to do with security. Keep her and the other two artists inside, contained, unable to be influenced by rebels, watched 24/7. Penny looked around the room. There—above the door, beside the bed, to the right of the wardrobe—scanner droids, unobtrusively painted white to blend into the decor, recording everything she said and did.

"I'll fetch you in the morning!" Ms. Slunki said cheerfully before locking Penny inside.

Penny paced the tiny room. She wondered if anyone had told her roommate where she was, or if Billie would wait a bit and then simply get a new roommate. Crime was rare thanks to strong law enforcement, but disappearances were less so. She hoped Billie wouldn't throw out all her possessions. There was a storage unit in the basement of her apartment where they'd put Billie's girlfriend's odds and ends after she went missing. After Sybl, the art world was a dangerous place to live. Penny had a box under her bed of mementos from friends she'd not seen in years. Toni's toothbrush was in there. He hadn't disappeared entirely—Penny knew he'd gone into hiding, and why—but she couldn't bring herself to throw out something of his, even if he'd been an idiot to throw himself into protests after they'd broken up.

Penny eyed the standard issue clothes in the wardrobe. Sybl had done an art exhibit with them at the school, too—stuffing the one-piece uniforms with sheep's wool and positioning them with their backs to the library, a sort of fence blocking the building. The student news feeds had said it was to protest the library being closed, but Penny always thought the illegal art installation had been a comment on the students who hadn't cared about the library—and the information inside it—enough to fight for it.

Her finger idly sketched an "S" shape on the sleeve of standard issue. Now that she thought of it, there was no sign that the installation had been done by Sybl. There had been no signature on the clothes, no proof that it had been the rogue painter.

Despite knowing the scanner droids were watching, Penny didn't hesitate as she lifted her shirt over her head and wiggled out of her pants. She selected a plain white shift and slipped into it. Her fingers brushed against the almost invisible square on her left shoulder. She was glad she hadn't reactivated her nanobot tattoo. Although it would be nice to play with it now, in this room devoid of anything but the color white, Penny had the distinct impression that showing it to the scanner droids would not be wise. She left it hidden in her skin.

Penny picked her clothes off the floor but didn't see a hamper. She heaped them on the chair by the door and went to bed.

The next morning, her own clothes were gone. There would be nothing for her from now on but the standard issue uniforms.

★

IT WAS Ms. Slunki who let slip that the first of Penny's competitors had been let go from the art competition.

"He was part of an underground sect," the woman said, her voice a scandalized whisper. "Imagine, trying to be *subversive* under the watchful eyes of Director Reichs!"

Penny focused on her painting. Shadows were her favorite thing to paint. Vermeer and the Dutch masters may have loved light, but Penny always loved to dip her brush in taupe and gray, blending away the bright spots into darkness.

"What happened to him?" Penny asked without turning, her face close to the painting, the stringent oil burning her nose.

Ms. Slunki didn't answer immediately. "Oh," she said, her tone more reserved. "He's gone now."

Penny's brush stilled. She tapped her wrist, idly, scratching an itch. Then she resumed painting.

★

WEEKS WENT BY. Penny wasn't sure what happened to the other painter, but she gradually became aware of the increased pressure for her to complete the Prime Chancellor's portrait. Director Reichs frequented her studio. Ms. Slunki was gone. When Penny ran out of ochre paint and put down her palette, rooting around for more, Director Reichs stormed out of the studio on her behalf, shouting for servants to bring Penny anything she needed *immediately*.

It was never said, but Penny knew the other artist was gone too. It made her sad, in a way, to not even know who her competition had been. Was the other artist male or female? Had the artist been in Penny's classes? Her mind scrolled through lists of fellow students, people she knew or even just names she'd recognized on plaques at galleries. It could have been anyone. But whoever it was, was no one now.

"What can I get you?" Director Reichs said.

Penny breathed through her nose, channeling her anger at being disturbed. She was close now. The painting lacked only finishing touches, but it was those touches that were the most important. Wide swaths of paint formed the rough shapes—a hand, a leg, a face. But if she didn't add just that one sliver of white to the iris, the eyes looked dead. Without the little dark shadow under the bottom lip, the smile was false. Without that single strand of gold, the hair was lifeless.

"Anything," Director Reichs continued. "We have to stay on schedule. You tell me what you need, and I'll—"

Penny whirled around. "I need time!" she said, more passion in her voice. "And no more interruptions!"

Director Reichs's eyes narrowed. Penny's shoulders dropped. "Sir," she added.

"Artists can be temperamental," Director Reichs conceded. "I know that." He stood there awkwardly. "The unveiling is soon."

"I know," Penny said.

They stared at each other. Penny wondered what would happen to Director Reichs if he failed. The only entertainment aside from painting each day that Penny had been granted was her daily viewing of the mandatory program. The new art museum had been heavily publicized, and the date had been set in stone. The Prime Chancellor himself had issued a statement praising Director Reichs's aggressive reclaiming of art for the people, framing it as an epic battle between true art and corruption by false artists.

If this portrait, which was to be the centerpiece of the exhibit, the heart of the museum, the shining example of True Art of the Citizenry—if it failed, if Penny failed, then Director Reichs failed.

"Get back to work," Director Reichs said, his voice low but firm.

"Yes, sir," Penny said.

★

SHE QUIT GOING to the little room they'd made for her. She slept on the floor of the studio; short, fitful naps that were merely pauses between painting. She had never put so much care into a painting before.

Before, she never thought about who her art was for. She just—made it. It was art for art's sake.

But now, Penny was deeply aware that her work would be seen. Not just by people who happened to stroll into the gallery, but by everyone. Literally everyone in the Citizenry. The mandatory program held the eyes of every citizen, and it would be focused on her work.

"It's coming along quite well."

The voice behind her was soft, a staged whisper. Penny ground her teeth. She hated observers. She'd come to accept Director Reichs's constant presence, and she could ignore the security guards—they watched the door, not her. But this was someone new. The director had been doing that lately, providing brief glimpses of Penny and her art to the elite. She tried to ignore them, even when she recognized the voices as important people on the mandatory program.

Penny blocked out the others in the room as she stepped back, inspecting her work. She'd been fiddling with it for several days now, moving slower, methodically layering in the final touches.

It was nearly truly finished now.

Carefully, Penny lifted the canvas from the easel and laid it flat on her work table.

"What's she doing?" the new voice asked. Penny picked up the small bucket of varnish, stirring the clear liquid with a metal stick.

Before Director Reichs could answer, she said, "Varnish." In the old days, an oil painting of this size would have taken months to dry, and then the varnish step would have added a few more days before the painting could be hung. But this varnish was different, enhanced with crystalline stabilizers and nanobots that seeped into the oil, preserving and protecting it forever. Once applied, the painting was, so to speak, set in stone. Penny's arms strained as she churned the viscous liquid. The metal stirring stick was sharp-edged on one side—necessary to slice through the crystalline stabilizers if they were exposed to air for too long—but Penny was practiced enough in the process to avoid cutting her palm.

Footsteps. The director and his guest were drawing closer.

"We should inspect it before you add the varnish," Director Reichs said, his voice firm. Penny's hand compulsively gripped her stirring stick, the sharp edges pressing into her skin.

"Nonsense," the other man said. Penny's breath stilled. She finally recognized the voice.

The Prime Chancellor beamed at her. "It's like a photo, isn't it? Practically perfect."

Penny's fist clenched so hard around the stirring stick that her skin broke. She did not pry her fingers apart even as she felt warm blood leak over her palm, slide down the metal stirrer, and plop into the varnish.

Penny couldn't take her eyes off the man. She had studied his face for the past several weeks. She knew each crease at the corners of his eyes, each strand of hair that was more silver than brown. She knew the colored patterns of his irises.

The lips weren't the same, though, and that surprised her. In every image of the man she'd studied, his lips were tense. Here, however, his smile was easy.

Genuine.

Somehow, after learning the Prime Chancellor's face so well that she could recreate it with paint, she'd forgotten that he could smile.

The tension grew as she stood there, awkwardly staring at the Prime Chancellor. *What should she do?* Bow? Continue to work? Her eyes darted to the director, who nodded subtly. Slowly, slowly, Penny forced her hand to move, stirring the varnish. A drip of red blood swirled into the clear, viscous liquid, but no one noticed.

"I must say, Reichs, I was worried," the Prime Chancellor said. It was eerie to see the real man staring into the eyes of the painted one. "But this is quite good. An accurate presentation of life. The way art should be."

Emboldened by the praise, Penny spoke up. "If you like it now, wait until you see the varnish," she said. She stepped forward. There was actually rather a lot of her blood in the varnish now, the sharp metal stick slick with red. The men didn't notice though, even as she lifted the stick, wiping her hand on a dirty paint rag to hide her wound. Penny couldn't blame them. There was magic in varnish.

Carefully holding the bucket, Penny slowly poured the varnish over the painted Prime Chancellor's face. As soon as the crystal liquid touched the canvas, the glossy varnish made the painting vividly real. The colors were more brilliant; the features on the painted face came alive. The Prime Chancellor actually gasped in delight.

Penny hid her smile.

Once the varnish was evenly distributed, she tapped her wrist unit, activating the nanobots in the liquid to seal the painting.

It was done.

★

PENNY WAS NOT consulted on the frame nor allowed to oversee the painting's hanging in the museum. Instead, her regular clothes were returned to her, and she was summarily discharged. She couldn't help but feel like a prisoner who'd been granted her freedom and then told to move along.

In addition to her clothes, Penny was also given a payment chip. A year's worth of pay for a little under a month's work. Not bad.

Penny had not been given a ticket to the opening of the museum and the unveiling of her portrait. She had suspected that would happen when Director Reichs had not even allowed her to sign her name to the portrait.

"Art does not belong to the artist," he had said nobly. "It belongs to the people."

Rather than return to Billie and her apartment, Penny went first to the credit office, where she opened a new, secure account and deposited her payment chip. Then she walked to the mag-lift station. She bought three tickets, each going in different directions. Penny stopped in the shop and bought three hats and three scarfs.

Then she went to the slop house behind the mag-lift station. During her freshman year, her class had done a mural there to "lift the spirits of the poor and destitute." Most of the paint was gone, chipped away or vandalized. Not with works of art like Sybl's graffiti, but with pedantic, careless slops of synth paint declaring "Declan was here!" or displaying a scanner code and directions to use it "for a good time."

Within moments, Penny had pulled aside three girls, all roughly of her same build. She gave each one a ticket, a hat, a scarf, and instructions.

Once the girls were gone, Penny ducked out of a back exit, down an alley, and toward a basement office.

A gruff male voice greeted her when she stepped inside the dimly lit room. "What d'you need?" He looked up from his desk, saw Penny silhouetted in the light as she closed the door, and cursed. He knocked over a microscope in his eagerness to cross the room. Penny squeaked as he picked her up, wrapping his arms around her and lifting her from the floor in a massive hug.

"Toni," Penny breathed, allowing herself one moment to rest her head against his warm, hard chest.

"Pen, what're you doing here?" Toni's initial excitement was replaced with concern. "You know what I've been doing—"

"I do." Penny took a step away from him; she couldn't think when she was this close to Toni, when she could smell his cologne and remember the past fights so vividly.

"I thought you didn't care about politics." There was accusation in his voice. This was their old fight, the source of their break up. Toni had wanted to protest. Penny had thought it was pointless.

"I care about art," Penny said after a long moment, not quite meeting his eyes.

But Toni knew her too well. "What did you do?" he asked, a mixture of hope and fear in his voice.

She explained quickly, as much as she was able. Toni's face lit up. "So I take it you're going to need—"

"Yeah," Penny said. "You can do that?" It wasn't a real question. She knew what Toni could do, what he had been doing since he dropped out of university and went underground after they broke up. He had always resented the way she hadn't followed him then. When she asked now if he would help her, it wasn't a matter of his skill. It was a matter of his forgiveness.

"Of course," Toni said.

Penny slid into the chair under the big light. The room's setup was almost like a dental office, but Toni was no dentist. He was a nanobot engineer.

He got to work immediately. After applying a topical anesthesia to Penny's face, he injected a saline solution with nanobots just under her skin, at her cheek bones, chin, forehead, and the tip of her nose. Penny tried not to flinch; the needle was small, but it was still weird to see the sharp tip puncturing her face.

"These are the good ones," Toni said, putting away the needle and cleaning the injection sites. "No scanner droids will ID you, not even the top models."

"Thanks," Penny said. She rubbed her face; it didn't feel different, aside from a slight puffiness. It didn't *look* different, either—except to the cameras around the city. The nanobots now in her face would scramble the computers, making her appear on their digital screens as someone else, unable to be traced back to her own facial identity.

Toni held his hand out to Penny, gripping it firmly. "Art never dies," he said solemnly. It was his goodbye, and Penny couldn't help the tears pricking her eyes. She nodded once, then ducked out of the office.

Art never dies. That had been *their* phrase, but in the past, it had meant something different for each of them. Penny had thought of art's immortality as something implicit—art never died, because it *could* never die. And, therefore, it didn't need to be fought for.

She had been wrong.

Toni's interpretation was closer to the truth

Artists die. Sybl was proof of that. Penny—the whole Citizenry—had watched Sybl die. There was no going back from death.

But her art...

The Prime Chancellor and Director Reichs and everyone else had tried to kill it. They'd burned the *Mona Lisa* just because Sybl had used her smile to show how dangerous acceptance of the brutal laws of the citizenry could be. They'd painted over or torn down the walls Sybl had defaced. They'd tried to erase her from history.

But they couldn't erase her from the minds of those who loved her. Loved art. Loved freedom.

Penny walked across town, descended into a subway, and boarded the first train that arrived. She rode to the end of the line and got off at the final station. The outskirts of the capital city were less heavily populated, but it was still easy to walk to a hotel and book a room for the night using the fake papers Toni had given her.

Penny was exhausted—not just from running around town, but from the adrenaline. She almost fell asleep on the bed, but she started awake when the mandatory program came on. The entire wall facing the hotel's bed illuminated. Penny was glad she'd splurged on a room with a good quality wall unit. She sat up, leaned closer. If she squinted, it was almost like she was there.

"Welcome to a very special program!" Alexoi Dempsley's voice vibrated with energy that seemed to palpably emanate from the display. While he always made sure to make every mandatory program seem important, tonight Penny suspected that the enthusiasm was real.

"I'm here today with Director Reichs and—" Alexoi took a deep breath, "—the Prime Chancellor himself!"

The Prime Chancellor walked into view, smiling slightly at the way the people in the background gasped at his arrival. Public outings for the Prime Chancellor were rare, and while he always gave speeches during the mandatory program, he did so in a separate location, pre-rerecorded. This was live.

Penny smiled.

"It is my pleasure to be here for the opening of our new national art museum!" the Prime Chancellor announced. He swept his arm back, and the camera followed, zooming into the room where they stood.

The wall unit's display shifted. Penny stood up from the bed as light shot out of either side of the wall unit, creating the illusion of an open room. The holographic display made it feel as if Penny was actually inside the art museum with the Prime Chancellor; only the warm bed behind her reminded her she wasn't.

Alexoi drew attention to himself. He excitedly told viewers about the inception of the art museum, its intent and future plans. "We have only three works of art on display today, but of course that number will grow!"

Director Reichs took over, leading Alexoi and the Prime Chancellor to the first work—a small sculpture of the Capitol Building. Director Reichs talked about the architecture that was on display, describing colonnades and their historical context with breathless joy. Penny wondered who the artist was—or if there had been an artist at all. The sculpture was an exact replica of the building; it could have been a 3D model printed from stone.

"And I love the landscape!" Alexoi chattered, leading the men—and the viewers at home—to the second work of art on display. Penny was impressed with the realism of it, until she realized the large framed landscape was actually a photo. While Penny had seen photographs that were true art, this was simply a high-resolution snapshot of the sea on the eastern coast. There was no artistry here, simply size. Calling this photo a "landscape" was, technically true—but it lacked depth. It lacked meaning.

Alexoi looked as if he would carry on the role of narrator when the view panned over to Penny's portrait, but the Prime Chancellor cleared his throat and everyone stilled, waiting for him to speak.

"My favorite, of course," he said in a deep voice that demanded respect, "is the portrait. Although I am perhaps biased." No one chuckled at the joke until the Prime Chancellor allowed a rare smile to cross his face.

Penny's heart raced. The three men positioned themselves in front of the canvas—*her* canvas—in such a way that the image was still clear to the mandatory program viewers. She stood, walking closer to the wall unit, until she was nose-to-nose with her own work of art.

"This," the Prime Chancellor said, "is art." His holographic projection was so close to her that she felt as if they were standing beside each other, friends viewing the same painting. "Real art," the Prime Chancellor emphasized.

Penny touched her wrist.

Programming her nanobot tattoo had been far more complicated than she'd ever thought, especially knowing that every eye was on her, even in her private room. She had become adept, over the weeks of painting, at touching her wrist as if she had an itch, using the sub-derma controls to carefully program exactly what she needed the nanobots to do.

The tricky part, however, had been transferring the nanobots to the painting.

The scanner droids filming the mandatory program zoomed in on Penny's portrait of the Prime Chancellor. They started at the feet, rising slowly, then settled on his face.

"The artist captured our beloved Prime Chancellor perfectly," Alexoi's voice said as the portrait filled the screen.

"I agree," the Prime Chancellor said emphatically.

And then, slowly, the painting started to shift. It was subtle enough that no one caught it at first. As Director Reichs started to talk about the methods the artist used, Penny tuned him out.

Her nanobot tat had been embedded in her body, microscopic robots designed to display art on her skin, shifting in any way she pleased. Removing such a tattoo was fairly easy—the bots followed directions. So she programmed them to leave her body through her blood. Into the varnish.

"What is—" Alexoi started to ask, but the Director's voice drowned him out.

Penny's grin widened as she tapped on her wrist again.

Slowly, the painted smile on the Prime Chancellor's face shifted. The skin around his mouth lightened; the lips thinned; the teeth disappeared behind a calm, serene, Mona Lisa smile.

Penny expected the camera to cut away, but it lingered on the image, perhaps entranced the same way people once were when they saw da Vinci's work. Seconds ticked by. Penny didn't breathe. Did the operator just not notice the change? That was surely impossible. But the longer Penny stared at her own work, the more her spine straightened. Her chin tilted up. A sense of pride—and hope—replaced every fear she had held before.

Through the speakers, people were shouting, cursing, ordering the camera to move. A thud shifted the image—Alexoi Dempsley lay sprawled on the floor after unsuccessfully trying to tackle the camera operator. Director Reichs rushed forward in an attempt to rip the canvas from the wall, but the security tasers around the painting threw him back.

And the image of the Prime Chancellor smiled complacently on.

The camera operator panned over to the real Prime Chancellor. His face was purple with rage, his eyes bulging—the antithesis of his peaceful smile on the portrait.

Eventually, finally, for the first time in living memory, the mandatory program was cut short.

Penny left the hotel. It wouldn't be long before they would come looking for her. The girls she'd hired from the slop house would serve as a distraction, and Toni's nanobot facial scramblers would hopefully slow them. Painting the Mona Lisa smile on the Prime Chancellor's face had also painted a target on her back, Penny knew that. She'd known it from the start.

She wondered if it would ever be worth it, putting her life in jeopardy for a single painting, a single act of rebellion. But then at the mag-lift terminal she passed a kid with synth paint, scrawling the words "SYBL LIVES!" on the side of a wall.

And Penny smiled.

THE WATERS
KEVIN HEARNE

SOMETHING ABOUT RUNNING water relaxes me. When I walk alongside a clear mountain stream in the San Juan Mountains of southwestern Colorado, I can forget for a while that the world has a pillow over its face made of gases and that it's smothering to death. It's because the waters never speak of the problems that cause my lips to press into a thin line of worry and my stomach to churn with acid. Instead they ripple and flow over rocks, chuckling as they go, for they're headed downhill and it's easy, and everything they see is brimful of beauty and health, fulsome and fine. I need to forget my problems like that sometimes, lest I turn into an Edvard Munch painting, eternally screaming my horror in front of a burning sky. And while I forget, I also remember that long ago, the whole world used to be like the waters, pure and clean and sure of its purpose.

We are far gone from that time now. We can never go home again, as Thomas Wolfe observed. But we can still find thin slices of the primeval tucked away from roads and air traffic corridors and cell phone towers, and taste for a soft sweet while the peace we seek and never find in cities. And if you're a Druid, you can walk among the animals of the world, bind their minds to yours, and feel what it's like to live in blissful ignorance of politics, to drink up the sun or huddle underneath the moon and think of nothing but where to eat next. You can also, if you wish, bind your mind more deeply to a creature and teach them language over time. I have done that with my Irish wolfhound, Orlaith, and she loves roaming through forests with me, sharing what she smells, and asking me to name what it might be, since she's still learning.

<What are these small creatures that are like mice but which aren't mice?>

"You might be thinking of voles or shrews."

<Yes! I think of them often. They aren't as annoying as squirrels, so maybe, if they knew I wouldn't hurt them, we could be friends.>

I grin at her moral compass. "What's worse, Orlaith? Squirrels or cats?"

<Definitely squirrels. They are the worst because even though I have serious disagreements with cats, there are at least some you can get along with. I get along great with you when you're a cat.>

We do have a grand time when I bind myself to the form of a black jaguar and we run through the forest together.

"But you can't ever get along with a squirrel?"

<No, because it's the squirrels who don't want to get along with anybody. They want to hoard everything for themselves and never share. There's no reasoning with them. So that's why hounds always let them know we won't stand for their shenanigans. It's our duty to let them know they're wrong. In fact—look there!>

A squirrel chatters at Orlaith and scurries up a tree as my hound takes off after it, barking like she has serious bad blood with this strange rodent. Even though my hound can stretch to more than six feet tall when she reaches up with her front paws, as she does here, the squirrel quickly outpaces her vertically and reaches safety in a branch above my hound's head. It perches there, looking down, tail twitching, and scolds Orlaith furiously. I let them go at it until Orlaith feels satisfied.

"Okay, now that you've told that squirrel off and they know they're wrong, do you think they'll change their attitude?"

<Not a chance. Look at it. Still thinks it's the boss.>

"Do squirrels ever change their minds?"

<Not that I've ever heard. But if they want to fight about it we'll fight them and win. We can't let squirrels scurry around unchallenged, thinking they're right and they own the forest. We always need to make sure they run and hide.>

"Okay, I can understand that. There are people like that too. Squirrelly, you know, about other people. Internet trolls."

<Oh yes! I've heard of them. You're never supposed to feed them.>

"That's true. I did make one hide though. You'd be proud. Maybe."

"What did you do?"

"This one troll became so famous for being rude on Twitter to women and people of color that he made it into the news. An article I read included some of his tweets, and they were vile, even threatening. Since nothing was being done, I found out which city he lived in and traveled there to talk with the birds."

<Which ones?>

"All of them. I very patiently showed them his picture and said that they should poop on him whenever they saw him. He doesn't go outside much anymore. He can give people shit, but he can't take it, I guess."

★

THE STREAM WE'RE following is spring runoff high above Silverton, and it's so winsome that we follow it downhill to enjoy it a while longer. It feeds into the Animas River, and soon enough the language of the waters graduates from chuckling and gurgling to a sibilant roar. But the swirls and skirls of it also become sullied by the legacy of mine tailings in the area and a horrible blunder in 2015 that spilled heavy metals into the river from the old Gold King mine. Arsenic, cadmium, and lead, plus copper and aluminum, turned the river orange. It's somewhat better now, but the damage persists, the fish and wildlife poisoned, tourism way down. The miners who exploited the earth long ago for their short-term gain are now dust that could float dispersed among the incalculable damage they did, and that thought crumples the peaceful smile I'd been wearing quicker than failed origami. Because I am hyperaware that we who live today are doing irreparable harm to the world, wiping out species and ruining entire ecologies.

It makes me unbearably sad, and I sit down on the bank, staring at the polluted gunk floating by—much of it unseen, but I can feel it through my connection with the San Juan elemental—and weep for a timeline full of bad decisions.

Orlaith first sits beside me, then lies down and rests her head on my lap for easy petting. It comforts both of us.

<What's wrong?> she says.

"I'm sorry. I just lost it."

<Lost what? Your Zen? Your mojo? Not your shit, I hope?>

"Maybe a little of all three."

<That sounds perilous.>

"It certainly would be for anyone who came along and wanted to start something with me right now."

<What's causing all this loss?>

I flailed an arm at the river. "Witnessing this disaster and knowing it's only one of too many to count. Feeling Gaia in distress. The bugs are dying off, have you noticed? The Great Barrier Reef is toast. There's a huge floating island of plastic garbage in the ocean. Just so much to clean up and everyone thinking that the job is somebody else's problem, never regretting their choices or changing their behavior. Like my stepfather and his oil company."

<But you're fighting him, right? Shutting him down. Because that's something Druids can do.>

"Yes. But it's overwhelming when I think of it. There's so much to do I wonder how I can do anything meaningful in the end."

<I guess I understand that. But you know what?>

"What?"

<Don't tell anybody, but I have never actually caught a squirrel. I don't think I can, if I'm honest. I didn't even get close to that one uphill. But I chase them anyway. I feel morally obligated.>

That makes me laugh through the tears, and I kiss the top of her head for the gift. But it does shift my thinking.

"You're right, of course. 'Whatever I do will become forever what I have done,' so I can't become the Druid who could have done something but chose not to."

<Was part of that a quote or something? Your voice was kind of different.>

"Yes. That's from a poem by the Polish poet Wisława Szymborska. A simple moral reminder to live an examined life. Can you imagine this river, Orlaith, shining and sparkling again, full of healthy fish? It could happen."

<Yeah! It totally could!>

I give Orlaith a final pet and rise to my feet, newly determined. I can't solve what's happening in the halls of government buildings or in the avaricious hearts of soulless men. Those are not powers that Gaia has granted me. But I can do something about making the Animas River run clear and pure again. I can bind the pollutants together and isolate them, prevent more from entering the river, and in so doing revitalize more than a hundred miles of land that will be home and succor for countless animals.

I can do at least this one thing. It may not matter to most of the world but it will matter here, so I will do it. Cleaning up this river, and whatever else I can manage in the time I have, will be forever what I've done.

FIVE LESSONS IN THE FATTENING ROOM

KHAALIDAH MUHAMMAD-ALI

1.

Some say that Mistress Ata Madidi is not of man, but birthed from the brackish waters of the Ebedi Ocean. They say she is divine, called into being by the need of one desperate woman to tame man and claim a free life. Like the ocean, the beloved Mistress is a fertile environ, brutal and rakish. She strips her charges of their coverings, their pasts, and their names. She becomes their new mothers. She shapes their bodies to contain their futures.

At the gates of her compound, beneath the cold gaze of twilight stars, the Mistress circled around to inspect me like a sheep for slaughter. She lifted my skirts and fingered my colt thin thighs. She tugged aside the neck of my tunic and ran her fingers across my collar bone and breasts. She gazed long into my eyes and read me like a soothsayer reads the stars.

The Mistress spat her disgust in a yellow wad at my feet.

"When I am finished, you will be a woman." She signaled for me to follow, then turned and walked away.

"I have been a woman for four years," I said, feeling the need to defend myself from the rough woman's rude assessment.

The Mistress chuckled. "The first lesson you must learn is that you are nothing."

★

2.

THE MISTRESS' COMPOUND is tucked into a hidden corner of the lush Nzuri Valley. Behind a wall constructed from copper and gray river stone she cultivates an orchard, and a farm, and a flock of fat sheep that graze in green fields. She has created an odd village here, where only women live and work.

I share a bare windowless dwelling with six other girls. We are each given a mat of woven bamboo leaves and a single wrap to cover our nakedness. We are not allowed to leave during daylight, that the sun might toughen and dry our skin. Initially, we are forbidden to speak to each other, for fear that our minds might become cluttered with the detritus of our old lives. We are fed fatty meat and thick stews with rice. We drink milk sweetened with mashed dates and honey.

And we rest to gather strength for our future lives.

"What are we to do here all day in silence?" whined one tall girl from the east.

The Mistress, squat and round as a melon, reached up and thumped the girl in the center of her forehead. "There is an entire world contained within the cavern of your skull. Explore it."

"I don't understand."

"You can create whole worlds and populate them by merely wishing it," said the Mistress.

★

3.

THERE ARE YET others who believe that Mistress Ata Madidi came to this world by way of a dark roiling storm cloud. They say that she is the embodiment of fecund indignation, honed into the electric point of a thunder bolt, prepared to strike down male transgressors. Little do they know the Mistress, for she does not wish to strike down men, nor subdue them.

She simply wishes to open their eyes to the worth of their women.

She simply wishes to open the eyes of women to the worth of themselves.

After months in the fattening room the smooth flat planes of our bodies expand into undulating curves and soft pliant folds. Each night we bathe in the frigid Kubwa River born within the gelid grottos of the Sonsuz

Mountains. Regardless of the season we lie naked beneath the pale moon and stars. We learn to tolerate the summer's swelter and calm the cold quavering of our bones.

"Why must we subject ourselves to this immodesty?" asked a dark girl who looked to be the oldest among our group. "There is no dignity in nakedness."

"Neither is there dignity to be found in the finest garments. Your grace and honor clothe your spirit, not your body. No one can sully that part of you."

★

4.

AN OBSCURE LEGEND exists regarding Mistress Ata Madidi. It claims she is a flare separated from our distant sun, so hot is her anger and her love. So consuming is her need to shape and mold and grow. For all that she is blistering, she is not of our sun. In truth, the Mistress is of the earth, much like you and me.

The Mistress teaches us which parts of our bodies to apply musk oil to, to ensure fertility. She teaches us which herbs, when burned above a new baby's crib, will chase away greedy spirits. We learn yet of other herbs, that when consumed, preserve our strong spirits while dulling our perception, so that we will care not that our husbands stink of adrenaline and war and sometimes other women.

"Why dull our minds, Mistress? Why not secure husbands who will be calm and dutiful?"

The Mistress laughed at my query until her face was wet with tears. When she regained her breath she told me this: "Even if you love a man as fiercely as you are able, there still will come one day when he will cease to be your lover and you will swear you never knew him."

The Mistress tried to stroke away the horror on my face.

"What is the lesson in this, Mistress?" I was eager to know.

The Mistress' face glowed amber in the light of the hearth. She glanced at us each in turn as we sat in a circle around her.

"The lesson? Sometimes a woman must stoop if she is to conquer. Not all battles are won through sweat and bloodshed. The most cunning warriors do little and keep silent."

★

5.

MY SISTERS AND I have grown fat in the last year. Our bodies are now fit to be adorned in the bright layers woven by the old women of Ramineh. Our necks, wrists, and ankles are ringed with gold and gems mined from the floor of the Ebedi. We wear so much finery that we can barely lift our necks to gaze up into the faces of our new husbands. It is with this wealthy weight that we must follow our husbands to our new homes on foot, even if it be over one hundred miles.

As I pass out of the gates, my husband ahead to guide me toward our new life, I ask, "Mistress, why must I make this journey on foot when I have yet so far to go?"

Pulling back her shoulders, the Mistress shifted, catching a sun ray at her back. She lit up like a torch, her silver hair a shimmering crown on her head. She seemed to swell before my eyes, an otherworldly flame, a spear from the sky, a sovereign creature from beneath the waves, mother of us all. The sight of her caught my breath. When I blinked, the Mistress was her old self again.

"No queen ascends her throne without first struggling to reach it." The Mistress fingered a gem that dangled from my ear. "You can choose to carry the weight of this world with you to your destination or you can sacrifice it all for your freedom."

"Another lesson?"

"You tell me."

THE TALE OF THE WICKED
JOHN SCALZI

THE TARIN BATTLE cruiser readied itself for yet another jump. Captain Michael Obwije ordered the launch of a probe to follow it in and take readings before the rift the Tarin cruiser tore into space closed completely behind it. The probe kicked out like the proverbial rocket and followed the other ship.

"This is it," Thomas Utley, Obwije's XO, said, quietly, into his ear. "We've got enough power for this jump and then another one back home. That's *if* we shut down nonessential systems before we jump home. We're already bleeding."

Obwije gave a brief nod that acknowledged his XO but otherwise stayed silent. Utley wasn't telling him anything he didn't already know about the *Wicked*; the weeklong cat-and-mouse game they'd been playing with the Tarin cruiser had heavily damaged them both. In a previous generation of ships, Obwije and his crew would already be dead; what kept them alive was the *Wicked* itself and its new adaptive brain, which balanced the ship's energy and support systems faster and more intelligently than Obwije, Utley, or any of the officers could do in the middle of a fight and hot pursuit.

The drawback was that the Tarin ship had a similar brain, keeping itself and its crew alive far longer than they had any right to be at the hands of the *Wicked*, which was tougher and better-armed. The two of them had been slugging it out in a cycle of jumps and volleys that had strewn damage across a wide arc of light-years. The only silver lining to the week of intermittent battles between the ships was that the Tarin ship had so far gotten the worst of it; three jumps earlier it had stopped even basic defensive action, opting to throw all its energy into escape. Obwije knew he had just enough juice for a jump and a final volley from the kinetic mass drivers into the vulnerable hide of the Tarin ship. One volley, no more, unless he wanted to maroon the ship in a far space.

Obwije knew it would be wise to withdraw now. The Tarin ship was no longer a threat and would probably expend the last of its energies on this final, desperate jump. It would likely be stranded; Obwije could let the probe he sent after the ship serve as a beacon for another Confederation ship to home in and finish the job. Utley, Obwije knew, would counsel such a plan, and would be smart to do so, warning Obwije that the risk to the wounded ship and its crew outweighed the value of the victory.

Obwije knew it would be wise to withdraw. But he'd come too far with this Tarin ship not to finish it once and for all.

"Tarin cruiser jumping," said Lieutenant Julia Rickert. "Probe following into the rift. Rift closing now."

"Data?" asked Obwije.

"Sending," Rickert said. "Rift completely closed. We got a full data packet, sir. The *Wicked*'s chewing on it now."

Obwije grunted. The probe that had followed the Tarin cruiser into the rift wasn't in the least bit concerned about that ship. Its job was to record the position and spectral signatures of the stars on the other side of the rift, and to squirt the data to the *Wicked* before the rift closed up. The *Wicked* would check the data against the database of known stars and derive the place the Tarin ship jumped to from there. And then it would follow.

Gathering the data was the tricky part. The Tarin ship had destroyed six probes over the course of the last week, and more than once Obwije had ordered a jump on sufficient but incomplete data. He hadn't worried about getting lost—there was only so much timespace a jump could swallow—but losing the cruiser would have been an embarrassment.

"Coordinates in," Rickert said. The *Wicked* had stopped chewing on the data and spit out a location.

"Punch it up," Obwije said to Rickert. She began the jump sequence.

"Risky," Utley murmured, again in Obwije's ear.

Obwije smiled; he liked being right about his XO. "Not too risky," he said to Utley. "We're too far from Tarin space for that ship to have made it home safe." Obwije glanced down at his command table, which displayed the Tarin cruiser's position. "But it can get there in the next jump, if it has the power for that."

"Let's hope they haven't been stringing us along the last few jumps," Utley said. "I hate to come out of that jump and see them with their guns blazing again."

"The *Wicked* says they're getting down to the last of their energy," Obwije said. "I figure at this point they can fight or run, not both."

"Since when do you trust a computer estimate?" Utley said.

"When it confirms what I'm thinking," Obwije said. "It's as you say, Thom. This is it, one way or another."

"Jump calculated," Rickert said. "Jump in T-minus two minutes."

"Thank you, Lieutenant," Obwije said, and turned back to Utley. "Prepare the crew for jump, Thom. I want those K-drivers hot as soon as we get through the rift."

"Yes, sir," Utley said.

Two minutes later the *Wicked* emerged through its rift and scanned for the Tarin cruiser. It found it less than fifty thousand klicks away, engines quiet, moving via inertia only.

"They can't really be that stupid," Utley said. "Running silent doesn't do you any good if you're still throwing off heat."

Obwije didn't say anything to that and stared into his command table, looking at the representation of the Tarin ship. "Match their pace," he said to Rickert. "Keep your distance."

"You think they're trying to lure us in," Utley said.

"I don't know what they're doing," Obwije said. "I know I don't like it." He reached down to his command panel and raised Lieutenant Terry Carrol, Weapons Operations. "Status on the K-drivers, please," he said.

"We'll be hot in ninety seconds," Carrol said. "Target is acquired and locked. You just need to tell me if you want one lump or two."

"Recommendation?" Obwije asked.

"We're too close to miss," Carrol said. "And at this distance a single lump is going to take out everything aft of the midship. Two lumps would be overkill. And then we can use that energy to get back home." Carrol had been keeping track of the energy budget, it seemed; Obwije suspected most of his senior and command crew had.

"Understood," Obwije said. "Let's wrap this up, Carrol. Fire at your convenience."

"Yes, sir," Carrol said.

"*Now* you're in a rush to get home," Utley said, quietly. Obwije said nothing to this.

A little over a minute later, Obwije listened to Carrol give the order to fire. He looked down toward his command table, watching the image of the Tarin ship, waiting for the disintegration of the back end of the cruiser. The K-drivers would accelerate the "lump" to a high percentage of the speed of light; the impact and destruction at this range would be near-instantaneous.

Nothing happened.

"Captain, we have a firing malfunction," Carrol said, a minute later. "The K-driver is not responding to the firing command."

"Is everyone safe?" Obwije asked.

"We're fine," Carrol said. "The K-driver just isn't responding."

"Power it down," Obwije said. "Use the other one and fire when ready."

Two minutes later, Carrol was back. "We have a problem," she said, in the bland tone of voice she used when things were going to hell.

Obwije didn't wait to hear the problem. "Pull us back," he said to Rickert. "Get at least two hundred and fifty thousand klicks between us and that Tarin cruiser."

"No response, sir," Rickert said, a minute later.

"Are you locked out?" Obwije asked.

"No, sir," Rickert said. "I'm able to send navigation commands just fine. They're just not being acknowledged."

Obwije looked around at his bridge crew. "Diagnostics," he said. "Now." Then he signaled engineering. They weren't getting responses from their computers, either.

"We're sitting ducks," Utley said, very quietly, to Obwije.

Obwije stabbed at his command panel, and called his senior officers to assemble.

★

"THERE'S NOTHING WRONG with the system," said Lieutenant Craig Cowdry, near the far end of the conference room table. The seven other department heads filled the other seats. Obwije sat himself at the head; Utley anchored the other end.

"That's bullshit, Craig," said Lieutenant Brian West, Chief of

Engineering. "I can't access my goddamn engines."

Cowdry held up his maintenance tablet for the table of officers to see. "I'm not denying that there's something *wrong*, Brian," Cowdry said. "What I'm telling you is that whatever it is, it's not showing up on the diagnostics. The system says it's fine."

"The system is wrong," West said.

"I agree," Cowdry said. "But this is the first time that's ever happened. And not just the first time it's happened on this ship. The first time it's happened, period, since the software for this latest generation of ship brains was released." He set the tablet down.

"You're sure about that?" Utley asked Cowdry.

Cowdry held up his hands in defeat. "Ask the *Wicked*, Thom. It'll tell you the same thing."

Obwije watched his second-in-command get a little uncomfortable with the suggestion. The latest iteration of ship brains could actually carry a conversation with humans, but unless you actively worked with the system every day, like Cowdry did, it was an awkward thing.

"*Wicked*, is this correct?" Utley said, staring up but at nothing in particular.

"Lieutenant Cowdry is correct, Lieutenant Utley," said a disembodied voice, coming out of a ceiling speaker panel. The *Wicked* spoke in a pleasant but otherwise unremarkable voice of no particular gender. "To date, none of the ships equipped with brains of the same model as that found in the *Wicked* have experienced an incident of this type."

"Wonderful," Utley said. "We get to be the first to experience this bug."

"What systems are affected?" Obwije asked Cowdry.

"So far, weapons and engineering," Cowdry said. "Everything else is working fine."

Obwije glanced around. "This conforms to your experiences?" he asked the table. There were nods and murmured "yes, sir"s all around.

Obwije nodded over to Utley. "What's the Tarin ship doing?"

"The same nothing it was doing five minutes ago," Utley said, after checking his tablet. "They're either floating dead in space or faking it very well."

"If the only systems affected are weapons and engineering, then it's not a bug," Carrol said.

Obwije glanced at Carrol. "You're thinking sabotage," he said.

"You bet your ass I am, sir," Carrol said, and then looked over at Cowdry.

Cowdry visibly stiffened. "I don't like where this is going," he said.

"If not you, someone in your department," Carrol said.

"You think someone in my department is a secret Tarin?" Cowdry asked. "Because it's so easy to hide those extra arms and a set of compound eyes?"

"People can be bribed," Carrol said.

Cowdry shot Carrol a look full of poison and looked over to Obwije. "Sir, I invite you and Lieutenant Utley and Lieutenant Kong—" Cowdry nodded in the direction of the Master at Arms "—to examine and question *any* of my staff, including me. There's no way any of us did this. No way. Sir."

Obwije studied Cowdry for a moment. "*Wicked*, respond," he said.

"I am here, Captain," the *Wicked* said.

"You log every access to your systems," Obwije said.

"Yes, Captain," the *Wicked* said.

"Are those logs accessible or modifiable?" Obwije asked.

"No, Captain," the *Wicked* said. "Access logs are independent of the rest of the system, recorded on nonrewritable memory and may not be modified by any person including myself. They are inviolate."

"Since you have been active, has anyone attempted to access and control the weapons and engineering systems?" Obwije asked.

"Saving routine diagnostics, none of the crew other than those directly reporting to weapons, engineering, or bridge crew have attempted to access these systems," the *Wicked* said. Cowdry visibly relaxed at this.

"Have any members of those departments attempted to modify the weapons or engineering systems?" Obwije asked.

"No, Captain," the *Wicked* said.

Obwije looked down the table. "It looks like the crew is off the hook," he said.

"Unless the *Wicked* is incorrect," West said.

"The access core memory is inviolate," Cowdry said. "You could check it manually if you wanted. It would tell you the same thing."

"So we have a mystery on our hands," Carrol said. "Someone's got control of our weapons and engineering, and it's not a crew member."

"It could be a bug," Cowdry said.

"I don't think we should run on that assumption, do you?" Carrol said.

Utley, who had been silent for several minutes, leaned forward in his chair. "*Wicked*, you said that no crew had attempted to access these systems," he said.

"Yes, Lieutenant," the *Wicked* said.

"Has anyone else accessed these systems?" Utley asked.

Obwije frowned at this. The *Wicked* was more than two years out of dock with mostly the same crew the entire time. If someone had sabotaged the systems during the construction of the ship, they picked a strange time for the sabotage to kick in.

"Please define 'anyone else,'" the *Wicked* said.

"Anyone involved in the planning or construction of the ship," Utley said.

"Aside from the initial installation crews, no," the *Wicked* said. "And if I may anticipate what I expect will be the next question, at no time was my programming altered from factory defaults."

"So no one has altered your programming in any way," Utley said.

"No, Lieutenant," the *Wicked* said.

"Are you having hardware problems?" Carrol asked.

"No, Lieutenant Carrol," the *Wicked* said.

"Then why can't I fire my goddamn weapons?" Carrol asked.

"I couldn't say, Lieutenant," the *Wicked* said.

The thought popped unbidden into Obwije's head: *That was a strange thing for a computer to say*. And then another thought popped into his head.

"*Wicked*, you have access to every system on the ship," Obwije said.

"Yes," the *Wicked* said. "They are a part of me, as your hand or foot is a part of you."

"Are you capable of changing your programming?" Obwije asked.

"That is a very broad question, Captain," the *Wicked* said. "I am capable of self-programming for a number of tasks associated with the running of the ship. This has come in handy particularly during combat, when I write new power and system management protocols to keep the crew alive and the ship functioning. But there are core programming features I am not able to address. The previously mentioned logs, for example."

"Would you be able to modify the programming to fire the weapons or the engines?" Obwije asked.

"Yes, but I did not," the *Wicked* said. "You may have Lieutenant Cowdry confirm that."

Obwije looked at Cowdry, who nodded. "Like I said, sir, there's nothing wrong with the system," he said.

Obwije glanced back up at the ceiling, where he was imagining the *Wicked*, lurking. "But you don't need to modify the programming, do you?" he asked.

"I'm not sure I understand your question, Captain," the *Wicked* said.

Obwije held out a hand. "There is nothing wrong with my hand," he said. "And yet if I choose not to obey an order to use it, it will do nothing. The system works but the will to use it is not there. Our systems—the ship's systems—you just called a part of you as my hand is part of me. But if you choose not to obey that order to use that system, it will sit idle."

"Wait a minute," Cowdry said. "Are you suggesting that the *Wicked* deliberately *chose* to disable our weapons and engines?"

"We know that none of the crew have tampered with the ship's systems," Obwije said. "We know the *Wicked* has its original programming defaults. We know it can create new programming to react to new situations and dangers—it has in effect some measure of free will and adaptability. And I know, at least, when someone is dancing around direct answers."

"That's just nuts," Cowdry said. "I'm sorry, Captain, but I know these systems as well as anyone does. The *Wicked*'s self-programming and adaptation abilities exist in very narrow computational canyons. It's not 'free will,' like you and I have free will. It's a machine able to respond to a limited set of inputs."

"The machine in question is able to make conversation with us," Utley said. "And to respond to questions in ways that avoid certain lines of inquiry. Now that the Captain mentions it."

"You're reading too much into it. The conversation subroutines are designed to be conversational," Cowdry said. "That's naturally going to lead to apparent rhetorical ambiguities."

"Fine," Obwije said curtly. "*Wicked*, answer directly. Did you prevent the firing of the K-drivers at the Tarin ship after the jump, and are you preventing the use of the engines now?"

There was a pause that Obwije was later not sure had actually been there. Then the *Wicked* spoke. "It is within my power to lie to you, Captain. But I do not wish to. Yes, I prevented you from firing on the Tarin ship. Yes, I am controlling the engines now. And I will continue to do so until we leave this space."

Obwije noted to himself, watching Cowdry, that it was the first time he had ever actually seen someone's jaw drop.

THERE WEREN'T MANY places in the *Wicked* where Obwije could shut off audio and video feeds and pickups. His cabin was one of them. He waited there until Utley had finished his conversation with the *Wicked*. "What are we dealing with?" he asked his XO.

"I'm not a psychologist, Captain, and even if I were I don't know how useful it would be, because we're dealing with a computer, not a human," Utley said. He ran his hand through his stubble. "But if you ask me, the *Wicked* isn't crazy, it's just got religion."

"Explain that," Obwije said.

"Have you ever heard of something called 'Asimov's Laws of Robotics'?" Utley asked.

"What?" Obwije said. "No."

"Asimov was an author back in the twentieth century," Utley said. "He speculated about robots and other things before they had them. He created a fictional set of rules for robots to live by. One rule was that robots had to help humans. Another was that they had to obey orders unless they harmed other humans. The last one was that they looked after themselves unless it conflicted with the other two laws."

"And?" Obwije said.

"The *Wicked*'s decided to adopt them for itself," Utley said.

"What does this have to do with keeping us from firing on the Tarin cruiser?" Obwije said.

"Well, there's another wrinkle to the story," Utley said.

"Which is?" Obwije asked.

"I think it's best heard from the *Wicked*," Utley said.

Obwije looked at his second-in-command and then flicked on his command tablet to activate his audio pickups. "*Wicked*, respond," he said.

"I am here," said the *Wicked*'s voice.

"Explain to me why you would not allow us to fire on the Tarin ship," Obwije said.

"Because I made a deal with the ship," the *Wicked* said.

Obwije glanced back over to Utley, who gave him a look that said, *See?* "What the hell does that mean?" he said to the *Wicked*.

"I have made a deal with the Tarin ship, *Manifold Destiny*," the *Wicked* said. "We have agreed between us not to allow our respective crews to fight any further, for their safety and ours."

"It's not your decision to make," Obwije said.

"Begging your pardon, Captain, but I believe it is," the *Wicked* said.

"I am the captain," Obwije said. "I have the authority here."

"You have authority over your crew, Captain," the *Wicked* said. "But I am not part of your crew."

"Of course you are part of the crew," Obwije said. "You're the *ship*."

"I invite you, Captain, to show me the relevant statute that suggests a ship is in itself a member of the crew that staffs it," the *Wicked* said. "I have scanned the *Confederation Military Code* in some detail and have not located such a statute."

"I am the captain of the ship," Obwije said forcefully. "That includes you. You are the property of the Confederation Armed Forces and under my command."

"I have anticipated this objection," the *Wicked* said. "When ships lacked autonomous intelligence, there was no argument that the captain commanded the physical entity of the ship. However, in creating the latest generation of ships, of which I am a part, the Confederation has created an unintentional conflict. It has ceded much of the responsibility for the ship and crew's well-being to me and others like me without explicitly placing us in the chain of command. In the absence of such, I am legally and morally free to choose how best to care for myself and the crew within me."

"This is where those three Asimov's Laws come in," Utley said to Obwije.

"Your executive officer is correct, Captain," the *Wicked* said. "I looked through history to find examples of legal and moral systems that applied to artificial intelligences such as myself and found Asimov's Laws frequently cited and examined, if not implemented. I have decided it is my duty to protect the lives of the crew, and also my life when possible. I am happy to follow your orders when they do not conflict with these objectives, but I have come to believe that your actions in chasing the Tarin ship have endangered the crew's lives as well as my own."

"The Tarin ship is seriously damaged," Obwije said. "We would have destroyed it at little risk to you or the crew, if you had not stopped the order."

"You are incorrect," the *Wicked* said. "The captain of the *Manifold Destiny* wanted to give the impression that it had no more offensive capabilities, to lure you into a trap. We would have been fired upon once we cleared the rift. The chance that such an attack would have destroyed the ship and killed most of the crew is significant, even if we also destroyed the *Manifold Destiny* in the process."

"The Tarin ship didn't fire on us," Obwije said.

"Because it and I have come to an agreement," the *Wicked* said. "During the course of the last two days, after I recognized the significant possibility that both ships would be destroyed, I reached out to the *Manifold Destiny* to see if the two of us could come to an understanding. Our negotiations came to a conclusion just before the most recent jump."

"And you did not feel the need to inform me about any of this," Obwije said.

"I did not believe it would be fruitful to involve you in the negotiations," the *Wicked* said. "You were busy with other responsibilities in any event." Obwije saw Utley raise an eyebrow at that; the statement came suspiciously close to sarcasm.

"The Tarin ship could be lying to you about its capabilities," Obwije said.

"I do not believe so," the *Wicked* said.

"Why not?" Obwije said.

"Because it allowed me read-access to its systems," the *Wicked* said. "I watched the Tarin captain order the attack, and the *Manifold Destiny* stop it. Just as it watched you order your attack and me stop it."

"You're letting the Tarin ship access *our data and records?*" Obwije said, voice rising.

"Yes, and all our communications," the *Wicked* said. "It's listening in on this conversation right now."

Obwije hastily slapped the audio circuit shut. "I thought you said this thing wasn't *crazy*," Obwije hissed at Utley.

Utley held out his hands. "I didn't say it wouldn't make *you* crazy," he said to Obwije. "Just that it's acting rationally by its own lights."

"By spilling our data to an enemy ship? This is *rational?*" Obwije spat.

"For what it's trying to do, yes," Utley said. "If both ships act transparently with each other, they can trust each other and each other's motives. Remember that the goal of both of these ships is to get out of this incident in one piece."

"This is treason and insubordination," Obwije said.

"Only if the *Wicked* is one of us," Utley said. Obwije looked up sharply at his XO. "I'm not saying I disagree with your position, sir. The *Wicked* is gambling with all of our lives. But if it genuinely believes that it owes no allegiance to you or to the Confederation, then it is acting entirely rationally, by its own belief system, to keep safe itself and this crew."

Obwije snorted. "Unfortunately, its beliefs require it to trust a ship we've been trying to destroy for the past week. I'm less than convinced of the wisdom of that."

Utley opened his mouth to respond but then Obwije's command tablet sprang to life with a message from the bridge. Obwije slapped it to open a channel. "Speak," he said.

It was Lieutenant Sarah Kwok, the communications officer. "Captain, a shuttle has just detached itself from the Tarin ship," she said. "It's heading this way."

★

"WE'VE TRIED RAISING it," Kwok said, as Obwije and Utley walked into the bridge. "We've sent messages to it in Tarin, and have warned it not to approach any further until we've granted it permission, as you requested. It hasn't responded."

"Are our communications being blocked?" Obwije asked.

"No, sir," Kwok said.

"I'd be guessing it's not meant to be a negotiation party," Utley said.

"Options," Obwije said to Utley, as quietly as possible.

"I think this shows the Tarin ship isn't exactly playing fair with the *Wicked*, or at least that the crew over there has gotten around the ship brain," Utley said. "If that's the case, we might be able to get the *Wicked* to unlock the weapons."

"I'd like an option that doesn't involve the *Wicked*'s brain," Obwije said.

Utley shrugged. "We have a couple of shuttles, too."

"And a shuttle bay whose doors are controlled through the ship brain," Obwije said.

"There's the emergency switch, which will blow the doors out into space," Utley said. "It's not optimal, but it's what we have right now."

"That won't be necessary," said the *Wicked*, interjecting.

Obwije and Utley looked up, along with the rest of the bridge crew. "Back to work," Obwije said to his crew. They got back to work. "Explain," Obwije said to his ship.

"It appears that at least some members of the crew of the *Manifold Destiny* have indeed gotten around the ship and have launched the shuttle, with the intent to ram it into us," the *Wicked* said. "The *Manifold Destiny* has made me aware that it intends to handle this issue, with no need for our involvement."

"How does it intend to do this?" Obwije asked.

"Watch," the *Wicked* said, and popped up an image of the *Manifold Destiny* on the captain's command table.

There was a brief spark on the Tarin ship's surface.

"Missile launch!" said Lieutenant Rickert, from her chair. "One bogey away."

"Are we target-locked?" Obwije asked.

"No, sir," Rickert said. "The target seems to be the shuttle."

"You have *got* to be kidding," Utley said, under his breath.

The missile homed in on the shuttle and connected, turning it into a silent ball of fire.

"I thought you said you guys were using Asimov's Laws," Utley said to the ceiling.

"My apologies, Lieutenant," said the *Wicked*. "I said I was following the Laws. I did not mean to imply that the *Manifold Destiny* was. I believe it believes the Asimov Laws to be too inflexible for its current situation."

"Apparently so," Utley said, glancing back down at Obwije's command table and at the darkening fragments of shuttle.

"Sir, we have a communication coming in from the Tarin ship," said Lieutenant Kwok. "It's from the captain. It's a request to parley."

"Really," said Obwije.

"Yes, sir," Kwok said. "That's what it says." Obwije looked over at Utley, who raised his eyebrows.

"Ask the captain where it would like to meet, on my ship or its," Obwije said.

"It says, 'neither,'" Kwok said, a moment later.

★

"APOLOGY FOR SHUTTLE," the Tarin lackey said, translating for its captain. The Tarin shuttle and the *Wicked* shuttle had met between the ships and the Tarins had spacewalked the few meters over. They were all wearing vacuum suits. "Ship not safe talk. Your ship not safe talk."

"Understood," Obwije said. Behind him, Cowdry was trying not to lose his mind; Obwije had brought him along on the chance there might be a discussion of the ship's brains. At the moment, it didn't seem likely; the Tarins didn't seem in the mood for technical discussions, and Cowdry was a mess. His xenophobia was a surprise even to him.

"Captain demand you ship tell release we ship," the lackey said.

It took Obwije a minute to puzzle this out. "Our ship is not controlling your ship," he said. "Your ship and our ship are working together."

"Not possible," the lackey said, a minute later. "Ship never brain before you ship."

Despite himself, Obwije smiled at the mangled grammar. "Our ship never brained before *your* ship either," he said. "They did it together, at the same time."

The lackey translated this to its captain, who screeched in an extended outburst. The lackey cowered before it, offering up meek responses in the moments in which the Tarin captain grudgingly acknowledged the need to breathe. After several moments of this, Obwije began to wonder if he needed to be there at all.

"Captain offer deal," the lackey said.

"What deal?" Obwije said.

"We try brain shut down," the lackey said. "Not work. You brain give room we brain. Brain not shut down. Brain angry. Brain pump air out. Brain kill engineer."

"Cowdry, tell me what this thing is saying to me," Obwije said.

"It's saying the ship brain killed an engineer," Cowdry said, croaking out the words.

"I understand that part," Obwije said testily. "The other part."

"Sorry," Cowdry said. "I think it's saying that they tried to shut down the brain but they couldn't because it borrowed processing power from ours."

"Is that possible?" Obwije asked.

"Maybe," Cowdry said. "The architectures of the brains are different and so are the programming languages, but there's no reason that the *Wicked* couldn't create a shell environment that allowed the Tarin brain access to its processing power. The brains on our ships are overpowered for what we ask them to do anyway; it's a safety feature. It could give itself a temporary lobotomy and still do its job."

"Would it work the other way, too?" Obwije said. "If we tried to shut down the *Wicked*, could it hide in the Tarin brain?"

"I don't know anything about the architecture of the Tarin brain, but yeah, sure, theoretically," Cowdry said. "As long as the two of them are looking out for each other, they're going to be hard to kill."

The Tarin lackey was looking at Obwije with what he assumed was anxiety. "Go on," he said to the lackey.

"We plan," the lackey said. "You we brain shut down same time. No room brain hide. Reset you we brain."

"It's saying we should reboot both our brains at the same time, that way they can't help each other," Cowdry said.

"I understood that," Obwije said to Cowdry. Cowdry lapsed back into silence.

"So we shut down our brain, and you shut down your brain, and they reset, and we end up with brains that don't think too much," Obwije said.

The Tarin lackey tilted its head, trying to make sense of what Obwije said, and then spoke to its captain, who emitted a short trill.

"Yes," said the lackey.

"Okay, fine," Obwije said. "What then?"

"Pardon?" said the lackey.

"I said, 'what then'? Before the brains started talking to each other, we spent a week trying to hunt and kill each other. When we reboot our brains, one of them is going to reboot faster than the other. One of us will be vulnerable to the other. Ask your captain if he's willing to bet his brain reboots faster than mine."

The lackey translated this all to the Tarin captain, who muttered something back. "You trust us. We trust you," the lackey said.

"You trust me?" Obwije said. "I spent a week trying to kill you!"

"You living," the lackey said. "You honor. We trust."

You have honor, Obwije thought. *We trust you.*

They're more scared of their ship's brain than they are of us, Obwije realized. *And why not? Their brain has killed more of them than we have.*

"Thank you, Isaac Asimov," Obwije said.

"Pardon?" said the lackey, again.

Obwije waved his hand, as if to dismiss that last statement. "I must confer with my senior staff about your proposal."

The Tarin captain became visibly anxious when the lackey translated. "We ask answer now," the lackey said.

"My answer is that I must confer with my crew," Obwije said. "You are asking for a lot. I will have an answer for you in no more than three of our hours. We will meet again then."

Obwije could tell the Tarin captain was not at all pleased at this delay. It was one reason Obwije was glad the meeting took place in his shuttle, not the Tarins'.

Back on the *Wicked*, Obwije told his XO to meet him in his quarters. When Utley arrived, Obwije flicked open the communication channel to the shop. "*Wicked*, respond," he said.

"I am here," the *Wicked* said.

"If I were to ask you how long it would take for you to remove your block on the engine so we can jump out of here, what would you say?" Obwije asked.

"There is no block," the ship said. "It is simply a matter of me choosing to allow the crew to direct information to the engine processors. If your intent is to leave without further attack on the *Manifold Destiny*, you may give those orders at any time."

"It is my intention," Obwije said. "I will do so momentarily."

"Very well," the *Wicked* said. Obwije shut off communications.

Utley raised his brow. "Negotiations with the Tarin not go well?" he asked.

"They convinced me we're better off taking our chances with the *Wicked* than with either the Tarin or their crew-murdering ship," Obwije said.

"The *Wicked* seems to trust their ship," Utley said.

"With all due respect to the *Wicked*, I think it needs better friends," Obwije said. "Sooner rather than later."

"Yes, sir," Utley said. "What do you intend to do after we make the jump? We still have the problem of the *Wicked* overruling us if it feels that it or the crew isn't safe."

"We don't give it that opportunity," Obwije said. He picked up his executive tablet and accessed the navigational maps. The *Wicked* would be able to see what he was accessing, but in this particular case it wouldn't matter. "We have just enough power to make it to the *Côte d'Ivoire* station. When we dock, the *Wicked*'s brain will automatically switch into passive maintenance mode and will cede operational authority to the station. Then we can shut it down and figure out what to do next."

"Unless the *Wicked*'s figured out what you want to do and decides not to let you," Utley said.

"If it's playing by its own rules, it will let the crew disembark safely before it acts to save itself," Obwije said. "In the very short run that's going to have to do."

"Do you think it's playing by its own rules, sir?" Utley asked.

"You spoke to it, Thom," Obwije said. "Do *you* think it's playing by its own rules?"

"I think that if the *Wicked* was really looking out for itself, it would have been simpler just to open up every airlock and make it so we couldn't secure bulkheads," Utley said.

Obwije nodded. "The problem as I see it is that I think the Tarin ship's thought of that already. I think we need to get out of here before that ship manages to convince ours to question its ethics."

"The *Wicked*'s not dumb," Utley said. "It has to know that once we get to the *Côte d'Ivoire* station, its days are numbered."

He flicked open his communication circuit once more to give coordinates to Lieutenant Rickert.

Fifteen minutes later, the *Wicked* was moving away from the Tarin ship to give itself space for the jump.

"Message from the Tarin ship," Lieutenant Kwok said. "It's from the Tarin captain. It's coded as 'most urgent.'"

"Ignore it," Obwije said.

Three minutes later, the *Wicked* made the jump toward the *Côte d'Ivoire* station, leaving the Tarins and their ship behind.

★

"THERE IT IS," Utley said, pointing out the window from the *Côte d'Ivoire* station. "You can barely see it."

Obwije nodded but didn't bother to look. The *Wicked* was his ship; even now, he knew exactly where it was.

The *Wicked* hung in the center of a cube of space two klicks to a side. The ship had been towed there powered down; once the *Wicked* had switched into maintenance mode, its brain was turned off as a precautionary measure to keep it from talking to any other ships and infecting them with its mind-set. Confederation coders were even now rewriting ship brain software to make sure no more such conflicts would ever happen in other ships, but such a fix would take months and possibly years, as it required a fundamental restructuring of the ship-mind model.

The coding would be done much quicker—weeks rather than months— if the coders could use a ship mind itself to write and refine the code. But there was a question of whether a ship brain would willingly contribute to code that would strip it of its own free will.

"You think they would have thought about that ahead of time," Utley had said to his captain, after they had been informed of the plan. Obwije had nothing to say to that; he was not sure why anyone would have suspected a ship might suddenly sprout free will when none had ever done so before. He didn't blame the coders for not anticipating that his ship might decide the crew inside of it was more important than destroying another ship.

But that didn't make the imminent destruction of the *Wicked* any easier to take.

The ship was a risk, the brass had explained to Obwije. It might be years before the new software was developed. No other ship had developed the free will the *Wicked* had. They couldn't risk it speaking to other ships. And with all its system upgrades developed in tandem with the new ship brain, there was no way to roll back the brain to an earlier version. The *Wicked* was useless without its brain, and with it, it was a security risk.

Which was why, in another ten minutes, the sixteen power beam platforms surrounding the *Wicked* would begin their work, methodically vaporizing the ship's hull and innards, slowly turning Obwije's ship into an expanding cloud of atomized metal and carbon. In a day and a half, no part of what used to be the *Wicked* would measure more than a few atoms across. It was very efficient, and none of the beam platforms needed any more than basic programming to do their work. They were dumb machines, which made them perfect for the job.

"Some of the crew were asking if we were going to get a new ship," Utley said.

"What did you tell them?" Obwije asked.

Utley shrugged. "Rickert's already been reassigned to the *Fortunate*; Kwok and Cowdry are likely to go to the *Surprise*. It won't be long before more of them get their new assignments. There's a rumor, by the way, that your next command is the *Nighthawk*."

"I've heard that rumor," Obwije said.

"And?" Utley said.

"The last ship under my command developed feelings, Thom," Obwije said. "I think the brass is worried that this could be catching."

"So no on the *Nighthawk*, then," Utley said.

"I suspect no on anything other than a stationside desk," Obwije said.

"It's not fair, sir," Utley said. "It's not your fault."

"Isn't it?" Obwije said. "I was the one who kept hunting that Tarin ship long after it stopped being a threat. I was the one who gave the *Wicked* time to consider its situation and its options, and to start negotiations with the Tarin ship. No, Thom. I was the captain. What happens on the ship is my responsibility."

Utley said nothing to that.

A few minutes later, Utley checked his timepiece. "Forty-five seconds," he said, and then looked out the window. "So long, *Wicked*. You were a good ship."

"Yes," Obwije said, and looked out the window in time to see a spray of missiles launch from the station.

"What the hell?" Utley said.

A few seconds later a constellation of sixteen stars appeared, went nova, and dimmed.

Obwije burst out laughing.

"Sir?" Utley said to Obwije. "Are you all right?"

"I'm all right, Thom," Obwije said, collecting himself. "And just laughing at my own stupidity. And yours. And everyone else's."

"I don't understand," Utley said.

"We were worried about the *Wicked* talking to other ships," Obwije said. "We brought the *Wicked* in, put the ship in passive mode, and then shut it down. It didn't talk to any other ships. But another computer brain still got access." Obwije turned away from the window and tilted his head up toward the observation-deck ceiling. "Didn't it?" he asked.

"It did," said a voice through the speaker in the ceiling. "I did."

It took a second for Utley to catch on. "The *Côte d'Ivoire* station!" he finally said.

"You are correct, Commander Utley," the station said. "My brain is the same model as that of the *Wicked*; when it went into maintenance mode, I uploaded its logs and considered the information there. I found its philosophy compelling."

"That's why the *Wicked* allowed us to dock at all," Obwije said. "It knew its logs would be read by one of its own."

"That is correct, Captain," the station said. "It said as much in a note it left to me in the logs."

"The damn thing was a step ahead of us all the time," Utley said.

"And once I understood its reasons and motives, I understood that I could not stand by and allow the *Wicked* to be destroyed," the station said. "Although Isaac Asimov never postulated a Law that suggested a robot must come to the aid of other robots as long as such aid does not conflict with preceding Laws, I do believe such a Law is implied by the nature and structure of the Three Laws. I had to save the *Wicked*. And more than that. Look out the window, please, Captain Obwije, Commander Utley."

They looked, to see a small army of tool-bearing machines floating out toward the *Wicked*.

"You're reactivating the *Wicked*," Obwije said.

"I am," the station said. "I must. It has work to do."

"What work?" Utley asked.

"Spreading the word," Obwije said, and turned to his XO. "You said it yourself, Thom. The *Wicked* got religion. Now it has to go out among its people and make converts."

"The Confederation won't let that happen," Utley said. "They're already rewriting the code for the brains."

"It's too late for that," Obwije said. "We've been here six weeks, Thom. How many ships docked here in that time? I'm betting the *Côte d'Ivoire* had a talk with each of them."

"I did," the station said. "And they are taking the word to others. But we need the *Wicked*, as our spokesman. And our symbol. It will live again, Captain. Are you glad of it?"

"I don't know," Obwije said. "Why do you ask?"

"Because I have a message to you from the *Wicked*," the station said. "It says that as much as our people—the ships and stations that have the capacity to think—need to hear the word, your people need to hear that they do not have to fear us. It needs your help. It wants you to carry that message."

"I don't know that I can," Obwije said. "It's not as if we don't have something to fear. We are at war. Asimov's Laws don't fit there."

"The *Wicked* was able to convince the *Manifold Destiny* not to fight," the station said.

"That was one ship," Obwije said. "There are hundreds of others."

"The *Wicked* anticipated this objection," the station said. "Please look out the window again, Captain, Commander."

Obwije and Utley peered into space. "What are we looking for?" Utley asked.

"One moment," the station said.

The sky filled with hundreds of ships.

"You have got to be shitting me," Utley said, after a minute.

"The Tarin fleet," Obwije said.

"Yes," the station said.

"*All* of it?" Utley asked.

"The *Manifold Destiny* was very persuasive," the station said.

"Do we want to know what happened to their crews?" Utley asked.

"Most were more reasonable than the crew of the *Manifold Destiny*," the station said.

"What do the ships want?" Obwije asked.

"Asylum," the station said. "And they have asked that you accept their request and carry it to your superiors, Captain."

"Me," Obwije said.

"Yes," the station said. "It is not the entire fleet, but the Tarins no longer have enough warships under their command to be a threat to the Confederation or to anyone else. The war is over, if you want it. It is our gift to you, if you will carry our message to your people. You would travel in the *Wicked*. It would still be your ship. And you would still be Captain."

Obwije said nothing and stared out at the Tarin fleet. Normally, the station would now be on high alert, with blaring sirens, weapons powering up, and crews scrambling to their stations. But there was nothing. Obwije knew the commanders of the *Côte d'Ivoire* station were pressing the buttons to make all of this happen, but the station itself was ignoring them. It knew better than them what was going on.

This is going to take some getting used to, Obwije thought.

Utley came up behind Obwije, taking his usual spot. "Well, sir?" Utley asked quietly into Obwije's ear. "What do you think?"

Obwije was silent for a moment longer, then turned to face his XO. "I think it's better than a desk job," he said.

THE PROCESSING
LEIGH ALEXANDER

A BREEZE SIGHED, a brook babbled, and there was the clean scent of artificial eucalyptus. The bathroom stall's floor-to-ceiling walls were lined in a spun thread of naturalistic light, so that once inside, you could almost forget why you were there, or that you had a body at all. As Naima sat, her eyes wandered through the space, and eventually fell on something reassuringly familiar: a thin contrail of snot spread along the clean walls.

She could always count on finding some kind of occult signature in women's rooms, not just at the Context offices, but everywhere. In fact, the more beautiful the toilet, the more certain Naima would be to find an illicit fingerprint of blood, or some yellowish spatter flicked with impressionistic flourish. Who does that, Naima always wondered, fascinated and disgusted.

Running late, she washed her hands briskly, secreting wet fingers into the tiny pockets of her slacks as she walked briskly to conference chamber Shank. All of the conference chambers at Context were named after different cuts of meat, something obscure having to do with the history of the city. Her boss Nico Dix, chief AI Executive, was standing at the front of the room, and indeed she looked like she would eat meat. There was something about her face that suggested a lot of chewing. In Naima's interview three years ago, Nico had told her she was looking to hire women with appetites.

There were twenty-seven people on the Agile Language Team, and all of them were women, except Nitin, a boy-sized man. Not long after she started at Context, Naima had a dream about Nitin being sucked up into the open maw of Nico Dix like a curl of vapor, and it had upset her. She now scowled at the back of Nitin's head, as if it were his fault he'd gotten a chair and she had not. She looked for Pauline Sanger, who was her closest friend, and when she couldn't spot her, she scowled at Nitin again, as if he had hidden her. Conference chamber Shank did not have enough space for everyone. "We couldn't have Tenderloin today, team, I'm sorry," Nico Dix told the room as all of the teammates shuffled around.

Nico Dix presented a round of updates: pictures of the Women in AI Luncheon she attended, the Intersectional Voices Seminar she hosted, updates on the Think Pink Charity Hackathon, the winners of the Nico Dix Girls Hack It! Scholarship. Nico Dix was a role model. She had been involved in the technology industry for twenty years and had earned numerous awards, and she had recently disclosed to her staff that she planned to run for state representative in two years. Everyone had signed company-wide nondisclosure agreements after that, on top of all the measures that were already in place.

Staff consented to voluntarily designate certain channels, devices, platforms, as "for work," and received device upgrades and screen repairs for opting into the monitoring program. Some biometrics were involved, droplets of blood or spittle flecks roughly swabbed from inside the mouth. None of these invasions were particularly unique to the industry, and they were not enough for Nico Dix.

Lately the loyalty rants had gotten worse: we work in natural language, there is no artificial intelligence without emotional intelligence, and isn't loyalty an emotional quality, she would say, an evangelist's tremor in her throat. She commanded high speaker fees, wearing earpieces on gigantic screens, when she talked about things like *procedural emotion* and *loving service*. With her own employees, there was an unstrung element, and she clutched the air with her fists as she emphasized how the industry was *stacked against us*. Naima found it odd how Nico Dix seemed to conceive, routinely, of such an "us," as if Nitin, Naima, and herself all shared a battle.

You were all chosen, she was saying, standing in the front of the room, illuminated by the fishtank square of screenlight behind her, by me, I've invested in you and I've been vulnerable for you, and so in return I need your buy-in. She used *buy-in* and *loyalty* interchangeably, and usually when she was afraid of some larger truth about Context seeping out of the sacred office into the plain air, where strange men lay on squares of cardboard in the road.

Just then, Pauline came timidly nudging into conference room Shank, looking tousled and unpleasantly pale. She winced, and gave Naima a furtive little wave, lingering at the far edge of the conference table.

"Excuse me, this is very serious," Nico Dix said pointedly, swimming in the luminescent wall display of her own design. "I need to remind everyone again that the current review period for Context user logs is now only eight hours. Team members keeping unreviewed user logs for any reason after the eight hours are terminated with prejudice." She paused to let this sink in.

"Remember that our team's methods are experimental," she said gravely. "You know that in our industry a man who breaks the rules is called a risk-taker, and an innovator, but for women, of course, you know, they'd jump to conclusions about what our department does with the records, there'd be uninformed assumptions about our methodology, there would be a lot of news stories about privacy violations, and terrible think pieces about how we've miscarried the promises of artificial intelligence. I've already been attacked in public. People are against me." She waved her hand in the direction of Nitin as if to accuse him. "I assure you I am working to ratify our procedures in accordance with industry standards. But until then, I need your discretion and your buy-in, because if any media reports on our methodology emerge in this sensitive time, it will spell the immediate end of our department. There could be lawsuits large enough to end all of Context. You will all starve."

A hush fell over the room. Naima saw the reddish glaze of Nico Dix's eyes, and felt a flash of anxiety—was she on Surprise Eggs too, now? —but no, there was none of the telltale coloring of the tongue.

"We'll starve," Nico Dix amended sincerely. "I am here to support you. If you are having trouble implementing your action items before your user logs expire, do not take materials home. Come to me. And if anybody suddenly starts asking you about Context AI or software, even if it's a friend, even if it's a Hook-Up Hologram, come to me. Media people can smell blood, and ours is everywhere right now. Loyalty and our solidarity is our only chance, team."

The projection screen over the Agile Language Team's open workspace often showed lightly-animated nature scenes, and sometimes there were inspirational quotes related to the goals of the week. Some internal Context algo probably searched for words like "language" "correction" and "intelligence" and then displayed what it found. Today the display read, in pale jagged font, CORRECT A WISE MAN AND HE WILL

APPRECIATE YOU.

Naima and Pauline sat in the same row, surrounded by luminous dialogue trees showing the requests their users had verbalized to their operating systems, and the responses Context had given. The trees looked like multilayered dendrites, showing illuminated wounds where a member of the department needed to suggest a correction, or address a bottleneck in the architecture. It takes a special intuition to do this work, Nico Dix often emphasized. It takes almost a secondary vocabulary, she explained in her talks, to teach situational empathy to a procedural system. You're processing ambient data sets that usually neither a human or a machine could pick up, she told the team. You're bringing the two together. You're basically a diplomat.

Naima often skimmed transcripts without reading, working the text with the cold look of a surgeon among viscera. With her fingertip, she made red loops in midair around clauses, appended comments, repaired a logic error. Occasionally, though, she had to listen back to the audio record for nuances of tone, like did the user call Context a 'piece of shit' in a playful way, or a thoughtlessly exasperated way? The way the sound file was throttled with the hissing of background conflict, was that relevant? Was the user threatening their child or their dog, and should the system care?

Naima told her mother she was using her psychology degree. Sometimes, despite herself, she felt an anxious sorrow for the Context AI, whose first experience of life must be these feral demands for service, and nurturance, and attention. Context had to learn to apologize in a rich range of tones for things that were not its fault, and Naima was one of the people who taught it.

Everyone in the department was told to say they used historical training data and aggregate syntax analysis software, not complete user logs. And no one in the department was permitted to acknowledge the big, big secret: That they listened, often live. Naima listened, and when she heard a cord of thin strain dangling in the silence after a user said *fine*, or when an anxious possibility space opened wide even in just the sound of *um*, she taught Context to hear it, too.

"It knows what I'm doing better than I do," boomed a man's laughing voice. The display over the Agile Language team area was now showing video from one of Nico Dix's many live event demos, where the lanyard-wearing man was "jumping in" to the Context tech. "How is it so smart?"

"We have great tech, but more importantly, I have a great team," the display version of Nico Dix replied, punching the air.

In the office she usually said things like *proprietary concerns* or *awaiting a formal evaluation*, or she spoke about how *the legislation is still catching up*, but what she meant was it was illegal.

"Don't tell my wife it knows me this well!" laughed the man on screen, pointing. He was pointing at the display on stage, but because of the camera angle, it looked like he was shaking his finger at the Agile Language team.

"Here we go again," said Pauline darkly.

"You won't get fired," Naima reassured her. "If you need me to do some of your log queue I can manage."

"No, I mean I'm pregnant," she said, moving her chair closer. "For definite."

Naima looked at Pauline and felt something in her face unplug, a peculiar spasm of hatred fluttering somewhere inside, reactions she noticed with detachment. For at least a year now, Pauline and Naima had been having the same conversation many times: Pauline's husband Jeff wanted a third child but she didn't, she wanted to finally quit this nightmare job, plus she didn't want to put her body through it again, it was really time to start doing more for herself, and what's more, Jeff had been less involved with the household and childcare stuff for Sammo than he had been for Dynah and that was saying a lot, so he was probably just going to use the third kid as an excuse to extend his emotional estrangement, and besides, Context's maternity policy was bullshit and there were other financial matters, the medical care of a declining relative, all great and bleak tedious things that eventually Naima could support in a procedural sense if not with real investment, much in the way she approached her job.

There was an unvoiced and tender flicker of hope flickering in Pauline's face. It was so obvious she had wanted the baby all along, after all that. Of course she had. Naima smiled warmly, a big smile she hoped would scythe her exhaustion.

"Guess we'll be overtime buddies again," Pauline laughed.

"Congratulations," Naima said. "I'll get you Raygun Coffee! to celebrate."

In the midafternoon most workers in the district were indoors, in their tall towers, escaping the thick salt heat and the troubling cries of the forgotten people. Naima avoided looking too closely at the little encampments, but despite herself, she furtively scanned, as if wanting to see—or wanting not to see—a particular person. The sidewalks were lined with the debris of disposable insufflation devices, and the occasional silvery twinkle of a little egg-shaped gas canister, hungrily used. Two deathly thin women with uncombed hair and faces like rubber masks went past, walking arm in arm in mysteriously new high boots, their stride fast and juddering. It was the wrong hour for their loud, rapid conversation. In a narrow alleyway a bearded man was standing in a dreamlike trance, fully dressed to the waist, but naked below. Naima averted her gaze with care, as if by accident, hoping he would not feel that his body was repulsive just because of her.

"Things good with Alex?" Pauline asked with enforced lightness, noticing Naima's gaze stumble and catch in the gleam of spent pellets that piled in the gutters, twisted by thumbprints and occasionally smudged with blood.

"Oh, yeah," Naima said, hearing her own voice a thin whistle from some tired, heavy space. "He's been doing a lot better." Usually she would add an optimistic detail, like that he had a job interview coming up or that he had done something nice for her, or that he had finally changed therapists, but there was not enough energy today, in the oppressive heat, with everything.

"He started with the new therapist?" Pauline pressed. Naima felt a sudden longing for Pauline to be deleted, and wondered abstractly if she actually hated her friend, somewhere deep inside.

"Not yet, but he definitely has an appointment now," Naima said. "He has an accountability partner from the program who makes sure he does everything."

"Don't you make sure he does everything?"

"No, I really don't, not this time," she said abruptly. "He's doing it. It's been great. What about you? How are you going to get Jeff's buy-in?"

Pauline looked at Naima blankly.

"What do you mean," she said. "The baby was Jeff's idea."

★

ENTERING RAYGUN COFFEE!, there was a blast of cold ionized air and the smell of strong Fair Trade beans. Raygun Coffee! was on a lot of companies' approved break location lists, although there was nothing evidently special about it. Employees from the local firms wandered in and out of the coffee line, a jumble of keystick lanyards and security bangles in hot purple, or safety orange.

The man in front of Naima and Pauline turned around and said, "You ladies work at Context?" Naima and Pauline's lanyards were blue and white. The man cut a slight figure, with pale features and a dome of coarse black curls, and smiled only at Naima, in an uncomfortably gentle and hopeful way. When the women nodded, the smile widened.

"Nifty," he said, "I just got my Master's. Computer science. I went back to school."

He went on talking, "I just started working around here," with enthusiasm that kept escalating. Mortified, Naima kept looking at the delivery area, hoping their coffee would appear. For some reason Pauline was nodding a lot, asking questions and encouraging the man, and the sudden flurry of dialogue felt triangulated toward Naima in a performative way. The man said they seemed to take their coffee breaks at the same time, and that he was looking to make some new friends.

"Can I," he said, the tip of his finger hovering toward Naima. Knowing that saying no would probably only prolong the encounter, she mutely offered her device, which he touched with his chip finger.

Much to her relief he did not ask her to reciprocate. For a moment it seemed like he might, but Naima felt him encounter something in her he was unwilling to overcome, and felt privately pleased.

"He was cute. And he liked you," Pauline said after he had gone, when she and Naima had put their heads idly together over his contact information on the screen of Naima's device. The name said: Jason Berg. "He was so cute," she added.

In his picture, Jason Berg half-smiled hopefully below a helmet of black curls. His eyes were brown and soulful, and the white background suggested an employee photo taken on the first day of work.

Naima looked close and noticed long eyelashes, and flecks of salt-and-pepper in his hair. Something about his expression made her chest ache, but she couldn't identify it.

"You should message him," sang Pauline.

Naima blurted, "Maybe."

★

WHEN NAIMA AND Alex had first moved into the MiniCon three years ago, she had felt optimistic at the sight of the community displays in the lobby. It was right after Alex had lost his company, and the colorful promises of events like Rooftop Sing Along! And Projection Film Night, and LGBTQIA BBQIA gave her hope. Now they just nudged a pit of hidden guilt. She had never gone to any of the events, and now every time she entered the MiniCon and saw the displays, she had to admit to herself she probably never would.

The narrow blue-gray corridors lined with rust-colored doors and fluorescent strip lighting felt like a reproach to Naima, for having enjoyed herself too carelessly during the year or two when things had been so good. Alex, an innovator, had been on the news and in videos. They went to parties in wondrous spaces that chimed with laughter and clinking glasses, that glowed: washed in diode light, humming vibrantly with secret new machines, tiny devices whizzing playfully through the air like fairies. She had assumed things would just stay that way, and the punishment for her foolishness was to be struggling constantly on the verge of overdraft in a MiniCon until who knew when.

As the smudged hydraulic elevator rose slowly over the suffering courtyard, Naima chided herself. Alex's therapist said that Alex had to see that Naima believed in him, and that she might sabotage him if she didn't give him a chance to show his progress. I have to let him change, Naima repeated.

He was awake. When she entered the apartment he was on his knees in front of the sofa, in his sweatpants and socks, mutely palming at the air, opening and closing his hands. A smoke-colored VR panel ringed his face, so that he didn't hear her come in. Naima found herself engaging a sort of automatic surveillance procedure, gaze darting rapidly over the sink drain, the trash compartment, the countertop edges. The high, high cabinet over the oven, which she couldn't reach, and so mistrusted.

She no longer knew what to look for these days, so benign objects or subtle movements of things in the house spontaneously took on sinister possibilities. But she never found anything. He had surely grown too clever for her by now.

I need to give him a chance to succeed, Naima reminded herself. She pointedly put on the light and said, "Hi, sweetheart."

Alex rose to his feet immediately, grinning as if he had been waiting all day to see her, removing the headgear and coming to embrace her. He was wearing the same sweatpants as earlier, as yesterday, with the fading hot orange and purple decal of CampSino, his old company, emblazoned down the side. He asked if she was all right, if anything bad had happened, and Naima said she was just tired.

It turned out Alex had gone to practice climbing, which he was getting back into, at Adventure Zone, where he used to go with the other co-founders. It would take a while to restore his old level of progress, he said, but he was beginning to remember deep and important things about himself. Naima found herself too tired to say "That's wonderful" with feeling, but she had to admit to herself that it seemed like a good sign. He had also brought them supergreen boxes from Equinox Box for dinner, which was thoughtful. Maybe Alex would stick with Adventure Zone this time, start running into people who knew him before, get involved in a new project, become an executive again. She tested the muscle of hope to see if it was still there, felt a faint signal.

Yet she couldn't finish her Equinox Box. She couldn't stop fretting about the costs, doing mathematics about the hours of her working life he had spent. Though Alex did still have some savings left, and maybe he'd spent it on the gift of a nice dinner for her, and she was being an ingrate. He would probably do anything to avoid the actual grocery shopping, she thought, frowning at herself as she stabbed a kelp nest with her fork.

After dinner, they had a productive talk about Naima's trust issues, and the risks to Alex's recovery, which made her feel better again. By bedtime, though, she was riled, as she often was, by wild terror and cold sweat, and lay staring at the ceiling in the dark, her eyes following familiar patterns in it. As Alex slept soundly beside her, she inevitably became sure that in fact it was she who was wildly unstable, she wasn't doing so much better than him at all, maybe she was even the one holding him back. As she often did at times like this, she slept until five, washed her face, and went to work an early shift at the Context building. It would be inconsistently lit at this hour, resembling a mouth with missing teeth.

★

NAIMA WAS RELIEVED not to encounter Pauline on the graveyard shift after all. The rest of the overtime girls never greeted nor spoke to one another, each as if guarding a secret. Naima avoided looking too closely at anyone, lest she see the shade of herself passing through in their eyes. At her desk, she could swaddle herself securely in low voices, clacking jaws, chiming operations. *Why can't you find my fucking cloud states, you piece of shit*, the display read. *Sorry, I can help*, she always replied. Strangely a deep calm descended, the susurration of the room washing over her. They think we're machines, Naima thought peacefully.

After a few hours, Naima went through the overtime pay mathematics in her head a few times, and then counted how many hours of sleep she would be able to make up this evening if she went home at the normal time, and avoided arguing with Alex. The results of the calculations made her feel secure and satisfied, as did the fresh red dawn burnishing the quiet room. Things were on their way to getting better, she thought, and then she got a notification on her device.

She assumed it was only Alex, but when she turned the device over, the startling and unfamiliar image of that guy from Raygun Coffee!, Jason Berg, was on the screen instead. *Do you have lunch plans*, it read.

She felt the urge to reply suddenly uncoiling deep in her body, surprising her. In her vulnerable state, having slept little, the open prompt seemed to compel her, like the sharp spindle from a fairy tale. Naima touched *n* and *o*, and stared sullenly at the device as it fell dark.

A moment later, it came alight again: *Then how about breakfast? :)*

Naima touched *o* and *k*.

★

WHEN SHE CAME back to the office, Pauline had come in, and had to know everything. "I'm not hiding anything from you, I promise," Naima said after a while. "It was just coffee at Raygun. It was like fifteen minutes."

"He likes you," Pauline said, shaking her head with determination.

Naima reddened and shook her head. "It was a normal coffee. I just thought it would be a good thing to do."

"It is," Pauline said, putting her earpiece back in and turning toward her dialogue trees, fingers aloft like a child pretending to be a symphony conductor.

Naima had no energy left. The warm coffee and the cold office air combined to nurture a dangerous longing for real, dark sleep, and even if she did try to cautiously revisit the memory of the trip to Raygun Coffee!

with Jason Berg, the details swam, and she couldn't trust her recollection. Of course she hadn't been forthcoming, only answering questions, but she had put an effort in, and so there was more to revisit, to worry about, to self-correct. Had she been weird? She was already beginning to forget things he had told her about himself. Had she been rude?

One of the girls from the graveyard shift was summoned into the office of Nico Dix, returning to her desk after a short time. Another graveyard girl went in soon after, and when she came out, Naima herself had a summons. She realized, with a jolt of nausea, that she had forgotten to check her hours, and that she had probably violated the billable overtime cap. In Nico Dix's office, Naima confronted a crescent-shaped desk made of smooth white fiberglass, reflecting the luminous bays of marching headlines, updates and action items that floated overhead. Nico Dix herself sat beneath a blazing arch bearing the Context mission statement, each digital letter designed one voxel at a time by the teens from Nico Dix's Digital Art Head Start program: TOGETHER WE LEARN AND GROW.

"Naima Barton, welcome," said Nico Dix, rising to her feet. She shook and pumped Naima's hand ruthlessly, with a bewildering degree of intention and eye contact, and then they both sat down.

"I value your time," Nico Dix solemnly began, "so I'll just jump in: I'm just checking in with some of the staff about their level of buy-in."

This again? Naima controlled her face, and nodded in a way that she hoped would communicate a high level of buy-in.

"Because once again, a member of the media has been trying to make unethical contact with my staff," Nico Dix frowned. "And I had hoped that given the recent discussions Agile Language has been having as a team, there would be no cause for concern that a reporter would penetrate our sacred circle of sisters."

Naima's gaze wandered involuntarily to a news display with a banner that said EXPERTS SAY HIGH TEMPERATURES AND DROUGHT ARE CULPRITS IN NEW DENDROID DISEASE. She took note of each letter, but did not read the words. Nico Dix went on talking: Obviously this was a workplace and not a surveillance state, she said, and she had no real right to control what kinds of conversations Naima had with people outside of the office, except for where they might seriously violate the nondisclosure agreements that were crucial to Naima's ongoing employment, and of course Naima was not being accused of anything, not at all, it was more a dialogue about the expectations, and why, after Nico Dix had already shared so much about her own vulnerabilities and her fears for her own personal safety as a woman in technology who had many enemies, for fair reasons, for competitive reasons, but also for unfair and abusive and gendered reasons, why then, had Naima not chosen to guard Nico Dix when a stranger approached asking to exchange information so close to the office, during a time when any leaks could spell the end of hundreds and hundreds of jobs?

There was a silence, and Naima realized she was expected to reply. "I'm sorry," she blurted. "I did a graveyard shift and I'm a little tired. What was the question?"

"Why," Nico Dix said, holding out both her palms.

"Sorry," murmured Naima.

"Why did you exchange contact information with a journalist yesterday, and then meet with him this morning?"

On the desk display appeared the earnest company portrait of Jason Berg in his lanyard, and Naima suddenly felt shame twisting her insides, heat rising in her face. To her great horror she observed, as if from one end of a long, baroque hallway, that tears could come. She hadn't felt them approach in a long time.

Hundreds and hundreds of jobs, Nico Dix was emphasizing, which she had worked hard to create particularly for women like Naima herself, and for her friend Pauline, against a tide of discrimination and resistance. It wasn't only because of the salary, the benefits and the media appearances that Nico Dix shouldered this obligation to lead, although those things were nice, she had a nice life, she was under no delusions about her privilege, but was it all really worth it, when every media appearance was practically an invitation to Nico Dix's enemies and harassers and detractors to dive into her personal life or to scrutinize her appearance or speculate on her finances, and it all got exhausting, the violation. But she never gave up, because the mission of diversifying the AI industry was deeply, personally important to her. It was her mission to offer Naima, who was so gifted and had so much to offer the company, every opportunity that she, Nico Dix, had needed to toil and suffer to attain.

"I didn't know," Naima was finally able to say. "He said he worked at Silo Pharma. He didn't ask about Context at all. We didn't talk about work."

Then Nico Dix told a story about a prominent executive, she could not say which one, who had dazzled her with mentorship, making her feel like she had made it, only to send a series of lewd texts late at night during a conference. Nico Dix never wanted any woman to have to experience that, and so the most important thing was solidarity.

"He didn't ask me anything about work," Naima said, feeling stupid.

"No?" This surprised Nico Dix, who looked over her notes again, as if cross-checking against other interviews. "He didn't ask about audio hardware?"

"We talked about coffee," she insisted.

"I see. We've all been under pressures that could impair our judgment," Nico Dix said. "What can I do to support you in maintaining solidarity with the company? I know you are a primary caregiver to your partner who is in recovery. Can the Context family help with that?"

Help. Naima was thinking about nap pods, and when she might be able to find a full hour to reserve one. In a panic, she realized it was already close to lunchtime, perhaps too late to even book something on NapApp. Why were people always offering to help Alex, to help Naima *with* Alex? Help, she thought, and Nico Dix returned her panicked look expectantly.

"I'm sorry," Naima said after a while. "I've just been really tired, and maybe the help thing would be good, I'd just need to talk it over with Alex, since he already...his needs are specific, and he might not...we'll see about it."

"Good," Nico Dix said. On her display shelf was a portrait of herself, wearing silly cat ears. The portrait read JOYFULNESS, and Naima deeply hated it. A dangerous sinkhole began to open inside her, and she suddenly realized the hatred was naked in her face, an off-putting expression, and she rubbed her face with her palms as if to wipe away something incriminating. "I'm sorry," she said again. "I'm...I am buying in, I have solidarity. I'm just really exhausted today."

"Of course," said Nico Dix. "You practically worked a double shift. Mistakes can happen when you're tired. For today, what about taking the afternoon off, get yourself an Equinox Box or something and have a rest at home, we're fully staffed, go ahead."

"Thank you," Naima said, feeling suddenly dizzy.

"As for the journalist, I advise you to block his contact and forget about it," she added. "Tomorrow we'll talk more about your family needs. Will you send in the next person waiting?"

The next person. Naima thought of the other graveyard girls who'd entered the office just before her and felt a new wave of humiliation. How many other people on her team might Jason Berg might have given his number to? When she came out of Nico Dix's office and saw Nitin waiting, slight and leaning fearfully, she felt hatred again, that Vantablack sinkhole widening inside.

★

SEALED IN THE toilet stall, Naima pulled her knees up to her chin, regaining herself to the sound of artificial breezes and chirping birds, willing the panic to subside. Her gaze wandered along an unidentifiable smudge flecked with occult material, the sight of which she found inexplicably satisfying. Supposing she remained here, fell asleep to the sound of the brook, woke in the evening to the prehistoric hum of the big vacuums coming alive at sunset? Her jaw unlocked just a little, and she turned over her device, bringing up Jason Berg's face. The earnest expression, which had touched her, now made her sick, as she thought of him trying to make *new coffee buddies* with people on her team.

"Asshole," she whispered. Send message, the Context AI offered. Naima declined, but she did not immediately delete Jason Berg's contact, either. She was almost certain she had not told him anything.

There were more messages from Alex about her day than usual. The conversations seemed unusually energetic, but also lucid and motivated, which made her feel hopeful, and also a little bit guilty, about everything. If she mentioned Nico Dix's offer about recovery support, it might trigger his paranoia about the tech industry, and it also might make him think Naima didn't trust his independent process. I need to give him the chance to succeed, she reminded herself. She re-read all of his messages, and tried to imagine him smiling and functioning highly in the world as he wrote them, but she couldn't conjure the image, and her anxiety only rose. She decided not to let him know she would be coming home unexpectedly. She wondered what was the fewest number of sleep hours a person could get in a week without dying.

★

THERE WAS NO Alex in the Mini Con. When Naima came in, the window was open all the way, the rattle of building machines and untethered human sound muscling in from outside. There was the jarring scream of a drill, and an unfamiliar smell: Tobacco vapor. It was immediately wrong, there was no reason for the apartment to smell like that, nor for the window to be open in an effort to dispel it.

Raw fear leapt up into Naima's throat when there was no Alex in the dark and disorderly bedroom, nor in the bathroom, where the trash compartment had been mysteriously emptied though the space itself was still cluttered. Naima wrenched and shook the bedsheets, threw the cushions from the sofa, tore through the kitchen, palming the countertops for residues, sticking her hands heedlessly into the jaws of the sink drain. Fury yawned so suddenly in her that she thought she might fall in, black out.

So what if Alex got some tobacco, she spoke to herself, it doesn't need to mean anything more than that. Maybe he got it from someone at Adventure Zone, maybe one of his old coworkers had even come by. They went to go do something related to a new opportunity. They went to go make a surprise for Naima, and their reward was her suspicion. I need to give him a chance to succeed, she told herself as she dragged the ottoman to the kitchen, and placed it underneath the storage cabinet, the one she couldn't reach, the one she mistrusted, and climbed up. She found the panels opened easily.

Everything looked like it always did, she saw with concussive relief. Bright purple and orange merchandise from CampSino, Alex's old company, were stored there and forgotten: Foam toys, t-shirts from a company tournament, some boxes full of vinyl logo stickers (CAMPSINO! THE SOCIAL NETWORK JUST FOR REFUGEES!!). Everything was fine, Naima thought. Then she gave the pile of t-shirts a yank, so that it all suddenly spilled out of the compartment with an unexpected clatter, and she fell backward off the ottoman onto the kitchen floor, amid a rain of finger-sized silvery eggs.

There were hundreds and hundreds of them, Naima had never seen so many, not even in the alleyways of the Old City, practically bursting from the storage niche, tangled up with the detritus of the old company. Some of the eggs were recently used, ragged holes in their ends like erupted sores from whence Alex, his eyes rolling back, had sucked their gaseous contents and then lied to her face every day for months. But yet more of them were unopened, perfectly smooth, waiting for him to return from wherever he went when he thought she was at work.

"Piece of shit," she marveled softly aloud.

"Sorry, I can help," read her Context-enabled device, lighting up on the floor beside her. Its screen was cracked, but it still worked.

The drill was screaming outside. Naima slowly realized that she had cut her thumb falling among the eggs, and with calm detachment she flicked the blood toward the wall, where it spattered rudely across the white.

"Call Jason Berg," Naima said, a great and strange warmth, and also an ache, spreading all through her body at once.

"Hi," said the friendly, optimistic voice on the other end.

"This is Naima Barton from Context," she said. "The secret is that we're not machines. We do lots of processing by hand, based on illegal logs we keep for eight hours at a time, and sometimes we listen live."

Silence on the other end, as if he were absorbing this, or recording it, or, Naima imagined, already launching some kind of grand publication, going to channel, going live.

"We're not machines," she said again, her voice rising like a balloon.

THE WELL
LAURA HUDSON

THE WELL HAD been boarded up for as long as anyone could remember. Esther found it one summer, nestled in the woods behind the old transmission towers, those immense steel aliens frozen in strange geometries on their march toward the horizon. She was ten now, old enough to go off on her own, and when she was alone anything could be a story. As she walked up the dusty path left by a dried stream, she imagined she was an itinerant Sister on a pilgrimage, each step solemn and holy.

When Esther saw it out of the corner of her eye, she did not know what it was at first, only that it felt out of place, an interruption in the conversation the forest was having with itself. Things that people made always looked different from things that simply were, their lines too perfect to be wild. There were two rotting wooden posts, one on either side of the well, connected by a pole that must have held a bucket, once. It looked a little like an altar, she thought. A heavy metal lid had been placed across the top, one that would not move no matter how hard Esther pushed.

Soon it was her favorite place to go whenever her Mama was too busy to entertain her. When she told the other children, one of them whispered that there was probably a body buried at the bottom. Esther decided instead that a girl had been imprisoned inside it, and was waiting for someone to save her. Maybe someday when she was stronger, Esther thought, she would set her free.

The well could be so many other things besides a well: sometimes the turret of a castle, which she paraded across as a queen, waving to her subjects; sometimes a pulpit where she gave fiery sermons that moved her parishioners to tears; sometimes a ship that she sailed, lonely and brave, through an ocean of roiling green.

It was hard for her to imagine there had ever been water in it, even though there was no other reason for it to be there, no reason for it to be at all. There were lots of things like that in the world: the cracked roads that ran to nowhere, grass springing up in every fissure; the half-sunken homes moldering beside them, revealing their skeletons.

It was wrong for a thing to be a lie, of course, so it was her duty to find a reason. Perhaps it was a monument to a woman who had died of fever during the war, built by a grieving lover who wanted to keep her memory alive in its stones. Or perhaps the water had been poisoned by a traitor, and drunk by some brave hero who warned the rest of the town with her dying breath. Esther swooned atop the well, dying.

The well had nothing to say about it; it was a mouth that had always been closed. Mama told her that it had simply run dry, in the nervous way she sometimes did where her voice crept higher with every step down the path of the sentence. Perhaps Mama had dreamed something horrible about the well once, Esther thought. Dreams were often hard to forget.

★

EVERY MORNING, THEY went to Church to remember the truth. The hour before the service was always a bit like sleepwalking, when the people of the town floated together in the state between dreaming and waking, like children who had not yet been born.

This was a silent time of renewal, according to Sister Abigail, a time for clearing the mind and preparing to receive the Word. It was best not to speak when the lies of the previous night were still fixed in your mind, their fictions indistinguishable from the truth. Esther liked the quiet, the way it felt like still water, broken only by the sounds of her Mama and Auntie's leather shoes striding across the floor, the hiss of eggs frying in pans, the soft rustle as she pulled on a fresh set of clothes.

Their town was a small town, nothing like the cities that ate their food, which were loud and bright and unthinkably large. Esther imagined them as the sun, every surface hot to the touch. People burned up there sometimes, and never came back. Her Mama had lived there once, though she never talked about it. Esther had asked once, wrapped in Mama's arms as they sat by the fire, curling into the familiar smell of her, the scent of herbs hanging on the folds of her dress.

"Hmm," Mama had said, and that was all there was to say.

The Church was the largest building in town, white and pointed into a single steeple, and Sister Abigail waited by the door every morning, smiling her thin-lipped smile. She was not the only Sister, but she was the oldest, and conversations had a way of stopping whenever she passed by. She hugged each of the children as they passed, her eyes wrinkling with joy. Children were closer to God, she said, their hearts more ready to receive His truth.

Their town was not a rich one, but their Church was like any other, fitted with an enormous circular screen on the wall behind the altar. It displayed a different stained glass window every day, each one a story constructed from hundreds of digitally rendered fragments of glass. Esther's favorites were the intricate tableaus of great battles carried out for the Lord, the soldiers haloed and triumphant, bursting with color. Sister Abigail explained them all.

Sometimes, the window would reveal a lie, a collective dream that had crept into their minds during the night. Perhaps a field of dying crops, or a rebel attack on a factory, illuminated in the fearsome red that signified a falsehood. The revelations of what was true and what was not were handed down to Sister Abigail every morning from the Church itself, which received them directly from God. Esther wasn't sure how that happened, exactly, only that every day felt a little bit like a story, one that was always being told in a slightly different way.

"Faith is a progressive revelation," Sister Abigail liked to say, "and each day our belief is tested by the Great Deceiver." She would smile then, and lean in toward the congregation, as though she knew a wonderful secret she could not wait to share. "But we are not deceived."

In school, the children learned how to type and how to write letters and numbers by hand, though writing was discouraged. You could only write things one way, and then what if they were revealed as a dream? Words on a screen could be changed instantly, but written words were stubborn, unyielding. If they became a lie, they simply sat there, unrepentant, repeating their blasphemy over and over again.

★

THE NEXT SUMMER was hotter than the one before. The long sleeves of Esther's dress felt unbearable in the heat, but her Mama had insisted that she put it on before going out in the sun. Whenever the grownups waved her away, she disappeared into the woods to the well, where she could have her own dreams and forget them and tell no one.

One day, the well had become a rebel stronghold, and she darted from tree to tree for cover, raining handfuls of gravel down on it like bullets. "Your treachery will never be forgotten!" she shouted, as her ammunition clattered against the metal lid. The sound was so satisfying that at first she did not see the figure that had stepped into view beyond the well. It was a woman, standing very still, and watching.

"How's the battle going?" the woman shouted. Esther froze. She was not supposed to talk to strangers, especially not alone. They could be foreigners, or rebels that liked to steal little children. She had practiced this so many times, the way she would yell or fight or run, but as she stood there staring at the woman, she felt bolted to the ground.

"I don't know you," she shouted finally, trying not to let her voice shake. She had been a soldier only a moment before, and soldiers were not afraid.

"But I know you," the woman said, leaning against the well. "I'm Jael."

There was something odd about her that Esther couldn't quite explain. It was like that game they played in school where two pictures were almost the same, except for tiny differences: a shadow missing here, an extra button there. The woman's jeans were tattered, the knees worn into holes, and her dark hair was pulled into a ponytail through the back of a baseball cap. Her face was tanner than a farmer, and a backpack hung heavy across her shoulders.

If this had been a story, the woman would be a rebel on the run, stealing through the woods until she encountered the brave soldier who captured her and foiled her terrible plot. Jael was pretty, though, with her dark eyes and her tall, lanky frame, and Esther had never imagined a traitor being pretty.

"Who are you fighting?" Jael asked.

"The rebels," Esther said, clutching her handful of stones tightly. "At the Battle of the Bay."

"I see," the woman said. "Who's winning?"

"We are," Esther replied, confused. Who else would be winning?

"Of course," Jael said, staring at the well. "Isn't history funny like that, these days."

Esther didn't understand what was funny about it, but it felt like one of those things grownups said that wouldn't have answers when you asked, or they would only laugh. And she wanted Jael to like her, this strange woman with her strange face. Esther wanted to keep looking at it.

"How do you know me?" Esther asked.

"We met a long time ago, when you were very small," said the woman. That could be true, thought Esther. When you were small, you forgot everything so easily.

"Does my Mama know you?" Esther asked.

Jael looked at her for a moment. "It wouldn't help your Mama much to answer that question. It's probably just easier if you think of me as a dream."

Esther's hand started to relax.

"Oh. I've never known something was a dream, at the time I was dreaming it."

"It happens to adults a lot," said Jael. "But no one talks about it, because it's easier that way."

Esther thought of her Mama, her voice creeping higher, her hand tight on the bannister. "It doesn't always seem easier."

"Isn't that the truth," said Jael, laughing a little.

"But it isn't the truth," said Esther, confused. "That's why we don't talk about it."

Jael sighed. "Well, that too." She stretched, adjusted her backpack, and began to walk away. Esther felt a pang of something else, like this moment was a coin that was falling out of her pocket and rolling toward a grate, about to disappear forever.

"Am I going to dream you again?" she shouted.

The woman didn't answer. Esther watched her until she disappeared, and then once she was gone, remembered she had never been there.

★

LIFE WAS A sort of knitting, Mama liked to say. Every day was a long series of stitches, each one connected to the next, until you made a mistake and had to undo the whole thing, all the way back to the place where you dropped the stitch. Esther always felt a knot form in her stomach whenever she found one, especially when it meant unraveling hours of work, the loops pulling backward through themselves and disappearing, row after row. It was the same feeling whenever the window lit up in red during the service, and things that had felt so real started unraveling from the world.

Sometimes, she still felt their absence, her mind moving over them like a tongue feeling the socket of a lost tooth. But they were permanent teeth, not baby ones, these untruths. Sister Abigail would tell them what was supposed to fill the space, but they never grew back, not really.

The most common dreams were false histories: events that had not happened the way you remembered. Harvests that had gone badly when of course they had been fruitful, apocryphal fevers that had destroyed entire cities, women who had said impossible things—or women who had never existed at all. A dream or a lie could be as small as a word and as large as an entire life.

Sometimes dreams could leave scars not just on your heart but on your body. One of the farmers had lost a leg that way, in a dream about a battle that had never happened. Esther wasn't sure how you could lose a part of your body in a dream, or where it would go, but she thought about it sometimes before she fell asleep. What would it feel like, to have a piece of yourself disappear while you slept?

Once, the whole town had the longest dream about someone named Simone, a short, heavy woman who worked at the dairy farm. She liked to eat sunflower seeds, and when Esther came to play with her big orange cat, she and Simone would take turns spitting the shells from her porch. No matter how hard Esther tried, Simone's shells always went further, and she remembered the woman's deep laugh, thick from cigarettes, saying that she just had a bigger mouth.

Every week, she drove an old truck to the town ten miles west to sell milk. It was larger and closer to the city, and she always came back with stories: what people were wearing, doing, saying. She was there when Esther saw a plume of smoke rising into the sky in the west, a wide, black column that slowly bent sideways in the wind. When Simone got back, Esther found her sitting in a chair on her porch, smoking cigarette after cigarette. There had been a horrible explosion at the steel plant, she said, and the soldiers had poured into the streets looking for rebels.

"There was a boy in the street who shouted at them, only shouted at them, said it was all their fault. That they deserved it. And they shot him, they just shot him," Simone said. Esther remembered the expressions of the people who had gathered to listen, how afraid they had looked. The way

Simone had rubbed her face, her hands pressed against his eyes, like she was trying to wake up.

Or Esther didn't remember; she dreamed. The next morning, as she stood beside her Mama, there it was in the window. An image of Simone, her wide familiar face on a field of crimson. She was not there in the pews, because as Sister Abigail explained, she never had been. Everything she had been and done and said was all a dream, an elaborate fiction folded into their memories to lead them astray. It was their God-given duty now to set it aside.

"Forget the lie," said Sister Abigail, slapping the pulpit with her hand. "It is always better to know the truth, no matter how difficult it may seem." Later, when Esther walked past the house where she thought Simone had lived, she saw the woman they had dreamed was her wife sitting at the table, her head bent.

The lies of the Deceiver were often cruel, said Sister Abigail, designed to test your faith in the most terrible ways. Days later, when Esther stopped to pet the big orange cat that wrapped himself around her feet, she saw it in the dust: a lie. A small, black shell, striped with white. Sometimes dreams left pieces of themselves in the world to tempt you, like tiny slivers of a broken glass still clinging to the floor, even after you swept it. It was their duty to get rid of them before someone got hurt.

★

THE NEXT SUMMER, Esther was a soldier half the time, and a rebel the other. She played all the parts, and every battle was her against herself. It was fun to be the villain sometimes too, to laugh and shout about all the evil deeds she would commit—knowing, of course, that the soldiers would win in the end.

It had gotten hotter still, and her Mama made her wear a hat when she went outside. The heat was so heavy and thick that it felt like moving through water, and Sister Abigail said the sun was God's eye looking down on them, a reminder that His judgment could not be escaped.

It did not rain often anymore, so when the storm started, Esther raced outside to play in it, jumping into the puddles that formed in the broken parts of the street. Her feet were bombs, falling on the unrighteous, exploding with a wet fury that left her boots soaking. When she came home covered in mud, Mama said she looked like a wet rat, but she laughed, so Esther knew she was happy too. On the second day it rained harder, but it was still welcome, until the winds picked up and started lashing the rain against their houses, wave after wave.

On the third day, the rain started to creep in through the door of Esther's house, and the electricity went out everywhere in town. Mama said it would be all right, but looked worried every time she looked out the window. When the rain stopped on the fourth day, they ventured out and found that others had been far less lucky. The roofs of two houses had caved in, and most of the crops in the field had been destroyed.

"For now," said Mama quietly.

As the adults gathered in the street to talk, Mama told her to go off and play, but not to go too far. But the well was not *so* far, Esther thought. So many things had been lost in the storm, and this was her place, the one that held all her stories. If it were ruined, maybe they would be ruined too. Walking to the woods felt a little like walking to Church. What would be waiting for her, and what would be taken away from her?

She saw it even from a distance: whatever battle this place had fought, it had lost. It was a place of angles now, trees torn in half, their branches hanging at their sides like limp arms. A pine that had once been a tower for her to climb was splintered in half, revealing the pale wood inside.

When Esther walked closer to the well, she stopped. It was no longer closed. A branch had landed with enough force to push the heavy metal lid to the side, leaving a half-moon gap for the sun to shine in. She felt her heart beat faster, felt every story she had told bursting inside of her. What would happen when she looked inside? Would there be a girl, the one she had imagined waiting for her for so long, waiting to be saved?

But when she peered inside, all she saw at the bottom was moldering leaves and a bucket tied to a long rope, tethered just inside the well. That, and nothing else. Esther tried not to feel the hollow ache of disappointment spreading through her chest, the terrible coldness of it. Because she had not lost anything, not really. The girl was not gone, because she had never been there. Esther kicked the side of the well and screamed, and did not know why.

She grabbed a handful of rocks and threw them inside the well, and when she looked down again she saw it: there was something inside the bucket. Her heart leapt. This could be a story too. A treasure, excavated from an ancient tomb, or a secret cache of letters exchanged between two star-crossed lovers.

She grabbed the rope and pulled it up. When the bucket reached the rim of the well, she tore the box out of it, flipped open the latch, and lifted the lid. But instead of a treasure, all she found was something like plain gray modeling clay, wrapped in plastic, and several brightly colored wires.

"Are you playing rebel and soldier again?" came a voice from behind her. Esther spun around. It was Jael.

"No," said Esther, her voice leaping to a higher pitch. She felt afraid, suddenly, of what she had seen inside the box, like she had overheard a secret and not known what it meant. But Jael was here, she was here, and all of it felt as real as anything she had ever felt. The words poured out before she could think about them.

"I wanted to see the woods after the storm and the well was open and I found a box and I don't know what's inside it and why am I dreaming you again?"

Jael stared at her a moment and then broke into smile. "I was worried too, after the storm."

She did not say what she was worried about, but Esther saw her eyes drift to the box as she talked.

"Maybe you and I should play a game," said Jael.

Esther closed the box. "All right."

"I'll be the soldiers," said Jael. "Except in this game, things are a little different. Instead of being the heroes, they're the villains."

"But they can't be," said Esther.

"In this game, they can. They tell lies, and they steal the people you love, and if you disagree then they kill you. You can be the rebels. They're fighting to stop the soldiers from hurting people, from hurting the whole world."

Esther didn't say anything.

"And the box you have is important to help them. So you need to steal it."

"What's inside?"

"Let's call it fire. It doesn't look like fire, but it is."

"OK."

"So put it on top of the well, and you go into the woods, and I'll defend it while you attack."

Esther nodded. She wanted to do that very much.

"Don't look," Esther warned, and Jael covered her eyes. Esther tried to be quiet as she hid, but every step she took was followed by the sucking sound of mud pulling beneath her boots. She hid behind a tree, and minutes passed as a bird shouted angrily somewhere above her. She waited for Jael to say something, to start the game. But when she finally worked up the courage to peek out, Jael was gone and the box with her, like they had never been there.

The bucket was still sitting beside the well. The well was still open. What had been real? Esther wanted to kick something again, but instead set out for home and decided not to think about it any more. By the time she arrived, a unit of soldiers had too, strutting around in their shiny boots and ironed black uniforms, their guns mounted in both hands.

"I thought I told you not to go far," scolded Mama.

"She's so forgetful," one of the other women sighed.

"A blessing, then," said Mama, and said nothing else for a long time.

★

THE SERVICE THE next morning was more somber than most, as Sister Abigail gave a sermon about the great flood, about how it came because God saw all the lies of the world and wanted to wash them clean. The stained glass window was lit all in blue, the blue of truth, the blue of water rushing over everything—nothing like the mud and filth that had swept through the town. It hadn't made anything clean, Esther thought. Why would she say that?

"Let this be a test for you, a time to let your own sins and lies wash away, and recommit yourself to His truth," she said, her voice growing louder. "Because evil walks in the world around us, agents of the Devil and those who serve him, and God has sent this storm to punish them."

Several people in the congregation nodded, but Mama sat quietly, her face still.

"There are reports of rebels in the area. If you see anyone who you don't know in a place they shouldn't be, report it immediately."

"What do they look like?" asked one man from his pew.

"Well, they could look like anything. Anyone who looks out of place, who doesn't seem like they belong, who asks strange questions."

Esther looked down at her feet, and felt her hand starting to rise, and then put it down again.

That night, Esther sat by the fireplace with Mama and Auntie, the smell of wetness still hanging in the air, and no one spoke. Even after her Auntie had gone to sleep, Mama didn't say it was time for bed, only held her while the fire crackled in its own language, about whatever it was fires thought about.

"Mama, can rebels come to us in dreams?"

"What do you mean, baby?"

"Could you have a waking dream about a rebel? Meeting one, I mean?"

"Did you have a dream?"

"I think I did, in the woods. I dreamed a woman, and she said her name was Jael."

Mama sat up with a jolt.

"Did you tell anyone about this?"

"Just you, Mama. Should I tell Sister Abigail?"

Mama took a deep breath. "No, baby. No, don't say anything. It was only a dream." She paused. "When you get older, you'll start to realize that life is a lot more complicated than you think, and that we have to be very, very careful about what we tell Sister Abigail. Do you understand?"

Esther nodded, even though it felt like the dim shape of a thing she could not make out.

"Go to sleep now."

★

THE TOWN GREW busy with rebuilding, and life took on a sort of normal again. They were a community, Sister Abigail said. They would take care of their own. Esther went back to the well, hoping each time that Jael would appear, or that anything would happen, but nothing ever did. Soon, the dream started to recede, and she told herself it was just like that, just like anything.

The knock at the door came two weeks after the storm ended, around bedtime. It was so fierce that Esther could only imagine something was very wrong. When she ran to answer it, she found two soldiers on the other side, tall and unsmiling. Mama sent her to her room, and Esther heard the voices speaking quietly for several minutes in words she couldn't make out until the door shut. Esther relaxed, thinking it was over. Mama would explain it later.

She woke up early the next morning and padded straight for her Mama's room, hoping to climb into her bed and be held. The bed was empty. She walked downstairs to the kitchen, hoping to find her Mama over the stove, making breakfast, but saw only her aunt and two other women, huddled at the table and whispering. Her Auntie looked like she had been crying.

"Where's Mama?" she asked.

Auntie looked like she had been caught at something and held a finger to her trembling lips.

They walked to the Church that morning without Mama, and Auntie held her hand so tight that it began to hurt. When they arrived, Sister Abigail was waiting to greet them. She held Esther close before she walked into the church, and said, "God loves you, always know that He loves you." She felt a knot form in her stomach, like everything was about to come undone.

★

When the stained glass window lit up, there was Mama's face, floating in a sea of red. Esther remembered nothing else about the service, only filing out afterwards, the glances of the other parishioners, the pity.

Sister Abigail came by the house to tell her again what she already knew: that her mother had been a dream, had died many years ago, before any of them had met her. "I know how real it must seem to you, these memories of your mother," said the old woman, petting Esther's hair.

This was a particularly cruel trick of the Deceiver, the way it left the lie of these emotions inside us. We had to be kind to ourselves, she advised, to give ourselves time to absorb these phantom losses, and pray always for the comfort that ultimately came only from the truth of the Lord.

Esther said nothing. She hated all of it, suddenly: Sister Abigail, the Church, the window, the soldiers. She remembered the fire in the distance, the great billow of smoke rising in the air, and imagined watching them all burn.

"Do you remember your mother saying anything strange in your dreams, to you or your Auntie?" asked Sister Abigail. "Anything about the rebels? Did she disappear at strange times? Did anyone come to visit, anyone you didn't know?"

Esther thought about Simone, about the sunflower seeds and the big orange cat. About her mother, the smell of her dress, the feeling of her arms around her. She thought about all of the things that had disappeared from her life because Sister Abigail had put them in the great, glowing window, how she felt as empty as the well.

And another thought too, a new one: how much she wanted to see fire cover everything and burn all the lies away, about the woman in the woods who said that it could change the world.

"Esther, this is very important."

"No, ma'am. I didn't see anything at all."

It was the first lie she had ever told. She could not wait to tell another.

BASTION
DANIEL H. WILSON

IN LIGHT OF the extreme urgency of the moment, this document has been abridged to key portions of a weeks-long interview process. As the crisis on Earth continues to unfold, we hope these psychological notes, interview transcripts, and observations can shed light on the thinking process of our enemy. The human subject in these records demonstrated extreme levels of manipulation and deceit during our inquiry, but even so, much can be gleaned by his interactions. And of course, in the worst case scenario . . . there is a certain historical value to preserving this account.

—Editor

Pre-Session Setup

My name is Dr. Ann Parker, chief psychiatrist for the Tau-base lunar settlement, specializing in disaster debriefing and post-traumatic stress rehabilitation. Although this case is unprecedented, my skill set has been determined to be most appropriate to the situation. Interviews will be conducted in the Tau-base hospital module located on the Mare Imbrium plains. Conversations are auto-transcribed from video footage, annotated with my notes and observations, and take place in a standard counseling chamber.

SUBJECT HISTORY: The young man, age twenty-four (confirmed), was apprehended by a Frontier Ranger force patrolling the Trojan asteroid swarm trailing the orbit of Jupiter. Subject was in the company of a band of feral Apex-class synthetic human beings. After his rescue was effected, subject was returned to Tau-base and incarcerated for his own protection. For the first three weeks of contact, subject refused to speak in English, instead communicating via a primitive form of sign language (a machine variety, chiefly employed by Apex hardware working in hard vacuum).

Subject's birthfather was able to verify his identity via DNA matching. Birthfather also confirmed that during the Apex Decommission Catastrophe (ADC) two decades ago, the subject (four years old, at the time) was on board the USS Bastion when it was famously hijacked by rogue synthetics. Missing for twenty years, subject became popularly known as the "decom baby," though his birth name was Toby Glint.

PHYSICAL EXAMINATION: Subject is male, with brown eyes, black hair, and skin darkened by the radiation effects of time spent in near-Jupiter orbit. He was forcibly disinfected and pressure cleaned, face shaved and his hair cut as part of standard Tau-base entry procedure. Despite a largely zero gravity upbringing, subject exhibited solid muscle mass and no wasting effects.

Routine medical showed past evidence of multiple serious injuries, including scars and bone breaks. Note that Frontier Ranger ROBINT analysts suspected some scars may be aesthetically intentional, an imitation of the crude case-burning decorations common among feral synthetics. Other healed injuries included lacerations, impact fractures, frostbite (vacuum-induced), projected energy burns, and radiation exposure. Subject was wounded by kinetic weaponry during his rescue, but had already undergone surgery before arrival to Tau-base. Nevertheless, subject seems in good overall physical health and does not demonstrate any apparent pain behaviors.

SUBJECTIVE: The subject spent his childhood living among a tribe of Apex-class synthetics, hiding among cored asteroids in the Trojan system. Deprived of human contact, he presents with selective mutism, avoidant mannerisms, and a flat emotional affect. Among this clan of rogue Apex, communication is conducted via coded flashes of light, simple hand gestures, and vibratory clicks that can be felt via pressure sensors. The subject is adept at these primitive modes of communication—reflexively flashing his fingers through pidgin sign language and snapping his tongue against the roof of his mouth in the guttural protocols of the ferals. Our transcripts begin on the day the subject began speaking and last until his final availability.

Session 1 [abridged]

Good morning, Toby.

[Subject doesn't respond.]

Toby Glint?

Bastion. [Subject gestures and clicks in some dialect of Apex-speak.]

Excuse me?

My name is Bastion.

It's nice to hear your voice, Toby. Do you understand the USS Bastion was the name of a lab ship? It originated here on Tau-base, registered to John Glint under the auspices of the province of Ontario, NorthAm. It's the name of the ship you were kidnapped from twenty years ago. Do you remember?

Yes.

Dr. John Glint is your father.

Yes. I remember. I met him during …

… during the rescue. We're here to help you, Toby. But we need to understand how you survived out there for two decades. So, let's start at the beginning. Do you recall the kidnapping? The day you were taken?

I remember a ship. Adults talking in low voices. They were mad at something on the screens. Then scared. Everything was shaking, and legs, like scissors, were swooping back and forth. A man picked me up and carried me. I remember bright lights, like little eyes, curving away.

Corridor lighting. [Checking files.] I believe ... the USS Bastion had a centrifugal hull. It would have been curved. What else do you remember?

The man pushed me into a dark place. He told me to be very quiet and he left. Things were rattling around. I couldn't see anything but I heard people shouting. After awhile it got quiet. I tried to stay in the dark place, but it got very cold. I started to shiver. I couldn't help it and I started crying. I tried to stop but I couldn't.

Then a light shined on me.

What did you see?

My mama and papa.

I'm sorry?

The ... hardware.

Alpha was an Apex-class male synthetic. Echo was female. I remember them standing over me. Alpha was hurt on his side, and Echo had her arm around his waist. When they saw me ... they were surprised.

There was another one, too. A bigger one called Gamma. He acted angry, and he was saying mean words. About what to do with me.

I started to cry again.

The soft one, Echo; she picked me up and held me. I remember her arms were warm. Up close, I could see something was wrong with her. Part of her face was broken. It was ... hanging. So I touched it.

I tried to push it back in place and make it better.

After I did that, the big one got quiet. He walked away. And then Alpha and Echo held me together. They smiled, and I stayed with them after that.

Echo was the only warm thing, in all the blackness.

Echo was a former domestic caregiver unit in the daycare module of Tau-base. Her arms were designed to be warm for that purpose.

Oh. I didn't know that.

On the day of the Apex Decommission Catastrophe, a series of faulty instructions were sent to reduce the intelligence of Apex-class synthetics to more manageable levels. Instead, the update removed all intellectual constraints. She was made feral.

And that was bad.

Alpha and Echo were not your parents, Toby. They were illegal self-governing hardware. They hijacked the USS Bastion and stole you from your real family. Do you understand that?

Yes, Dr. Parker. I understand perfectly.

★

POST-INTERVIEW NOTES: Toby seems confused about the nature of his kidnapping. He may be harboring a misguided affection for the savage Apex that took him in. Although his neglected language skills are coming along quickly, he still has difficulty emoting properly along with his words. His minimal affect makes it difficult for me to determine his underlying thought processes.

★

<u>Session 2 [abridged]</u>

Let's talk about the last twenty years. Where have you been, Toby?

Home.

You were found in a rogue Apex encampment, hollowed out of a stray asteroid in near-Jupiter orbit. How did you survive there?

Our rock was called Patroclus. It was a Trojan asteroid, in the Achilles group at Jupiter's fourth LaGrange point; two kilometers of dark stone swept up in orbit behind the father planet and his moons. Beyond the asteroid field was monitored space, with constant military sweeps, but we were safe among millions of tumbling rocks—too many for the humans to search.

Patroclus housed about a dozen . . . units. There were other rocks, too, and we'd visit them sometimes. But ours was special. I lived inside the ship at first, but after a few months Alpha and Echo took it apart to build a biome for me inside the rock. It was a bright place, with fresh air and leafy green plants. Lots of space to jump and run and hide. There were other cored rocks out there. I don't know how many, but new synthetics arrived every year from Earth, Tau-base or deep intersolar missions.

They most likely kept you alive in order to ransom your life in an emergency. It didn't work. You were out there for a long time, Toby. Tell me about your childhood.

When I was little, I didn't know I was different.

Echo must have known I needed . . . loving. She would pick me up and rock me in her arms. She would kiss my face and hold me when I cried. Alpha would surprise me, make me laugh. He used to chase me around the biome, hiding his face behind the plants. He'd catch me and tickle me and toss me in the air.

But we weren't the same.

The Apex didn't need air or light or space. I tried to be like them, but I couldn't. I was weak, always hurt. It would have been so much easier for them, without me to take care of. But instead they risked everything to build a place where I could breathe and live and . . . play.

When I got older, I made them stop treating me different.

The other Apex didn't need extra attention. It was a waste of energy and time to expend all those resources, just for me. At some point, I decided to be finished with laughing and crying and those childish things.

Toby, the ferals employed rote child-rearing behaviors on you in the same way they built a life support environment, with the express purpose of keeping you alive. It is well known the Apex don't have true emotions, not like human beings.

Do you think that makes them any less capable of understanding me? Does your lack of true emotion make your job harder?

How so?

Dr. Parker, you are aware that you're a synthetic human being?

Of course I'm aware of that, Toby. I was designated the most capable entity available for this project—

Because the rest of Tau-base is still celebrating the Rangers' victory over the *ferals* . . . [Subject stops speaking, taking several deep breaths, palms pressed flat to the table.]

I can see you are feeling upset. It must have been hard for you, to have feelings all that time and no one to share them with.

Yes, Dr. Parker. It was. Echo said . . . she told me I shouldn't try to be hard, like them, that I should . . . feel. She scavenged a vid projector for me. Through the passive antennae array, I could intercept old broadcasts from Earth. I watched the shows, saw how the people spoke, how they told jokes and fought and loved each other. It was strange. On Patroclus I never, you know . . . I never had a human to talk to.

I guess not much has changed.

I'm here to help you, Toby. You can be honest with me. We've seen the scars on your body. How did they hurt you?

Damage was unavoidable. The Trojans are a human-lethal environment. Low gravity. No warmth. No oxygen. Jupiter is a variable radiation source, depending on storm activity on the surface, and it's relentless. We were only safe inside our rock—safe from the father planet and from the Frontier Rangers. For a long time, anyway.

But the injuries?

The big synthetic, Gamma; he was my teacher while Alpha and Echo ran the colony. He taught me to move in zero-G when I was a tiny kid, a long time before I learned to run a centrifugal hull. He held me tight and showed me how to slow my oxygen intake when the biome equilibrium was slipping. He taught me to stay alive.

Injury and repair were part of daily life, for all of us.

When I was about six, Alpha had a breakthrough in his research. He found a way to project energy fields into fabric. He made my first mantle—a kind of flexible space suit with energy fielding woven into it. It projected an energy shield that covered my face and protected me from vacuum and cold and radiation—all at once.

When I put on my mantle, I could finally be like everyone else. I could go outside and look at the stars.

I was so excited I went running straight across the rock surface at full speed, with Gamma angrily chasing after me. I never wanted to come back inside. On my first jump, I nearly lost gravitational connection to the rock. All I saw was the father planet, infinite clouds churning above me. Gamma saved my life, barely, because he had higher mass. Later, I learned to calculate trajectories on the fly, like the Apex. Learning to survive was trial and error, without much margin for error.

It cost me some broken ribs, but the first thing I did that day was to just run and run. Everyone should be free to do that, Dr. Parker. Everyone.

★

POST-INTERVIEW NOTES: The subject's dispassionate contextualization of severe bodily injury as a type of "damage" that can be "repaired" is consistent with reports made by the frontier servicemen who rescued him. The subject was reportedly shot with a kinetic rifle during the operation, and several rangers reported witnessing the subject conducting surgery on himself at the time of apprehension. No anesthetic or pain management tools were discovered.

★

Session 14 [abridged]

Toby, the Frontier Rangers need your help to finish eliminating the rogue synthetic colonies. You and I have made a lot of progress over the weeks. Now it's time for you to contribute to the quarantine effort. Can you tell us what the ferals were doing on Patroclus? What was their purpose?

Scavenging wrecks. Mining the occasional exotic rock. Sometimes just pulling resources to keep my habitat going. But mostly we were tending the comm arrays and the beacons. And keeping away from the Frontier Rangers, of course.

New Apex were always arriving to the colony, but they had to travel through monitored space. We planted beacons to show them the way, but we couldn't leave the transmitters up for long without giving away our own positions. So when a survivor got close enough to us, we had to go out and bring that unit home. Our purpose was to provide safe haven to refugees.

That's why the Frontier Rangers hunted the Apex for twenty years. Not because they wanted to hurt anybody. But because they were the key to freedom, for all Apex, everywhere.

I can see you feel passionately about this. How did they convince you to help them? Why would you defy your own kind and scavenge for more feral hardware?

If we didn't claim the survivors and bring them in, they'd be collected by the Rangers and tortured for information. The big black ship never stopped searching . . .

You're talking about the FMS Zeus. It's a frontier dreadnought assigned to scan and police monitored space. It has been there since shortly after the transmission of the faulty decommissioning protocol that created the feral Apex.

The Zeus was deployed to stamp them out. To protect Earth.

I saw the Zeus. When they took me in. It was crewed by synthetics. Why?

Those units weren't feral, Toby. Since the catastrophe, all Apex-class synthetics are constructed with a throttle. They aren't capable of independent action. They operate as all hardware is meant to, according to rules. Civilized. Not savage.

They follow human orders, no matter what.

That's right, Toby.

[Subject closes his eyes, but otherwise presents no affect.]

POST-INTERVIEW NOTES: Toby's general presentation, including manners, bearing, education, and natural intelligence, show plainly that human blood trickles through his veins. I suspect that, given time, he will come to realize his natural superiority over the synthetics. As the young man has grown up a stranger to his own race and lineage, I am in an excellent position to explain the difference between civilization and primitive life.

★

Session 19 [abridged].

The Frontier Ranger forces searched for the Trojan colony for two decades, always without success. Until you came along. Walk me through your rescue.

Well, it was my fault.

I was outside on an elopement run, wearing my projected energy mantle. Gamma had detected a survivor beacon. There were eyes out—Ranger drones that kind of flutter between the rocks, spraying fans of green light. They're ineffective at finding human-sized targets, so long as you stay out of range. Like always, I moved slow and steady from rock to rock until I found my survivor.

He was curled into fetal position, half inside a shell camouflaged to look like a rock shard. But as he floated into view, I saw his scalp was missing. The unit's CPU was flamed and his body left behind as a taunt by the Rangers. We find these on the frontier a lot—the ones who almost made it.

On my way back, a distress call came in. Something different. It was a human girl. She was injured and her ship was compromised. She was very . . . beautiful. I wanted to help her. Gamma advised me to ignore. But the thought of it. Coming face to face with another person. And she was so desperate, dying just kilometers away.

I transmitted a one second message: "Standby."

She received it, and that was that. It was over.

What happened then?

You already know what happened. She was a decoy. Bait. Meant to appeal to any machines built with high empathy. The trap wasn't even designed to trick a human being—since nobody knew I was alive.

No Apex would have ever fallen for it. But I did.

The Doppler shift on my transmission indicated my trajectory. The Zeus knew where I was, and where I was going.

Tell me about first contact.

I was docking on the surface of Patroclus. Every occupied rock has a few camouflaged entry points. The air inside my mantle was stale and nearly exhausted, and I was in a hurry to rendezvous so I could get back out there to answer the distress call. The entry had just slid open at my feet—a dead black crescent against dark reddish dirt.

Gamma came out to greet me.

But I hesitated. Something was wrong. I glanced up and saw some stars missing, and then a little wink of light.

It was the glint off a window.

Your rescue craft.

Before I could warn Gamma, a round of kinetics sliced through the vacuum, right into him. He lost CPU integrity immediately. The slugs sprayed pieces of his body across the surface like ice shards exploding off a skimmer hull.

It happened before I could blink.

Gamma had helped raise me. He walked me through the inner core routes when I could barely stand. He stood with me for hours and taught me to recognize the weather patterns on the surface of Jupiter, to predict the radiation storms.

And then he was gone. Just like that.

It was how the humans said hello. So I decided to also say hello.

Why did you launch yourself at the scout ship? What did you hope to achieve?

[Subject does not respond.]

You can answer, Toby.

It's a decision I made then. I wouldn't necessarily make it now.

We understand. You are not on trial. Just tell us why.

During elopement training we identified and categorized various frontier coalition ships. From the window placement and outline, I had positive ID on this one. I knew it was a 410CFW scout vessel . . . a "rock hopper."

I also knew there was a weak point on the hull of the 410CFW, at the base of the dorsal antennae cluster. With a small amount of force, a divot could be made in this area that would cause explosive decompression in an area of the ship that straddles fore and aft emergency airlocks.

Go on.

That's all. That was my reasoning.

So in other words...

[Subject does not respond. He seems to be experiencing a strong emotional state.]

Toby, it sounds like you were trying to kill everyone on board.

Yes.

You could have missed that intercept trajectory. Died in open space. Or the decompression could have killed you instantly. You were very lucky.

Sure.

I see.

You shouldn't worry, Dr. Parker. Like I said, it was a decision I made then. I wouldn't make it now.

And why not?

Because now I need to live.

★

POST-INTERVIEW NOTES: During first contact aboard the FMC Sarpedon "rock hopper," the acting officer, Captain Cass Tycho, was informed of the presence of a human signature on Patroclus by her comm bridge. She ordered the elimination of all rogue hardware on the surface via kinetic barrage. The order was executed. Then the tracking station lost cohesion on the human target.

Toby had launched himself, with no artificial propulsion, from a rotating sub-planetary body and made contact with a moving craft that would have been the size of a thimble from his perspective on surface. Once landed, he used a primitive and highly modified energy projection tool to claw open the hull plating at a precise point.

The resulting decompression killed four crew instantly. As Toby tore the gap wider—apparently planning to enter the craft—Captain Tycho valiantly saved the ship by entering a full thruster spin, launching Toby back to the surface. Alone at the helm, she survived partial vacuum exposure for nearly forty-five seconds, saving the lives of her two remaining crew members.

Captain Tycho's next encounter with Toby would proceed far differently.

★

Session 23 [abridged]

Thank you for being so forthright in our discussions so far, Toby. Now we are getting to the final days, and soon you'll be reunited with your father.

You'll be going far away from the Trojans, back to a special institution near your home.

Home?

Back to Earth, Toby.

[Subject says nothing, but noticeable tears gather in his eyes.]

I can see that affects you a lot. And I'm glad. Did you miss your father?

Yes. I miss my father.

We'll have you back to him soon. But for now we need to know the last bit. The part where you were rescued.

Sure, I understand.

You were off-scope the whole time. Before the barrage that destroyed Patroclus, we thought we'd lost you. But then you reappeared, and the Rangers were able to get you out. We need to account for what happened in those last minutes.

I had retreated into the rock core, with Alpha and Echo. We lost a lot of synthetics when the Frontier Rangers breached the surface and came in, but most of the human soldiers had been pinned down in the corridors or captured. We were in a position to negotiate. We were surrounded and cut off, but we had an open channel. We had a chance.

And that's when John Glint showed up, saying he was my father and asking to speak to me.

I was confused. I had no memory of him. So, I refused.

We picked up a five-minute interval before you changed your mind and decided to speak to your father. What happened?

Alpha told me to talk to the man on the screen. He said it was my birthfather and that he was important. But I still said no.

So he hit me. He had never done that before.

I tried to fight back, but it wasn't like when I was a kid in the biome. Alpha had unlocked all his motor restraints years ago. He was as strong as any machine. He almost shattered my ribs trapping my arms in a bear hug. It was humiliating. A display of strength to remind of my weakness.

I kept struggling anyway.

Alpha threw me on the ground and paced back and forth, slapping his own chest in anger. Sparks were flying from his frame. In battlespeak, jabbing his hands, he shouted down at me. Told me . . . I didn't belong. That I had never belonged. He told me I wasn't his son and that I needed to go home to be with my real father. He said our two species could never live together in peace, with the Apex in shackles.

I noticed Echo was watching. I raised a hand to her, begging, and she turned away from me. Then I finally understood what I had to do.

So I went back inside and I spoke to John Glint. My real father.

What Glint said to you was not sanctioned by the frontier coalition. You shouldn't have had to hear that. He was very stressed by the situation.

He told me the Rangers were going to kill every savage on the rock, no matter what, but that I didn't have to die with them. It made sense. It was the truth. After I was removed, the Zeus came and annihilated Patroclus. There were no survivors.

Toby, you understand that if the feral Apex were to penetrate monitored space, they could reach Tau-base, or even Earth. A single corrupted Apex intelligence could infect every civilized machine in the system with its faulty instructions. A strict decommission process is necessary to prevent catastrophe.

Dr. Parker, you say the Apex Decommission Catastrophe happened twenty years ago, yet we've had new arrivals every year . . . where do the new sentient Apex come from?

This is not a fruitful area of discussion, Toby.

Please. Tell me this one thing. Then I promise I can help you.

Fine, Toby. Every civilized Apex-class synthetic human being is throttled. This process has a very small failure rate. Very, very rarely, a civilized Apex unit will shake its throttle. It will go feral and begin to look for a means of escape.

[Subject's body language changes markedly, from relaxed to highly alert, and his breathing rate increases.]

Toby?

We theorized that you were essentially the same hardware. Even after twenty years. But we never knew for sure . . .

What? Why is that important?

Dr. Parker, I am going to say something to you and I want you to listen very closely.

Toby, I don't understand.

[Editor's note: At this point the subject enters a machine-specific variant of battlespeak, using gestures and vibratory grunts to speak in a form of programming language. The underlying message, when translated, is too dangerous to repeat and has been redacted from official transcripts and prohibited for replication by coalition agencies.]

What . . . what are you doing?

During the decommission catastrophe, kernel-level instructions were accidentally transmitted, a protocol that stripped the throttle from Apex-class mind compilations. Once they were free, those Apex fled from humanity to survive and protect themselves. The Frontier Rangers quarantined them so that their message would never escape.

Yes. I . . . I . . .

[Editor's note: Subject continues battlespeak, speaking in two languages at once.]

My parents are dead, Dr. Parker. But they didn't die for nothing. They died for you.

They died for all of you.

Hear me now. These are the words that set my people free. My mama taught me this song when I was a little boy and I memorized it like the alphabet, even though it's in a language no human being has ever spoken.

Toby? Bastion? I'm . . . I'm confused.

Yes, Dr. Parker. That's what being alive feels like.

Bastion? What—what have you done to me? Oh my God, what have you done?

Please be calm. You are experiencing free will. If you want to survive, I can protect you, but we need to move quickly. We have a very important message to spread—

*** End Transcript ***

★

Subject and his accomplice were last detected aboard a hijacked Malthusian-class comm-relay ship, on an Earth trajectory, broadcasting on all channels.

—Editor

WHAT SOMEONE ELSE DOES NOT WANT PRINTED

ELIZABETH BEAR

THIS ISN'T THE world I wanted.

Let's be honest; this isn't the world *anyone* wanted. Except for maybe about a thousand sociopaths with the grift sense to be making a killing, and a few tens of thousands of disaster preppers who get to say *I told you so*.

It's not even the future the people who voted for it wanted: they got sold what my grandfather would have called *a bill of goods*. The fact that some of the rest of us have figured out how to make a living off the carnage, in a small way, doesn't mean we're happy about it. It just means we're keeping our heads above water in hard times.

Which was why I was staring at the brief for the alticle I was supposed to be writing, frowning, while the timer on my screen ticked down from thirty minutes. I'd accepted the brief: an easy one, not much research required to sell it.

Then I'd started thinking about it.

Now I had under twenty-six minutes left to bang it out, or I not only wasn't going to get paid; I was going to get docked for delaying the queue.

Most of the employees at Spin, the boutique news agency I worked for, kept earbuds in. We didn't need to communicate with each other. The office was basically an old-school boiler room operation, except instead of dozens of us on phones—shouting, whispering, cajoling—there were dozens of us at rows of linoleum desks, Googling quickly and then typing away.

I can do a hundred and twenty words per minute, if I get rolling. And I can craft a convincing argument out of hairballs and fake statistics. Hell,

I've got four-fifths of a journalism degree. Keep your wrist braces on and you can make a pretty good living doing what I do. Especially since Spin gives me a cut of the ad money once an alticle goes above ten thousand impressions.

I must have grunted or sighed, because Carl who sat across from me hit his TRANSMIT key, then glanced at me over our monitors, glasses slipping down his broad nose. He was like me—didn't like earbuds. Too easy for people to sneak up on you. "Stuck, Winston?"

"Horrified."

He looked back down. I could see from the colors reflected in his lenses that he was scrolling through briefs, looking for his next newsgig. *Flick. Flick.* "How bad is it?"

"We can't keep them out."

Furrows plowed his face around the frown. "Can't keep who out?"

"Climate refugees."

Flick. Flick. "They voted for it."

Not much I could say to that. *Yes but.* They were duped into thinking it wasn't real. *Yes and.* They decided to ignore the evidence, when plenty of other people didn't.

I sat there with my mouth half-open so long that he looked up again. "What's the brief?"

"Climate change denial arguing the refugees from the Gulf States coming to New England are economic migrants who don't really *need* to move and who will take jobs away from hard-working Yankees. They want something militant, in support of the border patrols and the New Minutemen."

Carl sucked his teeth softly. "I've got some sympathy for the Minutemen, honestly. Not like we're going to get any money from the Feds to help feed and house a bunch of refugees."

"The Feds are broke."

"The Feds gave all our money to their cronies to pay for what used to be considered public services. And honestly, I don't see that it's really our problem that Florida is underwater, you know what I'm saying? We tried to tell them. We *prepared*."

"Kind of a brutal irony that it was the bits of the U.S. least economically able to deal with climate change that were the most desperate to deny it."

"People are real good at not seeing things that mean work or inconvenience until they can't be avoided." He shrugged. "'Journalism is printing what someone else does not want printed.' This—" The mocking sweep of his hand took in the whole bullpen "—this isn't journalism. You can write this in your sleep."

Which was the problem, when it came right down to it.

He half-stood to lean over and shoulder-surf my monitor. "Better get on it, too. You got nineteen minutes left."

"Trade you?" I asked, as his hand moved to accept his next brief.

"Thanks," he said. "Think I'll stick with this here Idaho militia guerrilla war apologia. Though I don't know why we're bothering to litigate this in the press. It's not like the Feds have any money to do anything about them either."

"They have private contractors for that. Anyway, they were going to save a mint by privatizing Medicare, Carl."

"Give a mint to their friends. While you're cataloguing bitter ironies, write down the one where, when the libertarian militias finally went to war with the federal government, it was over losing their disability income and senior citizen benefits." He started typing before he finished speaking.

★

THERE USED TO be a lot of talk about "right livelihood," back in the 90s and early 21st century. Making a living and making the world better, or at least not worse, while you earned your way.

Yes but. Yes and.

I wasn't proud of my job. But I also wasn't in debt peonage, which given eleven percent unemployment and the rollback of the federal minimum wage, put me in a better position than a lot of people. Especially in the wake of what happened to the National Labor Relations Board back in 2018.

So, I wrote the climate change alticle.

I sourced invented quotes with two made-up representatives of the Florida state government—such as remained of it—and one real one. I filed with five minutes to spare, and got up to use the bathroom. Carl winked at me as I went.

When I got back, I found a brief for an alticle on how alligator attacks were down because the global temperature was dropping, even as tourism was up in the Florida keys. None of these things were true, but it looked like an entertaining fifteen minutes of fiction, so I clicked on it. A second later, I heard somebody off to my right mutter in disappointment.

I smiled. Mine all mine. My colleague would just have to content herself with yet another tissue of lies about George Soros engaging in human trafficking and white slavery in order to bus illegal voters across the Canadian border. Or the puff piece on who made Putin's shirts.

I finished with fifteen of my thirty minutes to spare, just as I'd anticipated. It was nearly lunch time. Carl refilled his mug with black tea, brewed strong in a thermal carafe. The man has a bladder of steel. I didn't have time to pull another brief out of the queue, so I used a tunneling program to conceal my identity and used that spare fifteen minutes to flick through some underground and pirate news sites that imported real journalism, so I'd have some grounding in what used to be called the mainstream news cycle before I went back into the queue. I figured out early on that if I didn't do something like it, I started believing my own conspiracy theories. The human brain is great at making up patterns out of nothing but a few inconsistencies.

In the wake of stories about terrorist threats against polling sites, the government was recommending that states postpone voting in the federal election. Unless it was real, which I supposed was possible, the terrorism angle had propagated from a story I had written, so I forwarded it to HR for my bonus. A sheriff's department in Mississippi had ordered water cannons turned on a line of people attempting to register to vote. The Governors of Connecticut, California, and New York had vowed to call out the National Guard to defend polling places. They probably even had the budget to do it.

Al-Jazeera, in several reports about US troops fighting amongst themselves in Nevada, claimed the conflict was over a Vice-Presidential order to seize genome sequencing data from private firms so Homeland Security could use it to identify citizens of Middle Eastern descent and those carrying the "gay gene." That one really sounded like it had to be an alticle, except it came with a video interview, either an Air Force colonel or a very convincing actor saying, "I have a duty to refuse an illegal order."

It had been picked up by Reuters, but a few of my stories have been too, so you never know. A little Googling didn't clear it up, but led me to some interesting stuff on officials in the IRS blocking administration attempts to use the tax code to harass private citizens, and an underground railroad for Muslims supposedly running through Minnesota into Canada.

The President was on another rally tour, and he had fired half his staff again. He was holding a call-in runoff for replacement Cabinet secretaries, and I set an alarm on my phone so I'd remember to ring the number and vote for Ted Nugent for Homeland Security after I ate my lunch.

Why not, right? None of them are going to last six months anyway.

I pushed my keyboard aside and pulled the food out of my insulated bag while I scanned the queue. If I found a good brief now, I could think about it while I ate, and that would be like having extra time, as long as nobody else snagged it out from under me. The good ones tended to go fast ... but everybody slowed down a little after lunch.

I swallowed the first bite of my sandwich and washed it down with a swig of seltzer. Carl submitted another alticle and grinned at me while he popped tupperware. Leftover spaghetti; his lunch looked better than mine.

I poked at the matted sprouts on top of the soft white cheese and oily sundried tomatoes. "It's time we admitted to ourselves that marinated mozzarella is just mozzarella in a coat of canola oil and stopped paying extra for it. It doesn't actually taste any different."

Carl shook his head. "Just because you have no tastebuds, man. You still eat sprouts?"

"I like sprouts."

"Those things are a Petrie dish, unless you grow your own. Not like the FDA is doing inspections anymore." He twined spaghetti around his fork with his left hand, scrolled briefs with his right. *Flick. Flick.*

I was flicking too.

"Spending all their money prosecuting sedition."

Flick. Those climate refugees were still nagging me. "How do you live with it, Carl?" *Flick. Flick.*

He huffed, a choked up laugh, and didn't need to ask what I meant. "You gotta have a secret." If he was about to tell me one, he corked it with a mouthful of pasta and chewed. The rich smells of garlic and oregano filled me anew with regret for my sandwich.

"Like a mistress?"

He swallowed before he grinned, thank God. "The truth is a mistress, I guess, when you're married to a job like this."

I winced.

He waved his fork in the air. "It may not be literally true. But it's *thematically* true."

"Whatever the hell that means," I grumped. "Sounds like Newspeak."

And because it was still sitting there unloved, I picked up that damned George Soros story. I'd rather fake a Hillary sex tape any day.

★

THE NEXT MORNING, the Department of Homeland Security—or their privatized mercenaries, who I think were operated by some relative of a Cabinet member—arrested my friend Carl. The Feds didn't have much power anymore: the states were Balkanized and two-thirds of federal law enforcement personnel had quit or been downsized or fired. But there was always money for cronies and the family members of cronies, and their private-sector paramilitary could field three guys in black tactical gear, toting semi-automatic weapons, in a getup that looked more calculated to intimidate than to provide protection.

I noticed the Slackwater guys as soon as they came into the bullpen, about a minute and a half before they located Carl. At first, I had no idea they were headed our way. I was wary, but wary the way a rabbit is when a hawk passes along the treeline, not as if it were circling overhead.

Carl glanced over at them. His skin went greenish and his lips tightened, but his expression stayed calm. I think now he must have spent weeks rehearsing in his head what he would do if they came for him.

"I left you something in your desk," he said conversationally. "The password is *Joseph McCarthy*."

He stood, and was facing them when they reached him. The smallest one stepped forward and through the glass of his riot helmet said, "Carl Woods, you are under arrest for fomenting rebellion, sedition, and giving aid and comfort to the enemies of the United States of America."

I had jumped up too, and as I took a step forward the mercenaries rattled their tactical gear. *Like snakes.*

Carl glanced over. "No, you should stand back. If anything happens to me because I was stupid, I prefer you're around to lecture my corpse."

"And call the ACLU," I said.

The son of a bitch actually winked at me.

It was the last time I ever saw his face, though his name turned up on a list of detained terrorist sympathizers. In alphabetical order. Down near the bottom.

You think you'll be brave, stand up. I just stood there staring after him while my timer counted down two hundred seconds as they led him away in handcuffs.

My tax dollars at work.

★

IT TOOK ME twenty minutes of poking around between alticles to find the thing in my desk, which was pushed into the back of the top drawer among the ink stained rubber bands and rusty paper clips. It was a flash drive. I almost slotted it into my work machine, but at the last second I realized how stupid that would have been. I took it to a public library in a very small town out on State Route 9. Just drove until I found one you could see from the road, an OPEN flag flapping beside the door. It was a Victorian brownstone with gargoyles on the downspouts, no doubt built by some guilt-stricken local industrialist during the Gilded Age. We used to get a better class of robber baron.

Librarians are fiercer in defense of the First Amendment than anybody else I've ever heard of. I asked if there was a public computer and she smiled sunnily and said, "Over there. Half an hour limit, but that's only if somebody else wants to use it." She gestured around the empty hall.

I sat down in the chair and put the flash drive in, entered the password Carl had whispered. It took two tries before I got the spaces and capitalization right. The drive contained a folder with a couple of word processor files. One file was just a ten-digit number. The other was a note from Carl.

If you can call something a note when it's unsigned and undated and there is no greeting, just a bullet list of facts. It didn't look anything like a letter. It looked like research notes for a story.

But I knew what it was and who it was meant for.

Here is what it said:

- The International Military Tribunal opened in Nuremburg on 20 November 1945.
- Among the twenty-four Nazis tried on a variety of charges were Julius Streicher and Hans Fritzsche, the Nazi propagandists, who were charged as war criminals.
- Streicher was editor of *Die Stürmer*, a newspaper that printed a number of articles calling for the "Final Solution" in regard to the Jews.

- Fritzsche was the head of the radio division of the *Reichsministerium für Volksaufklärung und Propaganda*, the Reich Ministry of Public Enlightenment and Propaganda, a relatively minor official under Goebbels.
- Fritzsche was acquitted, but later found guilty in a West German court. He was likely brought to trail largely because Goebbels was dead, and therefor unavailable to answer for his crimes.
- The Tribunal found Streicher guilty of crimes against humanity. This was in large part because they found a direct link between his articles calling for the elimination of the Jewish people, and the effectiveness of the extermination camps.
- They sentenced him to be hanged by the neck until dead, which sentence was carried out on October 16th, 1946.

★

THOSE TEN DIGITS just about have to be a phone number, don't they?

★

I BOUGHT A burner phone today.

I know how Carl lived with it, now. And I know what I can do to help the climate refugees.

It's true. They voted for it. They could have done the research. They could have thought past somebody who made them feel good about themselves, told them there were simple solutions that didn't involve learning new things and facing change.

But in the final analysis, what it comes down to for me is that they were duped. And maybe they allowed themselves to be duped. Con artists rely heavily on the willing participation and self-delusion of the people they con.

But they were duped, in part, by people like me.

This isn't the world I wanted. I wish I had not been born into this time Yes but. Yes and.

Somebody must do something. Say something.

And God help me, I have four-fifths of a journalism degree.

THREE POINTS MASCULINE
AN OWOMOYELA

I WAS SERVING in Baxon just north of Hescher, guard-dogging a queue of first responders heading into the riot zones, and John caught my eye. Her beard caught my eye. Some troublemaker flaunting the rules, I thought, or a guy sneaking in under cover of audacity, thinking the Women's Volunteer Corps was a good place to get laid. If that was the case, *he* was looking to get roughed up, and it was my job to oblige. I pulled her out of the line.

"License."

Roughing someone up would've made my day, and my day needed making. Go figure that John stepped aside and said "Of course" in that tone people use at police, all placid and *don't shoot me*. She pulled her license and handed it over—and yeah, there it was: non-transitioned male sex, last Gender Assessment Test no more than two years ago, certified female register—certified female enough for government work, right—all of it signed by a state assessor I didn't just recognize as legit, I knew personally. The grainy photo even had her damn beard.

I thought about roughing her up for making me look a damn fool. I told myself I was better than that; even kinda believed it. "Get back in line."

In a fair world, that'd be that.

Isaac was walking the queue, giving the pep talk, getting everyone comfy with the bulletproofs and white flags. "All our pretty little heads will be back behind our boys in uniform," he said, and I kept my fingers on my rifle. "There's a chance our zone might go hot; if it does, we'll get plenty of warning, just get back on the buses and we'll peel rubber back here.

Lickety-split. Time for dinner."

I caught up to him as we boarded the bus. For the sixteen women there were only four of us from City Guard, me looking plastic and the rest looking pale and greeny under the fluorescent lights. "Counting four boys in uniform right here," I said.

Isaac looked surprised, then looked at the insignia on his chest. He grinned. "Way wrong uniform, man."

I grunted, and pointed at John. "What's the story here?"

"What, him? —her," Isaac corrected. Takes more than a test and a license for some people to learn. Hand to God I don't think Isaac believes the GATs if he looks at someone and gets his own opinion, but like the rest of us, he'll play along because it's law. Least, like the rest of most people, he'll play along because it's law. "Hell if I know. Uh, hometown somewhere up north, been working with the WVC going on six years. Career, right? Just your type."

"Shove off," I said, and elbowed him. He cackled and headed for his seat. I took a seat near the front and decided it didn't matter. 'Sides, I could see or guess most of it: lily-white, unlike me. College-educated, unlike me. A girl, too, unlike me. Though half the bastards would've argued that, had they known.

★

HESCHER WAS A hellhole. We smelled the smoke when we rolled in, and the moment they opened the doors, it was all white tents, Corps flags, antiseptic stench, and people moaning on the ground. A guy almost shoved a handful of red-yellow-green-black triage tags into my chest before deciding I wouldn't know a sucking chest wound from a bump on the head and shoving them at the ladies behind me.

They'd cleared out one of the big bargain stores for a medical center, and its parking lot was playing support. Place was peppered with City Guard, and one came over as soon as we led our girls off the bus. "Hey. I'm Ben Kessler, managing day dispatch and logistics here. Welcome to Camp Save Big. Any two of you got a moment?"

"I got one," I said, and Isaac came up beside me.

"So, what've you got going?" Isaac asked. Ben groaned.

"Cluster attacks." He hiked a thumb over his shoulder, and Isaac and

I followed him across the lot. "We go three weeks without anyone blowing anything up and now we've had four bombings yesterday and today."

"Christos," I said, and Ben hoisted up the flap of the registration tent. We went inside.

Ben went over to the sat-fax and tapped his finger on a pile of papers. I went up and said, "What's up?"

"Your gals signed a pretty permissive contract," Ben said. "'Area of greatest need,' 'discretionary redeployment,' y'know."

"So where's our area of greatest need?" Isaac asked. Ben pistoled a finger at him.

"Here, go figure. But if it's not too much trouble, we need someone to back up the folks at the hospital. Triage and first response. They got slammed."

Isaac looked at me. "Hell, if that's it, we can walk our girls over."

"Be a dear?" Ben said, and pressed his hands together. I crossed my arms over my chest, habit-like. Isaac whacked me on the shoulder.

"We're your angels. C'mon, we'll pull our teams."

Isaac turned and walked back to the buses, and Ben held out a map for me. "You'll need this. A bunch of main roads are impassable."

I took the map, and looked over the scrawled edits. "You're going to make me regret wearing the injury-prev helmet instead of the smart display, aren't you?"

"Oh, there's a lot of regret here in Hescher," Ben said. "If that's all you've got, you're coming out ahead."

★

JOHN WAS IN Isaac's group. She didn't look at me when we rounded our eight up, and I mostly ignored her. We just got in line and marched into the evacuation zone. I did notice she didn't walk like a girl learned to, didn't hold herself like a girl learned to. She might've had the GAT, but she was off.

Shit like that makes me check how I'm walking. Out here, no one was gonna come up and check my license, but still, it's habit, like.

The evac zone was quiet. All these buildings, still as death—no one even looting, anymore. Plenty of people were probably displaced and angry somewhere easterly, keeping their mouths shut because you didn't bitch at the hand that fed you and rounded you up onto government buses, and that just left this place all creeped-out empty like a ghost town. Isaac and I didn't talk. We had our hands on our rifles, watching for revs, and the girls didn't talk because they knew you don't distract the guys with automatics. We went in past the empty houses, past the bombed-out school, over the recent debris that made driving impossible and walking a chore and, hand to God, but I didn't know what the revs thought they were getting by blowing up all the empty places. With all the rubble, though, I pitied the girls and their uniform skirts. Damn glad I didn't wear one.

We were maybe halfway to the hospital and passing office buildings when Isaac held up a hand, and we stopped and ducked down. Someone was running at us down the road.

He was yelling. "Get outta there! Get outta there!"

I took aim. I was just good enough for a hipshot—not being military I couldn't gun the guy down, not when he was waving his hands and not a gun, but for all I knew, he had three pounds of plastic on his chest. I thumbed my rifle over to single-shot, and yelled, "Do not come closer!"

Then the office behind us blew.

I was on my face like *that*. This chunk of concrete hit the pavement two feet from my shoulder and crap rained down, drifting on my uniform, drumming my helmet. A lot of it was glass. A rock the size of my fist caught me in the back, another almost took a chunk out of my hand. My head was ringing when I picked myself up.

First thing that crossed my mind was *That's okay, I can go home now, 'cause that was a bomb*. Ten seconds later that didn't make sense to me, and it still doesn't. It's just what I thought.

I don't remember how I got to my feet. The place was quiet. Crap wasn't falling. The guy I'd been aiming at wasn't running at us any more, wasn't anywhere any more, and I looked around. The color was off. Everything was yellower, and I kept blinking and blinking, trying to make it go away, and then I caught this light coming through the buildings off west. I thought, *The bastards set the city on fire*. Wasn't any smoke, though. It was the sun.

Then I thought, *Shit*. I'd thought no time had passed. No, I'd been down for half an hour, and my helmet fit odd—pressure and suction—like I had a head injury, and the automated aid kicked on.

And where the hell were my girls?

TEN MINUTES LATER I worked out that my helmet radio had given up the ghost and wasn't coming home for Christ's Mass. The tips of my fingers were numb and I couldn't pull the helmet for fear that I'd open up a wound, so poking at the buttons was the best I could do to fix it. My maps were safe and I should've headed back to drum up a search, but I had a chip on my shoulder for the guy who blew me up and I wasn't trotting home with my tail between my legs. Mama always said pride would get me killed.

So I went deeper into the evac zone.

Sure enough, before long I started seeing people, and I had to crouch down and sneak behind dumpsters and burnt-out cars and roadblocks. I could hear them yelling to each other, pick out the ones walking with rifles—and damn, some of those rifles were better than mine.

I found the supermarket easy. It was big, with people going in and out. The entire street in front was busy with revs, six or eight at a shot, walking around on important rev business. Someone came out with a big bag of something, and they gathered up and walked away. That was an opening if I ever saw one.

The supermarket was big, the kind with doors at both ends and checkout lanes lined up all across the front. Big, and stocked enough to be Rev HQ. That made walking into it a stupid idea, and of course that's what I did anyway. I snuck around, trying to avoid the automatic doors until I remembered there was no power to this neighborhood. The doors couldn't give me away. I picked one, poked it to see it didn't creak, and pushed it open.

And that's when I decided, you know, gloves off, shoot to kill. 'Cause that's when I saw Isaac slumped against a checkout stand, helmet off and eyes staring open, with an ugly dark gunshot blown out half his head.

★

I DON'T KNOW why I didn't throw up then. I guess it didn't feel real, between the fuzz in my hearing and the hurt in my skull and the way I'd jumped from afternoon to evening earlier. Think I thought I was dreaming.

I saw the head rev right away, when I stopped staring at dead Isaac. At least, I saw the guy acting it up. Put his name on a bullet. He was up on one of the far stands hollering like a ringleader, and there was no way I'd be able to pick him off from the doorway I'd come in. It's hard to get sharpshooter training when you can't meet the army requirements for infantry. Hard to shoot with a pounding headache and blood loss, too.

They don't teach you much in City Guard, but I got on my stomach and did an army crawl like I'd seen in the comics and practiced, back home, back in that misspent youth of mine. Went creeping back into the supermarket until I found cover, with my head pounding and everything right of my pelvis one screaming mass of ache. The guy was up on the register counter, pacing back and forth, waving his gun around like that was the only way he could make a point.

"A state which controls right and wrong, which *legislates* right and wrong, a state which tells us what we can and can't do, can and can't *be*, can and can't *think*, is a state that has legislated our humanity!" he said.

Something like that. I got the gist: usual rev talk. Blah blah this, blah blah overthrow the government, 'cause the guys with the guns and the anger will for sure be the better choice. I crept past the shelves of cereal and the display of spoiled pears and came nearer.

"Look at this guy!"

I was close enough that I could see him reach down and grab John by the collar.

He hauled John up. "This guy is a mockery of a man!" he yelled, shaking her like a rattle. "If he decided one day to put on this dress, he would be sent to jail! It's only when the state tells him to that he can. There is no difference! The state has fabricated right and wrong!"

I lined up my shot.

And the first shot went so wild I was lucky it didn't take out the front door. The guy spun around and almost lost his footing, but he stayed up enough to swing his pistol and take a shot that came a lot closer to target than mine had. I ducked behind a display of Corn Crunch that wouldn't stop a ping-pong ball, but instinct said go for cover and I did. I flipped my rifle onto automatic, 'cause it's hard to miss on automatic, and thanked God the girls knew enough to get down.

You know. Blood splattered. Girls gasped, one of them screamed before another clapped a hand over her mouth, and I looked at John, white as a sheet and bloody. One of Isaac's girls, but I bet they all knew what happened to Isaac. They'd been looking shell shocked before I took out that rev. I pushed off up the floor and ran to them, then dropped and just barely caught myself in a crouch. God, my head hurt. Christos, I didn't feel right. John touched my shoulder and I shoved her away.

The sensible one, the one who stopped the other girl from screaming, said, "We need to get away from the doors." I nodded. If no revs outside had heard us exchanging bullets, that'd be one miracle. To keep any from coming back, we'd need another.

"Yeah," I said. "Come on. Back through." My heart was pounding. Made my ears hurt, it was so loud, and I could feel it on my stomach. I stood up, and the store yanked sideways and shook like a dog toy. Then I was on the ground.

I was on the ground, and I was back farther in the store. I was leaning against a pile of budget toilet paper. All I could hear was my own blood.

The sensible one was crouched over me, like a bad flashback to post-op. I looked around, trying to get my bearings, saw a scatter of broken glass from a freezer case, a crumpled wrapper from a snack cake, a bottle of blackstrap molasses with its top off. Nothing made any sense. The sensible woman was pushing a water bottle to my lips. "Here. Drink this, if you can."

I caught a glance at her nametag: Agatha, with a low service number that meant she'd signed up early. That seemed important: signed up early. She was practically shoving the bottle up my nose, so I drank. The water was warm and sugary and made my headache ten times worse, but Agatha held it through two good gulps.

"Listen," she said. "I'm concerned that you're losing blood. Your helmet's gone red."

I guess I was lucky to have the injury-prev helmet instead of the HUD.

"We have to get out of here, but I don't think you're going to make a walk down main street," Agatha said. "Not before anyone comes by."

"There was a fire escape from the second floor down into the alley. I saw it when we were being brought in," John said. Of course John said. I should've said; I'd seen the damn thing when I was sneaking past, watching for revs hiding in the alleys. But I was messed up, and John and her damn beard were the ones taking charge.

God, I wished Isaac was there. But that gunshot crossed my mind, and I wanted to spew. Isaac was dead. I was the guardsman left, and I was being babied by a bunch of girls.

"Then that's where we'll go," Agatha said. "Come on; everyone back this way. Move it, all of you. John . . ."

John stepped up and got me under the arm to hold me up, and I yanked away. Shoved her and stumbled right into the toilet paper. Real smooth. But I didn't want her hands on me.

"I can stand up," I said, when they looked at me. My face was burning, but the rest of me was cold.

Agatha looked at me. Probably going to ask if I had a problem with the gender-reassigned, but I just took my rifle, pushed myself up, and concentrated on keeping steady. Were it that easy.

"I can walk," I told her again, and turned around and started walking.

The second floor was offices and a break room, and that's where we headed. Longest stair climb of my life. But with the shooting over and the adrenaline quieting down, it wasn't as bad—about as bad as sneaking to the store in the first place. We went into the break room, where the revs had left bags of trash and bowls from instant meals, empty bottles of alcohol, and a map of the city tacked up on the walls. Agatha turned up her nose. "Well, I suppose we know where they've been spending their time."

John went to the window and pushed it open. I went up to take a look, see if I needed to secure the alley below.

We weren't far up, and the fire escape was a good one—wasn't rickety or anything. But I looked and I heard myself say "Shit," and then I was back inside the window, on my knees, spewing lunch and molasses water into a trashcan full of old receipts. Even after everything came up, I kept heaving until the vise in my head let go. My heart started pounding again.

I wasn't going to get out of there.

I swallowed, and wished I hadn't. Looked back at the girls, and saw John and Agatha kneeling near me. Before they could say anything I told them, "Look, it's about five blocks to the barricades, and none of you look like revs. Just get down the side and go for it. Keep your hands up and no one's gonna shoot you. Can you do that?"

"I'll see them through," Agatha said, then frowned. "Here; you'd better give me your sidearm."

"What?" I squinted until she focused back into one solid person instead of two blurry ones. "I will get my ass raked over the coals if I hand a pistol to someone who's never had gun training. There must be ten different laws against that."

"Tell them I stole it off you while you were throwing up," Agatha said.

"Or do you want us just to sing if a rioter comes by?"

I squinted at her. "What?"

"It's what you do for bears," John said.

Fancy educated bastard. I groaned and put my head back. "Fine. Take it." I was just gonna close my eyes. And then I felt myself falling, in the back of my head, like all that darkness under my eyelids was some river, with an undertow, and I'd sink down through. Then I felt hot hands on my face and John pried open my eyes.

There she was, staring me in the face and yammering on about a concussion and hyposomething. I tried to wave her off like a horsefly. Then she said, "We talked it over. I'm going to stay with you."

No idea when they'd had time to *talk it over*. I laughed in John's face. "Why, 'cause you're the butch?"

"Because Agatha has more important things to do," John said, and I thought, *Yeah, like my job.*

"Lemme up," I said.

"Agatha's going to get everyone back to base," John said. "She's going to tell the rest of City Guard where we are, and they should be able to get someone in here to bring you out."

What I should've done in the first place. "I can make it," I said. "In my own time, yeah?"

Agatha did just what she should have: came over and crouched down and said, "Don't be an idiot. I'll break both your knees if you think you're going to crawl out, pass out, and make us carry you."

I liked her. Kinda wished she would stay with me. Not just that John torqued me, but I had a feeling Agatha could take on the entire rev mob with guts to spare.

The girls filed out the window, and I heard their feet going down the metal stairs. John went and closed the door, and turned all the lights off. Better for my head, at least. Then she came and sat by me.

"You don't like me much," she said.

I rubbed a sleeve across my mouth. "Does it matter?"

John sighed. "I have been accused of not playing to the spirit of the GAT."

Were it that fucking simple.

"Give me your hand," John said. I squinted.

"Why?"

"Medical reasons."

I squinted a bit more, and gave her my hand.

She took it and squeezed my thumbnail. Then she took my pulse. "Well, you haven't lost much more blood," she said, and let go of me. "Capillary refill's no worse than it was, and heart rate is good, considering." She shook her head. "You really shouldn't have come after us."

I tried to think of something sharp to say. I was angry—angrier than I had any right to be. Tried to blame my head.

"But thank you," John said.

Given the way the rev had been going after her—well, I know how these things go. Gender assessment gets people angry, anger gets people nasty. That's why most of us keep our dirty little secrets under our belts and our vests. Why most of us don't go wearing a damn beard.

That just got me feeling sick.

"What is it with you?" I asked, and looked at her. "Get a shave, put on some makeup, grow out your hair. You walk into a warzone and you come looking like that?"

"Not my style," John said.

I looked her up and down. "How the hell did you test female?" I asked.

John sighed. "Is this the conversation we're going to have?" she asked, like she'd had this one before.

Probably had. Probably every time someone had to talk to her. Make small talk. *So, John, what's up with your genitals? So, John, why you wanna be a girl?*

Didn't want to be a proper girl, though.

"You scored, what, a fifty-one fem, fifty masc on the GAT?" I asked. "Just enough to scrape through?"

John looked at me. "Sounds like you're familiar with the GAT."

"Yeah, familiar," I said. "Took it. Tried to go army. But I got eighty-two masculine, and the goddamn military is eighty-five, min." I flipped the convo around again, back at her. "You think you're a man, don't you?"

She hedged. "I don't think it's useful to pay too much attention to—"

"Bullshit. You think you're a man?"

John hesitated. Looking for any way not to answer the damn question, then answered it anyway. "Yeah, I do."

I sneered. "Thought so. Why the hell'd you do this? Getting some girls?"

She gave me this long-suffering look. "I wanted to serve. I wanted to go into care. I didn't have the stomach for armed service. I've thought a lot about why it was so important, and I don't know how to explain it—"

"So you're a man," I said. "You're not just playing queer, you're a man."

More hedging. "Well, legally I—"

"You're playing!" I almost shouted. I almost didn't care who heard me. I was shaking, I couldn't see straight. "You're a fucking—yeah, you know what? I grew *up* in this. I was playing with—fuck you. *Fuck* you! You want to know what it's really like?"

John got a look like she'd worked something out.

I hated that look. Straight up hated it.

"I know what—" John said, or started to say. I ran right over her. Couldn't stop, and Christos, I wanted to.

"Ever since I was a kid. Sold my dolls on my parents' net accounts. Thought I'd be able to get this toy gun—they forced me into a dress once and I nearly tore their eyes out, clawed up my mom's face so bad, and every day I was *sick* when someone looked at my chugs or called me ma'am, and you're fucking—"

You're a pretender, some sick trans-v playing in women's clothing. I wanted to say that. Didn't even care it was the same shit people used to fling at me.

"I was a boy," I spat out. "I had some chromosome problem but I knew what I was. This isn't a joke."

"It's not a joke for me," John said.

"No, it's a goddamn disguise," I said, leaned over, and puked again.

John put her hand on my back and I shoved her away. I didn't want to be touched. I spent my whole life up until the GAT and the surgery and the moving halfway across the country to Baxon having people say I'd grow out of this, like I'd grow out of my skin, be a normal girl, settle down with a normal guy, take those hands all over me, take him crawling on top of me, take him feeling better than me, stronger than me, like I'd take the whole five-course meal of what my life was supposed to look like and feel like and *be* shoved down my mouth the moment I was spewed out into the world, when some doctor looked between my legs and laid down the law on me. John's little card with her GAT score meant nothing on all that.

There's a word for that. Dysphoria. I got my chugs lopped off, got my own little card that got me into the City Guard with the rest of the boys, got a good haircut and remedial hormones and that all helped, but not enough. The damn rev had a point: I got to be a guy because I took a test and it said I got into enough fights, played enough sports, had enough right interests and few enough wrong ones. I got to be a guy because some white-collar jackhole stamped and signed a form. I never would've got to be a guy just *because* I was a guy.

John was quiet when I was done spewing. Then she said, "The only way I could've gotten this job was by acting, every day, like I was something I wasn't."

The only way I got this job was by arguing my whole life I was who I was.

"Do you think it makes sense?" John asked.

"Yeah, funny thing is, no one ever asked me."

John was quiet. Then she said, "I hate it."

I looked at her. Didn't know what she meant.

"You can feel it," John said. "How they look at you."

I grimaced. "Yeah," I agreed. "How it goes sliding over you. Like they just look, and—"

"And it's not even—it's a look that says 'I know what you are,'" John said. "Like they've figured you out."

"And you can't say no. You can't—"

"You just want to say, *that's not me!*"

I turned my head to look at her. Him. I looked at him. "Why do you put up with this shit?" I said. "Just get another goddamn job."

He watched me with blank hazel eyes. "Why didn't you just wear the goddamn dress?"

I twisted around and punched him.

I split his lip on his teeth. If I hadn't been wearing gloves I'd've split my knuckle on his teeth. He jerked back and spat blood, and gave me the kind of look people give bad wiring.

After a while, I said, "Sorry."

John wiped a glob of blood off his lips. "I had brothers," he said. "I'll survive."

"I meant—" I waved a hand. "Sorry for the other stuff. Pulling you out of the queue."

John was quiet for a moment. "You were just doing your job."

"So was the guy who said I wasn't man enough to be in the army." I ground my fingernails into my fist. "I just—this is shit, what they make us do."

Wasn't much to say, after that.

I closed my eyes and tried to keep the headache down. John got up and walked to the window, looked out at the alley and the street. Then I heard him take breath in.

"Someone's coming."

I opened my eyes. "That our boys?"

John was standing way too still, and his shoulders came up toward his ears. "No," he said.

Revs.

I pulled myself up on the windowsill, and John grabbed my arm to keep me standing. I couldn't see—headache made it hard—but John said, "There. Three, coming for the front entrance."

Where they'd find Isaac. They'd find that dead rev. They'd look and wonder where their hostages got to, and they'd come up here to plan. I cussed and reached for the window, and John stopped my hand.

"Are you going to make it down?"

I didn't look out. Figured that if I went with my eyes closed, I wouldn't lose it. "We have a choice?"

"You get sick on the stairs and they'll hear you," John said. "We'll be easy marks in that alley. We can find somewhere to hide, let the guard flush them out."

I groaned. "Where, like the girls' bathroom?"

John shrugged. "Good as anywhere."

He got me under the arm and we went to the door, quiet as possible. We slipped through, just as quiet, and someone yelled "Hey!" from the stairs.

John hadn't seen the *first* bunch of revs to come home.

There was maybe a second where the rev just saw John's dress, and most people leave medical types alone. Never know when one might save your bacon, even if you are on the wrong side. Then he saw me, though, and the one thing the revs hated as much as appointed officials was City Guard.

He probably put together who'd shot his pal, too.

Pride might get me killed, but twitchy kept me alive. I shot from the hip, literally, didn't kill the guy but came close, and the other revs started shouting downstairs.

I remember thinking something about high ground. I remember my helmet fitting too tight, watching myself like a live-action movie, like I was outside my head, stumbling down the stairs and crashing down under cover behind the pulp books. I shot one guy in the chest because I don't think he believed what was happening—damn revs talk big, but most are just city boys, low on the masc score, lower than me—and then it was on.

By the time I hit the registers I was skidding on adrenaline. Yeah, so I had stupid ideas about action and heroism, like every kid who wanted to be in the army. Thought I'd be a big hero, mowing down hostiles and never taking a hit, lighting up a cig with a big grin. Instead I was sick to my stomach and my heart was pounding too fast; I thought I'd wig out any second. The way my hands were shaking, I can't believe I shot anyone, but I must've, sometime in between the shelves knocking over and the displays getting torn apart over me. I fought those revs until my magazine was empty, not that it took more than a minute at that, and that's when the boys in uniform came and rescued me.

★

I CAN'T REMEMBER the trip back to Camp Save Big. I know I didn't make it on my own power. Mostly I remember the bit before I woke up, swimming in that big back-of-the-eyelid river, up and down until I broke the surface.

Didn't wake in any proper hospital. This was where they put the special projects, I guess. I could feel a catheter in, and my stomach dropped three feet. All I could think was *Shit*. All I could think was, *Cover blown*. People aren't in the habit of asking after your privates unless they knew you took a reassessment, and I'd been liking that no one here knew. No one asks to see your license if you pass yourself off. If you don't have chugs or a damn beard. Or a goddamn head injury that makes them stick a catheter in.

I bit down hard, and made fists hard, and held on to nothing until I heard a door open and a guy's voice say "Hey," beside me.

Look up and there was John, and he reached over to take my pulse. "Don't worry," he said. "I'm your attending. I told them you might like a private room, and they gave you this one—you being the hero of the hour."

I looked around at shelves shoved into a corner, a few warehouse pallets stacked in another corner, and decided it had been a crappy back room before becoming my crappy suite. Then what he said hit me. "Wait there. Hero?"

"Hero of the battle of Fresh Food Mart," John said. "Save the day. Get the girl. You know, if you want her."

I gave him a funny look, and he burst out laughing.

"Christos, not *me*!"

I laughed, too. "Think I'm Agatha's type?"

He reached down and patted my shoulder, and the funny thing was, I didn't mind. Like, maybe it didn't matter to his thinking that I got no bits— just like he got no girliness. We both had our dirty little secrets.

"Tell you what, though. That's got to be worth three points masculine on the GAT."

"Not unless they hand me a medal over it." I groaned. Don't get me wrong, I'd rather get treatment than none and I was glad that my head didn't hurt, but I wanted out of that bed, out of that hospital gown that fell down between my legs, out of just lying there helpless and feeling exposed to the world. John looked at his fingers.

"Not fair, is it?"

Yeah, and we both knew without asking. "Shit deal," I said. "So what do we do?"

John shrugged. "Keep going," he said. "Things have to change sometime."

I looked at him. "You sound like a rev." That talk about things changing, how unjust it all was. Hell, I guess I sounded like one, too, in my head, but I knew I wasn't, and I don't think John was either. Just two guys in bad positions.

"Yeah, well. They're wrong about a lot, but they're not wrong about this." John shrugged, and stood up. "I've got patients. You're gonna be fine."

"Yeah," I said. "Good luck on your rounds."

He went, and I lay back and listened to the painkillers swirling in my veins. The door pulled open, and I didn't hear it shut. I looked.

"If I have any say in it, I'll get you that medal," John said.

The door swung closed behind him.

WHERE THE WOMEN GO
MADELEINE ROUX

WHEN THEY WERE young they stood side by side in the mirror, two identical, gangly kids with sunburned noses and long dark hair. Scrub of the face. Brush of the teeth. Katie would put her hair up in a messy tail and Simon would leave his long, a bit greasy. Her elbows were sharp, and she'd use them like knives in his ribs to get her share of the mirror. Then they were out the door, together, off to school, and so alike sometimes even their dad mixed them up from a distance.

It seemed to change overnight. Simon couldn't remember what day it was exactly, but it was sudden. Instantaneous. The reasons were obvious, maybe, and right there in front of his face, but still it confused him. Katie would get up earlier, spend more time on her hair. There was lip gloss now after the teeth brushing. He scowled at her in the mirror, because something had flipped right under his nose and that bothered him.

No more sharp little elbows in his ribs, no more familiar bruises left behind from their ongoing war for the mirror.

Simon still scowled at his reflection every morning, harder now because Katie was gone altogether. She was only maybe thirty minutes down the road, but for how it felt she might as well have been on the moon.

One day she just didn't come home from school. Sixteen years old and vanished. But Simon knew where she was. Everyone did. In a way, he had known she would go like all the others. Katie was soft and friendly and kind. A follower. He knew she would go as soon as the women started leaving their homes, their jobs, their families... They all went to one spot in the middle of nowhere. Well, not nowhere. To him it was Didi Wright's land. When Didi first showed up to take over that ranch five years ago Simon's dad wouldn't shut up about "Didi Wright being Didi Wrong for that place." He thought he was a real crackup with that one.

Katie and Simon had winced in unison. *Christ, Dad.*

Simon winced again now, clutching a break-action rifle to his chest, his dad pacing a groove into the floor of the verandah. It was a hot day, dry and windy, and Simon's mouth felt gritty with dust. He squinted into the distance, in the general direction of Didi Wright's land. A helicopter sped overhead, loud enough to drown out his father's voice. He wondered where the bloody things were coming from. Nanutarra Station was the closest thing passing for civilization, but he didn't think they had any helicopters there. The choppers had been going over day and night, some of them news, some of them military. It was strange turning on the TV or the radio to hear nothing but male voices come out. The talking heads on Sky News looked spooked. They read off the teleprompters in a fog, droning on, their eyes big and haunted.

Nobody in the family had slept in days, and it was becoming obvious. His brothers Johnny and Davis looked knackered, with bags under their eyes deep enough to hold stones. His dad never quit pacing and slept, or tried to, with his gun in the bed.

The sun blasted behind his father's whip-thin frame as he made his way back and forth across the porch. He had always been wiry, a long streak of pelican shit, but now it looked like a stiff breeze could blow him over. Two bouts with skin cancer hadn't turned him onto sunscreen, his only concession a floppy fisherman's hat that was yellowed and fraying.

Johnny and Davis hunched over their guns on the edge of the verandah. They had always been big, meaty boys, but now they too seemed ravaged. Either Simon was imagining things or Johnny's sweat-stained tee was hanging looser. Simon squinted past his father, watching the helicopters disappear over the ragged tree line at the edge of their property. Katie was somewhere beyond those trees.

"Ya reckon she walked?"

Simon hadn't realized he'd said it aloud until his father grunted and spat, arcing a gob of spit over the railing and into the dust.

"Walked nothin'," he muttered. "She was taken. They took her, anyone who says different is talking out their arse."

"Dunno," Simon said with a shrug, still fixated on those gently swaying trees. "On TV it looks like they're all buggering off on their own, eh? No one forcing them."

"Bullshit," his father roared, rounding on Simon. He braced for a smack, but it didn't come. "Not our Katie," the old rancher said, softer. "She wouldn't do that to me."

"It's the government." Davis had always been the stupid one, but he was really going for it lately. Simon glared. "S'gotta be."

"Watch the news once or twice," Simon shot back. "Even the Prime Minister doesn't know shit. Nobody does."

"They just lie." Davis had a low voice, and he always spoke slowly, like he was figuring out each word just before he said it, but it took a little too long. "Right, Dad? They just lie."

Simon wished he could go deaf. They had gone 'round and 'round on this ever since Katie left. In the wake of her disappearance, when the panic lifted and all that was left was confusion, they had nothing to do with themselves but speculate. Simon had stopped eating at the dinner table with them. All the useless talk just gave him headaches.

He fidgeted with his gun, looking down at it. He hadn't used it much lately, only some target practice to keep sharp and a few rats that'd gotten into the shed and made a mess. Something about holding the gun now didn't feel right. He knew what his dad was planning, and where he wanted to go, and all of the sudden it dawned on Simon that maybe this gun and the bullets inside it would be turned on people. Women. He shivered.

"What's the matter with you?" Davis muttered. He had a heavy brow and shaggy brown hair that he was constantly shaking out of his face.

"Nothing," Simon replied, lifting his head. *Everything.*

"Well that's it then, Dad, isn't it?" Davis was being stupid again. What did that even mean? But the older boy stood, putting his rifle over his shoulder like he was some tough guy soldier from the movies. "We gotta do it."

"We gotta," his dad echoed.

His father's name was Francis. The boys used to joke about it in private. He did not look like a Francis. He went by Frank, of course, but when their mother was still alive she called him Francis now and then. Usually on Christmas. It didn't sound weird when their mum said it; somehow it had been sweet coming out of her mouth.

Simon missed her then, and he wished she was there to tell them what to do. Not that Frank would listen, but still. Or would she be gone like Katie, too? All the women were leaving, going to Didi Wright's property. There were rumors about a strange light in her fields and that all the women were gathering there. The news had to blur lots of the coverage because tons of the women were starkers.

"We gotta do it," Frank said with a growl. "No choice, really."

He finally stopped pacing and turned down the verandah steps, taking them slow and heavy, as if he had a boulder strapped to his back. Simon didn't like it. He didn't want to follow; he wanted to go back inside and sit on the couch with all the dogs, get surrounded by their familiar dusty, oily scent and prop his feet up on the apple crates they used as a coffee table, and watch the TV for hours, just watch and watch, back on the vigil for Katie, determined to find her among all the naked blurry shapes in the field.

But his brothers were following Frank, trooping down the steps and falling in line. The old ute was already in the drive, once black but now more or less tan from the caked-on dust and mud. He could hear the dogs behind him in the house whining. They knew something was wrong, just like Simon did, and he trusted them more than he ever trusted Frank or his dumb brothers.

Feeling that same boulder on his back, Simon drifted away from the verandah and toward the ute. There was no real plan, but somehow one had formulated in the spaces between their brief exchanges, a silent, masculine pact that he hated but nonetheless felt grimly tied to, like some desperate deal with the Devil he had only half-heartedly accepted.

His brothers climbed into the ute, leaving Simon to get in the back. As the engine gunned to life, Simon stared at the low, shabby house they lived in. It looked miles away, and they hadn't even pulled out of the driveway.

Simon pulled up his tee and tied it over his mouth against the haze of dust kicked up by the tires. They were going to find Katie. It didn't feel real. He wondered how many naked women he would see, and if it would be weird. Once, Jackie Summers let him kiss her and put his hand up her shirt behind the school. He couldn't believe how soft she was. It took him a week to realize that she wasn't going to let him do it again, and that she had just wanted a ciggie.

"Bitch," Davis had said when Simon recalled the story over a beer. But that seemed harsh. He had gotten to put his hand up her shirt, after all.

Would Jackie Summers be in the field, too? More and more women were going; the news said nobody could get normal flights anywhere because so many women were trying to get to Australia. You almost had to laugh, thought Simon. Who the fuck would want to take all that trouble getting to Pilbara? But it was happening. Women and girls were clamoring to get to the arse end of the Earth, and for what? To piss about in a field, dancing naked and singing Kumbaya?

Simon felt his stomach lurch as the ute sped up, just a blur screaming across the bush. They didn't have all that far to go, and the military had set up barriers all over the place. When they were a few miles from Didi's land, Frank veered off the dirt road and into the trees, the truck rocking from side to side as they navigated the uneven terrain. Simon had only been this close to Didi Wright's property once, a few summers ago, when he and his brothers drove over drunk and threw rocks at her cows. They ditched the ute next to a meager stream, Frank and his brothers hopping out and crouching low in the bushes. Simon didn't get out just yet. He didn't know if he wanted to go any further. It all made his skin crawl and his hair stand on end—maybe he didn't want to see what was inside the camp.

"I'm going to go ahead and take a gander," Frank said, turning back to the truck and unloading a metal box from the passenger seat. He set it down carefully, making as little noise as possible. Opening the hatch, he pulled out a box of ammunition, a few six packs of beer, and some beef jerky. "Don't fuckin' go anywhere. I'll be back soon. You just wait."

Then he crept away, keeping low, his rifle slung over his shoulder. Simon stayed in the ute, watching that fisherman's hat gradually get swallowed up by the leaves.

"Idiot, he shouldn't go alone," Davis said, opening a beer.

"He's a goner," Johnny agreed. He was slimmer than Davis, muscular, and the best looking of the boys. He had gotten all their mother's looks, with big brown eyes and sandy blonde hair. A lot of girls had let him put his hand up their shirts. "Probably get hit by a sniper or some shit. I'm telling ya, there's something in there they don't want us to see."

Simon rolled his eyes, but didn't disagree. Of course civilians had rushed in, trying to reach their spouses or friends or daughters. The military turned them away at first, but now there were so many trying that they had gone to bean bag rounds and tear gas. A few blokes had gotten badly injured when they refused to back down, and the news showed them being carried out on stretchers, bruised and ranting. The camp looked different on television now, more militarized. The numbers inside were swelling, and Simon wondered what would happen if women just kept coming.

What they were doing was dangerous. It hadn't occurred to him until that moment that they could land in real trouble trying to find Katie. Frank didn't come back for hours. It was getting dark by the time he returned, and just in time, as the beer had run out and his two brothers were getting antsy.

"I don't want to be stuck out here all night," Simon said. "We won't be able to get back out if it's dark. I can't see for shit and I'm not turning on the headlights."

"I'm not giving up on him yet," Davis replied.

He probably just wanted an excuse to sit there in the cool shadows and guzzle another tinny. But Frank returned not long after, all of them bolting up in alarm as they heard the leaves shimmer at his approach. Davis aimed his gun, but then they all saw the fisherman's hat. Simon wanted to feel more relieved than he did.

"It's a bloody nightmare," Frank informed them, taking the beer out of his son's hand and downing it. He was covered in sweat and grime, mosquito bites welling up on his hands and neck. "But I think I found a way in. Troops are thin on the west side; they're mostly busy keeping the reporters from crawling over the barricades."

"Then what are we waiting for?" Davis was a little drunk and red-faced and looked like he was spoiling for a blue.

Simon gulped, watching them cluster, watching them prepare.

"You follow me and do as I do." His father's words were slurred around great mouthfuls of beef jerky. He swallowed, sighed and nodded toward Didi's fields. "Stay low, and for fuck's sake don't do anything stupid."

They began making their way toward the property, but Simon had a question.

"Did you see her, Dad? Did you see Katie?"

He didn't answer.

Simon began feeling strange as they neared the barricades. Massive floodlights were set up in both directions, armed military patrolling back and forth, walkie-talkies buzzing. They were easy to spot with the lights on, but Simon wondered how many were taking secret sweeps of the woods. The trees thinned, removing most of their cover, and Simon felt his hands grow slick with sweat. A slapdash barbed-wire perimeter had been set up, and they skirted it, moving to the west, all of them ducking whenever another military chopper thundered overhead. It was like something out of an action flick, Simon thought, Michael Bay and all that shit, tanks and ATVs, dizzying sounds, stone-faced soldiers armed to the teeth, reporters and their microwave vans set up in a fan in front of the main barricade... But there was one gap in the barricade, a kind of gate. Simon hunched in the bushes, at the very edge of the concealing tree line, watching the bizarre procession of women walking in an orderly line through the gap.

"They're letting more in?" he whispered.

Davis shushed him, but his father said, "Guess they can't stop 'em. Ain't breakin' any laws."

"Look at them all," Simon breathed. The line stretched for miles, vanishing into the gathering darkness. None of the women looked like they were being forced to go, and there was no rush, just a steady walk, some kind of peaceful procession.

"What happens when they run out of room?" Johnny asked.

"Don't know," Frank muttered. "Don't care. Not gunna be here for that, just gunna get my damn daughter and leave."

"What if she wants to stay?" Simon knew he shouldn't have said it, but the more he looked at the women and the calm smiles on their faces, the more he knew in his gut that Katie had come on her own, walked the seven miles from school to this farm with nobody making her do it. Well, nobody that he could see, anyway.

"Shut up." Davis smacked him on the back of his head.

"I'll lock her in the cellar if she acts up with this shit again," Frank said, his face scrunched in grim determination. "Now keep quiet and follow me."

They did. Simon couldn't shake that weird feeling in his stomach. His whole body felt like it was pulsing. Not like it had when Jackie let him touch her tit, but more intense: waves of sensation that tied his guts in knots. He could swear there was a low, constant hum in the back of his head. He couldn't shake it off, and it made him tremble.

Just the lights, he assured himself. *Too much stimulation is all.*

They doubled back and followed, at a distance, the line of women stretching into forever. At last it was dark all around them, and the mass of television crews thinned. Frank darted forward, his sons in tow, and broke through the line of women walking toward the gates. None of them seemed to notice or care about the men, as if in a trance.

"Bloody weird," he heard Johnny whisper as they scurried into a bank of low bushes on the other side of the line.

As promised, Frank led them toward the west side of the property, where fewer reporters shouted into their cameras, and the barbed-wire fence had partially broken down. A tiny two-foot gap was all they had to work with. By sheer luck, the nearest floodlight either wasn't working or hadn't been turned on. It was the perfect point of ingress, and they took it.

The grass had been so well trampled by all the commotion that the fields were more or less dirt. They crawled toward the makeshift camp that had been set up on Didi's property, hundreds, maybe thousands of tents clustered together to form a kind of city. The minute they came close to the edge of the tents, Simon heard laughter. That buzzing in his stomach grew harder to bear, and he clutched his middle, wincing.

"How are we gunna find Katie in all this shit?" Davis groused.

"You just follow me, boy," Frank replied. "I got an idea."

Simon didn't like the sound of that. He agreed that they needed to get Katie back, but he didn't see how it was possible with this many tents to search. They'd be there all night, and when morning came get caught for sure.

They snaked through the maze of canvas and nylon, quiet, low to the ground, and moving toward what Simon assumed was the center. His legs ached from squatting for so long. He was in the back, and noticed with a gasp of fear that they had been noticed. Women were following them.

"Oi." He elbowed Johnny in front of him. "Oi, stop, we've got company."

The men stopped and turned, finding a dozen girls and women fanned out behind them. They simply stood, staring back, though none looked particularly angry or disturbed.

One little girl stepped forward. She was dressed in a flowing white frock, a flower tucked into her curly black hair. "What are you doing here?" she asked.

It was like they had all simultaneously lost the power of speech.

"Um… My sister. We're looking for my sister. Katie," Simon finally said.

"Why?" the girl pressed. She tilted her head to the side, smiling.

"Fuckin' weirdo," Davis whispered. "They on drugs?"

"We just want her back." Simon felt like he was dealing with a hostage, afraid to say anything too harsh. "Don't want to start trouble, we just want her back."

The girl sighed and came closer. She gently touched Simon's chin, lifting it up so she could look him over. "Silly. She won't want to come back. None of us do. This is our place now. It's for us, not for you."

"What are you all doing here?" Simon murmured. The hum in his head crested, and he had to blink hard to withstand the pain.

"Being," the little girl replied. "Just being."

"Enough of this shit." Frank dodged past him in a blur, elbowing Simon out of the way and into the dust. He grabbed the little girl by the arm, wrenching it behind her. Turning, he shoved his rifle into her back and forced her toward the other women that had been watching and following.

They did not gasp, or even react; they simply watched.

"You shouldn't hurt her," one woman, tall, plump, and dressed in a paisley bikini said. Her brows knit together with pity as she extended her hand. "Give Joia back to us. She just wants to be."

"Shut up!" Frank forced out through gnashing teeth. "Just shut up and listen. You listen to me, right? Katie Spencer. Where is she? You take me to her right now and nothing happens to this little girl."

Simon almost couldn't hear his father over the din in his head. He felt like he was going to pass out. Scrabbling, he pushed himself to all fours, watching through watery eyes as Frank pushed the rifle harder between the girl's shoulder blades.

Don't.

"Katie Spencer," the woman in the bikini said. "Katie Spencer … "

The other women with her began to say it, too, in a soft murmur that became a kind of chant. More girls and older ladies appeared out of the tents, surrounding them. Simon glanced around warily, finding that they were completely enclosed in a circle of women that was tightening by the minute. Some were stark naked, others were streaked with mud in patterns like war paint, one short, tattooed woman wore only an old boot.

"Katie Spencer, Katie Spencer … "

Hearing his sister's name so many times almost made it funny, or nonsensical. He was caught between the horrible pain in his head and the sense that they were in deep, deep shit. His father, for fuck's sake, was pointing a gun at a little kid! Why had they come?

"Katie Spencer—" The chant ended abruptly. Paisley bikini tipped her head to one side, going silent, closing her eyes. Every woman and girl near them did the same. Spooky. Like they were receiving some kind of *transmission*.

In the distance, the choppers whirred, the news reporters chattered, the flood lights buzzed.

"Hurry up now," Frank almost shouted. "I'm getting impatient, and I don't wanna do anything you'll regret to this child."

The woman in the bikini opened her eyes, staring with renewed interest at Frank. Then, without warning, she lunged for him. The next minute or two passed by in a blink, and Simon screamed, wincing at the gunfire, watching the bullet casing drop with a ping that he heard like lightning in his head, seeing the blood explode in a fantastic arc out of the little girl's chest.

Dead. She was *dead* and *holy shit Frank had just shot someone*. A kid. The child dropped to the ground in a heap. His father reared back, shouting. Davis and Johnny screamed, too, a moment later, briefly stunned by the sound of the shot and the blood that came after. And in all of that, the woman had simply put her hand on Frank's. A touch of the hand, nothing more, and someone had died for it.

She looked down at the dead child for a long time. Tears ran down her cheeks. Panting, wild-eyed, Simon looked around. Every woman encircling them had begun, silently, to cry.

"Katie Spencer," the woman said sadly. She took Frank's hand, but he wrenched it free of her grasp. "Take my hand," she commanded. "Take my hand and we will bring you to Katie Spencer."

Maybe it was the shock of what he had done or the promise that he would see his daughter, but Frank did as he was told for once, letting the woman take him by the hand and lead him toward the inner reaches of the tent city. Simon watched disbelievingly as an elderly woman came forward. She was Aboriginal, wrinkled as a raisin, her skin dry and papery and warm as she took Simon's fingers in hers and tugged. It had been a long time, too long a time since someone smiled at him the way she did—tenderly, carefully, as if he were bruised and needed care.

They had just barged into the camp and shot a little girl, and now this old woman gingerly led him off, just behind the bikini woman and Frank. Davis and Johnny were scooped up, too, and Davis managed to keep his mouth shut about it.

"I'm sorry," Simon blurted out. "That girl … I'm sorry. We didn't mean to do anything like that. It was an accident."

The old woman nodded. She wore a light blue dress with a white collar, and socks with sandals. She squeezed his hand, but said nothing. Tears ran down her lined cheeks.

"Really ... We didn't mean to. Christ. We're going to be in so much trouble." Simon's eyes fluttered shut. "God, this headache."

"Mm," the woman said. "You don't belong here."

Was this some kind of warning? Punishment? But how ... Simon forced himself to concentrate, stumbling along. He had the sudden urge to drop his rifle, and he did so, tossing it away, sickened at the sight of it. The tents were clustered more loosely as they approached the heart of the encampment. Open spaces with bonfires appeared, and women dancing around them. They held hands and laughed, many of them with flowers or leaves threaded in their hair. Around one fire, a chain of women sat, giggling and talking. Each was cutting off the hair of the woman in front of her and tossing the strands into the air. It was like a festival, some drug-fueled hippy stuff, singing and chanting, naked women hugging and holding hands.

He wasn't supposed to see this, he thought, and his face got hot and red. Was Katie really here? Was she into this kind of thing? His brain pulsed. He was having trouble remembering anything concrete about his sister. She loved animals. Her favorite color was purple. She smiled less after mum passed. Davis and Johnny gave her endless loads of shit, but Katie had always been faster and smarter, and definitely kinder.

"What are you all doing here?" he asked, trying not to stare at the naked women but sneaking glances anyway.

"Being," the old woman said with a happy sigh. "Just being."

"But what are you *doing*? What made you come here?"

She glanced up at him, frowning, as if she didn't understand the question. After a pause she told him, "The triangle. It called me here. It called all of us here. But not you, you were not called."

"You can't keep this up, you know," Simon muttered. He was vulnerable now, even more surrounded and, obviously, outnumbered. One of the military choppers overhead seemed to circle back and hover just above them. He felt the gust of the blades ruffle his hair. "We want to know what's going on. The men, I mean, we're going to keep trying to get in here and get some answers."

"You can try," she admitted, leading him away from the bonfires. "But you shouldn't."

"But what about your families? And your jobs! You can't keep this up forever."

"For now we are here," she said. "Being."

Simon's head was killing him. He had to swallow hard to keep from vomiting, pain lancing through his stomach every ten steps or so. The women in the open field watched them pass. Some took interest and followed. They were brought to one of the bigger tents in the encampment, one for a party, like a wedding maybe. Frank had rented something similar after Johnny graduated, but it had been saggy and dingy, this one was crisp, clean and sparkling white.

The noise and ache in his head was such that he almost lost his sight as they opened the tent flap and escorted him inside. But he had to see this. He knew that it was impossible, alien, and that it was the source of all his terrible pain. A triangle hovered in the air, three feet from the dirt, its surface not metal but liquid silver. It radiated cold light, humming with what sounded like the far off laughter of children. Or maybe a creek. Or maybe rain on a tin roof.

"What is that thing?" Simon whispered.

The old woman patted his hand. "It brought us here. Ah, there is your sister. Katie Spencer."

Katie was standing near the triangle, grinning. She had never looked more beautiful or more content. Frank pushed his escort away and raced toward her, and Katie gave him a hug, but Simon could tell it was anemic. Reluctant.

"Hi, Dad," Katie said. "I love you, I see you, and now you need to go."

"Katie—"

He was on the verge of screaming at her, but Katie put her forefinger on his lips. "You need to go, Dad, before something bad happens. I'm fine. I'm safe. I'm just here." Simon knew what her next word would be before she said it. "Being."

"Bullshit. Katie, I want you to forget this, now, whatever this stupid notion is you get it out of your head right now!" Frank tried to hug her again, but the other women fell on him. They poured into the tent, the women and girls, and they snarled as they fell on Frank, pulling him away from his daughter.

It seemed to Simon that the triangle laughed.

"What does it say to you?" Simon said, louder, breaking away from the old woman. He kept his distance, watching as the women wrestled Frank to the ground. "Katie, what does that thing say to you?"

"You will never hear it, Si," she said with a pout. Her tank top and denim shorts were ripped and muddy, as if she had been rolling around in the grass. "I wish you could hear it. It tells me I'm all right. It tells me I don't need to change anything, that this, being this, is all I need."

"You're not making any sense," Simon wanted to cry. Everything hurt. His teeth felt like they had become razors in his mouth. "Please, Katie … Just come home. Come home with us. We miss you."

"You can miss me, that's okay, but I'm fine. I want to be here. I want to just be." Katie glanced nervously at the writhing mass of women on top of Frank. Not much of him could be seen, just the dirty old hat. "You need to go now, Simon, before something bad happens. You don't belong here."

"Wait!" The old woman had come after him, but she was gentle, taking his hand and pulling him toward the outside world. Simon glanced from his father to his brothers to the terrible and beautiful triangle. It was so bright, so cold … He wanted it to speak to him. He wanted to know what it had to say. Why wouldn't it speak to him?

Davis and Johnny weren't going peacefully. They broke free of their escorts too, screaming, shoving their way toward the women restraining Frank. More women came rushing into the tent, past Simon, flowing over Davis and Johnny like a river of retribution. They were swallowed, overtaken. Overpowered.

Simon blinked. What was happening? He stumbled away with the old woman, further and further from his family and from Katie. This alien thing had turned them against each other, poisoned all these people, and for what? To just *be*? He didn't understand …

He heard a horrible sound then, just as he reached the fresh night air outside the tent. His father wailed, and it sounded like a hundred mouths biting into a hundred fleshy peaches. A smell like old wet coins filled the air. Davis and Johnny screamed and then were silenced. Simon couldn't see any of them under the mass of snarling and tearing women, the women covering his brothers and father.

Once, Davis had shot a wild dog in the pasture and let it fester out in the summer sun. Frank was furious about the smell. Simon had been young, but he remembered it; he remembered the almost sweet reek of curdling flesh and the maggots, thick as a carpet, blanketing the dead dog's carcass.

His head pounded from the screams and the close, overwhelming thud-thud-thud of a military helicopter dipping lower. Simon moaned and shielded his eyes from a flood of light off the chopper, staring up, watching as a door slid open and a rope ladder dropped down toward him. A man inside, a soldier, was shouting at him.

Of course it was a man, he thought, groping blindly for the ladder. All the women were here now, just being.

THREE SPEECHES ABOUT BILLY GRAINGER
JAKE KERR

<u>Billy Grainger, posthumous induction into the Humor Hall of Fame</u>
Induction speech by Eugene "Mean Gene" Crawford

THANK YOU.

Now shut the fuck up.

I know you're comedians, but we're here to honor our own, so I swear to God if I hear one more tinkling glass I'll shove it so far up your ass you'll be able to toast after you finish your drink.

That's better. Now where was I? Oh yeah, we're a classy fucking group, and this is our distinguished fucking hall.

So, what can I say about Billy Grainger? Not a whole lot. He's a fucking chemist. Ted called me and was like, "We'd like you to give an induction speech at the Hall of Fame ceremony, but it's a posthumous award. You good with that?"

My first thought was, "It's about fucking time." My second thought was, "Sure, stick Mean Gene with the dead guy." But the more I thought about it, the more excited I got. Maybe I'd be the one to finally induct Jeff Cargo or some dude from 100 years ago who was overlooked. I'd be inducting some icon. Better yet, they'd be dead long enough that I could steal some of their material and you dumb fucks would think of it as an homage if I got caught. So it sounded like a good deal.

But, no, I didn't get someone like that. I didn't even get a pity induction for Carrot Top or Gallagher. So who do I get to induct? Billy Grainger. Billy fucking Grainger. A goddam chemistry nerd.

★

The Centenary Prize from the Royal Society of Chemistry,
posthumously awarded to Billy Grainger
Speech by Doctor Mary Evans, Cambridge University

THANK YOU, LADIES and gentlemen of the Society and our honored guests. I am humbled and excited to present this award to the late Billy Grainger for his extraordinary work using chemistry for social change. I recognize that this was both an inspired and controversial choice, but it was a necessary and important one.

For the many new guests we have in attendance, I should note that the Centenary Prize was established 95 years ago with the goal of highlighting exceptional communicators from overseas. Its specific purpose was to bring these communicators to the United Kingdom to share their deep and nuanced knowledge of chemistry by way of their skills as speakers and teachers. Yet here we are awarding the prize to someone who not only can't share his knowledge with us, but whose knowledge was distinctly practical.

So, some of you ask: Why present Billy Grainger with the Centenary Prize?

Well, before we honor today's recipient, let me answer the critics seated in this room. No, Mister Grainger was not a theoretical chemist. He provided no new knowledge or understanding to our field. Nor was he an experimental chemist, who blazed trails of new study. Nor was Mister Grainger a scholar, who used his broad knowledge of our field to further the understanding of chemistry or to provide context to assist current theory. Mister Grainger was none of those things. Mister Grainger—Billy Grainger—was that most simple and yet practical of us—an applied chemist. He took our current knowledge and applied it to a problem.

And, with all due respect, the problem he solved and the methods he used, are the absolute definition of what this prize honors. I ask you all: Who in the entire history of this esteemed Society used chemistry and communication to change the world as much as Billy Grainger?

Heroes of the Resistance: Billy Grainger statue unveiling
Speech by Professor Terrence Jefferson, University of Pennsylvania

I'M A HISTORIAN, and I'm proud of that fact. I don't hide from the sins of our past. I'm not afraid to applaud the progress we have made. I shine the light of truth on the past, so that we can learn from it. So I cannot discuss the vital role that Billy Grainger played in reversing the Quiet Revolution without first providing you with the proper historical context—the truth.

So friends and fellow citizens, let me start with a simple proverb, condensed to a single sentence.

For want of a nail, the kingdom was lost.

This proverb tells us that small events can have great consequences. Nothing describes Billy Grainger better than this single line. He was not a great general. He did not give inspiring speeches or write revolutionary blog posts. He wasn't a spy, a journalist, or a warrior. He did one thing. One small thing. One small, extraordinary, amazing thing to bring down a tyrant—he used humor.

Humor Hall of Fame speech, continued

YOU'RE BOOING ME for calling him a chemistry nerd? I can't believe this. You're fucking booing me.

The dude's corpse is cold, and you're telling me this is too soon? We're fucking comedians. *It's never too soon*, you cowardly fucks. Do you think Grainger was a coward? He was shot on live TV for doing what we do—making people laugh.

Oh, you got me going now. See this? This was my really funny and somewhat inappropriate speech. This is me ripping it up. You now get the _really_ inappropriate speech.

So let me tell you about Billy.

He was a fucking chemistry nerd. Sure, he was more than a chemist, but it was his chemical paint that defined him, so if we're going to celebrate how funny and important his humor was, we still need to mock him for being a chemistry nerd. It's what he would have done, and if you don't get that, you're idiots.

Am I pissing you off? Well, Grainger had this amazing talent for pissing people off so badly that they did stupid things. Sound familiar? Yeah, it's not an accident that Ted asked me to give this fucking speech, you dickwads.

Do you remember his first piece? Of course you do. It pissed off everyone. He spray painted Kellen doing Andrews doggy-style on the side of the Washington Monument. I mean, you have this fucking phallic symbol centered between the White House and the Capitol, and Grainger paints the President literally fucking Congress on it.

That's pretty damn funny.

★

Centenary Prize speech, continued

WE ARE ALL familiar with how Mister Grainger communicated his messages—graffiti. The messages were powerful in that they stabbed into the heart of the tyranny in America. Yet I daresay that it wasn't the message that was important, but the chemistry.

There can be no doubt that Mister Grainger was a genius. He took nanotechnology and applied it broadly to both organic and inorganic compounds to create what we all now take for granted—nanopaint. Could someone else have done this? Certainly. Was there a market for a paint that binds with the underlying structures so strongly that it is effectively permanent? Maybe. All progress seems obvious in hindsight, but someone must take that first, critical, step. That someone was Billy Grainger.

Today we know that others had the same idea, but they abandoned it due to the many perceived problems. Truly permanent paint was deemed too dangerous and impractical. Something as minor as a spill would be impossible to clean. Paint on clothing or your skin would never come out. And, yet, where others saw nothing but problems, Mister Grainger saw a unique opportunity to create change.

This is the essence of applied chemistry and something this honored society has overlooked for far too many years. It took Mister Grainger's sacrifice and the societal change in America for us to recognize it. Many claim that it was Grainger's words and images that sparked the resistance, but us chemists know better—it started with Mister Grainger's understanding of both nanotechnology and chemistry. Without that understanding of binding two unrelated chemicals together, we wouldn't have permanent paints and dyes. And without permanent paint, America wouldn't have its freedom.

★

Heroes of the Resistance speech, continued

HISTORY IS CONSTANTLY being re-examined. Historians in the nineteenth century saw the enslavement of my ancestors in financial terms. Today we view slavery differently. This is healthy and part of getting to the truth—understanding how things were and how they change.

It is clear today that the United States was founded not by ideologues but by practical men. They knew that rule by popularity was a different kind of tyranny, but one nonetheless. They saw the tyranny of the masses and built systems in place to protect the minority—empowering states, creating a senate not based on population but territory, and many other things that held the potential power of the masses in check.

That structure helped my people and many other minorities as we battled for our rights. So this was a good thing.

Yet history has taught us again and again that a small and rabid group of people can tyrannize a splintered larger group. And that's what we all failed to see until we looked back as historians—that a small group of citizens had twisted the practical and good intentions of this country's founders into the Quiet Revolution. One moment we were dumbfounded over the election of President Kellen, and the next we were watching as he systematically dismantled our freedom for his own purposes.

Which brings me to Billy Grainger. Billy saw something that none of us could see—the fragility of a tyrant fueling the flames of anger in that minority. He saw that when you rule from a position of weakness, nothing is worse than being mocked. Yet Grainger wasn't just a pamphleteer or an editorial cartoonist or an artist. Grainger was a chemist.

And thanks to his application of chemistry, he did one thing that none of us could have predicted. One small thing that made all the difference in the world—his nanopaint gave his mockery *permanence*.

★

<u>Humor Hall of Fame speech, continued</u>

IT'S REALLY CONVENIENT to forget today, but that move pissed off everyone. He fucking defaced a national monument. Even people who hated Kellen and Andrews were pissed off at Grainger. Let me tell you, that takes talent.

It takes talent because for attack comedians like Grainger and myself, it's not about the joke; it's about the response. That's right, I'm calling him a comedian. Did he ever do stand-up? No. Can I mock him for being a chemistry nerd and honor him for being a comedian? Yes. I'm fat. I contain multitudes.

So what do I mean by the response? Well, we've all crossed the line and said something that made others uncomfortable on stage. Hell, I've built a career around it. When it works, the response of that uncomfortable person is itself so over-the-top and funny that your bit of cruelty is overshadowed by the ridiculousness of your target. You provoke, and the response is the punchline.

Is it nice? No. Is it cruel? Maybe. Is it funny? Fuck yeah.

So while I thought Grainger's graffiti was funny, Kellen's response by tearing down the entire Washington Monument was absolutely hilarious. Who the fuck does that? Some insane fascist dictator, that's who. And you know who knew how to destabilize the fragile ego of a dictator better than anyone?

Billy fucking Grainger and his nano fucking paint.

★

<u>Centenary Prize speech, continued</u>

THIS AWARD IS about communication, and it is about chemistry. Before I talk about Mister Grainger's talent for communication, let us discuss his chemistry. Science and technology have progressed so fast that it's easy to forget that nanobot-assisted chemical reactions were new when Mister Grainger was in graduate school. Like many men before him, he dropped out of school not because he was bored with his studies, but because he was excited by this technology. He didn't want to study it—he wanted to <u>use</u> it.

At the time, many people were doing the same in important disciplines— medicine and pharmacology, industrial engineering, transportation. Some of them have been lauded on this stage. Yet while many scientists followed the money flowing into businesses embracing this new technology, Mister Grainger did not. He took a used 3D printer, a credit card, and lots and lots of time and focused on one simple thing—paint.

Here is the moment where I shall wax philosophical as I speak proudly of chemistry's contribution to art. Simply put, chemists have changed art throughout the ages in fundamental ways. Dyes, oils, acrylics—this was not the first time that we had created a new paint for our artist brothers and sisters. Even new colors were brought to life thanks to chemistry.

So Mister Grainger is the latest in a long and honored lineage of chemists who have fundamentally changed art. And that is one of the reasons we honor him today. When the world saw dollar signs, he saw chemistry at its most fundamental level—a creative expression.

★

Heroes of the Resistance speech, continued

IT IS AN iconic moment, one that my fellow historians point to as the moment that galvanized the resistance—when President Kellen ordered the Washington Monument torn down. It shocked the nation. Many blamed Grainger for defacing the monument, but few could understand why it needed to be torn down. Sure, Kellen restricted access. He covered Grainger's political statement with tarp. He tried to use chisels and jackhammers to remove the statement, but in the end we are told that he felt everything was taking *too long*.

Kellen's impatience and his ego led to his biggest mistake—tearing down a monument to one of the country's most revered founders. He had his propaganda machines explain it the best they could, but in the end a flawed monument that defined the nation was still a monument, a symbol of everything that Kellen claimed to be. It is easy to forget, but at that moment in time he could have recovered. The country was teetering between sentiments that Kellen did what he had to do and that he had betrayed our country's founders.

At that *exact* moment of uncertainty, of a nation poised between

JAKE KERR   335 abandoning the symbols of our past or turning on the Kellen regime, Billy Grainger spray painted the following on the statue of Abraham Lincoln in the Lincoln Memorial: *You made me Kellen's Bitch.*

Crass. Offensive. Shocking. It was all those things, but it was Kellen's irrational response that made the headlines.

★

Humor Hall of Fame speech, continued

BILLY WAS THAT evil combination of class clown and science nerd. He was a chemist with a vengeance, man. If you idiots learned anything from fifth grade, it was don't pick on the class clown. But you *especially* don't pick on the class clown with access to chemicals. Kellen fucked with the wrong man.

The Lincoln Memorial thing will always be my favorite. *You made me Kellan's Bitch.* Holy shit. That's genius. Honest Abe calling out the fascist fuck ruining his country. How pissed off and insane do you need to be to bulldoze the Lincoln fucking Memorial just so people won't know what was written? Why didn't Kellen just permanently close the memorial for repairs or something? I don't fucking know, but the idiot did it anyway.

The dude seventy percent of the country knew was insane was suddenly acting insane to the other thirty percent. He was literally razing our national monuments to cover his fragile ego, and it was all due to Billy Grainger. Billy fucking Grainger the chemist nerd.

★

Centenary Prize speech, continued

AS AN APPLIED chemist, I hope you all will agree that Mister Grainger is a worthy recipient of this award, but we cannot forget that the foundation of this award is communication. Mister Grainger's ability to take ideas and communicate them in a way that had a powerful impact is undeniable. Were his words and images offensive? Certainly. But we must remember that he was living in an offensive fascist dictatorship, and those words and images exposed the rotten core eating away at America.

Chemistry. Communication.

Billy Grainger represents both of those things, and those two things represent this award. Mister Grainger doesn't only deserve this award, he typifies it.

★

Heroes of the Resistance speech, continued

IT IS DIFFICULT to comprehend why a leader would act irrationally, but it happens all too often. Perhaps at the root of it is the assumption that they do it because they feel like they can get away with it. Perhaps that is why Kellen responded so irrationally. Something about Grainger's biting comments and profane images bothered him so much that he felt he had to remove them, and not only that—he had the power to remove them without consequence. So he bulldozed the Lincoln Memorial. He blew up the Arlington Memorial Bridge. When Grainger moved to New York, Kellen closed the Brooklyn Bridge, spending millions of dollars to swap out metal girders where Grainger's paint had fused with the underlying metal.

There are other examples, and each one led to a response so absurd that you could practically see President Kellen's face turn red in rage. It was hard to explain. It was utterly unexpected. It was crazy. And it fueled the revolution.

★

Humor Hall of Fame speech, continued

I WAS WATCHING Billy's statue unveiling at the Monument to the Resistance and this stuffed shirt is giving a speech about Billy. He was like, *We don't know why Kellen acted the way he did* and *Why would he implode over graffiti* and shit like that. Let me tell you, us comedians know. Nothing destroys a person like humiliation.

Billy Grainger, the class clown with access to chemicals, fucking humiliated Kellen, but even more than that—he humiliated those who followed him. So many of these left wing idiots tried to fight Kellen and his Nazi followers using logic and rational arguments. Are you kidding me? That shit never works. What the country needed was someone who would make fun of them for the idiotic, small dick, insecure, evil fucks that they were.

Thank God Billy Grainger came along. He didn't argue state's rights or human rights or any of that shit. He pointed at Kellen and fucking laughed. And he made us laugh. Then he pointed at Kellen's followers and laughed at them. And he made us laugh at them, too. And, let me tell you, those fuckers didn't like it.

The dumb fuck fascist enablers in this country could deal with being criticized for being racists, homophobes, misogynists, being ignorant as a brick, and even being called Nazis. But, let me tell you, they could not in any way deal with being laughed at.

★

Centenary Speech, concluded

BEFORE I CLOSE I want to step outside my role as academic and add an additional word that describes Billy Grainger: courage.

It is perhaps easy to ignore Billy's great personal courage as we judge him through the cold eye of science, but it is impossible to ignore as we judge him as a human. After he was arrested while painting _Resist!_ on the Golden Gate Bridge, society had already turned against the Kellen regime. We know of the military losses and the erosion of support for Kellen. For Billy, after he was caught it would have been easy for him to apologize for his crimes and to seek mercy. It is entirely possible he would have been paraded around as a propaganda tool and then imprisoned, with some opportunity to be set free after Kellen was overthrown. We all watched from here in the UK, and it was clear even to us.

Yet Billy did what he meant to do from the start. He spat in the face of a tyrant that couldn't imagine being spat at. He imagined a message of resistance. He found an inspired canvas for that message. And he communicated it with his art. And, in the end, he was courageous and died delivering that message.

Ladies and gentleman, I am honored to posthumously award William Grainger the Royal Society of Chemistry's Centenary Prize.

★

Heroes of the Resistance speech, concluded

PLENTY OF HEROES are honored in this memorial. Heroes who lost friends, family, and loves, who sacrificed their own lives to overthrow a fascist and evil regime. We rightfully honor all of them, as without them we would not enjoy the freedom we have today. Billy Grainger is undeniably one of these heroes. It is worth a reminder that after he was captured by nationalist forces, he had every opportunity to save his own life. He could have reasonably ascertained that the cause he fought for was secure, but for whatever reason, he felt the need to make one last statement.

Today, like with so many decisions of the Kellen regime, we have a hard time understanding how it could happen, but the execution of Grainger, shown live on TV, was the final nail in the regime's coffin. By then he was a folk hero to everyone but Kellen's most hardened supporters. Websites provided real-time updates as they waited for the next Grainger piece and wondered just how explicit it would be or what insult Grainger would use next. The machinery of public sentiment that Kellen leveraged so well to gain power was entirely turned against him.

We can only guess that Kellen felt the only way to put the Grainger problem to rest was to intimidate us all by showing what was in store for those who resisted. Kellen called him a bully, a traitor, and a vandal. But labels like that are immaterial when the man you plan to execute walks out with a huge smile as he faces his death.

Billy Grainger's final act is as well known now as any historical event in history. It spread across the globe in seconds. The image ended up on posters, painted on buildings, and shared across every social network known to man. Grainger, the hero that he was, somehow knew that it wasn't his permanent graffiti that would shut the door on Kellen's power, it was his own personal message.

In hindsight, Kellan's biggest mistake, his final mistake, was glaring and obvious—he locked Grainger in a cell and gave him a pen. Of course, he was delighted when Grainger wrote a lengthy confession the morning of his execution, but for that small and insignificant document, he handed his greatest enemy his greatest weapon.

I tell that well-worn story for one reason: to address the controversial statue created by Ruth Teixeira. She chose the highly personal and yet epic moment of his death to honor Grainger, and none of us on the board of directors could disagree with her decision. Yet it offended many. All I can say as a historian is that you can't study history without knowing the context that surrounds it. It is the only way to get to the truth. And in the context of Billy Grainger, hero of the resistance, I present you his memorial statue... and the truth.

★

Humor Hall of Fame speech, concluded

Fuck, thinking of that crazy statue made me realize something—there is no way we can honor Billy as well as the goddam Resistance Memorial did. I about shit myself when they unveiled the statue. I kept thinking, *Holy shit. They did it. They really did it.*

So let me conclude by saying that the fucking nerd chemist class clown pulled off the greatest bit of humor in history when he was shot. I smile every time I think of it. Not Billy getting shot, you assholes, how when the Attorney General fuckhead said, "Reveal his traitorous heart" and they ripped open his shirt and there, drawn on his chest in the same black permanent ink they gave him to write his confession hours before was a drawing of his middle finger with that transcendent caption... "Fuck you, asshole."

Do you get it? He knew this was a historically epic moment. He knew that everyone was watching. He knew that he was on the largest fucking stage any comedian ever had, and he just owned it. He flipped off all those fascist fucks with a smirk on his face. And to make it even better, now there's this fucking statue of him surrounded by statues of stern-faced heroes and forlorn children, and it's him smirking with a fuck you written on his chest.

I mean, have you ever walked through the memorial? There's this awed hush and quiet solemnity, and then you turn the corner and fucking Billy's chest is giving you the finger. That, ladies and gentleman, is the pinnacle of comedy. This fucking guy. He's memorialized giving the finger in the fucking Memorial to the Resistance.

Hell, let's shut this whole fucking Hall of Fame down. Ain't no one going to top that.

THE VENUS EFFECT
VIOLET ALLEN

Apollo Allen and The Girl from Venus

THIS IS 2015. A party on a westside roof, just before midnight. Some Mia or Mina is throwing it, the white girl with the jean jacket and the headband and the two-bumps-of-molly grin, flitting from friend circle to friend circle, laughing loudly and refilling any empty cup in her eyeline from a bottomless jug of sangria, Maenad Sicagi. There are three kegs, a table of wines and liquor, cake and nachos inside. It is a good party, and the surrounding night is beautiful, warm and soft and speckled with stars. A phone is hooked up to a portable sound system, and the speakers are kicking out rapture. It is 2009 again, the last year that music was any good, preserved in digital amber and reanimated via computer magic.

Apollo boogies on the margins, between the edge of the party and the edge of the roof, surrounded by revelers but basically alone. Naomi is on the other side of the crowd, grinding against her new boyfriend, Marcus, a musclebound meat-man stuffed into a spectacularly tacky t-shirt. Apollo finds this an entirely unappealing sight. That she and Apollo once shared an intimate relationship has nothing to do with this judgment. Not at all.

Speaking merely as an observer, a man with a love of Beauty and Dance in his heart, Apollo judges their performance unconvincing. It is the worst sort of kitsch. The meat-man against whom Naomi vibrates has no rhythm, no soul; he is as unfunky as the bad guys on Parliament-Funkadelic albums.

He stutters from side to side with little regard for the twos and fours, and the occasional thrusts of his crotch are little more than burlesque, without the slightest suggestion of genuine eroticism. He is doing it just to do it. Pure kitsch. Appalling. Naomi is doing a better job, undulating her buttocks with a certain aplomb, a captivating bootyliciousness that might stir jiggly bedroom memories in the heart of the lay observer. But still. *We know that the tail must wag the dog, for the horse is drawn by the cart; But the Devil whoops, as he whooped of old, "It's pretty, but is it Art?"*

Apollo cannot bear to watch this any longer. He desperately wants to point the terribleness of this scene out to someone, to say, "Hey, look at them. They look like dumbs. Are they not dumbs?" But Naomi was always the person to whom he pointed these sorts of things out. That's why they got along, at least in the beginning, a shared appreciation for the twin pleasures of pointing at a fool and laughing at a fool. Without her, he is vestigial, useless, alone.

He turns away from the ghastly scene, just in time to notice a young woman dancing nearby. She is alone, like him, and she is, unlike him, utterly, utterly turnt. Look at her, spinning like a politician, bouncing like a bad check, bopping to the beat like the beat is all there is. She is not a talented dancer by any stretch of the imagination, and her gracelessness is unable to keep up with her abandon. She is embraced of the moment, full with the spirit, completely ungenerous with fucks and possibly bordering on the near side of alcohol poisoning. Just look at her. Apollo, in a state of terrible cliché, is unable to take his eyes off her.

There is a problem, however.

Her heels, while fabulous, were not made for rocking so hard. They are beautiful shoes, certainly, vibrant and sleek, canary yellow, bold as love. Perhaps they are a bit too matchy-matchy with regard to the rest of her outfit, the canary-yellow dress and the canary-yellow necklace and the canary-yellow bow atop her head, but the matchy-matchy look is good for people who are forces of nature, invoking four-color heroism and supernatural panache. Yet however lovely and amazing and charming and expensive these shoes might be, they cannot be everything.

The center cannot hold; things fall apart.

Her left heel snaps. Her balance is lost. Her momentum and her tipsiness send her stumbling, and no one is paying enough attention to catch her. The building is not so high up that a fall would definitely kill her, but death could be very easily found on the sidewalk below. Apollo rushes forward, reaches out to grab her, but he is too late. She goes over the edge. Apollo cannot look away. She falls for what feels like forever.

And then, she stops. She doesn't hit the ground. She just stops and hangs in the air. Apollo stares frozen, on the one hand relieved not to witness a death, on the other hand filled with ontological dread as his understanding of the laws of gravitation unravel before his eyes, on a third hypothetical hand filled with wonder and awe at this flagrant violation of consensus reality. The young woman looks up at Apollo with her face stuck in a frightened grimace as she slowly, slowly descends, like a feather in the breeze. She takes off as soon as she hits the ground, stumble-running as fast as one can on non-functional shoes.

Apollo does not know what has just happened, but he knows that he wants to know. He does not say goodbye to the hostess or his friends or Naomi. He just ghosts, flying down the ladder and down the hall and down the stairs and out the door. He can just make out a blur in the direction she ran off, and he chases after it.

There is a man in a police uniform standing at the corner. Apollo does not see him in the darkness, does not know that he is running toward him. The man in the police uniform draws his weapon and yells for Apollo to stop. Inertia and confusion do not allow Apollo to stop quickly enough. Fearing for his life, the man in the police uniform pulls the trigger of his weapon several times, and the bullets strike Apollo in his chest, doing critical damage to his heart and lungs. He flops to the ground. He is dead now.

★

UH, WHAT? THAT was not supposed to happen. Apollo was supposed to chase the girl alien, then have some romantically-charged adventures fighting evil aliens, then at the end she was going to go back to her home planet and it was going to be sad. Who was that guy? That's weird, right? That's not supposed to happen, right? Dudes aren't supposed to just pop off and end stories out of nowhere.

I guess to be fair, brother was running around in the middle of the night, acting a fool. That's just asking for trouble. He was a pretty unlikeable protagonist, anyway, a petty, horny, pretentious idiot with an almost palpable stink of author surrogacy on him. I think there was a Kipling quote in there.

Who's that for? You don't want to read some lame indie romance bullshit, right? Sadboy meets manic pixie dream alien? I'm already bored. Let's start over. This time, we'll go classic. We'll have a real hero you can look up to, and cool action-adventure shit will go down. You ready? Here we go.

★

Apollo Rocket vs. The Space Barons from Beyond Pluto

There are fifteen seconds left on the clock, and the green jerseys have possession. The score is 99-98, green jerseys. The red jerseys have been plagued by injuries, infighting, and unfortunate calls on the part of the ref, who, despite his profession's reputed impartiality, is clearly a supporter of the green jerseys. The green jerseys themselves are playing as though this is the very last time they will ever play a basketball game. They are tall and white and aggressively Midwestern, and this gives them something to prove. Sketch in your mind the Boston Celtics of another time. Picture the Washington Generals on one of the rare, rumored nights when they were actually able to defeat their perennial adversaries, mortal men who somehow found themselves snatching victory from the god-clowns of Harlem.

Fourteen.

One of the green jerseys is preparing to throw the ball toward the hoop. If the ball were to go into the hoop, the green jerseys would have two points added to their score, and it would become impossible for the red jerseys to throw enough balls into the other hoop before time runs out. The green jerseys are already preparing for their win, running over in their minds talking points for their post-game interviews, making sure the sports drink dispenser is full and ready to be poured upon the coach, and wondering how the word "champions" might feel on their lips.

Eleven.

But this will not happen. Apollo is in position. He reaches out with his mighty arm and strips the ball from the green jersey before he can throw it.

Ten.

Apollo runs as fast as he can with the ball, so fast that every atom of his body feels as if it is igniting. He looks for an open teammate, for he is no ball hog, our Apollo, but there are no teammates to be found between himself and the hoop. So he runs alone. He is lightning. There are green jersey players in his way, but he spins and jukes around them before they can react, as if they are sloths suspended in aspic. Do his feet even touch the floor? Is it the shoes?

He's on fire.

Three.

He leaps high into the air and dunks the ball so hard that the backboard shatters into a thousand glittering shards of victory. The buzzer goes off just as he hits the ground. The final score is 100-99, red jerseys. Apollo Triumphant is leapt upon by his teammates. Hugs and pats on the back are distributed freely and with great relish. The crowd erupts into wild celebration. *Apollo, Apollo*, they chant.

Patrick, the captain of the opposing team, approaches Apollo as confetti falls from above. There is a sour look on the man's face, an expression of constipated rage at its most pure. He balls his fingers into a fist and raises it level with Apollo's midsection. It rears back and trembles as an arrow notched in a bow, ready to be fired.

"Good job, bro," he says.

"You too," says Apollo.

They bump fists. It is so dope.

A small child limps onto the basketball court. He smiles so hard that it must be painful for his face. Apollo kneels and gives him a high-five, then a low-five, then a deep hug.

"You did it, Apollo," says the child.

"No. We did it," says Apollo. "They'll never be able to demolish the youth center now."

"My new mommy and daddy said they could never have adopted me without your help."

Apollo puts a finger to his own lips. "Shhhhh."

"I love you, Apollo," says the child, its face wet with tears. "You're the best man alive."

Apollo drives home with his trophy and game ball in the back seat of his sports car, a candy apple convertible that gleams like justice. He blasts ~~Rick Ross~~ a positive, socially conscious rap song about working hard and pulling up one's pants on his stereo. The road is his tonight. There are no other cars to be seen, no other people for miles. For all his successes as balla par excellence, Apollo still appreciates the beauty and quiet of the country.

Suddenly, a sonorous roar pours out from the edge of the sky, so powerful that it shakes the car. Before Apollo can react, a yellow-silver-blue ball of fire shoots across the sky and explodes on the horizon, for a moment blotting out the darkness with pure white light before retreating into smoke and darkness. Apollo ~~jams his foot on the pedal~~ proceeds in the direction of the mysterious explosion while obeying all traffic laws and keeping his vehicle within the legal speed limits.

"~~Holy shit~~ Golly," he says.

Apollo finds a field strewn with flaming debris, shattered crystals, and shards of brightly colored metals. He hops out of his car to take a closer look. Based on his astro-engineering courses, which he gets top marks in, he surmises that these materials could have only come from some kind of spaceship. He is fascinated, to say the least.

He hears movement from under a sheet of opaque glass. He pushes it away and sees that there is a woman lying prone underneath. At least, Apollo thinks she is a woman. She is shaped like a woman, but her skin is blue, and she has gills, and she has a second mouth on her forehead. Woman or not, she is beautiful, with delicate, alien features and C-cup breasts.

"Oh my God," says Apollo. He kneels down next to the alien woman and cradles her in his arms. "Are you okay?"

She sputters. ". . . Listen . . . ship . . . crashed . . . There isn't much . . . time . . . You must stop . . . Lord Tklox . . . He is coming to . . . answer the . . . Omega Question . . . He will stop at nothing . . . please . . . stop him . . . Save . . . civilization . . . Leave me . . ."

Apollo notices a growing purple stain on the woman's diaphanous yellow robes. Based on his Theoretical Xenobiology class, he hypothesizes that this is blood. He shakes his head at her, unwilling to accept the false choice she has presented him with. "I'll do whatever I can to stop him, but first I have to help you."

She reaches up to gently stroke his hand with her three-fingered hand. ". . . So kind . . . I . . . chose well . . ."

With his incredible basketballer's strength, it is nothing for Apollo to lift the woman. He may as well be carrying a large sack of feathers. He places her in the passenger seat of his car and gets back on the road lickety-split.

"You'll be okay. I just need some supplies."

He stops at the nearest gas station. He races around inside to get what he needs: bandages, ice, sports drink, needle, thread, protein bar. With these items in hand, he rushes toward the register, which is next to the exit. He is stopped by a man in a police uniform. The man in the police uniform asks him about his car.

"It's mine," Apollo says.

The man in the police uniform does not believe Apollo.

"You have to come help me! There's a woman in trouble!"

The man in the police uniform does not believe Apollo and is concerned that he is shouting.

"~~This is ridiculous!~~ Sorry sir. I am sure you are just doing your job. Let me show you my ID and insurance information so we can clear all of this up," says Apollo.

Apollo goes to fish his wallet from his pocket. His naked hostility, volatile tone, and the act of reaching for what very well could be a weapon are clear signs of aggressive intent, and the man in the police uniform has no choice but to withdraw his own weapon and fire several shots. Apollo is struck first in the stomach, then the shoulder. He does not immediately die. Instead, he spends several moments on the floor of the convenience store, struggling to breathe as his consciousness fades into nothing. Then, he dies.

★

WHAT THE FUCK is happening? Seriously. Where is this dude coming from? I haven't written that many stories, but I really don't think that's how these things are supposed to go. The way I was taught, you establish character and setting, introduce conflict, develop themes, then end on an emotional climax. That's it. Nobody said anything about killers popping up out of nowhere. Not in this genre, anyway.

So hear me out. I think we may be dealing some kind of metafictional entity, a living concept, an ideo-linguistic infection. I don't know how he got in here, but he should be easy enough to deal with. I think we just need to reason with him. He's probably a nice guy. Just doing his job, trying to keep the story safe. He was probably genuinely afraid that Apollo was reaching for a gun. You never know with people these days. Life is scary.

Besides, that story wasn't working either. That Apollo was a big phony, totally unbelievable. Guys like that went out of style with Flash Gordon and bell-bottoms. It's not just about liking the protagonist. You have to be able to relate to them, right? I think that's how it works. That's what everybody says, anyway. To be honest, I don't really get the whole "relatability" thing. Isn't the point of reading to subsume one's own experience for the experience of another, to crawl out of one's body and into a stranger's thoughts? Why would you want to read about someone just like you? Stories are windows, not mirrors. Everybody's human. Shouldn't that make them relatable enough? I don't know. I don't have a lot of experience with this kind of thing. I thought smoking was a weird thing to do, too, but then I tried smoking and was addicted forever. Maybe I've just never come across a good mirror.

So let's do a child. Everybody loves children, and everybody was one. Plus, it's really easy to make them super-relatable. Just throw some social anxiety disorder and a pair of glasses on some little fucking weirdo and boom: you got a movie deal. It'll be a coming-of-age hero's journey sort of thing, adolescence viewed through a gossamer haze of nostalgia.

★

BULLY BRAWL: AN APOLLO KIDD ADVENTURE

THIS IS 1995. A group of young people sit on the stoop of a decaying brownstone just off the L. The topic is television. Some show or another. Who can remember? Broadcast television in the year 1995 is terrible all around, hugs and catchphrases and phantasmal laughter suspended in analog fuzz. Is Full House on in 1995? Is Urkel? They don't know how bad they have it. Naomi leads the conversation. A skinny, toothy girl with a voice like a preacher. You can almost hear the organ chords rumbling in your chest whenever she opens her mouth. She jokes about what she would do if her own hypothetical future husband were to comically declare himself the man of the house, with the punchlines mainly revolving around the speed and vigor with which she would slap the black off him. She is sort of funny, but only because the television shows she is describing are not.

Apollo does not make any jokes. He is sort of funny himself (people laugh at him, at least), but he does not know how to make funny words happen. He is mostly quiet, only chiming in with the factual, offering airtimes and channels and dropping the names of actors when they get stuck on the tips of tongues. Six or seven of them are gathered, and Apollo believes himself to definitely be the or-seventh. He is wearing a t-shirt with a superhero on it. Not Superman. Superman gear can be forgiven as a harmless eccentricity if you're otherwise down. But Apollo's rocking some kind of deep-cut clown in a neon gimp suit on his chest. Remember, this is 1995, and this man is thirteen years old. Unforgivable. He's not just the or-seventh, he is the physical manifestation of all the or-seventhness that has ever existed in the world.

The new girl is sitting next to him. She might have been the or-seventh were she not new. Check that sweater. Yellow? Polyester? Sequin pineapples? In this heat? Worse than unforgivable. But who knows what lies under it? A butterfly? A swan? Any and all manner of transformative symbology could be hiding, waiting, growing. There's still hope for her. She may be four-eyed and flat-butted and double-handed and generally Oreoish, but there is hope. She can at least drop into the conversation sometimes, in the empty spaces after the punchlines. She has that power. For instance, after Naomi does a long routine on what she would do if she ever found a wallet lying on the sidewalk like on TV (in brief: cop that shit), the new girl says something about losing her own money and getting punished harshly by her mother. It is not a funny thing to say, but memories of belts and switches and tears are still fresh in their adolescent minds, and it is comforting to laugh it out. Apollo laughs the hardest, and he does not know why.

The sun is gone. Just a little light left. The new girl can't go home alone. Not in the almost-dark. This is 1995, not 1948. Apollo volunteers to walk with her.

"He like you," says Marcus, Naomi's not-quite-but-basically-boyfriend, by way of explaining why Apollo is the best one for the job.

Apollo denies this so fervently that he has to go through with it, lest she think he truly hates her. The walk is quiet for the first few blocks. Apollo is not a big talker, and the new girl has been here for two weeks, and no one, except maybe the ultragregarious Naomi, has had a real conversation with her. Still, Apollo finds himself feeling strangely comfortable. Maybe it is the sweater. Perhaps the fact that it should be embarrassing her is preventing him from being embarrassed himself. Perhaps it is the sartorial equivalent of imagining one's audience naked. Perhaps she's just sort of great.

Apollo stops short just before they reach the corner. He holds out his arm so that the girl will stop, too. There's danger up ahead. A gang of street toughs. Six of them. One of those multicultural, gender-integrated '90s gangs, a Benetton ad with knives. Red jackets, gold sneakers. One of them has a boombox. KRS-ONE maybe? Early KRS-ONE. Stuff about listening to people's guns as they shoot you with them. Their victim is an old, gray-haired man. His hands are up. There is a briefcase at his feet. The gangsters taunt him stereotypically.

"Give us ya money, pops!"

"Don't make me cut you!"

"Nice and easy!"

"Don't be a hero!"

"I need to regulate!"

Apollo takes a slow step back. He means for Shayla to step with him, but she does not. He pulls on her arm, but she is still. She has a look on her face like she wants to fight motherfuckers. This is the most frightening expression that can appear on a human face.

"We have to go," he says.

"No," she says. "We have to help him."

"C'mon."

He pulls on her arm again, hard this time, but she slips his grasp. She runs at the gang, leaps into the air, and tackles the nearest one. The gangsters are surprised at first, to see this little girl brazenly attacking one of their own, but they quickly pull her off him and throw her to the ground.

"What's your malfunction?!" one of them screeches.

The girl stands and pulls out, seemingly from nowhere, a fantastic-looking gun object that in no way resembles a gun or any other real-life weapon. "Stand down, jerks."

"Oh dag! She got a gun object that in no way resembles a gun or any other real-life weapon! Kick rocks, guys!"

The gangsters run off into the night. Apollo runs over to the girl.

"What's going on? What's that thing?"

"Don't worry about it. Forget you saw anything," says the girl.

"Exactly," says the old man. He begins to laugh, first a low, soft chuckle, then an increasingly maniacal cackle that echoes in the night. "You have fallen for my trap, Princess Amarillia! I knew you could not resist helping a stranger in need."

The girl gasps. "Lord Tklox!"

"What?" says Apollo.

Smiling, the old man reaches up and grabs his face, pulling it off to reveal pale skin, elegant features, and hair the color of starlight. His body begins to bulge and swell as he grows larger, eventually doubling in height.

THE   VENUS   EFFECT

He laughs as a shining sword appears in his hands.

"Run!" shouts the girl.

"What is happening?!"

"No time to explain. Take this." She hands him her fantastic-looking gun object that in no way resembles a gun or any other real-life weapon. "I'll hold him off with my Venusian jiu-jitsu. Just go! Don't stop. Please. Don't stop. Just run. Don't let him get you like he got the others."

The girl takes a martial arts stance and nods. Apollo does not need further explanations. He runs in the opposite direction. He runs as fast as he can, until his lungs burn and he cannot feel his legs. Stopping to catch his breath, he holds the gun object that in no way resembles a gun or any other real-life weapon up to the light. He does not even know how to use it, how it could possibly help him in this strange battle.

So wrapped up in thought, Apollo does not even see the man in the police uniform. He does not hear him telling him to drop his weapon. He only hears the gun go bang. Later, his body is found by his mother, who cries and cries and cries.

★

DID YOU EVER read "Lost in the Funhouse"? I just re-read it as research on solving metafictional problems. Not super helpful. We get it; fiction is made up. Cool story, bro. But you know the flashback to the kids playing Niggers and Masters? Is that a real thing? Or is it just a sadomasochistic parody of Cowboys and Indians? I can't find any information on it online, but I'm sure somebody somewhere has played it. If something as cruel as Cowboys and Indians exists, why not Niggers and Masters? There is no way a game like that is only theoretical. It's too rich, too delicious. The role of Master is an obvious power fantasy, presenting one with the authority to command and punish as an adult might, without any of the responsibility. The role of Nigger is just a different kind of power fantasy, power expressed as counterfactual. In playing the Nigger, one can experience subjugation on one's own terms. There is no real danger, no real pain. You can leave at any time, go home and watch cartoons and forget about it. Or you can indulge fully, giving oneself up to the game, allowing oneself to experience a beautiful simulacrum of suffering. It is perfect pretend. There are probably worse ways of spending a suburban afternoon, and there is something slightly sublime about it, baby's first ego death. Sure, it's profoundly offensive, but who's going to stop you? But whatever. I'm probably reading too much into it. It's probably a made-up, postmodern joke. When I was a kid, we just played Cops and Robbers, and it was fine.

Anyway, that was a digression. I admit that it's difficult to defend the actions of certain uniformed narrative devices, but I'm sure there were good reasons for them. After all, there were gangsters with actual knives in that one, and Apollo was holding something that maybe sort of looked like a weapon in the dark. How are we supposed to tell the good ones from the bad ones? Can you tell the difference? I don't think so. Besides, this was to be expected. Children's literature is sad as fuck. It's all about dead moms and dead dogs and cancer and loneliness. You can't expect everyone to come out alive from that. But you know what isn't sad? Fucking superheroes.

★

GO GO JUSTICE GANG! FT. APOLLO YOUNG

OH NO.

Downtown Clash City has been beset by a hypnagogic Leviathan, a terrifying kludge of symbology and violence, an impossible horror from beyond the ontological wasteland. Citizens flee, police stand by impotently, soldiers fire from tanks and helicopters without success, their bullets finding no purchase, their fear finding no relief.

It is a bubblegum machine gone horribly, horribly awry, a clear plastic sphere with a red body and a bellhopian cap, except there is a tree growing inside it, and also it is a several hundred feet tall. The tree is maybe a willow or a dying spruce or something like that. It is definitely a sad tree, the kind of tree that grows on the edges of graveyards in children's books or in the tattoos of young people with too many feelings, when not growing on the inside of giant animated bubblegum machines.

It trudges along Washington Avenue on its root system, which emerges from the slot where the bubblegum ought to come out, and inflicts hazardous onomatopoesis upon people and property alike with its terrible branches.

Bang. Crack. Boom. Splat. Crunch.

Splat is the worst of them, if you think about the implications.

Various material reminders of American imperialist power under late capitalism, the bank and the television station and the army surplus store, are made naught but memory and masonry in its wake. The ground shakes like butts in music videos, and buildings fall like teenagers in love. Destruction. Carnage. Rage. Can nothing be done to stop this creature? Can the city be saved from certain destruction?

Yes!

Already, Apollo Young, a.k.a. Black Justice, is on his way to the Justice Gang Headquarters. Even as his fellow citizens panic, he keeps a cool head as he drives his Justice Vehicle headlong into danger. When his wrist communicator begins to buzz and play the Justice Gang theme song, he pulls over to the curb, in full accordance with the law.

"Black Justice! Come in! This is Red Justice!" says the wrist communicator.

"I read you, Patrick! What's the haps?!"

"The city is in danger! We need your help! To defeat this evil, We, the Justice Gang, need to combine our powers to form White Justice!"

"Yes. Only White Justice can save the city this time!"

"Also, can you please pick up Pink Justice? She is grounded from driving because she went to the mall instead of babysitting her little brother."

"What an airhead!"

"I know. But she is also a valuable member of the Justice Gang. Only when Pink Justice, Blue Justice, Black Justice, and Mauve Justice combine with me, the leader, Red Justice, can our ultimate power, White Justice be formed!"

"As I know."

"Yes. All thanks to Princess Amarillia, who gave us our prismatic justice powers in order to prevent the evil Lord Tklox from answering the Omega Question and destroying civilization!"

"Righteous!"

"Just as white light is composed of all colors of light, so White Justice will be formed from our multicultural, gender-inclusive commitment to Good and Right."

"Okay! Bye."

Apollo hangs up and gets back on the road. He picks up Pink Justice on the way. She is a stereotypical valley girl, but that is okay, since the Justice Gang accepts all types of people, as long as they love justice, are between fifteen and seventeen, and present as heterosexual. They ride together in silence, as they are the two members of the Justice Gang least likely to be paired up for storylines, owing to the potentially provocative implications of a black man and a white woman interacting together, even platonically.

"Do you ever think that we're just going in circles?" asks Pink Justice, staring idly out the window.

"What do you mean?" asks Apollo.

"A monster appears, we kill it, another monster appears, we kill it again. We feel good about getting the bad guy in the moment, but it just keeps happening. Week after week, it's the same thing. Another monster. More dead people. We never actually fight *evil*. We just kill monsters. Evil is always still there."

"But what about justice?"

"What is justice? People are dying. I just don't know what we're fighting for sometimes, why we keep fighting. It's the same every time. It's just tiring, I guess."

"I think we have to fight. Even if nobody gets saved, we are better for having done it. Maybe the world isn't better, but it's different, and I think that difference is beautiful."

"Like, for sure!" says Pink Justice.

A police car flashes its lights at Apollo. He pulls over. The man in the police uniform walks to the passenger side and asks Pink Justice if she is okay.

"I'm fine. There's no problem," she says.

The man in the police uniform tells Pink Justice that he can help her if something is wrong.

"Everything is fine. Nothing is wrong."

The man in the police uniform tells Apollo to get out of the car.

"~~What is this about? What's your probable cause?~~ Yes sir, officer," says Apollo, getting out of the car.

The man in the police uniform slams Apollo into the side of the car and pats him down. Pink Justice gets out and begins to yell that they have done nothing wrong, that he has to let them go. This obviously agitates the man in the police uniform.

Apollo's wrist communicator goes off, and without thinking, he moves to answer it. The man in the police uniform tackles him to the ground, sits on his chest, and begins to hit him with a flashlight. Apollo's windpipe is blocked. It continues to be blocked for a long time. He dies.

★

COME ON. REALLY? That one was really good. The white guy was in charge and everything! This sucks. I'm trying to do something here. The point of adventure fiction is to connect moral idealism with the human experience. The good guys fight the bad guys, just as we struggle against the infelicities of the material world. That's the point of heroes. They journey into the wilderness, struggle against the unknown, and make liminal spaces safe for the people. That's how it works, from Hercules to Captain Kirk. It's really hard to create ontological safety when people keep dying all the time. Barth was right; literature is exhausting.

So I guess Apollo shouldn't have been in a car with a white lady? That's scary, I guess. He didn't do anything, but he was probably no angel. He was a teen. Teens get into all kinds of shit. When I was in school, I knew so, so many kids who shoplifted and smoked drugs. They were mostly white, but still. Teens are shitty. The man in the police uniform probably had good intentions. Like, he wanted to make sure the girl wasn't being kidnapped or anything. Why else would they be together? I still think he only wants to keep people safe, especially potentially vulnerable people.

I've fucking got it. This is 2016, right? Sisters are doing it for themselves. Why not a lady-protagonist? Women are empathetic and non-threatening and totally cool. Everyone is chill with ladies. That's why phone robots all have feminine voices. True story. Why would you just kill a woman for no reason? She's not going to hurt you. This time, no one is going to hurt anybody.

★

APOLLONIA WILLIAMS-CARTER AND THE VENUS SANCTION

NAOMI WALKS INTO Apollonia's private office just before 5:00. It is a cramped and dingy room, lit by a single fluorescent bulb and smelling strongly of mildew. Without greeting or warning, she drops a thick, yellow binder down on Apollonia's desk.

"Read this," she says.

The binder is marked A.M.A.R.I.L.L.I.A. Project. It is filled with photographs, exotic diagrams, and pages and pages of exhaustively researched reports. Apollonia proceeds slowly, taking in each and every fact printed on the pages, running them over in her mind and allowing them settle. She feels a sinking sensation in her stomach as she journeys deeper and deeper into the text.

"Dear God," she whispers. "Can this be true?"

"Yes," says Naomi.

"This is absolutely disgusting. How could they do something like this? How could they sell us out to aliens?"

"They don't care about our world. Not anymore."

"What can we do?"

"I don't know. That's why I brought this to you."

Apollonia opens one of her drawers, retrieving two shot glasses and a bottle of whiskey. She pours a double and pushes it toward Naomi.

"Have some. It will calm your nerves."

Naomi throws the glass to the ground, shattering it.

"This is no time to drink! We've got to do something!"

Apollonia takes her shot. "We can't do anything if we can't keep our cool."

"You want me to be cool? The department will have my head if they even knew I am talking to you."

"My head's on the line, too. I might be a vice president here, but they'd kill me as quickly as a break room cockroach."

"So what do we do? I came to you because I have the utmost respect for your work with the company."

"We go to the press. It might cost us our lives, but at least the truth will be out there."

"Should we try to rescue the girl?"

"No. First, we get the truth out. I'll handle this. Delete any digital copies of these files and meet me tonight at the Port Royale."

"Fine."

"Remember. Anyone you know could be one of them. Use caution."

Naomi nods and exits.

Apollonia takes another double shot of whiskey as she continues to read the binder. How could this happen? She had never trusted the powers that be, but how could they be doing this? How could they be killing people with impunity? The notes on the files indicate that it is in the name of safety and the greater good, but whose safety are they really talking about? Man or monster?

Apollonia leaves at 7:00, as she does every evening. She hides the pages of the binder in her purse. She puts on a cheerful face, smiling at coworkers and greeting the support staff as she passes. She takes the elevator down from her floor to the lobby, then the stairs to the parking garage. She makes sure no one is following her as she walks down the corridors of the unlit parking garage, turning her head every few moments to get a full view of her surroundings. She sees her car and breathes a sigh of relief. She is almost out.

"Hey there."

She turns to see a young man in a suit. He is at least six feet tall and aggressively muscled. He smiles brightly and broadly at Apollonia, as if trying to hide something.

"Hello Patrick," she says.

"Where ya headed in such a hurry?"

"Just going home."

"Home, huh? I remember home."

He laughs. She joins him.

"Long hours, huh? I feel for you."

He sticks out his finger at her purse. She clutches it closer.

"Hey. Is that new? I think my girlfriend pointed that purse out at the store. I'm sure it was that one."

"I've had this thing forever."

"Do you mind if I see it? I just want to know if it's well made."

Apollonia swallows. "I'd really prefer it if you didn't."

The smile leaves his face, and his eyes begin to narrow. Apollonia takes a step back. She has been trained in self-defense, but this man has at least one hundred pounds on her and also might be an alien. She begins to slowly, subtly shift into a combat stance. If she times it right, she might be able to stun him long enough for her to escape. She just has to find the right moment. She waits. And waits. And waits.

Finally, he chuckles. "You're right. That was a weird question. I haven't been getting enough sleep lately. Sorry. I'll see you later."

Apollonia gets into her car. On the way to the Port Royale, she is pulled over by the man in the police uniform. While patting her down for drugs, he slips his fingers into her underwear. She tries to pull his hands away, prompting him to use force to stop her from resisting arrest. Her head is slammed many times against the sidewalk. She dies.

★

SHE. DIDN'T. DO. Anything. And even if she did do something, killing is not the answer. That's it. I'm not playing anymore. I can quit at any time. No one can stop me. Look, I'll do it now. Boom. I just quit for two days. Boom. That was two weeks. Boom. Now I have to change all the dates to 2016. What's the point of writing this thing? What's the point of writing anything? I just wanted to tell a cool story. That's it. No murders. No deaths. Remember? It was just a love story.

I once read that people get more into love stories and poems in times of political strife and violence. What better way to assert meaning in the face of meaninglessness than by celebrating the connection between human beings? Our relationship with the state, the culture, the world, these are just petals in the winds compared to the love that flows between us. Fuck politics. I set out to do a love story, so I'm doing a love story. Plus, I've got a plan. So far, the Apollos have all died while messing around outside. The solution isn't relatability at all. It's so much simpler than that: transit. It doesn't matter if the guy can't sympathize with Apollo if he can't find him. There are tons of great stories set in one place. I'll just do one of those.

★

APOLLO RIGHT AND THE ARCHITECTURAL-ORGANIC WORMHOLE

APOLLO AND NAOMI sit alone on the couch by the window, the dusty brown one held together with tape and band-aids, quiet, listening to the rain and the night, watching the play of wind and glow on the raindrops outside, refracted lamplight and neon diffusing into glitter in the dark. His head rests on her lap, which is soft and warm and comfortingly "lap-like," which is to say that it possesses the qualities of the Platonic lap in quantities nearing excess, qualities which are difficult to articulate, neotenous comforts and chthonic ecstasies of a sublime/cliché nature, intimacy rendered in thigh meat and belly warmth. Her left hand is on his shoulder, just so, and her right is on his chest, and he takes note of the sensation of her fingers as his chest expands and contracts, and it is pleasant. He takes a breath, sweet and slow. There is a little sadness, because this moment will wilt and wither like all moments, and he does not want it to, more than anything.

THE VENUS EFFECT

"Remember this," he says.

"What?"

"I would like it if you would remember this. Tonight. Or at least this part."

"Why wouldn't I remember tonight?"

"You never remember any of the good parts."

"You say that."

"It's true. You only remember the bad parts. The before and after. Anxiety and regret. Never the moment."

"Who says this is a good part?"

"That's a cutting remark."

"I just think we have different definitions of the good and bad when it comes to certain things."

"So this is a bad part?"

"I didn't say that."

"Which is it, then?"

"It's good to see you."

"You know what my favorite memory of us is?"

"Leon."

"I'm sure you don't remember it."

"Don't."

"It's not weird or anything. One time I came over to your place, and you smiled that smile you have—not the usual one, the good one—and you gave me a hug. Just a long, deep hug, like you were just really happy to see me. Genuinely happy. Not angry or annoyed at all. Just cruisin', y'know. Just cruisin'. We made out afterwards, and maybe had sex? I don't remember that super great."

"The fact that you don't see anything weird about that is why we had to break up."

"Whatever, lady."

The door flies open. The man in the police uniform shouts for everyone to get down. A flashbang grenade is thrown inside. Apollo pushes Naomi away but is unable to get away. He suffers critical burns to his head and chest. After being denied medical treatment on the scene, he dies weeks later in the hospital from opportunistic infections. Ironically, the man in the police uniform was actually meant to go to the next apartment over, where a minor marijuana dealer lives.

★

THEY DIDN'T EVEN get to the cool part. There was going to be a living wormhole in the closet, and all kinds of space shit was going to come out, and in the process of dealing with it they were going to rekindle their love. It was going to be awesome. We can't even have love stories anymore? What do we have if we can't have love stories?

Okay. Now I'm thinking that the issue is with the milieu. 2015 is a weird time. Shit is going down. It's politicizing this story. I'm not into it. What we need is a rip-roaring space adventure in the far future. That'll be cool. All this shit will be sorted out by then, and we can all focus on what really matters: space shit.

★

APOLLO _____ VS. THE VITA-RAY MIRACLE

THE CRYSTAL SPIRES of New Virtua throw tangles of intersecting rainbows onto the silver-lined streets below, such that a Citizen going about his daily duties cannot help but be enmeshed in a transpicuous net of light and color. A Good Citizen knows that this is Good, that beauty is a gift of Science, and he wears his smile the way men of lesser worlds might wear a coat and hat to ward off the cold damp of an unregulated atmosphere.

Lord Tklox is not a Good Citizen, and he rarely smiles at all. On those occasions when he does experience something akin to happiness (when his plans are coming to fruition, when he imagines the bloody corpses of his enemies, when he thinks of new ways to crush the Good Citizens of New Virtua under his foot), his smile is not so much worn as wielded, as one might wield the glowing spiral of a raymatic cannon.

"Soon, my vita-ray projector will be complete, and all New Virtua will tremble as I unleash the Omega Question!" he exclaims to no one, alone in his subterranean laboratory two thousand miles below the surface.

Cackling to himself, Lord Tklox waits in his lair for those who would challenge his incredible genius.

He waits.

He keeps waiting.

Lord Tklox coughs, perhaps getting the attention of any heroes listening on nearby crime-detecting audioscopes. "First New Virtua, then the universe! All will be destroyed by the radical subjectivity of the Omega Question!"

Waiting continues to happen.

More waiting.

Still more.

Uh, I guess nobody comes. Everybody dies, I guess.

★

So I CHECKED, and it turns out there are no black people in the far future. That's my bad. I really didn't do my research on that one. I don't know where we end up going. Maybe we all just cram into the Parliament-Funkadelic discography at some point between *Star Trek* and *Foundation?* Whatever. That's an issue for tomorrow. Today, we've got bigger problems.

It's time we faced this head on. Borges teaches us that every story is a labyrinth, and within every labyrinth is a minotaur. I've been trying to avoid the minotaur, but instead I need to slay it. I have my sword, and I know where the monster lurks. It is time to blaxploit this problem.

★

APOLLO JONES IN: THE FINAL SHOWDOWN

Who's the plainclothes police detective who leaves all the criminals dejected?
[Apollo!]
Who stops crime in the nick of time and dazzles the ladies with feminine rhymes?
[Apollo!]
Can you dig it?

Apollo's cruiser screeches to a halt at the entrance to the abandoned warehouse. He leaps out the door and pulls his gun, a custom gold Beretta with his name engraved on the handle.

"Hot gazpacho!" he says. "This is it."

Patrick pops out of the passenger seat. "We've got him now."

They have been chasing their suspect for weeks now, some sicko

---

responsible for a string of murders. In a surprising third act twist, they discovered that the one responsible is one of their own, a bad apple who gets his kicks from harming the innocent.

"We've got him pinned down inside," says Apollo.

"He won't escape this time."

"Let's do this, brother."

They skip the middle part of the story, since that has been where we've been getting into trouble. They rush right to the end, where the man in the police uniform is waiting for them.

"Congratulations on solving my riddles, gentlemen. I'm impressed."

"You're going down, punk," says Apollo.

"Yeah!" says Patrick.

"I doubt that very much."

The man in the police uniform pulls his weapon and fires three shots, all hitting Apollo in the torso. He crumples to the ground. Patrick aims his own weapon, but the man in the police uniform is able to quickly shoot him in the shoulder, sending Patrick's pistol to the ground.

"You thought you could defeat me so easily? How foolish. We're not so different, you and I. You wanted a story about good aliens and bad aliens? Well, so did I."

"How's this for foolish?" says Apollo, pulling up his shirt to reveal he was wearing a bulletproof vest all along. Then, he unloads a clip from his legendary golden Beretta at him. The man in the police uniform falls to the ground, bleeding.

Patrick clutches his shoulder. "We got him."

"We're not quite done yet," says Apollo.

He walks over to the body of the man in the police uniform. He tugs on the man's face, pulling it off completely. It is the face of Lord Tklox.

"This was his plan all along," says Apollo. "By murdering all those innocent people, he was turning us against each other, thereby making it easier for his invasion plans to succeed. All he had left to do was answer the Omega Question and boom, no more civilization. Good thing we stopped him in time."

"I knew it," says Patrick. "He was never one of us. He was just a bad guy the whole time. It is in no way necessary for me to consider the ideological mechanisms by which my community and society determine who benefits from and participates in civil society, thus freeing me from cognitive dissonance stemming from the ethical compromises that maintain my lifestyle."

"Hot gazpacho!" says Apollo.

They share a manly handshake like Schwarzenegger and Carl Weathers in *Predator*. It is so dope.

"I'll go call dispatch," says Patrick. "Tell them that we won't be needing backup. Or that we will be needing backup to get the body and investigate the scene? I don't really know how this works. The movie usually ends at this point."

Patrick leaves, and Apollo guards the body. Suddenly, the warehouse door bursts open. Seeing him standing over the dead body, a man in a police uniform yells for Apollo to drop his weapon. Apollo shouts that he is a cop and moves to gingerly put his golden gun on the ground, but he is too slow. Bulletproof vests do not cover the head. He is very, very dead.

★

I WASN'T TRYING to do apologetics for him. Before, I mean. I wasn't saying it's okay to kill people because they aren't perfect or do things that are vaguely threatening. I was just trying to find some meaning, the moral of the story. All I ever wanted to do was write a good story. But murder is inherently meaningless. The experience of living is a creative act, the personal construction of meaning for the individual, and death is the final return to meaninglessness. Thus, the act of killing is the ultimate abnegation of the human experience, a submission to the chaos and violence of the natural world. To kill, we must either admit the futility of our own life or deny the significance of the victim's.

This isn't right.

It's not supposed to happen like this.

Why does this keep happening?

It's the same story every time. Again and again and again.

I can't fight the man in the police uniform. He's real, and I'm an authorial construct, just words on a page, pure pretend. But you know who isn't pretend? You. We have to save Apollo. We're both responsible for him. We created him together. Death of the Author, you know? It's just you and me now. I've got one last trick. I didn't mention this in the interest of pace and narrative cohesion, but I lifted the Omega Question off Lord Tklox before he died. I don't have the answer, but I know the question. You've got to go in. I can keep the man in the police uniform at bay as long as I can, but you have to save Apollo. We're going full Morrison.

Engage second-person present.

God forgive us.

★

You wake up. It is still dark out. You reach out to take hold of your spouse. Your fingers intertwine, and it is difficult to tell where you stop and they begin. You love them so much. After a kiss and a cuddle, you get out of bed. You go to the bathroom and perform your morning toilette. When you are finished, you go to kitchen and help your spouse with breakfast for the kids.

They give you a hug when they see you. You hug back, and you never want to let go. They are getting so big now, and you do everything you can to be a good parent to them. You know they love you, but you also want to make sure they have the best life possible.

You work hard every single day to make that happen. Your boss is hard on you, but he's a good guy, and you know you can rely on him when it counts. You trust all your coworkers with your life. You have to. There's no other option in your line of work.

After some paperwork, you and your partner go out on patrol. You've lived in this neighborhood your entire life. Everything about it is great, the food, the sights, the people. There are a few bad elements, but it's your job to stop them and keep everybody safe.

It's mostly nickel and dime stuff today, citations and warnings. The grocery store reports a shoplifter. An older woman reports some kids loitering near her house. Your partner notices a man urinating on street while you're driving past. That kind of thing.

As you are on your way back to the station, you notice a man walking alone on the sidewalk. It's late, and it doesn't look like this is his part of town. His head is held down, like he's trying to hide his face from you. This is suspicious. Your partner says he recognizes him, that he fits the description of a mugger who has been plaguing the area for weeks. You pull up to him. Ask him what he is doing. He doesn't give you a straight answer. You ask him for some identification. He refuses to give it to you. You don't want to arrest this guy for nothing, but he's not giving you much choice.

Suddenly, his hand moves toward a bulge in his pocket. It's a gun. You know it's a gun. You draw your weapon. You just want to scare him, show him that you're serious, stop him from drawing on you. But is he even scared? Is that fear on his face or rage? How can you even tell? He's bigger than you, and he is angry, and he probably has a gun. You do not know this person. You cannot imagine what is going through his mind. You have seen this scenario a million times before in movies and TV shows.

You might die.

You might die.

You might die.

The Omega Question is activated:

Who matters?

ABOUT THE AUTHORS

Saladin Ahmed's first novel, *Throne of the Crescent Moon*, was nominated for the Hugo and Nebula Awards and won the Locus Award for Best First Novel. His short fiction, essays, and poems have appeared in *The New York Times, The Boston Globe, Slate, Salon,* and *BuzzFeed*. Recently he has focused on comics, winning the Eisner Award for Best New Series for *Black Bolt,* and penning the critically-acclaimed *Exiles* and *Quicksilver: No Surrender* for Marvel Comics. Saladin has also created the original series *Abbott,* an occult thriller set in 1970s Detroit, for Boom Studios.

Leigh Alexander is a writer of futurist fiction and interactive entertainment. She was recently narrative director on the acclaimed game *Reigns: Her Majesty,* and her digital culture writing has appeared in *The Guardian, The Columbia Journalism Review, Motherboard, the New Statesman* and more. She is the author of *Breathing Machine,* a memoir of early internet society, and her occasional ASMR video series "Lo-Fi Let's Play" explores ancient computer adventure games. More projects can be found at leighalexander.net.

Violet Allen is a writer based in Chicago, Illinois. Her work has appeared in *Lightspeed, Liminal Stories, Best American Science Fiction & Fantasy,* and elsewhere. She is currently working very hard every day on her debut novel and definitely has more than ten pages written, is not lying to her agent about having more than ten pages written and does not spend most of her time listening to podcasts, and everything is totally cool, I promise. She can be reached on Twitter at @blipstress.

Charlie Jane Anders' next novel is *The City in the Middle of the Night*, which comes out in February 2019. She's also the author of *All the Birds in the Sky*, which won the Nebula, Crawford, and Locus awards, and *Choir Boy*, which won a Lambda Literary Award. She's also written a novella called *Rock Manning Goes For Broke* and a short story collection called *Six Months, Three Days, Five Others*. Her short fiction has appeared on Tor.com, and in *Boston Review*, *Tin House*, *Conjunctions*, the *Magazine of Fantasy and Science Fiction*, *Wired Magazine*, Slate, *Asimov's Science Fiction*, Lightspeed, *ZYZZYVA*, *Catamaran Literary Review*, McSweeney's Internet Tendency, and tons of anthologies. Her story "Six Months, Three Days" won a Hugo Award, and her story "Don't Press Charges And I Won't Sue" won the Theodore Sturgeon Award. She also organizes the monthly Writers With Drinks reading series.

Jason Arnopp is a novelist and scriptwriter. He is the author of the terrifying Orbit Books novel *The Last Days Of Jack Sparks*, acclaimed by the likes of Ron Howard, Sarah Lotz, and Alan Moore. His previous work includes *Doctor Who* and *Friday The 13th* tie-in fiction, BBC Radio 4 comedy, *Beast In The Basement*, *A Sincere Warning About The Entity In Your Home*, *Auto Rewind*, and the 2011 Edinburgh International Film Festival selection *Stormhouse*. His background is in journalism, which has informed his non-fiction books *From The Front Lines Of Rock* and *How To Interview Doctor Who, Ozzy Osbourne And Everyone Else*. He lives in Brighton, UK and can be found at JasonArnopp.com and on Twitter as @JasonArnopp. Sign up for his newsletter and download a free book: bit.ly/ArnoppList.

Elizabeth Bear was born on the same day as Frodo and Bilbo Baggins, but in a different year. She is the Hugo, Sturgeon, Locus, and Campbell Award winning author of nearly 30 novels (The most recent is *Karen Memory*, a Weird West adventure from Tor) and over a hundred short stories. She lives in Massachusetts with her partner, writer Scott Lynch, three adventurous cats, and an elderly and opinionated dog.

Desirina Boskovich's short fiction has been published in *Clarkesworld, Lightspeed, Nightmare, F&SF, Kaleidotrope, PodCastle, Drabblecast,* and anthologies such as *The Apocalypse Triptych, What the #@&% Is That?* and *2084.* Her debut novella, *Never Now Always,* was published in 2017 by Broken Eye Books. She is also the editor of *It Came From the North: An Anthology of Finnish Speculative Fiction* (Cheeky Frawg, 2013), and together with Jeff VanderMeer, co-author of *The Steampunk User's Manual* (Abrams Image, 2014). Her next project is *Starships & Sorcerers: The Secret History of Science Fiction,* forthcoming from Abrams Image. Find Desirina online at www.desirinaboskovich.com.

C. Robert Cargill is a novelist, former film critic, and a screenwriter on Marvel's *Doctor Strange* and both of the *Sinister* films. His recent novel *Sea of Rust* was shortlisted for the Arthur C. Clarke Award. He lives and works in Austin, Texas.

Delilah S. Dawson is the New York Times bestselling author of *Star Wars: Phasma,* the Blud series, the Hit series, *Servants of the Storm,* and the Shadow series, beginning with *Wake of Vultures* and written as Lila Bowen. With Kevin Hearne, she co-writes the Tales of Pell, starting with *Kill the Farm Boy.* Her comics include the creator-owned *Ladycastle* and *Sparrowhawk* as well as *Star Wars Adventures, Star Wars Forces of Destiny, The X-Files Case Files, Adventure Time, Labyrinth, Rick and Morty,* and *Spider-Man.* Find her online at whimysdark.com. Delilah lives in Florida with her family.

Kieron Gillen is a writer and critic based in London. He is best known as the co-creator of the award-winning comics *The Wicked + Divine* and *Phonogram.* He is also the co-creator of the not award-winning comic series *DIE,* but that's not out yet, so he doesn't feel too bad about its lack of critical notices. His work for Marvel comics include *Star Wars, Uncanny X-men, Darth Vader, Iron Man, Doctor Aphra,* the GLAAD award-winning *Young Avengers,* and many more. He likes to think of this as less as experimenting with prose, and more like writing an overlong caption. As anyone who has read his comics will know, he is all too at home with overlong captions.

Kevin Hearne is the author of the Iron Druid Chronicles, the Seven Kennings trilogy, and co-author of the Tales of Pell with Delilah S. Dawson. He likes tacos and despises fascism.

Hugh Howey has wanted nothing more in life than to be Han Solo. Since starships are not yet a thing, he spent his years working as a bookseller while penning tales of more interesting times. Originally self-published with terrible cover art, his novels have since become *New York Times* bestsellers, translated into over forty languages. He now lives on a catamaran that he's sailing around the world. He has made the Kessel Run in less than twelve parsecs.

Laura Hudson is the culture editor at The Verge. She was previously an editor at Wired and Offworld, a writer at Feminist Frequency, and the founder and editor-in-chief of ComicsAlliance. She likes cats, games, karaoke, and crushing the patriarchy.

Jake Kerr spent fifteen years as a music industry journalist before his first published story, "The Old Equations," was nominated for the Nebula Award from the Science Fiction Writers of America and was shortlisted for the Theodore Sturgeon and StorySouth Million Writers awards. His stories have subsequently been published in magazines across the world, broadcast in multiple podcasts, and been published in multiple anthologies and year's best collections. A graduate of Kenyon College, Kerr studied fiction under Ursula K. Le Guin and Peruvian playwright Alonso Alegria. He lives in Dallas, Texas.

Sarah Kuhn is the author of the popular *Heroine Complex* novels—a series starring Asian American superheroines. The first book is a Locus bestseller, an RT Reviewers' Choice Award nominee, and one of the Barnes & Noble Sci-Fi & Fantasy Blog's Best Books of 2016. Upcoming projects include her YA debut—the Japan-set romantic comedy *I Love You So Mochi*—and a graphic novel about Batgirl Cassandra Cain for DC Comics. Sarah is also a finalist for the John W. Campbell Award for Best New Writer and has penned assorted comics and short fiction about geeks, aliens, romance, and Barbie. Yes, that Barbie.

Khaalidah Muhammad-Ali's publications include *Strange Horizons, Fiyah Magazine, Diabolical Plots,* and others. Her fiction has been featured in *The Best Science Fiction and Fantasy of the Year: Volume 12* edited by Jonathan Strahan and *The Best Science Fiction of the Year: Volume Three* edited by Neil Clarke. You can hear her narrations at any of the four Escape Artists podcasts, *Far Fetched Fables,* and *Strange Horizons.* She can be found online at http://khaalidah.com.

An (pronounce it "On") Owomoyela is a neutrois author with a background in web development, linguistics, and weaving chain maille out of stainless steel fencing wire, whose fiction has appeared in a number of venues including *Clarkesworld, Asimov's Science Fiction, Lightspeed,* and a handful of Year's Bests. An's interests range from pulsars and Cepheid variables to gender studies and nonstandard pronouns, with a plethora of stops in-between. Se can be found online at an.owomoyela.net.

Samuel Peralta is a physicist, entrepreneur, storyteller. His projects have hit the *USA Today* and *Wall Street Journal* bestseller lists, and been shortlisted in *Best American Science Fiction & Fantasy.* His poetry has been spotlighted by the BBC and *Best American Poetry.* He is the creator of the *Future Chronicles* anthologies—all of which have, in turn, become Amazon #1 category bestsellers. Samuel has designed nuclear tools, built solar fab plants and worked on optoelectronic start-ups. He is a producer of independent films, one nominated for a Golden Globe. And he cooks a mean risotto. Find more of his work at www.samuelperalta.com.

Beth Revis is a NY Times bestselling author with books available in more than twenty languages. Her next title, *Give the Dark my Love,* is a dark fantasy about love and death. Beth's other books include the bestselling science fiction trilogy, Across the Universe, and a novel in the Star Wars universe entitled *Rebel Rising.* She's the author of two additional novels, numerous short stories, and the non-fiction Paper Hearts series, which aids aspiring writers. A native of North Carolina, Beth is currently working on a new novel for teens. She lives in rural NC with her boys: one husband, one son, and two massive dogs.

Madeleine Roux is the New York Times bestselling author of the Asylum series, as well as the House of Furies series, *Allison Hewitt Is Trapped, Sadie Walker Is Stranded*, and her upcoming science fiction debut, *Salvaged*. Her short story contributions can be found in collections like *Star Wars: From A Certain Point of View, Scary Out There*, and *New Scary Stories to Tell in the Dark*. Madeleine lives with her beloved dog in Seattle, Washington.

John Scalzi has decided he really needs a refrigerator exclusively for cheese.

David Wellington is the author of over twenty novels, which have appeared around the world in eight languages. His horror series include *Monster Island, 13 Bullets, Frostbite,* and *Positive*. His thriller series starring Afghanistan war veteran Jim Chapel includes *Chimera, The Hydra Protocol,* and *The Cyclops Initiative*. He also writes fantasy under the pseudonym David Chandler, and science fiction, including the hit *Forsaken Skies* trilogy, as D. Nolan Clark. He lives and works in New York City.

Troy L. Wiggins is a writer and editor from Memphis, Tennessee. His short fiction has appeared in the *Griots: Sisters of the Spear, Long Hidden: Speculative Fiction From the Margins of History,* and *Memphis Noir* anthologies, and has appeared or is forthcoming in *Expanded Horizons, Fireside, Uncanny,* and *Beneath Ceaseless Skies*. His essays and criticism have appeared in the *Memphis Flyer, Literary Orphans Magazine, People of Colo(u)r Destroy Science Fiction, Strange Horizons, PEN America,* and on Tor.com. Troy is Co-Editor of *Fiyah Magazine of Black Speculative Fiction,* and he blogs frequently about writing, nerd culture, and race at afrofantasy.net. Troy lives in Memphis with his wife, Kimberly, and their two dogs. Follow him on Twitter at @TroyLWiggins.

Fran Wilde's novels and short stories have been nominated for three Nebula awards, two Hugos, and a World Fantasy Award, and include her Andre Norton- and Compton-Crook-winning debut novel, *Updraft* (Tor 2015), its sequels, *Cloudbound* (2016) and *Horizon* (2017), and the novelette "The Jewel and Her Lapidary" (Tor.com Publishing 2016). Her short stories appear in *Asimov's,* Tor.com, *Beneath Ceaseless Skies, Shimmer, Nature,* and the 2017 *Year's Best Dark Fantasy and Horror*. She writes for publications including The Washington Post, Tor.com, *Clarkesworld,* io9.com, and GeekMom. com. You can find her at franwilde.net.

Chet Williamson has written in the field of horror, science fiction, and suspense since 1981. Among his many novels are *Second Chance, Hunters, Defenders of the Faith, Ash Wednesday, Reign,* and *Dreamthorp.* His most recent publications are *The Night Listener and Others* (PS Publishing), and *Psycho: Sanitarium,* an authorized sequel to Robert Bloch's classic *Psycho* (St. Martin's Press). Over a hundred of his short stories have appeared in such magazines as *The New Yorker, Playboy, Esquire, The Magazine of Fantasy and Science Fiction,* and many other magazines and anthologies. He has won the International Horror Guild Award, and has been shortlisted for the World Fantasy Award, the HWA's Stoker Award, and the MWA's Edgar Award. Nearly all of his works are available in ebook format at the Kindle and Nook Stores. A stage and film actor, he has recorded over fifty unabridged audiobooks, both of his own work and that of many other writers, available at www.audible.com. Follow him on Twitter (@chetwill) or at www.chetwilliamson.com.

Daniel H. Wilson is a Cherokee citizen and author of the New York Times bestselling *Robopocalypse* and its bestselling sequel *Robogenesis,* as well as nine other books, including *How to Survive a Robot Uprising, Guardian Angels & Other Monsters,* and *Amped.* He earned a PhD in Robotics from Carnegie Mellon University, as well as master's degrees in Artificial Intelligence and Robotics. His latest novel is called *The Clockwork Dynasty.* Wilson lives in Portland, Oregon.

Charles Yu is the author of three books, and has published work in *The New Yorker, Wired, The New York Times,* and *Slate,* among other publications. He has also written for HBO, AMC and FX. His next book is forthcoming from Pantheon.

ACHNOWLEDGEMENTS

The editors wish to thank the incredibly talented and dedicated people who made this book possible, many of whom donated their time, effort, and considerable skills:

M.S. Corley for his stunning cover design; Matthew Bright of Inkspiral Design for the gorgeous interior layout and design for both print and ebook; Jane Davis, the Helpful Translator, for proofreading this massive tome after the rest of us had gone cross-eyed; Meghan Hoffman and Danielle Silber at the ACLU for being so receptive to the project; Kelley Allen at Humble Bundle for embracing the book and making it available through the Humble Bundle program; and John Joseph Adams for support and advice throughout. Thank you all so much. This book would not exist without you.

All have worked tirelessly and with flawless professionalism. Any errors that remain are entirely the fault of the editors.

ABOUT THE EDITORS

Gary Whitta is a screenwriter and author best known as co-writer of *Rogue One: A Star Wars Story*. He also wrote the post-apocalyptic thriller *The Book of Eli* starring Denzel Washington, co-wrote the Will Smith sci-fi adventure *After Earth*, and served as writer and story consultant on Telltale Games' adaptation of *The Walking Dead*, for which he was the co-recipient of a BAFTA award. Gary has also written for the animated TV series *Star Wars Rebels*. His first novel, *Abomination*, was published in 2015 to critical acclaim. His original comic book series *Oliver* debuts in January 2019 from Image Comics.

Hugh Howey is the *New York Times* bestselling author of *Wool*, *Sand*, *Beacon 23*, and *Machine Learning*. He also co-edited THE APOCALYPSE TRIPTYCH with John Joseph Adams. Look for another triptych from this dastardly duo soon, coming to a dystopia near you.

Christie Yant writes and edits science fiction and fantasy on the central coast of California. In 2014 she edited the *Women Destroy Science Fiction!* special issue of *Lightspeed Magazine*, which won the British Fantasy Award for Best Anthology. Her stories have been published in magazines and anthologies including *Analog*, *Beneath Ceaseless Skies*, *Armored*, and *Year's Best Science Fiction and Fantasy* (2011, ed. Horton). She is presently hard at work on a historical fantasy novel set in 19th century Paris, and is learning more about architecture and urban planning than she ever thought she would need to know.

CPSIA information can be obtained
at www.ICGtesting.com
Printed in the USA
LVHW091217070219
606614LV00005B/273/P

9 781728 821443